SANDSTORM

The Arabian Storm
Series Book I
by
Samantha Mattocks

Sandstorm: The Arabian Storm Series Book I

First edition 2020
First published 2020 by TAM-Publishing
www.thearabianmagazine.com
ISBN 978-1-5272-6846-3

For Glenn... Never
forgotten, always missed.

Sandstorm

The Arabian Storm Series
Book I

by

Samantha Mattocks

Preface

Sandstorm has been a long time in the writing. The first nugget of the idea formed on one of my many travels around the world with *The Arabian Magazine* – the Arabian horse publication I co-founded at the end of 2004, and which I have run solo since August 2008.

The Arabian horse showing world is one rich with stories – but none of them have made it into this book! I must stress at this point that any similarities to any person, living or dead, is purely coincidental. I have had a vivid imagination since I was a young girl, and all it takes is a moment watching palm trees rustling on the Middle Eastern breeze and a whole chapter is written.

I began *Sandstorm* over a decade ago – and I do feel that this shows. Time, accidents, injuries, lack of belief, and a host of other reasons all contribute to my not publishing this novel before now. Indeed, I finished it in the last decade but for reasons best known to myself, I chose to sit on it. Until now. COVID-19 has pushed me to release the book, which so many of you have asked for, and I shall now let loose with *Firestorm*, the second book in the series, with the characters and plotline pushed to the back of my mind for far too long.

I hope that you enjoy *Sandstorm* – happy travelling to new and distant lands!

Samantha

1

In the north of Belgium, in the municipality of Baler, found less than forty miles from the city of Antwerp, was an impressively grand house. Set in fifty acres, the grounds included lush pastures, a lake, and various clusters of trees huddled together against the vicious north wind that frequently blew across the land. Next to the house, which was built in the 18th century and remained as powerful and impressive today as it was three hundred years ago, was an indoor school, a show presentation area, and two beautiful barns that were filled with Arabian horses. The house was home to Arjan Vermeulen, having been in his family for many generations, and it was from here that he ran his world-famed training centre for Arabian horses.

Standing in the doorway to the house, the bright sunshine of early spring falling at his feet, Arjan lit a cigarette and walked outside, heading down a gravel path that curled around a vast pond. Going under the cover of chestnut trees for a few paces, which cast vast shadows on the path as birds soared overhead on a gentle breeze, Arjan emerged once more into the warm sunlight. He stood for a moment, watching the ducks paddling on the pond, took a breath, and relaxed. As far as he was concerned, things were good; very good. Arabian horses, those magnificent animals that had enchanted him for as long as he could remember, were now such an important part of his life that they truly had become his everything, including his career. He was now one of Europe's top trainers of Arabian horses for the halter ring, and he had clients queuing up to send their horses to him, both from Europe and the Middle

East. As a result, the collection of Arabian horses that he had here at his beautiful farm was developing in depth and quality as each season passed. And as the quality improved, so did the number of wins and championship titles that he won. With everything on the up, Arjan was very much a man in demand.

Arjan smiled to himself as he walked across the yard, heading for the main stable block, which was also the horse breeding barn. At 6'3", he was broad and muscular, and he was an impressive sight – it was no wonder that he constantly had a string of girls after him. His mysterious, dark brown eyes were the colour of conkers and they captivated people when he spoke to them, almost adding their own version of events to the conversation. Add to that Arjan's dark, unruly hair and haunted expression, at first glance he was almost Heathcliffesque to look at. That was where any similarities stopped though. While the Heathcliff of *Wuthering Heights* was also dark and brooding in character, Arjan had a playful nature. He loved to be the centre of attention and it was rare to see him without a smile on his face. He also loved nothing more than to play the big man whenever he could, and his friends had deemed him the Lord of Misrule within their group, always looking to him to be their leader. There was no doubt that he was charismatic, and people were easily attracted to him and his easy-going manner.

For the past eight years, Arjan had been dating the beautiful Rin Risley, who was an ice maiden to his lord of misrule. She, too, was an Arabian horse trainer and together, they had travelled across Europe and won every title going. Since she had moved into the house in Balen seven years ago, they had proved to be the dream team, and everyone wanted this glamorous pair to show their horses for them. Arjan had decided that today was the day, he was going to ask Rin to marry him. It was time; he was 36 years old and he wanted to settle down and start a family. Smirking as he remembered some of his more memorable conquests around the world, Arjan acknowledged that he hadn't always been the most faithful of partners, but in this kind of business, what did one expect? Bed-hopping was part of their way of life as one country after another was visited, one show after another. However, deep down Arjan knew that the one-night stands here and there meant absolutely nothing to him, or any of the men on the circuit; it was just sometimes easier to go to bed with someone than being alone. Like so many men before him, he knew that these women meant nothing, and he frequently forgot their names, let alone what they looked like, within an hour of leaving their hotel room. For him, there was no question that Rin was the love of his life, the one that he wanted to be with, and she was the only person who he had ever loved. They had been through thick and thin together, had followed their dreams together, and she was the one he turned to, day after day, for comfort and friendship. He loved her and besides, he also liked the idea of becoming a dad.

Pausing to stub out his cigarette before he went into the breeding barn – all horse areas were strictly no smoking – he had a final look around for Rin. Not seeing her, he stepped out of the sun and into the relative cool of the barn, stopping first to pat one of his old mares, scratching her neck and chuckling as she nibbled him back. As he stood there, enjoying a quiet moment with this precious mare, Arjan heard a noise coming from one of the stables at the other end of the barn. Stiffening, he listened again and worried that it could be a horse stuck in the stable or suffering a colic, he walked purposefully down the barn. Arriving at the stable door, he anxiously looked over and what Arjan saw made him take a step back in shock: Rin, lying on her back in the straw with her legs thrown over the shoulders of Yves, the young good-looking groom that had been working with them on and off over the years. As Rin brought her hips up to meet Yves, she spied Arjan standing in the doorway. Swearing under her breath, she began to bang Yves on his back, trying to get him to stop.

'Arjan,' she groaned.

'My name... Is not... Arjan!' Yves growled as he thrust into her.

Failing to notice Rin's gestures to the door, Yves suddenly had the feeling he was being watched. Before he could fully register his boss's presence, he felt the icy cold of a full bucket of dirty water hitting him in the face.

'GET OUT!' Arjan roared as, shaking with anger and betrayal, he turned on his heels and marched out of the barn, towards the house, dust coming off the gravel as he tried to put as much distance between himself and Rin as possible.

Slamming the vast and solid wooden door behind him, where he had been stood so happily just minutes ago, Arjan ignored the dogs twisting around his feet seeking attention and leaned back against the door with his eyes closed, trying to remove the images of Rin and Yves from his mind. She had not only betrayed him with someone they knew, someone in their lives, but she had done so at their own farm in their own private – and sacred – space.

Failing to erase the sight and thought of Rin and Yves together, Arjan opened his eyes and glanced into the sitting room, looking at the lamps lighting up the dark oak interior. Seeing Rin's books, clothes, make up, and photographs everywhere, he ran up the great solid wooden staircase into the bedroom and slammed the door shut behind him so fiercely that it made the house shake and the dogs cower.

The bedroom. Their bedroom. Arjan looked at the unmade bed where, just a few hours before, he and Rin had made love before discussing their plans for the day. He looked at her lotions and potions, her diary, her pills... With a cry of rage, he swept all her belongings off the side table and onto the floor. Grabbing her diary, he sat on the corner of the bed before beginning to search through it, looking for clues as to the true extent of her betrayal.

Still searching, Arjan did not hear the footsteps leading up to the bedroom. The door opened a fraction and Rin appeared. Just 5'4, she was very petite, with big, dark amber coloured eyes and dirty blonde hair the colour of old straw. Despite being in her mid-thirties, Rin looked frail and childlike, something that had always appealed to Arjan's cavalier attitude. But looking at her now, Arjan could only see her and Yves. 'Who else have you been fucking?' he shouted. 'Who?'

Rin had the grace to blush as she stared at the floor. Her silence hit Arjan like a wall and he collapsed back on the bed, tears starting to form in his eyes as he stared at a silent Rin. He had always known that she had an icy, detached side to her, but he felt that he barely recognised the woman standing in front of him – she was so cold, so clinical, giving nothing away while his world seemed to be collapsing around him.

'I wanted to marry you. I wanted us to start a family.'

'No children. Not yet anyway,' Rin answered, still staring at the floor.

With a massive effort, she lifted her gaze to meet his. 'And no marriage. What we have works; why change it?'

Amazed at what he was hearing, Arjan closed his eyes and, with a superhuman effort, managed not to scream out loud.

"But we always wanted children. That was always part of

13

our dream!"

Lowering her gaze, Rin stared in silence at the floor.

"Rin… I love you…."

Again, silence greeted Arjan's comment and it hung in the air unanswered. The longer the silence went on, both Arjan and Rin felt more and more uncomfortable.

Rin leaned against the doorframe, all the energy knocked out of her. Looking at Arjan, she thought, just for a moment, that he might hit her. Although not his style, rage did strange things to people and Rin could see his knuckles whitening as he tried to contain his emotions. She sighed. 'Maybe… Maybe we just don't love each other enough….'

Standing, Arjan looked around their bedroom one last time. Knowing that things would never be the same again, he pushed past Rin and ran out of the house. Seeing Yves hovering around the barn door, Arjan gave a bellow of rage before jumping into his car and heading for Balen and his favourite bar. Total oblivion was now his only goal.

Waking at first light, Arjan recognised first the pain of a hangover, swiftly followed by the agony of a shattered heart. Wincing as the sun pierced through his eyes and straight into his skull, Arjan took bearing of his surroundings. He had slept in the driver's seat of his state of the art BMW X5, and as he tried to move his head, Arjan winced again as the pain of a stiff neck filtered through the haze of the immense hangover he was suffering.

Fumbling around on the seat next to him Arjan found, amid the detritus of his mobile office, his Ray-Bans. Groaning to himself, he put them on and then pulled an unopened bottle of water from underneath the pile of papers, show halters, rosettes, coats, and empty crisp packets. There were definite advantages to living life on the road, he thought grimly. Downing the bottle of water in one, Arjan found his mobile phone and checked it phone for messages; nothing.

Groaning again, he turned the ignition on and switched the car from park to drive, pausing for a second to try and gather his senses. Carefully and cautiously, Arjan eased his car out on to the deserted streets of Balen and began to slowly head for home.

Arriving, he found the place empty. The horses were stamping in their stables, some whinnying, all demanding breakfast. The dogs were locked up in the kitchen, desperate to get out and sniff for fox scents across the fields as well as doing their morning business. Of Rin, there was no sign. Amazed that she had not tended to the dogs' needs, Arjan let them out of the door and they playfully yapped at each other as they ran off towards the paddocks.

Leaving the kitchen door open, stumbling slowly up the stairs, Arjan made his way carefully to their bedroom. Empty. The wardrobe doors were open, showing only one half full of clothes – his. A check into the bathroom showed that all of Rin's things had gone. Angrily, Arjan smashed his fist into what left on the shelf, bottles of aftershave smashing on the ceramic tiles, and he then leant over the sink, bile rising in his throat. Looking up into the mirror, he gazed at his own reflection: red eyed, unshaven, haggard, empty…

Hating what he saw, and hating the events of the past day, he smashed his fist into his reflection, cracking the mirror into a thousand pieces. Staggering downstairs, knuckles bruised and bleeding, Arjan went into the kitchen and pulled a bottle of whiskey from the cupboard above the sink. Not bothering to get a glass, he unscrewed the top and took a huge slug from the bottle. Trembling, lighting a cigarette, Arjan headed through to the lounge, blood from his bleeding hand leaving a trail on the floor behind him.

Collapsing on to the sofa, Arjan listened to the noises of everyday life going on around him, totally incapable of joining in.

It would be three days later that Arjan finally came out of the stupor he had been in since that Sunday afternoon when his world had come crashing down around him. Rin had been the love of his life, even if he hadn't always shown it at times. Seeing her betrayal – right in front of him, without even the excuse of being thousands of miles away, drunk and lonely – had hurt him far more than he ever imagined possible. The grooms, realising that Rin had vanished and having not seen Arjan for days, but knowing he was in the house steadily drinking, had continued to look after the horses as usual. The training centre had several grooms, headed up by Suzanne and Zoë, two local girls with a passion for all things equine. Arjan didn't yet realise, but Rin had taken Zoë with her when she left, leaving Suzanne in charge. Having briefly entered the main house and seen first, the state of Arjan, and then the state of the house, Suzanne had moved the dogs temporarily to her flat above the office block attached to the stables, and then taken over the yard. It was Suzanne who would ensure that Arjan was carried during these dark days and clients' telephone calls were deflected away from him and, after three days of solid drinking, it was Suzanne who would call his best friend, Leap, and get him to come and help his friend.

Arjan had known Leap since they were teenagers, with both preferring to skive off school and go to the local pony club than sit in a classroom and learn about the world from a textbook. Christened Leopold, Leap was nicknamed at the pony club for his ability to jump any horse, over any height, and the name stuck. He was a breeder, owning

16

Leopold Arabians, and Arjan regularly showed his horses with great success. For over 20 years, Leap had been by Arjan's side as they had travelled around the globe together and they got into more scrapes than the men in *The Hangover*. Whereas Arjan was dark, Leap was his exact opposite, having almost white-blonde hair, eyelashes the envy of women everywhere, and incredible green eyes the colour of a forest canopy, reminding those ladies lucky enough to stare into them of their abandoned days from their misspent youth. Matching Arjan in height, the pair made a dramatic contrast. Many a woman had been known to pause mid-sentence when these two tall, impressive men walked into a room, commanding instant attention from the opposite, and sometimes same, sex. Constantly leading the other astray, not that either needed much encouragement, Leap was always there to support Arjan, and at show parties, they were like a double act, joined at the hip. They had been through so much together, and they were as loyal as the closest of brothers.

They were also there for each other in times of trouble, and it was now that Leap came speeding into the stable yard, slammed shut the door of his car before going into the house. Taking in the haze of stale cigarette smoke and seeing a number of empty whiskey bottles lying next to overflowing ashtrays, Leap grimly shut the door behind him, knowing that he needed to take Arjan to task before he drank himself to death.

Meanwhile, in another part of Belgium, Rin looked through the list of clients that she and Arjan shared, working out who she could claim for her own. Yves was sleeping on the bed of her hastily-rented apartment and, as she watched him stretch in his slumber, she read again a text message from Zoë, saying that reportedly Arjan was drinking himself to oblivion; Zoë and Suzanne had stayed in touch since their bosses had fallen out so spectacularly, each helping the other to fill in the blanks. Zoë was passing all the information she got to Rin, who she had known for many years and felt great loyalty towards.

Putting her phone down, Rin idly wondered why Arjan was so upset. She knew that he had never been faithful to her apart from during those first few heady months when they had met each other at a show in Germany. A local girl from Düsseldorf, Rin had been new to the showing world and Arjan, who had been showing Arabian horses since he was a teenager, captivated her. She watched him from the side-lines before she took her friend's chestnut gelding, Adventurer, into the ring for the penultimate class of the day. Arjan also had a gelding entered in the same class, and he noticed the pretty Rin as she trotted alongside Adventurer around the show-ring. She won the class, and also his heart, and he invited her to his stables at the showground for a drink after the day's judging had finished. That night, he had used all his considerable charm to devastating effect, and Rin was lost. Having been a playboy since he was a teenager, Arjan amazed his friends by being faithful to Rin for seven whole months before he finally cracked and indulged in his favourite, a threesome, at Leap's 28th birthday party. Rin, however, who loved Arjan unconditionally, remained oblivious for many years to his deceit and it was only two years ago, when one of Arjan's conquests thought herself to be pregnant, that he'd had to come clean and break the news to Rin. The fact that it was a false alarm made no difference to how Rin took the news, and she felt utterly betrayed. While Arjan significantly played down just how many women there had been since he had got together with Rin, she knew that things could not go back to the way they were. Deep down, she knew that it was over between them the moment that the other woman had thought that she was pregnant. It had marked the beginning of the end for them – for her at least. Like so many before her though, it was easier to go through the motions and show the horses together than face any reality, such as trying to break up not only their lives but their careers as well. For Rin, the love had gone and as much as she may have wanted to turn the clock back, it was impossible. Somehow it just seemed easier to get up every morning and deal with running their training centre together, before sharing a bed at night, than splitting up and dividing up the business. She wryly acknowledged now, however, that it had just been putting a plaster over a gaping wound – it was bound to come off in the end, and it certainly had done so with style. In fact, Rin was amazed that the plaster had held that long.

Sighing, Rin returned to both reality and the client list, making a note of those she thought she could convince to join her in her solo training centre. Not continuing with a passion she had enjoyed since her teenage years was not an option, and she was determined to make it work. Looking once more down the list, Rin's concentration was interrupted by Yves who, with all the vibrant energy of youth, had enjoyed his cat nap and wanted Rin to join him back in bed. With the thought of enjoying an orgasm easier than the alternative – that of ringing up clients and either begging them to stay with her or having them put the phone down on her – Rin allowed herself to be pulled back into Yves' energetic embrace once more.

'Come – I will take your mind off things,' purred Yves as he pushed Rin back on to the bed, kissing her neck and moving his hands down to her breasts. Yves was such a contrast to Arjan's stature, being shorter, thinner, and somehow more virile. With his mop of blond hair and

19

smattering of freckles giving him a permanently cheeky look, Yves had honey brown eyes that seemed to smile with mischief rather than being brooding as Arjan's were.

Yves' kisses became more insistent and his mouth began to tease Rin's nipples. Sighing deeply, she succumbed to his passion and groaned as he moved his mouth slowly down her body, stopping only for a moment as he explored her belly button, before pushing her legs open and burying his face between them.

'Oh Yves…,' gasped Rin, as she pushed her hands into his hair, and allowed herself the freedom to be totally lost in the moment. 'Yves!'

The next few months for Arjan were pure hell. Not only did he have to endure watching Rin enjoy herself with Yves – who was in turn cheating on her – she had then openly began an affair with one of their major clients, Juan Ricciardo from Spain. Arjan felt like his soul had been ripped out without anaesthetic. He guessed that when it came down to it, men and women were wired differently. To his mind, his one-night stands didn't count because he loved Rin and no matter how tempting the girl in his bed was for that night, it was always Rin on his mind when he woke in the morning, and it was she that he wanted to go back to. He truly believed that his flings were not as much of a betrayal as Rin's affair with Yves was – and to see her now with Juan, who naturally had taken his horses from Arjan and moved them to Rin, made him feel physically sick. He had learned from Suzanne, who had spoken to Zoë, that Rin and Yves had been carrying on together for months. Not only had their affair overlapped Arjan's own relationship with her, he now knew that she had been seeing Yves and Juan at the same time. To know that Rin was going around, warming one bed after another, left Arjan cold.

Arjan had always been a proud man, and he had taken Rin's betrayal hard, much the surprise of both Leap and Suzanne. While he may have had a cavalier attitude towards faithfulness, he had truly loved Rin and thought that they would spend the rest of their lives together. It hurt his pride to think that she had been off with other men behind his back – that it was double standards never occurred to him – and he truly felt as though his life would never be the same, and that he would never find happiness again.

Grimacing as he thought about Rin, Arjan felt like she had walked off with everything. It was his reputation that had been left in tatters as everyone assumed he had dumped her to be able to live his playboy lifestyle without reproach, and friends, clients and grooms had started to treat him accordingly. While a player to the end, Arjan had a strong chivalrous streak and although he wasn't happy with this turn of events, he was content to let people think that it was he who had left Rin if it spared her any blushes. He knew that he didn't owe her any favours and late at night, as he sat alone in his room with a glass of whiskey tightly clenched in his hand, he often wondered why he allowed this to happen. It seemed that his life had turned into a parody, and he was now seen to be the wild person, not just sometimes was at show, but all the time. Draining his glass, Arjan realised that he didn't know how to change this, and so he continued to go through the motions, day after day.

Leap had been a great support to Arjan, checking in on his friend on an hourly, and then daily, basis until finally, he seemed more like himself. Leap had never had any time for Rin, something Arjan had never understood. He desperately wanted his best friend and his girlfriend to get on. Unbeknown to him, however, Leap despised Rin for a very good reason and had, very early on in her relationships with

Arjan, realised exactly what type of person she really was.

Arriving at Arjan's farm a few years before, Leap had headed straight into the house, calling out hello as he pushed open the solid wooden door.

'Up here!' Rin had called. 'I need your help – can you come up?'

'Sure. Isn't Arjan around?' called back Leap as he began to climb up the vast staircase.

'He's not here – he's gone to Germany to collect some semen. I'm in here…'

Pushing open the bedroom door, Leap took a step back in shock at the sight that greeted him – Rin lying back on the bed, wearing just the briefest pair of white lace knickers. Her small breasts were pointing upwards and as Leap entered the room, Rin spread her legs suggestively.

'Hello Leap… I wonder if you can help me out with something?' said Rin as she licked her lips lasciviously.

'What the…!'

'Oh, come on. I know you want me, you always have. Arjan need never know…'

As she said this, Rin sat up and seductively moved from the bed over to Leap, placing her hand on his chest, starting to toy with the top button of his shirt as her other hand began to play with the belt of his jeans.

Leap angrily slapped her hands away.

'No! I don't want you! And I would never betray Arjan!'

'Are you sure about that?' said Rin as she stepped away and, turning around, slowly pulled her knickers down until they were around her ankles.

Before she had the chance to make another move, Leap had grabbed the duvet and, with a cry of rage, wrapped Rin up in it.

'You are nothing but a common little whore!' he spat at her. 'How dare you do this to Arjan! I will be watching you now – you had better watch your step!'

Pushing Rin back on the bed, Leap turned on his heels with disgust and walked out of the house. Slamming the door behind him as he got in the car, he slammed the steering wheel with a howl of rage. How could she do that to Arjan! And how dare she be so bloody desirable, too? Slamming the car into gear, Leap scattered gravel as he raced down the driveway and back to the sanctuary of his own house.

From that day on, Leap never trusted Rin, and he always watched her carefully for signs that she would break Arjan's heart. As for Rin, she never spoke to Leap again and would barely register his presence when they were in company together. Arjan, not understanding why there was so much friction between them, unsuccessfully talked to each, trying to persuade them to be friends. Leap always evaded the subject while Rin tried to blame Leap, telling Arjan that he was a bad friend and not to be trusted. However, deep down Arjan knew that there must be some serious reason as to why one day, they all laughed and joked together, and the next Rin and Leap ignored each other.

Not wanting to face either truth – that one had made a pass at the other, or that they had slept together – Arjan dealt with the fall out in his usual way, that of drinking and smoking his way through the nights, turning back into the Lord of Misrule and being the life and soul of any party, ignoring any fears or worries that he might have. It was always easier to turn a blind eye and pretend, rather than face the truth. As for Leap, he remained cold towards Rin and now he could not help but feel relieved that the timebomb, ignited years ago, had finally gone off.

2

Having made it through the immediate post break-up fall out, Arjan was now at the last show of the European season, the World Championships held in the beautiful city of Paris in December. With Christmas around the corner, the cold crisp air outside was the perfect contrast for the heat of expectation that went with this show, all combining to create a heady, almost giddy atmosphere of excitement, anticipation and romance.

Paris was the show where everyone tried to outdo each other, and not just in the show-ring either. Not only did the quality of horses brought to the show have to be the very best possible, but clothes had to be more expensive and glamorous, hair, nails and make-up had to be perfect, and your winter holiday plans must be the most elaborate, outshining everyone. If you weren't dripping with fur and diamonds, then no one would look twice at you unless, of course, your horse was the next big thing. The Paris show also provided the last chance of the season to bed your lust for the year before moving on to next year's younger, fresher model, and this resulted in a lot of late night knocking on hotel room doors and slinking down hotel corridors at 5am. The show had a reputation among many as being the highlight of the season, even if it was not always renowned for the exceptional quality of horses presented during the three days the event ran. Rather, it was so talked about for the extra-curricular activities that went on around the stables and at the hotels.

At these elite shows, known as title shows, the focus was all on halter classes; ridden was almost a dirty word, with just one title show offering such classes. The irony, of course, was that most of the trainers had got into horses through riding a part-bred Arabian at their local riding school. It was through these horses and the long weekends they spent down at the school, surrounding themselves with all things 'horse', that they developed love for the breed. From those early days, they would then seek out a pure-bred Arabian to ride and compete with. To make the lack of ridden classes at the shows even more ironic, many of the trainers continued to ride and would use ridden work as a way to get their horses fit for the show season ahead.

However, at these major shows, all the attention was on the halter – or in-hand – classes. Top show trainers around the world were paid extraordinary amounts of money to lead a horse into the ring and trot it around on the end of a long leather lead rope. With this done, the horse was then posed – stood up – in an artificial, unnatural and exaggerated way for the judges to assess the conformation - overall Arabian type, head and neck, body and topline, legs, and movement.

Points were awarded from a pool of judges – ranging from anything between three, from a pool of four, to six, from a pool of eight – per class. The scores ranged from one to twenty points, although judges the world over tended to stay in a safe zone of 17-19, going as high as 19.5 and 20 for something exceptional, and down to 16 for the leg scores; everyone always joked that four points were awarded for each leg. These scores were then added up to give a total out of 100 for each judge. The overall average score was calculated for each horse, and that average score was what was used to decide the horse's place in the final line up; the higher the score, the higher up the horse was placed. Thus, a horse receiving scores of 19, 19, 18, 16, 19 across all five categories from one judge would receive an average score of 91 points. If there were three judges, and they scored that horse 91, 89, and 92 respectively, then the overall score was 90.67 points.

If you won or placed second in a class, or were placed Top Five at the bigger shows, you then went into the championship classes, where the stakes were even higher. The horses here were assessed against each other by every judge – all at the same time rather than individually as in the class – and this was known as comparative judging. From this group of horses, the judges chose their Gold, Silver and Bronze Champion. They placed each horse in the medal positions and these placings were then tallied, with the horse receiving the highest allocation of Gold votes taking the title and then so on down the line to Bronze.

There was so much at stake at every show but as the year went on and the three main title shows – the All Nations' Cup in Aachen, the European Championships, and the Paris World Championships – approached, both the standard of horses, as well as the kudos they achieved with each title, increased dramatically at each show. With so much at stake, especially for stallions who could command huge stud fees if they won several prestigious titles, it was little wonder that by the time that the World Championships came around, vast sums of money were changing hands behind the stables as owners sought to secure the coveted title of World Champion for their horse. It was well rumoured that, at some shows, sponsorship in the region of €100,000 or above secured you a title, and the more you gave, the higher the accolade your horse received. However, this very much remained just a rumour as no one could ever prove exactly what happened behind closed doors, despite many trying to uncover evidence.

Arriving at the hotel in Paris, ready to endure another

show and get through it in one piece, Arjan caught sight of Sienna Stevens for the first time. She was checking in with clients and looking uncomfortably out of place. Arjan had heard all about her, the new girl in the spotlight. In her late twenties, Sienna was an Irish girl who was slowly, and not easily, settling into her newfound recognition. While she had been around horses all her life, she had emerged on the international scene earlier that year when she had set up her own Arabian horse marketing company, Essentially Arabian. To the surprise of many, not least Sienna herself, her fledgling business had really taken off and here she was, at another of the major shows, selling her promotional offerings. Acting as a liaison between breeders, owners, trainers, agents and magazines, she worked hard for her clients to get them the best coverage possible for their horses, and for the best price. Sienna would repeatedly work late into the early morning hours as she negotiated around the world through the different time zones to ensure that the right horse would be on the right cover of the right magazine at the right show. Combining a passion for horses, more recently the Arabian, with an ability to convey how much they moved her through an occasional written feature for a magazine, Sienna very quickly became hot property among those in the know in the Arabian world.

Sienna seemed overawed by the attention she received. She had gone from invisible to everyone knowing exactly who she was overnight. It seemed that being even slightly known in the Arabian horse industry meant that everywhere she went, people recognised her and there were few who did not know who she was. Add to that the gossip that people liked to share as they stood ringside – was she married and did she have a partner, being the top two questions – and rumours about Sienna were rife as people continued to fall over themselves in a bid to bed her, buy her, claim her, and control her.

'Likeable enough,' Arjan thought as he saw Sienna laughing with her clients as they made their way over to the bar for a drink. She stood out immediately for her obvious differences to the rest of the women at the bar. Where they all had the seemingly regulatory straightened, over-peroxided hair, Sienna's hair was long, slightly wavy, and brunette, making for a refreshing change. While many others were covered in fake tans, sometimes to hide the t-shirt and short lines that naturally developed as they worked their horses, Sienna's naturally fair skin made her look almost angelic against the rest. Not for her were the hair extensions, false nails and eyelashes. Instead, she looked dewy fresh. Those that she was laughing with looked older and harder, due to their heavier make up and added fakeness; instead, this girl looked so different to anyone that Arjan had seen before that he found that immediately, he was becoming captivated the more he looked at her. While she looked overwhelmed at the attention she was receiving, it seemed that Sienna was also comfortable just being herself and not trying to change herself to fit in. In an industry where so many of the women paid so much attention to what they wore, how their hair looked, whether they had a chip in their nails and so on, Sienna stood out for her naturalness. She was not tall, barely 5'5", and she had curves in all the right places. Blue, all-knowing and slightly cynical eyes, the colour of a brilliant summer sky, gave way to full lips that twisted into a smile at just the merest suggestion of something amusing or in welcome to the stream of people that came over to her to say hello. 'A breath of fresh air,' Arjan decided to himself as he continued to blatantly stare at Sienna, as if silently challenging her to turn her head around and look at him.

Lighting a cigarette, Arjan noted that Sienna was standing with clients who had been in the Arabian horse industry for a long time. He watched her cautiously, aware that if he was to stand any chance with her, he would have to get to her first. He couldn't have them telling her of his reputation with women, something that when he was alone and being honest with himself, he fervently wished he didn't have.

Calling to the barman to refill his glass, Arjan downed the last of the whiskey. The oblivion that he had sought so much when he split up with Rin was now becoming a permanent feature and this show was no exception. If anything, with its end of season feel, oblivion was even more tempting than ever as owners were already looking to the year ahead, deciding whether to move their horses from one trainer to another. Thankfully, Arjan had only lost a handful of clients when Rin left but it was enough to hit him hard, and he knew that he had to be careful not to lose anymore. Looking down at the fresh glass in his hand, Arjan knocked the liquor back in one mouthful.

His eyes roved around the bar, looking for a suitable woman to screw that evening. His eyes cast back to Sienna… No, not yet. There was plenty of fun to be had with her over the coming months, and plenty of time to get her just where he wanted. His eyes fell on to Katherine, one half of a very rich Scottish couple who had patronised Arjan on occasion by sending their horses to him before moving on to someone else just a few months later, a tactic they used on every trainer. A wry smile crossed Arjan's face as he looked at Katherine smoothing her hair and checking that her furs were hanging straight. It would be very entertaining to sleep with her and would bring the haughty bitch down a peg or two, as she stood there, draped head to toe in furs, full of airs and graces that belied her humble beginnings.

Assessing her slowly, Arjan decided that like Sienna, Katherine would wait. Glancing around once more, he spied a pretty German groom sitting on her own, texting someone on her phone. Arjan signalled to the barman for an extra drink before making his way over to her, a smile plastered on his face, and ready to move in for the kill.

It didn't take long for Arjan to be tired of being bollock-deep in faceless whores. He wanted that stability back of having a regular girlfriend but now, of course, he had the playboy reputation and while girls fifteen years younger than him were throwing themselves at his feet, it seemed wrong to say no. Besides, his friends expected it. They thought that he was a legend and Arjan liked nothing more than being the big man, sharing stories with his friends and being clapped on the back for being a stud. Standing in his room at the Holiday Inn in Aachen, home to the much loved All Nations' Cup, Arjan downed his vodka. Checking his reflection in the mirror, he smoothed his hair and straightened his shirt, before grabbing his jacket. Tonight was the Breeders' Party, and once again, it was time for some fun.

Arriving at the showground after the short walk from the hotel, Arjan headed straight for the bar. Spying Katherine and her monotonous husband, Crispin, as he went in, Arjan made a bee-line for them; Crispin was always good for a drink, and Arjan enjoyed winding him up, pretending that something had happened with Katherine. 'In her dreams,' he thought as he reached them. Still wearing the furs that she favoured so much, Katherine was a tall, willowy brunette, with long limbs and a natural style. Brown eyes, freckles, and a sly smile gave the impression of a friendly person but in reality, Katherine was only ever after her own gain.

Born outside of Glasgow, she had taken elocution lessons in a bid to improve her accent. A passionate Scot, she refused to go to England for university, instead heading to Edinburgh in a bid to snare herself a rich husband. A social climber of the worst kind, Katherine did not hold back when it came to getting what she wanted. Sleeping with most of the first squad for the Edinburgh University Rugby FC team, she thought that she found what she was after at one of the matches. Crispin Arbuthnot was the son of a Viscount and, easily led as well as incredibly rich. It did not take Katherine long to ensnare him. One small prick in a condom and before Crispin knew it, his elegant girlfriend was pregnant and, coming from a strong religious family, he knew that he had no option than to do the honourable thing. Married on an Arctic winter's day, the wind blowing a gale through the beautiful city, Katherine wore white fox furs to cover her growing bump.

Alas for her, it was only after they were married that she discovered Crispin's father, Viscount Arbuthnot, had gambled away the family title and that it would pass to the eldest son of his fiercest rival upon his death. Furious, a six-month pregnant Katherine screamed and beseeched Crispin to do something about it. More interested in watching Scotland thrash England in the Five Nations Championships, and take home the Calcutta Cup, Crispin merely shrugged, saying that according to old Scottish lore, there was nothing that they could do. Shorter than his wife, Crispin reminded many of Ratty from Wind in the Willows – small round glasses hid small brown eyes that helped frame a small round face. He was also incredibly old-fashioned in many ways, wearing a waistcoat at all times, regardless of the weather, and carrying a pocket watch and handkerchief. Prematurely balding, he had been nothing but a disappointment to Katherine. Their only child, the one conceived through dubious means, was a brooding daughter who had gone travelling as soon as she reached 18 years of age. The occasional postcard home from some far-flung corner of the world was all that they had heard from her in two years, and there was many a time when Crispin even forgot that they had a child.

The only thing that had kept the couple together was Crispin's construction company. Always interested in putting things together, he fell into this industry as soon as he left university, firstly through an apprenticeship and then starting his own business. As the bank account began to fill up, Katherine decided that staying was probably an option after all, and she looked for different ways to spend her husband's thousands. It was a chance conversation with a friend that led to them discovering the world of Arabian horses. To Katherine's surprise, Crispin was equally enthusiastic.

Realising that Arabian horses opened a whole new world to them, one full of luxury travel, of meeting Princes and Sheikhs, and visiting some of the most amazing places they had ever seen, the Arbuthnots embraced this new passion and thus it was that they found themselves in Germany, enjoying the applause that constantly seemed to be coming their way.

Arjan hated the Arbuthnots but he knew that Crispin had deep pockets, as well as some beautiful young horses. He knew that he had to be friendly to them. Bracing himself for the patronising conversation that would no doubt follow, Arjan made his way over to the couple. It was only as he reached them and started to say hello that he realised Sienna was there too.

'Mmmm – finally time to properly meet my new challenge,' he thought, feeling a rush of excitement course through him.

'Hello Arjan, want a beer? We were just talking about you. Do you know Sienna here?' Crispin smiled blandly at Arjan, his Scottish accent coming out thick and fast as he gripped the glass of champagne in his hand. Encouraged by Katherine, Crispin tried to be a cut above his other Scottish friends and was always keen to outgrow his roots. He scorned whiskey for champagne on a regular basis, even though he couldn't stand the stuff and would be happier with a stiff double, and he worked hard to keep up the act that Katherine had developed for them.

Katherine was equally bland underneath her falseness, but they were a rich couple and every trainer knew to stay on the right side of them in order to be on the receiving end of the big cheques that were handed over whenever they won a championship class.

Fixing his face with his winningest smile, Arjan stole an arm around Sienna's shoulders and pulled her in towards him as he looked into her eyes. Christ, he thought, they were as brilliant a blue as his were a sultry brown.

'We've met a couple of times before,' he charmed and was almost immediately shocked as Sienna didn't respond in the normal way, that of knees giving way, girlish giggles and blushing. Arjan, however, was more shocked at the way he responded – as he looked into her eyes, he felt himself begin to blush as he smiled at her, his stomach tightening into a knot as he continued to stare at her. Mildly registering that this was a complete role reversal to his normal reaction – with the girl simpering and he more laid back about it all – he was shocked to the core and he felt seriously jolted.

'Interesting. And even more of a challenge,' he thought to himself as he decided to put Sienna well and truly on the back burner and to look to get his somewhat easier kicks elsewhere that night.

Sienna was immediately aware of the allure of Arjan, and she had been for some time. She had seen him in the ring countless times and their eyes had also met across the bar at the various shows around Europe. He was incredibly handsome, and he had that manner about him that made women want to look after him, no doubt each believing that they would be the one to change, and tame, this lovable rouge. However, Sienna had also seen Arjan going off with woman after woman and she wasn't prepared to be just another easy fling for him. So while his smile, as he looked into her eyes, was tantalising and she could feel herself melting, her mind wandering, she was not going to give anything away when it came to how she felt. Not yet, at least. He had allure, there was no two ways about it, and she knew that Arjan would prove hard to resist.

As Arjan left, however, Sienna followed him with her eyes, taking in the way that he walked and his swagger, as he went back to Leap. 'That man is trouble,' she thought to herself before returning her attentions to the Arbuthnot's once more.

The following day, Arjan stood in the show-ring regretting shagging one of the trainer groupies the night before who seemed to be trying to complete a full set before the end of the season. Nursing a massive hangover, he felt sick, and Rin was openly flirting with Juan, who was still on the scene. Arjan himself had to be more than nice to Juan as he owned countless beautiful horses, many of whom were potential big winners, and that thought blackened his mood even further.

Feeling sicker by the minute as the heat grew in the ring and the pounding in his head became more intense, Arjan caught sight of Sienna sitting with Crispin and Katherine, with Crispin waving his hand around idly in the air as he loudly pointed out the horses in the class that he was planning to breed to. Sienna's hair had curled into soft waves and she was gazing, unseeingly, into the distance, nodding every now and again whenever Crispin paused for breath. As he looked over at her, Arjan felt his heart race. As he continued to stare, he wasn't sure whether it was his hangover, the heat of the show-ring on an hot late autumn afternoon, the brightness of the many spotlights bearing down on him, the double espresso he had downed before he came into the ring, or Sienna that caused the reaction in him. He could hardly draw his eyes from her and again, he felt himself willing her to turn around and look at him.

'One day, that girl will be mine,' he vowed. It was only when his horse was called forward to collect the Silver Championship sash that he realised that he hadn't meant just for a fuck. Somehow, he had a hunch that Sienna was worth more than that.

3

The Arabian horse showing circuit was certainly a curious one. While Sienna had grown up with horses, the more she went to shows on the continent and, as her job grew, to further afield in the Middle East, she was increasingly baffled and amazed by the Arabian industry in equal measures. The beauty of these horses captivated her – they were enchanting in the way that they moved, so fluid and effortless, and their intelligence continued to astound Sienna. However, it was the social aspect surrounding this breed that confounded her so much. Everyone was so keen to be better than the person next to them, although she recognised that this was something that could be true in all walks of life, not just the Arabian horse industry.

Growing up in rural Ireland had meant that Sienna was quite happy just to sit there and entertain herself as there were no cinemas or shops on her doorstep. This meant that she loved to people watch, something that continued to this day, and she was intrigued and baffled by those in the Arabian industry in equal measure. Many of the trainers were incredibly egotistical and determined to outdo each other, although she also appreciated that they had to be this way in order to do their job – to stand in front of the judges, as well as a vast audience, challenging them not to place their horse first. While to many, it may have looked easy, this was not a job for the faint hearted. Physically, it could take a lot out of a person as they showed horses in one class after another, running around and around the arena, all the time with a 600kg animal on the end of the lead, something that was especially challenging in the stallion classes with all the testosterone flying around. Add to that, if the show was an outdoor one, then the handlers would be out in the elements and they had to endure anything from baking heat to rainstorms. They showed, class after class, from 9am until gone 5pm, with no chance to rest in between, running around the ring countless times in one day. The lunch break was inevitably filled with speaking to clients, charming and placating them accordingly, with little chance to do more than take a couple of bites from a sandwich and gulp down some water. So, while it may have seemed like a very glamorous job, invariably it was anything but – especially if you didn't make the top of the line-up and had to slink away back to the stables empty handed, avoiding angry owners as you did so.

Sienna had decided that the trainers were very much like tribes. Each trainer had his own set of friends around them, as well as their own team who worked for and with them – grooms, managers and sometimes photographers – and there was very rarely any crossover. This sometimes made Sienna feel uneasy when she travelled as it meant that she never really fitted in wherever she went. The Germans always stuck together, as did the French, and the Flemish trainers, of which there were many, also had their own small groups within the one big, general tribe. Sienna had to mix with all of them because of her work, and everyone was always very friendly to her. But she never felt as though she quite belonged and instead was on the outside. Frequently, she would slip away from bars and parties so that she could go back to her hotel and Skype her friends back home, many of whom couldn't travel with her due to their day jobs although they would join her for a weekend show if they could. As time went on, however, and her company Essentially Arabian grew in reputation, Sienna was beginning to learn who she could and could not trust. It was not always easy.

The season was a long one, starting with the Ajman Show in the United Arab Emirates in January and lasting through until Paris and then Sharjah, back in the Emirates, in December. While many of the grooms and hangers on seemed to be permanently on holiday and partied wherever they went, their bar bill often being unwittingly picked up between their big clients, the schedule was still exhausting, especially packing up to go to the next show after a big night in the bar.

Add to the pressures of showing and the exploits in the bar every night, there were also many deadlines to be met for the multitude of different magazines being printed around the world, such as *The Arabian Magazine*, *Arabian Horse Times* and *Tutto Arabi*. This created a trial for editors and trainers alike, and Sienna found that she was now claiming this headache as her own as she had to organise publicity for the different magazines, all for different shows, and all on different deadlines. And then, there were the many farm brochures, stallion cards, new and innovative advertising campaigns, and so on. Sienna found that she had demands coming in from clients at all hours; she had a true tiger by the tail as she had to run herself to the point of exhaustion to keep everyone happy and, being so new to the business, she could not afford to turn any work down while her reputation grew.

Having left Ireland when she was 18 to study Business at University College London, Sienna went straight into working for a FTSE-100 company. Having previously worked just nine hours a day, five days a week, Sienna found the change of pace she was experiencing now difficult to adjust to. She knew that she had to be seen at all the right parties to help build up her reputation and her business, and that the parties were where the main contracts came from, but she was permanently exhausted.

Having been back in London for a month after the Aachen Show, where she had first been properly introduced to the brooding depths of Arjan Vermeulen, Sienna was rushing to pack for another show. As she was deciding what to wear for yet another breeders' party, an event that seemed to be held at every show she went to, her thoughts couldn't help but go to Arjan and she wondered whether a low-cut top was a good idea. Even before she was introduced properly by the Arbuthnots, Sienna had been aware of Arjan; who wasn't. He kept fixing her with his piercing, yet melting, stare and he was so suggestive when he smiled. But she knew of his reputation and besides, it seemed that man after man seemed to be throwing himself at her at the moment. She just wasn't interested, having just come out of a torrid break up. She had been with her previous boyfriend for a few years, a real City type, and having briefly ended things when she started her business, Sienna wondered whether she had been too hasty in splitting up with Toby and so decided to give things another chance. However, she returned from a European show to find her long-term boyfriend getting his short-term kicks elsewhere and had duly, and very finally, sent him packing. So while a relationship was the furthest thing on her mind, and in spite of her coolness around Arjan, she still found his interest in her difficult to ignore.

Throwing a Liberty-print wrap into her case, Sienna reflected that the way her business had grown seemed nothing short of miraculous. People, she discovered, had responded well to her and she was being introduced to the best names in the business at every show she went to. If only Arjan would stop creeping into her dreams at night, something that surprised her the first time it happened, then life would be perfect. There was just something about him, something that kept drawing her to him – his melting brown eyes, for one thing.

A beeping horn from the driver waiting outside for her interrupted her thoughts and, zipping her case shut and gathering her bags, she rushed out of the front door of her flat, on to the streets of London and into the waiting car, which was all set to whisk her off to Belgium and the European Championships.

Loading up his horses a little over 60 miles away, just south of Colchester, was Guy Tindall. Like most of the men in the Arabian horse industry, he assumed that he was God's gift to women, and his bedpost was covered in notches from his conquests. One of the top trainers in the UK, Guy was prepared to do whatever it would take to get to the top and he was more than happy to oil the palms of judges and owners the world over. He would sell his own grandmother if he thought it would get him further in his career, and he frequently went behind friends' backs in order to get what he wanted. Guy had definitely been at the back of the queue when morals and ethics were being handed out, and he was extremely ruthless and bloody-minded to the end.

At 6'3', Guy had straw-blond hair and steely blue-grey eyes, which could cut a rival dead at 20 paces, while at the same time, turn any potential squeeze into a simpering wreck. Guy took pride in his appearance and would rise at 5.30am every morning so that he could go on a 10-mile run through his woods, before completing 50 lengths in his pool. Over breakfast of an egg-white omelette, Guy would trawl his phone for updates from countries across the world, looking for tip offs from agents about people going bust, horses about to come on the market, and of those new to the industry who he could manipulate into buying the horses that he wanted for the prices he liked. All the time, Guy would be taking his cut, a minimum of 20% of each deal done, and sending the money to offshore accounts around the world. If the tax man ever caught up with him, he would be in trouble, but for now he was living the life of Riley and was determined to enjoy every single minute of it.

Guy's long-suffering girlfriend, Ally, seemed as plain as he was vain, and she merely served as someone to look after the clients' horses while Guy was away on the show circuit. She also kept Guy warm on the cold winter nights when he had to stay in the UK and he couldn't be bothered to leave the house. Sexually demanding, Guy needed regular servicing and despite Ally's laidback manner and constant availability, he continually hopped from bed to bed in the UK as well as abroad in order to satisfy his ever-increasing urges.

Having grown up with a love of horses, Guy had seemed like an ideal partner for Ally. The reality, however, was that he had worn away her confidence non-stop over the years. Now, she just agreed to go along with whatever he said, and whatever he did, just for a quiet life. Having left school at fifteen to work at the local stables, helping with riding lessons for the younger children, Ally had no qualifications and at least by staying with Guy, she had an easy life most of the time, as well as a roof over her head. She was also able to be near the horses that she loved so much all day, and they gave her so much love back, love that her boyfriend seemed to continually deny her.

They had met when Ally had won a raffle prize to attend the local Hunt Ball. Tall and thin, with dirty straw blonde hair that always looked like it needed a wash, Ally had slipped into a satin ball gown for the first time in her life. A deep violet, which brought out the blue of her eyes, Ally felt awkward and gauche as she arrived at the party, accompanied by the male owner of the local stables, who was more interested in the male riders than in Ally herself.

Wandering outside, Ally saw Guy surrounded by young bloods, all roaring with laughter at his dirty jokes. Hovering, uncertain whether to carry on outside to the fresh air or retreat inside, Guy looked up at her and grinned.

"Hello, I don't think I've ever had the pleasure. Guy Tindall," he said, as he made his way to her side, clicking his fingers to a waiter at the same time, ordering him to bring a fresh bottle of champagne.

Instantly at ease, Ally relaxed into Guy's company and they spent the night dancing away together, breast to chest, hip to hip, with Guy's fingers weaving circles on the small of her back.

"Do you live far," he murmured in her ear as the clock stuck midnight.

"No – just in the village," she whispered back at him, smiling as he gazed into her eyes and brought his lips down to kiss hers.

Racing down the roads in his Lotus Esprit, Guy reached Ally's ground-floor flat in record time, and he rushed to open the car door for her. Kissing her all the way up the path to her flat, Guy had practically undressed her by the time she managed to get the key in the lock. Slamming the door shut behind them, Guy pinned Ally up against the door, thrusting into her. That first sexual coupling was brief, urgent and insistent – something that Ally had loved as she thought it a measure of how much he wanted her. It was only now, so many years on, that she realised it was purely as Guy wanted to come as quickly as possible, and then sleep or leave. He was not interested in small talk, or in the woman he had just fucked once the urge was over.

Wowed by Guy's constant assault on her – flowers, champagne, rides out around the countryside either in his car or, occasionally, on horseback, Ally slowly fell for his considerable charms.

"I need you in my life Ally," he would tell her, realising that she had run the riding school almost single handed and that she would be a great asset to him and his busy life. "You are everything to me – I cannot exist without you. Move in with me."

Finally, Ally agreed and she sold her small flat, taking up residence in Guy's vast estate. It did not take long for the rot to set in – with Guy's frequent travelling, he expected Ally to orchestrate everything at home, including taking care of all his horses and overseeing the yard, as well as making sure that his clothes were freshly washed, ironed and packed, all ready to go the minute that he was, too. Ally longed for the heady days when Guy had first wooed her, but it seemed with each passing month that it was nothing more than a distant dream. Guy still made love to her, if she could call it that: his perfunctory fucking never lasting more than a couple of minutes, and she was always left wanting more.

As Guy's business grew, Ally increasingly spent her time outdoors, taking care of the horses. Frequently, Guy would come home and finding his once sexy girlfriend stinking of stables, and dressed to suit, so he would fire up one of his sport cars and race off to a local pub for amusement. On the rare occasions that Guy would actually ask Ally to join him, it would take her so long to get ready that, by the time that she had come down the stairs, all resplendent and shining, he would have already left. Standing at the door, looking out into the night, Ally's heart would sink as, yet again, she realised Guy had gone without her. Tears falling, she would go back upstairs and slowly begin to wipe off her make-up, smearing the mascara across her face as she wondered when it was that he fell so drastically out of love with her, and sometimes, even if he had ever truly loved her. She also wondered quite why she felt that she had no voice when it came to her irrepressible boyfriend – and just why she still loved him so very much.

On this bright October morning, Guy was tense and full of impatience to get on the road. Watching his grooms load up the last of the horses, an impressive black stallion called Cabernet Noir – his owners were vineyard owners in Italy – of whom he had high hopes, Guy checked his phone. Ally had tried to use it this morning to call the vet and was shouted at for her trouble. Guy, ever cautious, was thankful that he named all his squeezes after men. Miranda, his latest, was labelled under 'Mike Dann' and he quickly fired off a text to her, going into detail about all the things she could do to him later once the lorry was cleared of horses. Cabernet Noir whinnied as the ramp was raised, and Guy settled into his sports car to follow the lorry, immediately putting his phone onto hands-free so that he could start calling stud farms in America.

Across the Channel, Rin was in a bad mood as she loaded up her clients' horses. In the aftermath of leaving Arjan, as well as during the latter stages of the relationship, she had started the affair with Juan, and she had only come clean about to Yves about this two months after she left Arjan. Yves, who saw himself as her saviour, was crushed, calling her every name under the sun. Storming out, he refused to speak to her, and all her calls and messages were ignored. It made no difference, Rin reminding Yves that he had his own girlfriend while he had been with her, he still called her a whore and he would frequently sit in corners at the shows, his dark eyes full of hate for the way he had been treated by Rin. Naturally, since her revelations, Yves had gone back to his girlfriend permanently and was being holier than thou about Rin's relationship with Juan.

Rin surprised herself by being upset about her split with Yves. He had been good for her ego, severely dented following all of Arjan's philandering's, and her confidence had soared as she, in her 30s, had bedded someone 15 years younger than her. With their shared passion for the Arabian horse, Rin had enjoyed both Yves' youthful energy and insight into showing, with both learning from each other. His response to uncovering her affair with the client had shocked her – as did his ongoing refusal to ever speak to her again.

However, Rin's affair with her client, Juan Ricciardo, had not gone to plan and her heart was broken. Juan was a proud man born in Venezuela and who had moved to one of the Spanish islands after falling in love with an heiress while she was trekking through South America. Easily bored, but tied to his wife, mainly because of her money but the fact that they had children was also a consideration, Juan had wooed Rin with his easy-going charm and charisma, which was such a contrast to Arjan's ever frequent black moods. At 5'8", Juan wasn't that much taller than Rin but he still made her feel precious. With his dark eyes, skin that tanned to the colour of a conker after just a few minutes in the sun, and his salt and pepper hair, as well as great humour and a love of all the finer things in life, Rin had fallen heavily for him.

Juan promised Rin that he would leave his wife at the end of the current show season and, with riches and diamonds dangled before her, Rin had joined him at his palatial marital home that summer while his wife was spending a month on mainland Spain, showing off their children to doting aunts. After two blissful weeks of making love, siestas, riding out along the white sandy beaches, and dining under the stars, Rin was convinced that Juan loved her and would follow through on his promise. They had returned to Belgium together for the late summer and early autumn shows, sharing a bed both at her home and in hotels, and Rin knew it would only be a matter of time before Juan left his wife for good and put a ring on her finger.

After the tempestuous relationship with Arjan, followed by her fling with Yves, Juan made Rin feel secure. When she lay in bed next to him, wrapped up in his strong arms, Rin felt safer than she ever had in her whole life. For the first time, she finally fell truly and deeply in love. While she knew that, with Arjan, they had the dream partnership in terms of their job, as a couple they had just about got along together rather than being a deep and passionate love. Rin never regretted leaving Arjan, and now that she was in Juan's all-encompassing embrace, she had never felt happier.

But Rin found that as time went on, Juan's promises to leave his wife had become ever-more distant and now, with just two shows left this year, it became clear that Juan had gone back to his wife. Despite the pain she felt inside, it seemed that Rin was meant to just smile sweetly, show his horses and still allow him into her bed at shows. With Arjan still sulking over their break up from over a year ago, she needed Juan more than ever, and yet it seemed now that even when they made love, Juan was completely removed from her. Like so many before her, Rin had believed that Juan truly loved her, and she conveniently forgot how she herself had cheated on Arjan with Juan and Yves.

Even after all this time since Rin and Arjan had gone their separate ways, rumours were continuing to fly around the circuit about what had happened between them – how this couple who had won championships around the world in partnership and had seemed to be so completely together one day, in spite of Arjan's shenanigans, had brutally split up the next, destroying their business in the process. While gossip tended to move on very quickly in this industry, the news of Arjan and Rin splitting up in such a volatile fashion was still rippling around the Arabian horse world.

'Come on Claude,' she said, as she led a chestnut colt, full of Arabian type, out of his stable.

With the more flattering show name of Sparkle of Justice, Claude was one of the horses she had persuaded Juan to buy from her friend, and so far, he had not lived up to his promise. Unless he put on a good show this weekend – and the judges liked him and favoured Rin – he would be on his way to a new home. Pausing for a second, Rin dared to publicly show a rare emotional side as she buried her face in Claude's flaxen mane, fighting against the tears that continually threatened to overwhelm her in private these days. As she collected herself and led Claude up the ramp of the lorry, she wondered where, and how, her charmed life had gone so very wrong.

From across Europe, the horse boxes filed into the Zilveren Spoor Equestrian Centre outside Moorsele, Belgium. Held in Belgium every other year on the last weekend of October, the European Championships was among the favourite events for many on the Arabian showing calendar, not least as its Saturday night party was legendary. Grey skies, rain, a clock change to wintertime and a chill in the air seemed to go hand-in-hand with this show, but exhibitors, spectators and judges alike did not mind. For it was inside the centre, among the dark wood surroundings and sand of the arena, where champions were made, and dreams came true.

Pulling his sports car into a parking space, Guy was

satisfied to have just sprayed Arjan with the contents of a very big, very dirty puddle. There was no love lost between these two men, not least as, when Guy first decided to enter the Arabian show scene and make some money, he had poached one of Arjan's bigger clients, Jean Janssens, with promises of riches and wins while wining and dining him on a friend's luxury yacht. Guy had promptly ruined the client's horses, mainly because he used them as guinea pigs to practice his training methods, and they were sold on quietly at local markets across the UK and Ireland. Jean, heartbroken and very much out of love with the industry after such horrors, quit Arabian horses for good and moved to southern Spain to open a hotel, far away from any reminders of the Arabian showing world.

Arjan never forgave Guy for not only poaching his client, but also ruining a good man, and he vowed never to forget what Guy had done. Jean had long been a good influence on Arjan, teaching him much about the old ways of horsemanship and of showing, breeding, and competing. It was Jean who gave Arjan his first show champion and even when he had no horses to compete with, Jean still supported the young Belgian in all that he did. Surprised and a little bit hurt that Jean had moved his horses to Guy, Arjan was upset. When he spoke to Jean to ask why, the older man brushed it off lightly.

"We are too close now, you and I," he had said. "I see you more as a son than a trainer, and I don't ever want you to feel that you owe me. This will be a good thing. Just see."

Sadly for Jean, Guy had destroyed his lifelong passion for the Arabian horse and while he still sent Arjan the odd letter from his Spanish retreat, there was never any more mention of horses.

With this determination to avenge Jean, Arjan was

determined to beat Guy in the ring at every opportunity. The rivalry between the two was terrifying to watch, and spectators could never take their eyes off the pair when they were going head to head for a championship, each moving their horse closer and closer to the other, dangling whips over their shoulders and into the other's face, and trying to get their horse to intimidate the other. Neither gave an inch and many a time, a judge or ringmaster had to jump out of the way to avoid being hit by a whip as each man tried to outdo the other.

Markedly, neither would congratulate the other when they won. Rather, they muttered snide curses when they walked past each other in the collecting ring or stables. For Guy, this was all water off a duck's back – he was harder than Arjan and used to winning at any cost. Arjan, however, would brood into the night on how to beat Guy and how get horses away from him. For while outwardly, Arjan was the Lord of Misrule, he was a good person inside although he very rarely let it show. Raised in Belgium near Baler, where he still lived, Arjan came from a very close family and they were very proud of all his achievements. Those people that came into his life and were true found that they had a true ally in Arjan, but those people were few and far between.

Parking his car, Guy laughed as he got out and watched a muddy, soaked Arjan, cigarette hanging limply out of his mouth, walk towards the main building. Guy went around to where his horses were being unloaded. Sending one of his grooms down into the vaults of the building to collect the horses' show numbers, as well as the VIP table tickets for his carefully selected guests, he oversaw the horses being settled into their stables, constantly barking orders to have more hay, more water, more blankets and fresh tail bandages at once. As Holly, a particularly comely and buxom groom of his who had enjoyed the dubious pleasure of working for Guy for many years, finished putting the finishing touches to his hospitality area, he smiled and grabbing her, pulled her inside an empty stable for his first away-from-home fuck of the weekend.

Holly was still pulling the top door of the stable shut when Guy grabbed her from behind, pulling her over to a hay bale. Roughly kissing the back of her neck, desperate to have his own needs met, Guy unzipped her jeans, and yanked both them and her knickers down. Barely bothering to check whether Holly was ready for him, he thrust into her, enjoying the feeling of welcome tightness around his cock as Holly obligingly spread her legs further apart and leant further over the hay. Guy came in seconds, such was his need, and as he gave a final deep thrust into her, he moaned loudly into Holly's shoulder.

'God, I needed that,' he said as, pulling his flies up, Guy left the stable, and Holly lying resplendent over the hay bale, while he went to charm the first clients of the weekend. Winking at Miranda as she strutted past with a dancing chestnut filly with a flaxen mane and tail, Guy turned his attention to his new clients, Pierre and Marcia DuPont, who had just arrived nervously at the stables. With his lust stated, for now, Guy intended to make as much money as possible through selling horse flesh before the day was out. While he might pretend to have favourite horses, to him, they either just held dollar signs or were destined for the meat man. Pouring three glasses of high-quality Bordeaux and motioning to the DuPont's to sit down, Guy checked his hair in the reflection of a framed photograph of himself winning a coveted World Championship title four years earlier and settled down to do business.

Coming from a non-horsey family, Guy had bucked the trend and rather than follow his brothers into the FTSE-market, he had decided to make his millions through horses instead. His parents, official and polite, were short on affection and they paid each son £1 pocket money a month for each year of their age. Guy, the youngest, had received £5 as a five-year-old boy while his older brothers received £8 and £11 respectively, something that grated on the young boy. Their parents, however, had then split the pocket money, putting half of each month's allowance into a high-interest bank account that each boy could access when they were 21 years of age; 18 was deemed too young by them to know what to do with it and not fritter it away.

Guy had already been drawn to horses instead, and he cajoled his uncle, who had a passion for all things equine, into giving him a horse for his 13th birthday. Guy did everything for 'Monty', a six-year-old pure-bred Arabian gelding. They did everything together, Guy learning to ride and spending his afternoons out on the Brecon Beacons, undisturbed for miles. The bond he formed with Monty would be like no other he ever had in his life, and the two were inseparable.

It was during this time that Guy discovered that his mother had a weakness for horses. He played on this and together, they would drive across the UK to compete in shows. Having saved up enough money from county show wins, Guy purchased a filly and so his path with the Arabian breed was set. His father, finally acknowledging his success, begrudgingly allowed the old cattle barns at their Brecon Beacon home to be turned into stables, and Guy began to take in show liveries, where he would train the horses and show them for clients.

Guy's heart hardened, however, when he lost Monty at nine years of age. A freak, unexplained paddock accident left Monty with a broken leg and nothing could be done. Devastated, Guy vowed to himself that he would never allow another horse, or human, to get that close to him again. This hard, ruthless streak continued and turned Guy into the bitter person that he was today – one that always believed he could cajole money from even the poorest breeder, and one that could sell oil to the Arabs.

Guy spent the next few years building up his business in the UK, but he had his sights set higher than that. An invitation from a friend to visit him in Dubai just after his 18th birthday made Guy even more determined than ever. Visiting the famous horse race, the Dubai World Cup, he was amazed at both the high standard of woman readily available and the beauty of the Thoroughbreds that were racing. Realising that his good looks and charm could open many doors to him, Guy had soon found and secured some Arabian horse breeders to send their horses over to the UK for him to show in Europe.

Those within the industry were wary of Guy. They knew that he always had his eye on making a fast buck – and a quick fuck. Men sent their wives and daughters shopping for the day if Guy came to visit as he was notorious for seemingly just smiling at a woman and she would open her legs straight away. As for the fast buck, Guy excelled at this, buying a horse at 9am for £10,000 and selling it two hours later for £50,000.

Shallow, intent on winning at all costs, and with a cruel, ruthless streak to him, Guy was not a man to cross, as many found out to their detriment. As soon as he had come into his money at 21 years of age, there was no stopping Guy. He cut all ties with his family and, apart from sending his mother flowers for her birthday, he forged on through life alone, which was just the way he wanted it. 'Less complicated,' he muttered to himself. As far as he was concerned, people were only there to service his needs - either by lining his bank balance or satisfying his sexual demands. As for Ally, she was just an irritating convenience to look after the horses while he got his kicks all around the world.

Settling himself down on the sofa across from his clients, Guy was focused. For him, business meant money. He was always on the lookout for the next big thing, a way to exploit the innocent horse owner and to line his own pockets in the process. While other trainers always claimed a percentage of horses they helped to sell, Guy ensured that he took the maximum amount of commission possible. If he bought a stud fee for £1,500, he would sell it for £2,000 along with conditions that the foal would be registered as being co-bred with him should he like it. And if the foal was co-bred with him, then he would also be the one to show it. Just because he part-owned the horses didn't mean that he would charge any less – the co-owner would still be expected to pay full board and training expenses. The only consideration Guy ever made when making a deal was how soon he could get the money, and then get it out of the UK. Scrupulous to the end, Guy had few friends in the industry; rather just a steady stream of sexy blondes to warm his bed as he travelled around the world.

The DuPont's were new to the industry although Marcia had been into horses for many years. They had met when Pierre was 21, Marcia 19, and had very much fallen in love. Marcia rode regularly, and she had long held a dream to own a white Arabian mare. When they married three years later, Pierre had surprised her with a Polish mare as a wedding present. Deeply in love with his wife, Pierre allowed and enabled Marcia to fulfil her dreams, and he loved nothing more than seeing the look of joy on her face when she began talking about the horses.

With this in mind, they had tentatively begun a small breeding programme and had been looking to expand their farm. A trip to the Menton Show, held on the French Riviera in June, had further ignited that passion and they began to ask around as to which trainer they should use, and where to buy the best horses. Guy, overhearing a conversation, masterminded for them to visit him in England, here he had impressed Pierre with the wonderful, almost military-like set up at his training centre. Fully engaged, Guy had invited them along to the show this weekend as his guest, fully planning to have sold them a horse or two by the time the show was over, and to move on to Paris with a World Championship contender in his barn.

As day turned into night, trainers, clients and grooms migrated to the bar. In spite of the windows down one side of the room and the view into the arena the other side, the dark wood and the snug-like dividing compartments made the area seem more intriguing than it actually was. There was always the sense of wondering who was talking in the booth next to you; were they selling a horse, buying a horse, stealing a wife or bribing a judge? With one ear on the conversation in front of you, the other on what was going on around you, it was little wonder that there were few true friendships in the world of the Arabian horse. Friendship, it seemed, was a word used to promote yourself and get what you wanted from others. Only a handful of friendships were genuine, and while most accepted that as a way of life for the world they moved in, others struggled and it was not unusual to find someone sobbing in the toilets during the show, wondering just what they had done to their supposed best friend who, having got what they wanted, had dropped them like a hot potato and moved on to the next person to charm, captivate and con.

The night before a title show started was always a relaxed affair. There would be people drinking and standing at the bar, laughing late into the night, but many would have just a couple of drinks and enjoy an early night. With the breeders' party on the Saturday evening, several of the exhibitors and trainers decided to save themselves for that instead. The result of this was it was just a hardcore group of people left at the bar gone midnight – and you could always guarantee that Arjan would be at the centre of them. Guy, however, very rarely entered the bar, preferring to drink at his stables before taking clients out for dinner, invariably adding the cost of the meal on to their next bill.

Rising early on the Saturday, as the cold October night gave way to morning and clouds hung over the showground casting an incessant mist over anyone walking outside, Guy was at the stables early to check his horses, criticising everyone around him for not carrying out his orders in the exact way that he asked. Holly, po-faced as she listened to him rant and rage, tried to let it all sweep above her head. She knew that Guy was always uptight before a show and would shout continually. Everything had to be done to perfection: the water the right temperature for bathing the horses, the tails plaiting in a certain way, the bridle-path – the bit of the mane directly behind the ears – clipped to exactly the right length as prescribed by him – not a millimetre shorter or longer or there would be trouble. A new set of show products was purchased for each show to ensure that Guy never ran out – talc, chalk for the legs, shimmering spray for the body, hoof oil, insect repellent, detangler for manes and tails, and shampoo were all part of the standard set. Then there were clippers and blades, for when they clipped a horse's face or coat to make their coat appear fine; slicker hoods to put over the horses faces and necks to keep them warm and clean, as well as to stop their coat growing back; a variety of rugs, all of different weights; in addition, there were also bandages for tails and legs to stop them rubbing and to protect them respectively.

With so much at stake, including that European Championship title, Holly could understand why Guy got so uptight. She just wished that he wouldn't always take it out on her, and she also wished that, just sometimes, the sex could be more tender and caring. Not for the first time she envied Ally, as she got to stay at home and be out of the firing line, which became increasingly fierce as the weekend went on.

As Holly groomed one of the young fillies that Guy was showing in the first class for a client, she thought back to when she had first been captivated by his charm. Guy had been a regular on the showing circuit around the UK for many years, first entering the show-rings as a young boy. Just a couple of years younger than him, Holly, horse mad since she was a little girl, thought that Guy was dashing and divine, and she and her friends frequently swooned and giggled whenever he walked past.

It would be many years later that Holly, finally an owner of her own purebred Arabian mare, decided to breed to a stallion that Guy owned. At that time, the Tindall family had lived in Wales, located up steep mountains in the Brecon Beacons National Park. Guy's mother decided that it would do her sons good to live surrounded by such nature and encouraged the whole family out of the house for bracing walks every weekend during the holidays. Their father, keen to keep up their education, ensured that the boys boarded at the top schools in the country during term time. They tolerated Guy having horses, but only just.

Holly loved the stallion that Guy had at stud that year and was desperate to use him on her mare, affectionately known as Rosie. Having saved up enough money for the stud fee, she borrowed a small horse lorry from a friend and began the 300 plus mile round trip from her home in Hampshire to the Brecon Beacons. Her journey there, anticipated to take four hours or so, ended up being a nightmare as the lorry had a terrifying tyre blow out on the M4 and she had to sit and wait to be rescued, praying that her treasured mare would be okay. Already more than halfway, Holly continued her journey to the Tindall's into the evening. It was March, it was dark, and it was cold and, upon calling ahead, she discovered that the family had already headed out for the evening. One of the grooms was still at the farm, but also heading out, and told Holly that Mrs Tindall insisted that she stay the night once after such a terrible journey. Holly was to unload her mare and make her way into the farmhouse by a side door. A light would be left on for her above the door and in the kitchen, as well as the barn where she was to put her mare.

However, no one had anticipated the heavens opening just as Holly began the long drive up the mountain. Already nervous about getting her mare and the lorry up the 1,000 metre plus ascent, Holly's palms were sweating as she coaxed the vehicle up the mountainside. Finally arriving into the open space of the Tindall's farm, Holly groaned as she realised that there were no lights on anywhere; all she could see through the rapidly-moving wiper-blades was the pitch black of night and the glow of the light from the barn; she would later learn that they ran off their own circuit and so were not affected by the main power cut.

Bracing herself against the insistent rain that was drumming down outside the dry haven of her lorry, Holly opened the door and was immediately soaked through. Running through the night to the stables, she quickly found Rosie's stable, which was all ready for her.

Having ensured that Rosie was settled and had enough water, Holly took in her surroundings. The barn was cold. Holly was just wondering about sleeping in the stable with Rosie for the night rather than trying to find a way through the darkness and into the Tindall's house when she spied a torch on the floor near the tack room.

Relieved, she turned it on, and its powerful glow lit up a clear path through the darkness outside. Racing across the yard towards the house, Holly once again became completely soaked to the skin as the rain permeated through her supposedly waterproof jacket as well as her jeans and shoes.

Finding the key under the milk bottles as directed, Holly let herself into the house and shut the door on the very drenched night outside. She immediately felt the warmth of an aga reaching her very cold hands and she could see a glow of light coming through the door straight in front of her. Following it, she realised that it was the dying embers of a fire in what appeared to be a snug room. Putting the torch down on the floor, Holly quickly stoked up the fire with wood from the basket and as it sparked back into life, she warmed her hands up in front of the smouldering flames.

Shivering, Holly cast the light of the torch around the room once more and saw a sofa just to the left of the fire, piled up with blankets. Stripping her body of her soaking clothes, arranging them as best she could on the fire guard, Holly lay down on the sofa and piled blankets over her shivering, underwear-clad body. With the crackle of the logs on the fire creating a hypnotic lullaby, Holly soon fell into a deep and dreamless sleep.

Barely a few hours later, Holly woke with a jump. The sound of more logs being thrown on the fire had woken her and opening her eyes, she saw a tall figure standing in front of the fire, warming their own hands in a scene so reminiscent of herself just a few hours ago. Catching her breath, Holly's first thought was that the person was a burglar but just as she was beginning to panic, the crisp tones of Guy's voice cut through the half-darkness.

'Who's there?' he said. 'I know someone is here. Come on – show yourself.'

Turning towards her, Guy took a step and lowered himself to Holly's eye level.

'Guy… It's me… Holly,' she mumbled, the combination of waking terror and longing of being so close to him making her quiet and shy. Relief, exhaustion and lust all combined into one and Holly raised herself up into a sitting position rather than staying lying down. Before she even realised what she was doing, she threw her arms around his neck and hugged him, knocking him slightly off balance as she did so. As she held him to her, the pile of blankets barely concealing her near-naked body, she realised that he was soaked to the skin and shivering slightly.

Anticipating her question and relishing the feel of her warm back under his hands, Guy explained that he had gone out as planned but a telephone call from a local farmer had alerted him that some of his yearlings had broken through a fence and were loose.

'He and I have been out in this weather for three hours trying to catch them – we finally caught the last one half an hour ago, and I decided to come back here for some dry clothes,' he said, silently adding to his own mind that it looked as if he had made the right decision.

Standing up, Guy made his way back to the fire and threw some more logs on. Turning around, he said to

Holly: 'I am just going to get some candles and out of these wet clothes. Stay there.'

With that, he was gone and Holly lay back in the relative darkness, feeling the heat from the now roaring fire coursing through her body. Remember how many years she had secretly longed for Guy, she anticipated his returning footsteps as she lay there, her mind wandering constantly as to what might happen.

In a matter of minutes, Guy returned to the room. He had changed his clothes, but Holly could see that he was still shivering. In his hands, he carried a bottle of whiskey and a couple of glasses, as well as some candles which he quickly lit and placed on the low table in the middle of the room.

Turning, he half-smiled at Holly; she hadn't realised that her blankets had slipped down, exposing some of her body.

'Shift over,' he said. 'I need some of your body heat to warm me up. I'm chilled to the bone and you're all I've got.'

Without waiting for Holly to answer, Guy lay down next to her and as Holly shuffled over, he wrapped his arms around her and shuddered. 'God, I'm freezing,' he said, hoping that Holly would take the hint and wrap her arms around him too.

Guy had noticed Holly around the show-rings – most of his friends had. She wasn't tall, being just 5'4", but her curvy body, fluttering brown eyes and long, naturally curly blonde hair had attracted many admirers. Not that Holly had ever known it – she kept herself to herself and Guy had always liked that quality in a woman. Lying wrapped up together with her for a couple of minutes, listening to the crackling of logs on the fire and the sound of their breathing, Guy reached for the whiskey.

'Made with water straight from the Brecons,' he said as he poured two incredibly generous measures into the glasses. 'Definitely the best thing to warm us up right now.'

He handed Holly her glass and, raising it slightly to her, immediately downed it and poured himself another. Holly tentatively sipped hers, feeling the warmth from the liquor slowly filter down through her body. 'Drink up,' said Guy as he downed his second glass. Holly hesitated for only a moment before knocking back the rest of the drink in her glass. Eyes watering slightly, she dutifully handed her empty glass to Guy, who put it on the floor next to his. Immediately, he rolled back towards Holly, put his arms under the blankets and wrapped them tightly around her.

'Now, are you going to tell me why you are lying here in my front room wearing nothing more than your underwear and a blush please?'

Blushing even more furiously in the half-light, Holly closed her eyes as she felt Guy inch ever closer to her.

'I had a blow out on the way here, and then I got soaked putting Rosie in the stable. I was so tired and my clothes were soaked. It was easier just to lie here on the sofa for a while and warm up by the fire…'

Her mind, and stomach, in turmoil, Holly's skin felt hot under Guy's touch, even though his hands were intensely cold still. Whiskey making her put her normal voice of reason to one side, Holly pulled Guy closer to her, wrapping a leg over his hip as she did so, whispering 'you're freezing…'

She could feel Guy's breath on her neck, and she involuntarily pulled him even closer to her.

'Finding you here… It really is a most unexpected pleasure…' said Guy, the feel of his breath as he spoke making Holly shiver.

'Are you cold?' he asked innocently, fully aware of the effect that he was having on this young, voluptuous, sexy girl.

Dreading that he might pull away from her, Holly lied. 'Perhaps a little…,' she murmured.

'Here, put this on,' said Guy as he suddenly sat up and removed his t-shirt, handing it to Holly. She couldn't help her eyes lowering to his torso and she admired his bare, toned chest by the light of the fire.

Sitting up, Holly pulled the t-shirt on, struggling to get it to get down past her breasts. Admiringly, Guy poured them each another whiskey and toasted her.

'Looks good on you,' he smiled. Pulling her to him, the pair lay down once more and without saying a word, Guy reached his hands up underneath the t-shirt and began to slowly caress Holly's stomach.

'God, you've got such soft skin,' he whispered as he moved in closer.

Continuing to stroke her, Guy leaned in and slowly kissed Holly's neck. 'I've been wanting to do this for years,' he said. 'I've always wanted you…'

Amazed, Holly turned to look at Guy and, taking advantage, he immediately kissed her on the lips. Slowly, languidly, Guy's tongue danced its way into her mouth and Holly immediately responded, wrapped her arms around Guy's neck and parting her legs slightly.

'I didn't think you knew who I was!' Holly gasped as Guy finally stopped kissing her and came up for breath.

'Of course I did… And I am going to enjoy every single minute of this…'

Holly was suddenly brought back to the here and now from her trip down memory lane by Guy marching in the stable and shouting at her to hurry up. Sighing, she led the filly out towards the arena, wishing that perhaps she didn't love Guy quite so much.

4

Back at the show, the wives and mistresses of the trainers, or 'WAMS' as they were somewhat derogatorily referred to by the grooms, made their way to the VIP tables. Here, clients would have paid tens of thousands of euros for a front row seat while often not bothering to turn up at the show themselves. It would be the WAMS that would sit pristinely at these tables. Having been tanned, manicured and coiffured before the show, with new clothes and jewellery brought for every title or 'A' Show, the WAMS sat smugly knowing that they were taking centre stage on the live feed that was being streamed around the world. With a bottle of white wine in front of them by 11am, they sat writing down the scores and messaging each other on their telephones – all in an effort to look busy and important and not because they were actually interested in the outcome. As long as their man won, that was all that mattered; a win meant a bonus from a happy boss, and these could sometimes include cars and even luxury holidays. It also meant that they would have sex that evening, and it would be a happy occasion rather than the one-sided angry sex that happened so often when they lost. That, or their husband or boyfriend would disappear into the bar, returning to their hotel room at 4am, smelling of cigarettes, beer and perfume, and covered not only in lipstick around their mouths, but sometimes also around their cock.

At 9am exactly, the DJ changed the music from ambient background to something more stirring and the first horses could be seen gathering in the collecting ring. The

Disciplinary Committee, or the DCs as they were called, were busy checking everyone and every horse against their equine passport. They also invariably turned a blind eye when one of the big trainers whipped a horse, instead bearing down on a timid amateur, who was busy wondering just what they were doing there in the first place and whether it was too late to load up their horse and go home.

No show is complete without a commentator and the dulcet tones of Peter Gilliard, known among his admirers as Mr Smooth, began to welcome people to the show. Peter had a huge string of female fans, who hung on his every word and stared into his hazel-brown eyes as they hung off his arm. Peter loved to be the centre of attention and with his sleepy Devonshire accent, laid-back manner, and salt and pepper hair, he lured people into thinking that he was a gentle giant while he in fact preferred to go out with the boys and large it up until 5am.

Peter had spent his life being a dreamer. Growing up in Brixham, a small fishing town south of Torquay on the Devon coastline, he would spend his days watching the fishing trawlers return to dock, soaking up the limited sunshine and occasionally wondering where his life would take him.

Peter finally discovered that girls were more interesting than fish when he was 15 years old. One hot, balmy day, an older girl with a knowing smile came up to him as he sat on the wall overlooking the sea. She was doing highly suggestive things to an ice lolly and Peter's attention was caught. She grabbed Peter's hand, pulling him off the wall, and he followed her down to behind the gutting sheds. There, throwing the lolly away and without saying a word, she dropped to her knees, unbuttoned his flies and turned the ministrations of her cool tongue to his hot cock.

Grasping the back of her head, Peter looked up to the sky and groaned as he enjoyed what would be the first of many orgasms achieved this way.

As the months progressed, Peter earned something of a stud status throughout the town and the local arena and by the time he was 16, he walked with a swaying swagger and a confidence that he never knew he possessed. Shirking any offers of relationships, Peter's heart was finally won when he was approaching 18 years old as during one night in The Queens Arms, Esme walked into the bar and into his life. At 5'7", Esme was a 16-year old willowy blonde with a shy smile and captivating brown eyes. Peter was instantly hooked and he made his way over to her. Buying her a lime and lemonade, Peter discovered not only love for the first time in his life, but also the Arabian horse. Esme spent her weekends working at a local farm and she invited him to join her at a show. One glimpse of these majestic, proud horses with their terrific movement and incredible type, and Peter knew that this was the life for him.

Proposing to Esme just a few months later, Peter began to travel further and further to the shows, the couple finally ending up at Ascot one glorious summer in late July for the British National Championships. Class after class of beautiful horses fuelled Peter's imagination further and there was no stopping him. Speaking to one of the owners of a big farm in Wales, Peter went to spend the rest of the year with them, learning about the industry, the horses and what it meant to be a winner.

Esme stayed behind in Brixham, sending letters to Peter on a weekly basis and loitering by the telephone box on the Quay at 8pm every night as she waited for Peter's call. Despite the distance, their romance grew and grew, and at the end of 1979, Peter was invited to go to Scottsdale for the Scottsdale Show, travelling out at the end of December and staying until the end of February.

The couple quickly arranged their wedding, a simple affair with Esme wearing a short, white dress with a lace veil that belonged to her grandmother. Peter, meanwhile, wore a suit loaned from his sponsors in Wales. The reception was held in the pub where they first met – all curled sandwiches, soggy crisps, and warm wine – and they honeymooned for the weekend in Torquay. The days were long and the nights were hot, as if scorched by their intense love for each other. It came as no surprise to anyone, least of all themselves, when Esme fell pregnant immediately.

Torn between spending time with his beautiful young, and now pregnant, wife and his future with the horses, Esme made the decision for him. She sent Peter west, across the ocean to America while she stayed living with her mother. Just a few weeks after Peter left, Esme miscarried and she suffered from complications. Unable to reach Peter due to the eight-hour time difference, Esme's mother sent a telegram. By the time Peter received it, Esme had died, and he was left to mourn this huge loss alone, and over 5,000 miles away.

From then on, Peter vowed that he would never allow himself to love again. Outwardly, he was still the life and soul of the party but come the nights, he would rather go out with the boys and be one of the lads than risk falling in love and getting so hurt again. Of course, this sparked many rumours that he was gay, but Peter just laughed them off, keeping the truth to himself. It was far easier that way. He never visited Brixham again.

Now in his 50s, Peter took his role as a commentator very seriously – at least until lunchtime when he enjoyed the first of the many beers that he would consume during the day. If he had one too many, his legions of fans would giggle as his commentary became more and more outrageous as the afternoon went on.

Peter was the main commentator for several shows across Europe and the Middle East. After losing Esme while he was in Scottsdale, he had turned his back on that particular land of opportunity and never returned. However, he was kept more than busy where he was, travelling around the world and earning frequent flyer miles wherever he went.

Each country had local shows, which were generally affiliated to the country's Arabian horse registry. Bigger shows, however, fell under the jurisdiction of ECAHO, the European Conference Arabian Horse Organizations. The smallest of these shows were 'C' shows, followed by National Shows, then B Shows, which could be international or national, then A Shows. Among these were the title shows, based around the European Triple Crown of the All Nations' Cup in Aachen, the European Championships, and then the Paris World Championships. Peter loved to commentate at these shows. Being a bit of a wide boy, he knew all the handlers by name and would regularly tease them in the show-ring through his commentary. Sometimes, he went a bit too far, especially if he had enjoyed one too many at the bar, but on the whole, he was good entertainment and well worth the money.

This year's European Championships had over 200 horses entered, and the Sheikhs themselves had many horses entered, using the fact that they were bred in Europe to enable them to show. While the sponsors loved this, as it meant that there was more money available to them to put on the best show possible, it pushed out the smaller breeders and they frequently wondered why they should bother showing, knowing that they were certain to just make the top six if they were lucky.

Anticipation at this year's show was very high, however.

A grey filly had been sold by small breeders in Italy for astronomical amounts of money, and she would be making her debut here. Named Passionate Presence, this yearling filly had the showing world talking, not least for the much-rumoured €2,000,000 she was sold for. Before the show, Sienna had been busy co-ordinating publicity about the filly for her new owners, a young Middle Eastern couple new into the breed, and such was the level of interest that the grandstand was packed for the first class of the weekend.

Part of the condition of the sale was that Passionate Presence would be shown by an Italian trainer and so it was Luca Lucchetti who proudly led this dancing grey filly into the arena. Adored by women – and men – the world over, Luca was tanned, dark and very handsome. He only had to raise an eyebrow at a woman, and they would go weak and the knees and, in the show-ring, this often worked to his advantage as he gave a beaming smile to a female judge. Her hand, hovering between 19 and 19.5 points, would suddenly select the 20 instead, and Luca would, once more, claim another championship. However, such was the beauty of Passionate Presence that the high scores were automatically reached for. When she was standing up before the judges, her neck came up beautifully from her shoulders, arching in just the right places. Her head was elegant, refined, chiselled, with deep pools of black for her eyes, showing the way into her soul. As she walked, her tail automatically lifted. When she trotted, her tail flagged over her back and she powered from behind to cover the ground effortlessly. While, typically, the higher scores are reserved for later on in the show, today Presence received a glut of 20s from the judges and finished with an incredible 93.8 points. The crowd, understandably, went mad at the scores and Luca proudly led the beautifully filly around the ring for an extra parade lap, before being collared by fans the moment he left the ring, each eager to touch this amazing horse.

"That, ladies and gentlemen, is how to open a show!' laughed Peter over the announcers' speaker, ever the master of understatement.

The show continued, and Rin was not enjoying herself. It seemed that everything she touched at the moment turned to dust and her stalls were decidedly empty of people. Guy's stables, located a little further down than hers, were crowded with people as he schmoozed with everyone that he could lure in.

Meanwhile, a terrific party was still going on outside Luca's stables, with everyone delighted at Passionate Presence's win.

'Claude's class is coming up Rin. He will show well for you, he always does,' said Zoë, trying to raise her boss's spirits. Nodding vaguely, Rin moved to her hospitality area and collapsed in one of the chairs.

'I hope so. He needs to do well. If not, his owners may take him somewhere else,' said Rin, nervously looking down the corridor to Guy once more. She had been caught in the crossfire of Arjan and Guy on previous occasions when they were having one of their gigantic battles in the show-ring. As a result of Guy's wheeling and dealing, she and Arjan had lost clients to Guy. While she was nothing to do with Arjan anymore, she knew that the Englishman would still delight in putting the boot in wherever, and whenever, possible, such was his determination to succeed.

'It's time,' said Zoë as she led Claude out of his stable. In spite of the lateness in the show season, his chestnut coat looked vibrant and as he danced his way around to the collecting ring, Zoë had to admit that her boss certainly knew how to train and condition horses, regardless of what was going on in her personal life. Rin paid a great deal of attention to how the horses looked, regularly reassessing their diet and exercise regime. If any horse had an issue with its teeth or feet, Rin was immediately aware, and she took the day to day health of each horse very seriously.

Unfortunately for Rin, however, she had not looked after her own health so well. Sparkle of Justice, a huge mover, found himself being restricted during his flamboyant trot and Rin struggled to keep up with him. When it came to the stand-up however, Claude, thoroughly fed up with being held back, refused to stand still and the judges gave up, awarding him a lowly 89.2 points.

Defeated, a white-faced Rin left the arena having not even made the class Top Five let alone the championships. Ignoring a waiting Zoë, Rin led Claude back to the stable herself, locking herself in with him and crying once more into his mane.

'Rin, let me in,' Zoë pleaded.

Ignoring her, Rin sank to her knees, wondering where her golden life had gone so wrong, and had become so ruined.

'Rin, please. Claude's owner, Juan, is here... I'm sorry.'

What followed was short and swift but no less painless as Claude was immediately removed from Rin's care to Guy's stables. The fact that Juan and Rin had once been so close had no bearing in Juan's considerations, nor was the fact that he had helped put her in such a state.

'You lost,' was his final comment as he motioned to Holly to come and take Claude, the girl unable to meet the eyes of either Rin or Zoë as she did her job.

As Rin watched this most lovely of horses trot down the stables so trustingly, oblivious to the fact that he would never be able to nicker at her again in delight as she trained him and rewarded him, her heart broke. She knew that she had hit the bottom; she just hoped that she didn't have any further to fall.

As the first day of the European Championships came to a close, people made their way back to their horseboxes or hotels to get ready for that evening's breeders party. A firm favourite of all the parties on the circuit, this was the one that everyone wanted to be at and enjoy the most. With the clocks also going back an hour that weekend, there was either an extra hour's partying or an extra hour's sleeping, depending on your point of view.

As people slowly began to arrive at the showground, no one noticed as Rin and Zoë closed their empty horsebox and headed for home. Acutely aware that her boss, but most importantly her friend, was in meltdown, Zoë was only too happy to leave Zilveren Spoor for home. Messaging Susannah, Zoë told her that she was worried for Rin's wellbeing, adding that Juan's deceiving her had finally tipped her boss over the edge.

Luca also decided to give the party a miss. His beautiful wife, Alessandra, had left their children at home with her mother so that she could come to the show with him. Having left the showground while the celebrations were still going on, Alessandra had returned to the hotel to prepare for Luca's arrival. Stopping at the shops to buy Prosecco and scented candles, she awaited Luca's return.

She didn't have long to wait as, feeling incredibly horny after such a win, Luca cut short the party to head back to the hotel. Going into their suite, Luca stopped in his tracks at the sight of his curvaceous wife, her long auburn curls tumbling down over her shoulders while her sloe-black eyes started intently at him, lay naked on the bed wearing just Presence's garland for first place and nothing else. The room was lit by candles, the Prosecco in an ice bucket on the bedside table, and Luca immediately felt his crotch stiffen.

'Ciao amore," Alessandra purred, opening her legs a fraction to give Luca a tantalising glimpse of her neatly trimmed bush, lips already glistening as she was so excited for what was to come. Raising her hands above her head, she waited for Luca to gather himself.

'My darling…,' he whispered, shedding his clothes with lightning speed and crawling on to the bed astride her. 'My angel… My beauty…'

Picking up the Prosecco, he popped the cork and allowed some of the bubbling liquid to pour over his wife's naked body before he bent his head and started licking the rivers of liquid from her breasts.

'My angel…,' Luca said as he continued to lick, lower and lower until Alessandra was writhing beneath him, legs opening further and further each time his tongue touched her body.

Having brought her to a shuddering climax, Luca carefully removed the winner's garland and placed it across the headboard and rolled over, allowing Alessandra to climb on top of him and begin to rock back and forth.

'Amore! Amore!' he cried as, staring at the garland, he exploded into her, before pulling her down on to him and into his arms, muttering words of endearment into her hair. 'My angel…,' he sighed, one more time, as he fell into a deep and very satisfying sleep.

Alessandra lay there, gazing at his long eyelashes flickering against his cheek as he dreamed. They were childhood sweethearts, and she knew that she was lucky enough to be married to one of the few true men in the industry, and that she was more than enough for her sweet, sweet Luca. But they both knew that if he ever looked anywhere else, she would kill him.

Arjan, meanwhile, had been downing neat vodkas with Leap since the moment the show ended for the day. Since his break up with Rin last year, when Leap had pulled up outside Arjan's home and dragged the whiskey bottle away from him, the two had become completely inseparable. With Leap enjoying bedding the inevitable friend of Arjan's latest conquest, with the girls constantly turning up in twos and threes, he was pleased to see that his friend had recovered his mojo. As they downed another vodka shot, Leap laughed to himself as two German girls walked in, wearing identical barely-there outfits, and positioned themselves deliberately next to Arjan, eyes wide in anticipation that tonight could be their night to sleep with this legendary womaniser who was not only reputed to be hung like a horse but who knew how to pleasure a woman as well.

The Europeans in Moorsele was Arjan's favourite show of the year, not least as it was almost on his doorstep, and there was always a great atmosphere at the party. Held on the middle night of the show, it almost had an end of term feeling before the pressures of the World Championships got too much. Everyone was in a party mood and everyone was willing – and able – to let their hair down. Eyeing up the girls next to him, Arjan turned around to make some joke to Leap but was distracted by seeing Sienna. She had clearly drunk too much, caught up with a man and a woman who were obviously trying to get her into bed. Watching, he realised that Sienna was totally oblivious to what was happening and as he watched the woman go to kiss her and the man slap her on the backside, he decided that he should be the one to rescue her. Nothing like being a knight in shining armour, he thought wryly to himself as he walked over to where she stood next to the bar.

'Hey Sienna,' he said as he leaned in to place the

obligatory and highly perfunctory three kisses on her cheeks. 'Want a drink?'

Handing her a vodka, Arjan realised that Sienna was more drunk than he had realised. "Tonight could be the night", he thought as he led her over to introduce her to Leap.

'Ah – you are Sienna! Arjan is always talking about you,' said Leap as he looked Sienna up and down, assessing this woman before him who seemed to have his friend so transfixed. Over the past months, Arjan had deliberately mentioned this woman's name in conversation as much as he could and Leap was certainly intrigued by her, despite having never met her. Apart from anything else, she seemed to be able to resist Arjan's charms, something that not many women, if any, could lay claim to.

Sienna returned Leap's stare with a cynical look on her face. "Pissed, but not that pissed," thought Arjan, his arm naturally moving around her waist and settling on her hips. God, she was curvy! To his delight, her arm crept across his waist, initially as a form of support for herself until gradually, she began to return his pressure. Smiling to himself, Arjan began to stroke Sienna's arse, wondering how she would respond. As she caressed the side of his waist and returned his squeeze, Arjan was delighted. "Good good," he thought to himself as he kept his arm around her and brought her further and further into the conversation.

Leap was still talking to her. 'Sienna! He never stops talking about you!'

'Mmmm – whatever,' Sienna replied, leaning into Arjan and enjoying the feeling of his arm around her through the haze of vodka she had drunk. She recalled that first time he spoke to her in Aachen, when she just coolly smiled and ignored his winning gaze; secretly, she had been glad that she had been sitting down – so few women could resist when he fixed his gorgeous brown eyes on them, and Sienna knew that she would just another notch on his bedpost. Now, however, she felt her resolve weakening. It had been a long day and for once she felt like letting her hair down and having some fun. Slowly, Sienna allowed the amount of alcohol that she had drunk to take over her feelings, and she leaned into Arjan, enjoying the feel of his hand caressing her backside.

Time seemed to be suspended and the hands on the watch around Arjan's wrist seemed to be moving slowly, with the atmosphere between Sienna and Arjan building. Leap kept smiling to himself, and winking at Arjan, as it was obvious that tonight would finally be the night. Maybe then Arjan would move on and forget about this alluring brunette who seemed to have him wrapped around her little finger. Sienna was clinging to Arjan more and more, and Arjan was showing no sign of letting go of her, now that he finally had the woman who he had lusted after for so long in his arms.

Arjan was just wondering when to make his move, pulling Sienna ever closer and waiting for the moment when he could capture her full attention so that she would turn her head to him, and he could try and kiss her, when Guy came into the bar. Drunkenly looking around, Guy saw Sienna, grabbed her arm and, before anyone could say or do anything, he had dragged her out of the room and bundled her into a taxi, heading back to the hotel in Kortrijk.

"And that's that," thought Arjan to himself angrily, wondering quite what Guy had that he didn't. If anything, his reputation was far worse and the fact that Sienna had left with Guy had not escaped Leap, who was now outwardly laughing at Arjan, fouling his friend's mood further. Not only that but the party was now starting to wind down, with many people already left for their own, or other, beds for the night. The time that Arjan had spent with Sienna had apparently been wasted, and he would be sleeping alone tonight.

5

Waking the next day, Arjan was still furious with Sienna, and even more so with Guy. Always, that man got in the way! Having hated him already for so many years, the animosity he felt towards the supposed English gent had increased tenfold overnight, and he was more determined to beat him than ever. His heart played other tricks, however. Barely bothering to talk to his groom, Suzanne, Arjan went through the motions in the ring, hardly registering where the horses placed. Leap, watching from the sidelines, was surprised to see his friend so dispirited, as he just half-trotted the horses around the arena instead of his normal powerful run. As for the stand-up – Arjan just stood there and let the horse do its own thing. Lighting a cigarette, Leap felt nervous for Arjan as, if he continued like this, he would quickly lose clients. Thankfully, he still had good horses at the training centre, and with the normal backhanders having been paid before people arrived at Moorsele, Arjan still managed to be at the top of the line. Guy, to Arjan's immense satisfaction, left the show empty handed.

The last that Arjan saw of Sienna during the show was that lunchtime. Having been acutely aware of her location every time he walked around the arena, he stopped by the gate as he was leaving to briefly talk to Leap, who was holding out a cigarette for him; he still hadn't forgiven him, either, for laughing at him so much the night before. With the last class before lunch finished, there was now a presentation of birds of prey. Looking around, Arjan saw Sienna talking to a falconer as a bird of prey flew in to rest on her arm. The very last thing Arjan saw was Sienna's smile and the look of sheer delight on her face as the bird of prey got closer to her in those two seconds than all the stalking he had done at the previous two shows had achieved.

Thinking that Sienna had spent the night in bed with Guy, Arjan's heart hardened and he turned away, marching grimly to the stables, clearing a path before him as people almost crossed themselves, so fierce was the look on his face.

As for Sienna, she was unaware of the drama surrounding her departure last night, although she certainly wished that Guy hadn't dragged her away from Arjan so soon. Quizzing him in the taxi on the way back to the Park Hotel, she had found out that there was a 'looking after Brits abroad' rule that Sienna was unaware of, whereby if any of the male trainers were out at a party abroad, and one of 'their' women was there, they would always ensure that she got back to her hotel safely. Deciding that it was a good thing as she realised that she was drunk enough to have done something she might have regretted, Sienna kept thinking back to the feel of Arjan's arm around her waist, and how good it felt. While she was glad that she had left when she did, she did think that perhaps a small kiss would have been okay – but for now, she would never know. Sienna couldn't help but look forward to seeing Arjan again very soon. However, she had to leave the show early to fly to the Middle East and meet up with some sheikhs who, new to the industry, wanted her advice on the best people to speak to. Having chatted with the falcon handler, she looked around for Arjan but there was no sign of him. Smiling to herself once more as she recalled last night, she walked out of the main entrance and stepped into the black Mercedes, waiting to take her to Brussels Airport and her next adventure.

Guy, meanwhile, was determined to beat Arjan in the afternoon's championships and he showed Cabernet Noir to the very best of his abilities. The stallion that Arjan had in this class was one trained by someone else – he was just on the end of the rope as the regular trainer was injured – and out of the corner of his eye, Guy could see that the horse and Arjan did not understand each other. The stallion was called Sundos, and he had enjoyed success before, but today would not be Arjan's day. In such a situation, t wasn't difficult to win, and Guy was smugly delighted when Noir was announced as Gold Champion Stallion. With the World Championships just around the corner, there was every chance that he would carry this momentum forward and claim a World title, one that he felt was well overdue.

There was six weeks to kill between the European and World Championships and everyone chose to prepare, or relax, in different ways. For Sienna, there was a lot of work for her clients as the glamorous Paris show came around once more. E-blasts had to be organised and timed with meticulous detail; online articles about breeding farms had to be finalised; and that all important cover shot had to be decided upon once and for all, as the various magazine editors around the world chased her for copy. Some clients were easier than others, but there was always one who gave Sienna a terrible headache, changing their minds at every stage of approval and sign off, often reverting to the original option after 10 different versions. So, while others relaxed on a beach somewhere before the pressures of the World Championships got too great, Sienna burned the midnight oil as she dealt with all the clients flying in from Australia, the US and the Middle East – all on their different time zones – and all wanting everything to be

150% right.

Arjan, meanwhile, spent a lot of his time pacing around his house and his farm. He was still furious about Sienna and Guy, but deep down, he was also worried about the future. With most of the stable block now empty, Suzanne was able to give meticulous care to the horses that they still had – and she desperately hoped for a good Paris show for Arjan so that he could start to build himself up once more.

Ringing Zoë for a chat, Suzanne shared her concerns about her boss: 'He's always been a drinker, Zoë, but he's taking things to a whole new level right now. He and Leap are worse than they have ever been – out in the strip clubs every night, bringing girls back here in the small hours and partying until dawn, when they pass out. I've stopped going to the house, you never know what you're going to find…'

'How much longer can he keep it up? Rin is struggling too – you never would have thought that they were the "golden couple" who won everything going. I seem to spend my days on the phone to clients, convincing them that all is well while Rin just fades away. It's like she is not there, half the time.'

'It's catching – Arjan seems to have forgotten how to eat properly, and he's certainly in denial about how serious things are at the farm. He seems to live on indigestion relief and chain smoking. It's scary. He's half the man that he was – but still the girls throw themselves at him.'

'Well, he is rich – and he does have a big cock!'

Suzanne laughed, remembering how she and Zoë had walked in on Arjan changing in the stables one time.

'He certainly does – although I'm amazed that it's not fallen off by now!'

Giggling, the girls carried on their conversation, with Zoë oblivious to her boss, Rin, next door, listening to every word that was being said. Rin, however, barely took in a word that was being said as she sat staring out of the window, looking through the rain coming down in rivulets. Broken hearted after losing both Juan and Sparkle of Justice, Rin spent each day barely going through the motions, wondering whether she should even try to carry on. Having only ever known this life, however, and having failed every exam at school, Rin knew that she had no choice but to try.

Peter, meanwhile, spent his time between shows travelling with friends. He had a flat in Battersea, London, and that was his base, but he was very much a free spirit with a sense of adventure. This November would see him go to Australia to spend a few weeks surfing off the Gold Coast – a far cry from his days at Brixham – and with beach babes and beer everywhere he looked, Peter was in his element. Checking in occasionally with Guy, Sienna and the other Brits for news, Peter was very much a lone wolf in a world where no one really liked to be alone.

As for Guy, he was typically wheeling and dealing, trying to build on the success of Cabernet Noir at the Europeans. Knowing that November in Europe meant that some farms were looking to cut back their numbers before the new season arrived, he jetted around the capitals, hiring a car and driving for hundreds of miles just to see if he could beat everyone else to the deal of the century. Ally, meanwhile, stayed at home and, exhausted from looking after the horses all day, every day, fell asleep on the sofa each night, a glass of wine untouched on the table beside her and the fire dying in the embers before it even had a chance to thrive.

All were on the countdown to Paris, to the World Championships, and to the next episode in this merry saga that continually propelled them around the world at an unrelenting – and, at times, unforgiving – pace.

6

So it was that the show circuit had arrived back in Paris for the crème de la crème of the shows and the one place that everyone pretended to love, but actually hated – the World Championships.

Arjan came out of his room and looked down at the bar below him. The hotel was such that you could walk around each floor, which was open plan, so that the noise of the revellers below rose up towards you. It was easy to lean against one of the columns, light a cigarette, and peer down through the smoke haze below and see who was there, and who was talking to whom.

Thursday night and the pre-show bar was heaving with people. Arjan quickly clocked Sienna, laughing with her parents and a group of friends, drinking cocktails. With Arjan standing up high, Sienna hadn't seen him yet, so he was able to watch her unnoticed for a few moments before making his way down in the lift. He went straight to Leap and their friend John, who came from England but lived in Belgium. Downing the beer that Leap had already ordered for him, Arjan kept half an eye on Sienna as she chatted with people. For once, he was curiously still as he watched and, following Arjan's gaze, Leap realised why. Having had a huge row after Moorsele, however, when Leap's jibes had got too close to the bone, he decided now was not the time to tease Arjan and instead, Leap focused on selling a horse to John as a wedding present for his bride-to-be.

Grabbing his chance, Arjan went over to see Sienna as she was leaning over a table to look at some photographs a client was showing her. Putting his arms around her waist, he pulled her back into his body, his groin connecting with her backside, and whispered in her ear 'Have you got a minute? I'd like to introduce to you to someone.'

Excusing herself, heart a flutter, Sienna followed Arjan across the room. Seeing John, she laughed and before she could help herself blurted out: 'Him? He owes one of the magazines money from last year!'

'Really?' Arjan couldn't help but laugh at that titbit; John was always very particular about getting other people to pay their bills but nothing surprised Arjan these days. 'Well, that's nothing to do with me!'

'I never said it was', replied Sienna, somewhat cautiously, somewhat haughtily.

Arjan introduced her and Sienna had a quick chat with John. She was aware of Arjan being distant and he had turned away from her and was talking to Leap. Only by his stillness did he betray how alert he was to Sienna's presence and how he was straining to hear every word she said. Sienna herself was confused as to why Arjan had made a point of coming over to introduce her to one of his best friends, why he had put his arms around her in such a way, and he was now clearly ignoring her. Chatting away to John, she was aware of Arjan vanishing to the other side of the room as a wealthy future client called him over. Feeling uncomfortable, she retreated to the safety of her own friends.

Waking the next day, exhaustion hit Sienna like a train. Having done two presentations on Arabian horses back to back, one in the Netherlands and one in Germany, she had then come straight to Paris and she was now reaching the end of her limit. Tired of the falseness, tired of people such as Crispin and Katherine telling her that she should do this and try that and be someone other than she was – someone that Sienna had no desire to be. Just because many people in this world were superficial did not mean that Sienna needed to join them.

Everyone thought that they knew Sienna but in reality, she limited herself to a very small group of people. Born into a middle-class background, she was blessed with having Arabian horses all through her life. Her earliest memories were of these special animals, and she could ride before she could walk. Naturally artistic, Sienna could also draw horses before she could write her own name.

Having followed the expected and somewhat conventional route of her older brothers, that of A levels, university, and then a good job in the City, mixed in with a perfect boyfriend and walking holidays in the Lake District. The horses were sold, and her parents had moved to a house in Andalusia, living out their own dream.

Sienna always yearned for more – something away from convention. She longed to be more creative, and she dreamed of being able to spend time with her beloved Arabian horses rather than running around putting press releases together on insurance product launches, timed for perfect delivery to the London Stock Market. One Sunday, tired of her boyfriend, who was more interested in having lager-drinking competitions with his friends in a Chelsea pub than with doing anything more active, Sienna made her way to the riding school at Hyde Park. By chance, her steed for the next hour was an Anglo Arabian – sired by a thoroughbred stallion but out of the daughter of a pure-bred Arabian mare – and Sienna's passion for the breed was once more reignited.

After a quick search on the internet, she discovered that the Paris World Championships were taking place the following weekend and, fed up with damp, soggy, dank London, she booked a flight and hotel on a whim and headed to the show on the Friday morning.

Three days later, eyes and heart dazzled with excitement and full of enthusiasm for the breed, Sienna returned to her London flat. Located off Piccadilly, the space was a haven and Sienna had created a peaceful sanctuary away from the hectic world that she lived in. Entering the front door, there was an easy table to the right where she was able to drop her keys and paperwork before heading into the kitchen on the left. Small and practical, it served Sienna well and there was always a bunch of flowers in a vase on the window to brighten the room. Coming out of the kitchen, you turned left into a walk-round loop. First was Sienna's bedroom, painted in faded aubergine and duck egg blue, with heavy, ornate gold curtains to shut out the noise of London life. Continuing round, there was a bathroom off to the right before arriving in what was a box room. Sienna had knocked down the wall to make it a dining area with the lounge seen over a low coloured wall, made up of violet, azure and gold squares. The lounge was very Middle Eastern in style, with intricate silk rugs picked up in Dubai on the floor and Arabic coffee cups and tea glasses making a vibrant display in the corner of the room. A huge deep burgundy sofa covered one wall of the room, the kind that could be easily sunk into at the end of a long day. At the end of the sofa, was a pile of deep grey marled knitted throws, ready to be pulled over to keep off the chill on a cool evening or just for curling up under on the rare nights that Sienna was home and able to watch a film.

Arriving back from Paris that cold, London evening, rather than sleep and prepare for what was going to be a busy week at work, Sienna sat up all night, glass of Malbec in one hand, notebook in the other. She scribbled away furiously, coming up with all sorts of ideas as to how she could combine her own natural creativity – wasted at putting together a press release about car insurance – with her love for the Arabian horse. When her boyfriend turned up, late at night and drunk, he found himself locked out. Sienna ignored the persistently ringing doorbell and instead, scoured the internet, finding out as much as she could about the breed, and all that she had missed out on during her 'conventional years'.

The following day, Sienna dumped her boyfriend, only to allow him to come creeping back later, a decision that she regretted when she returned home from a show a few months later and found him in her bed with another woman. Back on that cold December day, however, she spent the weeks before Christmas alone in her flat, coming up with a plan, finally deciding to set up an Arabian horse marketing company. This would cover everything from advertising – print and video – to magazine coverage, written features, organising photo shoots, as well as giving lectures on the breed itself and what it could do for people, how they could be involved.

Spurning the advice of her family, Sienna handed in her notice on 2 January and that March, she flew out to the Middle East for the first time, to the Dubai International Arabian Horse Championships. The moment she landed, she was captivated by the Middle East; the heat that hit you the minute you stepped off the plane, the air that was fragrant with exotic flowers and spices, the 'call to prayer' that sounded out over the city at certain times of the day, a very evocative call by a man, or muezzin, from the minaret towers of the mosques.

Watching the show that year, Sienna knew that she had made the right decision. The quality of the horses captivated her mind and, as she stood in the collecting ring watching the horses before they made their way into the ring for their class, Sienna was spellbound. It was there, unbeknown to her, that Guy first saw her, with many of the male trainers and hangers on wondering among themselves who she was but not caring enough to find out as she was never in the bars in the evenings.

Sienna did, however, talk to the owners. Her quiet, unassuming way of speaking to them held their attention as she stood apart from the 'I am', 'I have' crowd, and instead listened to them, and to their story.

Rin was one of the few trainers who approached Sienna on that first visit – directly curious as to who she was, having heard Guy and Peter talking about the new 'hot totty' at the show. Liking her immediately, Rin became one of Sienna's first clients as she promoted a young filly called Dance of Glory through a series of e-blasts under the Essentially Arabian banner. As Sienna made more and more connections around the world, more clients came to her and the stage was set.

It was now exactly two years from that first Paris Show she went to and, tiredly, Sienna sat ringside watching the female classes on the Friday morning. She was fully aware of Arjan scowling every time he walked past her, unsure quite what she had done to cause such a reaction, especially after his behaviour the night before when he called her over to meet John. Arjan was so hot and cold towards her but she just couldn't get him out of her mind. Try as she might, he kept creeping into her thoughts, both waking and sleeping. She knew that he had a reputation but part of her thought that, as he had been after her for so long, they might actually be able to have something together. In Moorsele, he had been so attentive but since then, he'd done nothing but glare at her and she didn't know why. And right now, she was too tired to even care why.

Losing her friends after the last class, who had probably

gone into the centre of Paris in great excitement while Sienna spoke to clients, Sienna found herself with no option but to join Crispin and Katherine for a drink at their trainer's stables as they collared her and wanted to talk shop. It seemed that while the young trainer they had been using all season had done a good job for them, Crispin was bored of him and was trying to find someone new to train their horses. But being Crispin, he just removed the horses and criticised the trainer to others, hugely damaging their reputation in the process. And, as always, he was trying to find out everyone else's opinions on all the different trainers, the good and the bad, so that he could repeat it to others and lay another finger of blame in the process.

'Sienna, you really should put highlights in your hair. You'd look so much better.' Katherine was on the assault again, playing and fluffing Sienna's hair in a way that seemed so friendly, yet Sienna was more than aware of the tarantula underneath, ready to pounce any second and sink in its venom. Tiring by the minute, Sienna wanted to vanish into thin air as Katherine maliciously called Arjan over to join them. Glancing over with hardly a smile, he merely grunted and carried on striding past. He couldn't believe that Sienna was sat with the Arbuthnots! Crispin and Katherine ridiculed Sienna the minute her back was turned, but they still seemed to have her under their spell. As he banged the exit door against the wall in a bid to get outside into the cool December Parisian air, he wondered why he was so angry and why he cared so much about Sienna. She was nothing to him. And he had more important things to worry about – such as beating his arch rival Guy in the championships.

Later that day, Arjan strode into the bar, still in an unexplainable bad mood about Sienna and the Arbuthnots.

Ready to argue with anyone he saw, he headed straight for the bar and began downing shots. Leap and John were there with him, along with a trampish hooker friend of Leap's who was promising acts beyond even Arjan's wild and experienced imagination.

As he ordered another round, realising that he needed to get a grip and control of the situation, Arjan spied Sienna being comforted by some friends. She seemed to be crying and idly, Arjan wondered if she had finally found out the truth about the Arbuthnot's and the way they were towards her. He watched, intrigued, as Sienna fled to the toilets, followed by a South African judge, a Welsh matriarch and a man hovering with a very big glass of beer. After watching the door intently for two minutes, Arjan's attention span lapsed and he began ordering Penicillin cocktails – an intriguing yet deadly mixture of scotch and malt whiskies with ginger, lemon and honey, although Arjan frequently went without the honey and added a gin instead – downing them as if there were no tomorrow. He was determined to get drunk this evening and blot out his anger about Sienna. He had no idea why she was getting under his skin, but he was determined to put an end to it tonight. As he watched her, Arjan realised that, ironically, it was two years since he had first seen Sienna, when she made that first journey to the World Championships. Determined to be the first to bed her, his wings had been clipped by Rin reaching Sienna first and talking at length to her. Wary, he had retreated, and he wondered whether he had missed his chance with her for once and for all.

Picking up a fresh Penicillin, Arjan listened in on the hooker describe a vivid sexual act to Leap and decided to join in the conversation. 'You think you can fit me in later?'

The hooker licked her lips as she looked Arjan up and down, assessing him, her eyes resting on his crotch. 'I'm sure I can squeeze you in – somewhere...' she smiled. Arjan just nodded without smiling and ordered another drink. "Where is Sienna?" he wondered to himself, angry at his continuing obsession with her whereabouts.

Finally, he saw her – with the bloody Arbuthnots again! Katherine was stroking Sienna's hair again – oh, to be the one doing that, Arjan was shocked to find himself thinking – and Crispin was buying them champagne. "Always flashing his cash," Arjan thought angrily, seemingly ignorant of the number of times he had played the big man in a bid to seduce a woman. Leap followed Arjan's gaze. 'The Irish girl still getting to you?' he asked, speaking quickly in Flemish so no one could understand them.

'Of course not. I was just thinking what Katherine would look like with no clothes on.'

Both men knew that Arjan was lying, but with his continued position as Lord of Misrule, Leap was not about to challenge him.

Several Penicillins and a blow job in the toilets later, Arjan leant against the bar, his head spinning slightly. Before he realised what Leap was doing, his friend had jumped off his bar stool, rushed over to Sienna and pulled her over to join them at the bar.

'Arjan is in love with you – he never stops talking about you,' he started, almost continuing where he had left off in Moorsele, pushing Sienna into Arjan's arms and taking a photo of them together. 'He wants to marry you.'

Looking into Sienna's eyes and seeing the remains of her mascara under her eyes, Arjan remembered how Sienna had been crying earlier and he suddenly felt like a shit, and sorry for her. She looked like a rabbit caught in the headlights – she didn't know whether to stay or to go and she was aware of Leap, the hooker and John all laughing at her. Cursing herself for even looking at Arjan once that evening, never mind the hundred times she had, she tried to go, but Leap had her arm in a vice-like grip.

'I told you – he wants you,' he repeated, before reeling off a string of Flemish which caused the hooker to fall off her chair with laughter and both Arjan and John to chuckle and look embarrassed at the same time.

'I'm sorry for my friend,' said John. 'He is very drunk.'

'He loves you!' laughed Leap again, before once more launching into Flemish.

Trying to smile, her throat tight with unshed tears, Sienna turned to Arjan and said goodnight. Walking over to the lift, she was aware of Leap's laughter ringing around the foyer and she only just made it to her room before she broke down completely. Closing the door and leaning against it, hearing the laughter still ringing in her ears, Sienna slid down the back of the door, head resting on her knees, with her arms wrapped tightly around them, and sobbed. Arjan Vermeulen was no good for her – when would she realise that?

Sienna sat rigidly at the VIP table watching Sunday's championships. The upset of the night before had passed – she had embarrassed herself by crying when a judge made a kind comment. She was just so tired, had been working too hard, and she felt so low and alone. One nice word was all it took before the barricades broke and she couldn't stop the tears from falling. And then, if that wasn't enough, Arjan had, again, got to her and this time, humiliated her. A piece of ice entered her heart against him.

Sienna focussed on the classes. There were some truly special horses entered this year, including the darling of the European Championships, Passionate Presence. As widely anticipated, she had won her qualifying class on the Friday and everyone expected her to take the championship. However, the politics of Paris came into play, with each Middle Eastern stud having to take home their share of the spoils, and despite Luca's best efforts, this grey beauty was awarded a Bronze Championship title behind two perhaps lesser horses.

Also taking Bronze was Guy with Sparkle of Justice. This chestnut colt seemed to have lost some of his joie de vivre, but Juan was happy to be in the championship placings once more. As long as he had another trophy to take home, that was all that mattered.

Guy was delighted to have won a medal in Paris, but he really wanted Cabernet Noir to take a title. He had showed well in the qualifying rounds, but he seemed out of sorts during the championship class. One judge gave him a vote for Bronze, but none of the rest placed him. Dejected, he had already watched Arjan take the Junior Female Championship with Dance of Glory, the filly that Rin had asked Sienna to promote two years ago and who had gone to Arjan during the split, the client preferring the good-looking Belgian to the slightly bitter Rin. Now, he was in the ring with the same stallion he had shown at the European Championships, but it was like a different horse! The pair had a bond now and as the crowd cheered, the stallion, Sundos, showed off more than ever. Guy, meanwhile, had to settle for the back row as it was Arjan with Sundos who took the title home.

As the show finished, Arjan left the ring and threw the reins to Suzanne, who led Sundos back to the stables, patting him repeatedly. Waiting for him was Sundos' owner, who was still overwhelmed. 'I think I am going to retire him now,' the man said. 'He can never better this – than x you!'

Shaking hands goodbye, Arjan triumphantly rounded the corner, heading slowly back to his stables. He was thrilled to have beaten Guy and pleased with the big roll of euros in his pocket, his bonus for winning two World Championship titles at the same show. He understood that Sundos would never reach the same heights again, but he was somewhat miffed that the owner of Dance of Glory had decided to sell her to the Middle East where she would join a breeding programme and likely never be shown again. However, rounding the corner, Arjan was thrilled to see a queue of women, all waiting to talk to him about his brilliance and to have their photograph taken with him. Puffing out his chest, he leaned into the first girl, ensuring he made eye contact and taking her phone number for use later. Ah, the perks of being a trainer!

As the queue dwindled, he was aware of Sienna standing defiantly at the back, and the look on her face unnerved him slightly. 'After you,' she muttered to a young girl in a clinging dress who was keen to get to Arjan. 'I can wait.' Folding her arms, she leaned against the wall, staring over at Arjan's feet, waiting calmly for him to finish talking to the great and good and no doubt, making plans to meet them later behind the stable block.

'Sienna?' he said, almost nervously as the last hanger on withered away.

Drawing breath, Sienna looked up at him.

'Don't you ever treat me again like you did last night!' Sienna launched angrily, not holding back.

'It wasn't me, it was my friends…' Arjan interrupted pathetically as he looked over his shoulder for support.

'Don't give me that! You were there, you could have stopped it. People have feelings; you can't just treat them like that. You can't walk all over them. That is all you seem to do – you don't actually seem to care about people. You cannot carry on doing that.'

'I'm sorry, I…'

'Just don't ever do that again, okay?'

Sienna paused and Arjan could see her physically pulling herself together. He wanted to reach out and take her hand, and explain that when he got drunk, he acted like a moron. He also wanted to tell her that he was so drunk last night, he couldn't even remember what was said not just to her, but to anyone. Arjan didn't get a chance to do or say anything, however, as, gripping her hands into fists, Sienna looked up at him once more and said in a controlled voice, 'Congratulations on winning the World Championship. Have a good Christmas, see you next year.'

Dropping a kiss on his cheek in an attempt to maintain some attempt at formality, Sienna turned on her heel and walked off outside and into the snow, her tears feeling like they were turning to ice as they slowly ran down her face in the freezing wind.

Hidden from view around the corner, Rin had watched the whole exchange with great interest. Her show season had gone from bad to worse, with Sparkle of Justice being just one casualty. She would never quite get over how Juan had moved him to Guy's training yard after the Europeans and to see him claim a championship title today had hurt. Through her own pain, she idly wondered whether Arjan and Sienna had slept together yet. While she was all for girl power, Rin didn't want to lose her position as lead female in the Arabian industry, something that she was swiftly realising she was in danger of doing; she hoped it wasn't too late but, with a shock, she had discovered she had enjoyed being there for too long.

7

Christmas meant different things to different people in the Arabian horse industry. Many of the trainers took the chance to have some time out. Those with wives and children often went to Mauritius or Brazil for holidays. Those wives, however, heading to Brazil, flying first class with their husbands, knew that Arabian horses would end up on the agenda at some point. The area was known for breeding top quality horses that, when exported to Europe, commanded the show-rings, and no trainer could pass up the chance of being the one to find the next superstar. So while their husband promised family time for them all, the wife would wearily pack extra swimming costumes and bikinis, knowing full well that he would vanish for days on end, leaving her with two over-excitable children to contend with.

Those without families, or even in the first flush of love, would head to Scottsdale, Arizona, located on the western side of the United States. Another place known as a Mecca for Arabian horses, Scottsdale held a series of New Year parties and tours, masterminded by Arabian horse aficionado and entrepreneur Scott Bailey.

Flights in and out of Scottsdale during the holiday season weren't only busy because of regular visitors; the first-class cabins were full of people flocking to the area to, again, find the next big thing and to organise clients for the forthcoming European season ahead. There was also the party side of it, with this the Scottsdale New Year Tours being a great social occasion and one that many enjoyed, year after year.

Meanwhile, other trainers headed to the Middle East early and trained horses out there in readiness for the upcoming show season. After the hectic run of title shows in Europe, as well as visiting Egypt, Morocco and Italy to show there, the more laidback and relaxed pace of the Middle East was bliss for many.

All in all, the rule was simple for this eclectic group of people: escape from the bitter northern European winter and follow the route to sunshine and horses. No one could be without their fix for more than a week and the WAMs often had to have the patience of saints as yet another supposedly romantic break was changed to a horse-hunting exercise.

Sienna chose to stay in England for Christmas. Stunned, shocked and horrified at Arjan's actions towards her in Paris, and still unsure as to why he acted like that, and was such a contradiction in his personality to her, Sienna needed to surround herself with family and friends, and with those that she trusted. She had known her best friend Sally Watson since she went to high school and it was she that Sienna turned to now. Sally sprang into action, booking them to a gorgeous Highland retreat for New Year, where they celebrated Hogmanay into the early hours of 1 January. The retreat was everything that the Sienna could have hoped for – they had a log cabin nestled against the backdrop of a forest and surrounded by a small cluster of similar cabins. Log fires, frothy hot chocolates, and long walks through the forest and highlands were the order of the day, and they could even go skiing if they wanted to. "Too much like hard work," laughed Sally as she looked through the brochure and Sienna had to agree. After a fast-paced trip around the world, several times over, this year, it felt wonderful to just sit and relax without the weight of her clients on her shoulders.

Hogmanay was a wonderful night, spent at the resort's pub, with carolling and shrieks of laughter coming out from the doors until the girls staggered home at 4am. Sienna enjoyed spending time with real people focused on having a good time, playing the pipes, and dancing a jig and she did not miss anyone from the showing circuit at all.

Waking much later the next day, Sally cooked them both bacon and egg sandwiches, and feeling hungover but revitalised, they went for a walk through the snow. The sun was out and the snow sparkled like crystals as it hung off the boughs of the trees.

Sienna, captivated by the beauty of it all, gave a deep sigh. Once again, her thoughts turned to Arjan and she couldn't help but start to talk about him.

'Honey, I really think you need to forget about him,' said Sally. 'He sounds like he is no good for you or to you. And he certainly doesn't seem to treat you with much respect.'

Sienna kicked the snow in front of her with her boot and nodded slowly.

'I know. I do know. I know you are right. But oh Sally! It's just the way he looks at you – making you feel that you are the most special woman in the world, the only woman that exists for him. I know he's not the one for me. I think I know that anyway… It's all just so hard.'

'Hmmm, a bit like him,' said Sally wryly. 'Come on, let's go to that cosy pub down the road and have a brandy laced hot chocolate. And please darling, no more talking about Arjan bloody Vermeulen!'

Agreeing, Sienna linked her arm through Sally's and they headed off to the warmth of the bar.

Guy's New Year hadn't got off to the best of starts. Having spent the holidays with Ally's parents, an event that he found increasingly tedious as the days wore on, not least as he had no Wi-Fi or mobile signal where he was, Guy had left early on the pretence that he had a client visiting from the Middle East.

Arriving home, he found that his plans for the New Year had gone very wrong – he had planned to go skiing in Austria with Miranda, but she broke her leg in a fall during the Boxing Day Hunt. With the prospect of spending New Year with Ally, Guy had changed his ticket and headed to Dubai, where he planned to charm some of the local Arabian horse owners into letting him show their horses that season.

Unfortunately for Guy, although not for the local owners, many of them were out of town and so he saw the New Year in, by himself, in the Irish Village, a place that is on the list of every Dubai 'must-see' for every tourist. While the talent was plentiful, Guy just felt angry with the world and surprisingly, for once, tired as the exploits of the past few months took a toll on him. With a hangover pounding his temples, Guy took a flight back to the UK. At least Holly would welcome him with open arms – and legs – he thought wryly to himself as, taking a sleeping pill, he collapsed back in his British Airways first class seat and slept all the way back to a very grey and damp England.

Arjan, meanwhile, had spent a quiet Christmas and New Year in Belgium. He had taken his confused feelings about Sienna out on Leap and the two had not spoken since that Sunday in Paris. He wanted the girl and the way that she had got so far under his skin unnerved him. Shouting at Leap, he had finally gone a step too far and went to punch his friend. Leap had stormed off and refused to answer any of Arjan's calls since.

Normally, Arjan would have thrown a big party for New

Year at the stables, with alcohol flowing, and a pile of coke there for those that wished to indulge, but this year, he locked himself away, brooding into bottle after bottle of whiskey and chain-smoking the old year out. As the New Year bells rang out, he toyed with calling both Leap and Sienna, cancelling the call each time before it could finish dialling. Throwing his phone across the room, frustrated with himself and his own lack of gumption, Arjan staggered over to the bar and pulled another bottle of whiskey open. Not even bothering to find a glass, he sank on to the floor and drank his way into oblivion.

On 2 January, his own hangover finally abated, Leap rolled up with a bottle of whiskey and a crate of beer.

'Amends?'

Arjan nodded, too broken inside to even argue, and instead, welcomed Leap in through the front door and sat down in front of the fire to catch up. Sienna's name was never mentioned, and neither was their argument.

Rin decided to go away for Christmas and headed to the warmer climates of Argentina to enjoy some horse riding and days with the famed gauchos. She was so exhausted at the end of each day that she barely even registered that it was New Year. However, fate has a funny twist at times, and it was while she was in Argentina that Rin met some Arabian horse breeders from Australia. They had chatted incessantly to her about their horses and breeding programme, as well as the horses across Australia. They were keen to share their horses with the world, and this had sparked Rin's interest.

Much to Zoë's approval, Rin returned tanned and fit, and with more fire inside her than she had left Europe with. There was still something missing though, and Zoë knew that there was a way to go yet before her boss was back to being close to 100%. However, unknown to Zoë, Rin had come back with a plan and she mistook her boss's preoccupation for brooding. In fact, Rin was feeling inspired and wondering whether she could make her plan happen.

Keen to develop a new market, Rin was beginning to wonder if, for those times when she had no horses to show in the Middle East, she could retreat to the even warmer weather of Australia, and in particular New South Wales, and train horses there. With the Australian show season running from October – March, there would be plenty of time for her to escape the European winter and build a base for herself Down Under. For now, however, she was determined to try and salvage her fallen career. It would be an uphill struggle, but she was determined to continue with the Arabian horse, and this was the only way that she knew how. Her only hope at the moment was a young colt that she had spotted during her time away; her new Australian friends had bred him and Rin, deciding to be reckless for once in her life, flew the 7,000 miles to the Sydney suburbs to visit their farm. Straight away, she knew that she had made the right decision; from the moment she saw him, the two-year old Ibn Shahja had captured her heart and imagination. Grey and tall, he had an elegance to him in the way that he moved that Rin could not ignore. His eye was so soulful, and he seemed to drink Rin in as she stood assessing him. Having then taken the colt and trotted him out, Rin found herself in harmony with a horse for what felt like the first time in years, and she felt a surge of long-forgotten excitement as she rediscovered her passion for the breed.

Coming back from Australia, exhausted but with her mind full of ideas, Rin was determined to find a buyer, or group of buyers, for Ibn Shahja. Her plan was to bring him to the Middle East from Australia and show him there, before importing him to Europe for the coming show season. Rin knew that she needed to get the wheels in motion as quickly as possible, not just to get Ibn Shahja purchased, but also marketed. There was no time to lose.

With the New Year truly begun, all the trainers put aside any lingering thoughts of relaxing and, after trying on their show suits, began to regret eating – and drinking – quite so much over the festive break. Only Guy had maintained his fitness levels, his daily run akin to a religion for him.

"'Ally!'

Guy marched through the yard, the collar of his Barbour coat turned up to protect him against the cold and the rain.

'Ally!' he shouted once again. 'Where the hell is she…'

Sticking her head out of the top of a stable door, Ally looked exhausted.

'Yes?'

'I have to leave in an hour to Abu Dhabi – I've just had a call that there's some horses up for sale and I need to look at them. Pack me a case.'

'But there's the ball tonight…'

'Tough. I'm going. You can do what you want to. Now pack my case!'

Glaring at her, Guy turned on his heel and headed back to the house, texting Miranda as he did so.

"Be at Heathrow at 8pm – I have first class tickets for us for a week in the sun. Pack nothing but bikinis… G"

Ally, meanwhile, pulled the wheelbarrow from out of the stable, and sighing, headed to the house. As she walked, head down against the stinging rain, she felt her first rebellious surge for years. As she kicked off her muddy boots, a plan slowly began to formulate in her mind...

The Ajman Show in the middle of January came too soon for some. Still trying to work off their Christmas excesses, many of the trainers could be seen going for a run on the white sands of the Ajman beach, right in front of the Kempinski Hotel, where so many stayed for the show. As they ran, the turquoise waters of the Arabian Gulf sparkled and shone to the right of them, while to the left, the WAMS lay in the sunshine, iPods plugged into their ears and oil glistening on their skin.

This first show of the New Year offered a chance for those visiting the Middle East for the first time since October a chance to see the new youngsters, the foals born in late October and making their way into the ring in the foal classes. More importantly, it also gave trainers, buyers and breeders a chance to see the foals from the previous year, now yearlings, make their debut in the show-ring.

Guy dropped Miranda off at the airport. With his skin already as brown as a conker from his week doing nothing but lie in the sun on the Dubai beach, or have sex with Miranda on their balcony, he was very eye-catching, with his blond hair providing a sharp contrast to his tanned limbs. Having kissed Miranda goodbye, Guy made his way back to his hired Ferrari, turning more than a few heads as he did so. Putting the roof down, ready for the drive from Dubai to Ajman, with music blaring out of the speakers, Guy enjoyed being on the receiving end of lingering looks from locals and tourists alike.

Guy wasn't showing any horses in Ajman, but he wanted to see who had what so that he could start finalising his campaign for the coming season in Europe. Driving up outside the Kempinski, Guy threw the car keys at the bell boy and swaggered into the reception, barely registering the golden richness all around him. As he waited for the keys to his suite, Guy caught sight of Arjan and Leap heading to

103

the bar. "Christ, Arjan looks rough," Guy thought to himself as, taking his key and grinning at the receptionist, he headed to his sumptuous room complete with a balcony and breath-taking views of the Arabian Gulf. Opening the doors to the balcony, he threw himself on to a chair, taking in the sights and sounds before and around him.

The show began at 2pm, and having had a light lunch at the hotel, Guy made his way to the collecting ring to see the horses up close. A bay filly, Angelina OL, caught his eye. She had a natural poise and attitude and, as she made her way into the ring for the first of three yearling filly classes, she shone. Before the judges were able to even judge Angelina OL in her individual show, Guy had already sought out her owner and purchased her for £10,000. The filly won her class easily, beating the nearest horse by over three points, a huge margin at this level of competition and stage in the show. By the time of the championship the next day, Guy had sold her on to a client in America for £250,000, and the Ajman Gold Yearling Filly Champion, Angelina OL, would be making her way to Guy's barn in England. Part of the deal was that he would show the filly in Europe over the summer before deciding whether to take her to Paris for the World Championships, or to send her to the US straight after Aachen so that she could compete in the US Nationals at the end of October, and then prepare for the Scottsdale season. Racing back to Dubai airport after Angelina OL's championship, Guy mentally congratulated himself on a deal done well. He would receive over £3,000 a month for having her stabled with him, and Guy knew that his filly was a part to further riches.

Rin didn't fare as well in Ajman. She was cold showing

for a local breeder, where they prepared the horses at home, conditioning and training them, and then Rin flew in and showed them. Arriving at the farm the day before the show, Rin discovered that the condition of the horses was not as promised, and they looked as if they had walked straight from a sand paddock to the show-ring. Rin found herself at the bottom of the line time and time again as the classes went on, although sometimes she would scrape a seventh or eighth place. More often than not, however, she would get the gate having placed last yet again. As soon as the last of the classes was over, Rin made her way straight to the airport in Dubai and flew back to Belgium. As the plane took off and Rin pulled the flimsy blanket over her, she wondered not for the first time just where it had all gone so very wrong for her. She knew that things had to change - and fast.

Landing back into Brussels, Rin turned on her phone and gave a cry of delight. One of her clients had put up the money and purchased Ibn Shahja, the fantastic colt that she had seen while she was in Australia over Christmas and had been at the front of her mind ever since. The deal was now being arranged and Ibn Shahja would enter quarantine before going to the Middle East. Rin made a quick call to a regular contact in the Middle East in order to arrange transportation and stables for Ibn Shahja for the coming weeks, once he had arrived in the region. Stepping out into rare January sunshine in Belgium, Rin felt the first glimmer of hope for a long while. Getting into her car, she turned up the volume on the radio and sang wildly and tunelessly - but happily - all the way back to her farm.

8

Just a few weeks later and Sienna once more found herself in Belgium. John had e-mailed her, inviting her to visit and see his farm, and Sienna had warily accepted. She knew that, while Arjan was still based in Belgium, he was in the Middle East more and more, especially over winter, and so need not worry that he would be there to show John's horses to her. She didn't understand why he was so friendly in Moorsele and then so cold in Paris. Even knowing that Arjan was away, she was still apprehensive about visiting.

Still, as she packed her bag once more, Sienna couldn't help but think of him. While she might have played it cool with him over the past few months, but there was no denying that, deep down, she did fancy him. Every time she saw him, her stomach twisted and turned and while she didn't want to be another notch on his, or anyone's, bedpost, she couldn't help her basic primal reaction to him. Even with his reputation, Arjan was irresistible and while he was known for being a player, you couldn't help but feel flattered that he wanted to play with you.

Having got so close to him in October, before Guy came in and dragged her back to the hotel as part of the 'Brits abroad' rule, she had been eagerly anticipating Paris. The reality had been a massive shock to her system, and she was glad that she had spent New Year in Scotland, licking her wounds, with Sally. As she finally zipped up her case, Sienna decided that she was pleased to have this chance to get to visit Belgium without Arjan getting in the way.

Arjan. The name played continually on her lips. She had only had one communication from him since Paris, when he mailed her two days after the show to say sorry again for what he and his friends had done and to say that they appreciated all that she did for them – the way that she promoted their horses and helped get the best advertising exposure possible, on a global scale. While pleased that he had done so, she also knew that, like many, he had to stay on the right side of her as he needed her to promote him and his clients. So it was only a small victory in the end and might only have been done because of a business need rather than a personal feeling.

Sienna had decided to go over to Belgium on the Eurostar rather than drive, and John had promised that there would be someone there to meet her in Brussels. I will send a driver with a sign saying 'John' – it's easier, he had simply said over a text message. Sitting back into her first-class seat and accepting a glass of champagne, Sienna relaxed and looked out of the window as the train left the glamorous St Pancreas Station in London and headed east through France and towards the open Flemish countryside.

Pulling into Brussels just two and a quarter hours later, Sienna alighted from the train and made her way through the exit, pulling her weekend case along behind her. She pulled her coat around herself as, now late afternoon in Belgium, it was beginning to get cold, and stepped out on to the concourse. Looking around for a sign bearing John's name, she finally located a figure holding up a board standing by a concrete pillar. Sienna made a step towards the sign and the driver, then stopped in horror as she realised that the man holding the sign was Arjan. Slowly, Sienna tried to gather herself and walk towards him calmly, in spite of all her instincts telling her to run. She knew that it was at least a two-hour drive to their farm near Antwerp and the knowledge that she was going to be in such an enclosed space with Arjan for such a period of time... It was too much to bear.

Arjan's face gave nothing away as he stared at Sienna in shock. Deep down, he wanted to either go home and kill John for doing this to him, or to throw down the sign and run towards the Sienna, take her in his arms and kiss her on and on until the end of time. John had planned this deliberately, he knew that, and he suspected that Leap may have played a hand in it too. John's wife, Bethany, had found Sienna crying in Paris and she had taken Arjan to task for upsetting her.

Knowing that he was in the wrong didn't make him feel any better about the situation. His tentative apology sent by email, partly forced by Bethany and also from his own guilt, had not been acknowledged and he wasn't even sure whether Sienna had received it or not. Standing in the February cold and dark gloom of Brussels Midi/Zuid Station, seeing Sienna walk towards him, Arjan felt unsure of what to do, and all these thoughts ran through his mind in the 20 seconds it took for Sienna to leave the platform and be by his side. When John had said to pick up a guest, he certainly had no idea what a nightmare he was about to walk into.

'Hello,' he said coolly as he gave Sienna the perfunctory three kisses on the cheek as she finally reached him. 'How are you?'

'Fine,' replied Sienna in a small voice as Arjan took her case and headed outside to the waiting car, his long stride covering so much ground that she almost had to run to keep up. The sun was already beginning to set, and stars were starting to appear in the cold night sky. Just a few clouds scuttled overhead, turning magenta as the setting sun warmed them, before they faded once more into darkness.

Sliding into the 4x4, Sienna decided that maybe the best

plan was to feign sleep. The atmosphere in the car was already icy, despite Arjan turning the heat on to full blast, and she was not sure if she was ready for two more hours of this.

'Have you eaten?' Arjan asked as he looked over his shoulder into the oncoming traffic before pulling out on to the motorway.

'Yes. Thank you.'

Grunting a reply, Arjan set off on the long road to Antwerp. He kept his eyes on the road ahead and didn't look to the right once to see what Sienna was doing. For a few moments, it was as if she wasn't there. Sienna, however, felt the tension and stared fixedly out of the window at the changing scenery, even though in the almost faded light, all she could see was the occasional flash of a lit-up farmhouse in the distance.

After twenty minutes of driving in silence, Arjan coughed slightly and then started talking about nothing; horses he had seen in the Middle East and shared news of mutual friends Sienna hadn't seen since last year.

'It has been a long time since Paris, Sienna...' he finished, looking over at her warily. Damn his idiot friends for dragging Sienna over that night, and damn himself for being too fuelled on alcohol to do anything other than to join in and tease her mercilessly.

'Yes...' Sienna answered, not sure of what else to say. Having barely spoken since she uttered hello at the station, her voice sounded small and lost.

Arjan sighed and looked over to her. 'Sienna. I am...' he began, but whatever else Arjan was going to say was lost in a string of swear words as his car suddenly veered to the right and down a slight embankment at the side of the road. Coming to an abrupt halt, the seatbelts tightened against both passengers, pulling them back into their seats.

Realising they had stopped, Arjan shook himself slightly and glanced over to Sienna, who had a shocked expression on her face and her hands braced out in front of her.

'Shit! Stay there,' he said to her as he undid his seatbelt and opened his door. Leaping out, Arjan ran around to Sienna's side of the car and saw he had a burst tyre on the front and a slow puncture on the rear. Glancing into the gloom back down the road, he saw a piece of wood – one he had missed as he had been too busy looking at Sienna and working out how to apologise once more – and he had obviously hit it hard, causing an instant puncture.

Looking at Sienna through the car window, all he wanted to do was reach out and hold her. Kiss her. Make love to her. 'Get a grip,' he thought to himself, before opening her door more brusquely than was needed and saying 'two tyres are gone. We need to phone for help.'

Sienna just looked at Arjan, not believing her ears and neither trusting him nor wanting to be anywhere near him. She hopped out of the car and looked at the damage, while Arjan paced down the road talking animatedly on his phone. He looked like a tiger, pacing without the confines of a cage, and there was an increasing look of frustration on his face.

'They can't get here for three hours, and we can't stay in the car in case someone crashes into it. I hope you've got some warm clothes in that case of yours.' Opening the trunk, he pulled out the obligatory warning triangle and set it up behind the car, made sure that the hazard lights were switched on and pulled out two fluorescent jackets for them to wear. Having delved even further into the trunk, Arjan pulled out a couple of blankets, a horse rug and a torch.

Sienna waited for him to finish, then opened her case, pulling out a thick jumper and scarf. Putting the fluorescent jacket Arjan handed her on over the top of her extra layers, she followed him over the barrier and up the side of the bank. There, Arjan folded the horse blanket into half and laid it on the ground, motioning for her to sit down on it, before passing her a thick blanket to wrap herself in.

All of this was done in silence, each lost in their own thoughts. Sienna almost laughed out loud as she realised that she was probably living out every woman's fantasy - being stranded and alone with Arjan for hours on end on a cold, dark night. The reality of this particular fantasy was very different however, and Sienna questioned herself for the thousandth time, wondering why on earth she had accepted John's invitation. She could be back at home in London now, enjoying a large glass of red wine in front of a warm fire, chatting to a girlfriend, and not worrying about the hopefully resistible temptation that was in front of her right now.

For Arjan's part, he was furious. John had tricked him into collecting Sienna and now he was going to be on his own with her for at least five hours if not more. Taking out his phone once more, he texted Leap: 'With Sienna. Double puncture. Three hours before rescue.'

Almost instantly, his phone beeped in answer. 'Ha ha! This must be killing you, my friend. I bet you have her by the end of the night – stud!'

Angrily, Arjan pushed his phone into his pocket, glaring through the growing darkness to Sienna, who quickly looked away as she felt the force of his look. For once, he felt all the fight go out of him. Sienna didn't realise it, and neither did Arjan, but for the only time in her life, she was about to experience him at his most vulnerable.

Moving closer and watching her, he saw that Sienna's eyes had gone a grey-blue and that she was very pale. She had taken the blow out very stoically, but he could tell that she seemed to wish that she was anywhere but near him. Suddenly feeling the need to make her smile, Arjan sat down next to her.

'Hey, look at this.' Tugging the phone out of his pocket, which offered the latest in technology and was one of the many gadgets he had picked up in Dubai over winter, he scrolled through the gallery and found the photo of himself and Sienna which Leap had taken in Paris.

'See?'

Sienna looked at him as if he was offering up a viper for slaughter rather than just showing her that photo on his phone. Unsure what to say, she couldn't believe that he thought that being reminded of that night would cheer her up or make her smile; it made her want to thump him. She also couldn't believe that he had the photo on his phone. Why on earth would he still have that?

'Mmmm,' was all she could say, before looking away quickly. Her stomach was in knots as she wanted to be a million miles away from Arjan right now but was also relishing the feeling of him sitting beside her in the gloom, his face lit by the motorway lights. Conflicted, she glanced up at him again before looking back to the ground in front of her.

Sighing, Arjan leaned back on the rug, fixing Sienna with his chocolate-brown eyes. 'I am getting old Sienna,' he said, stretching his legs out in front of him. 'I look at all my friends and I'm surrounded by all these young people, friends who are married, friends with children. I want that. I'm tired of the life I lead, screwing around every weekend. I want to be settled with someone. I thought I had that, but it went. I just want to find someone special of my own and settle down with her…'

Sitting very still next to him, Sienna wasn't sure if Arjan was trying to send some hidden message to her, telling her

112

that she was the kind of woman he was after. Or was he just trying to seduce her, add her name to the many notches carved on to his bedpost. And if he wasn't trying to seduce her, then why on earth was he opening up to her so much?

'Right...' was all Sienna could think of to say in response.

The pair sat in silence for ages, the tension between them finally beginning to bubble up. The cars raced by, headlights turning to red streaks as they faded from them, heading down the road and to their homes and lives.

Sienna sat huddled up, knees to her chest, arms wrapped around them, and face turned away from Arjan, she rested the side of her face on her knees. Keeping her mind on other things, she tried to ignore the closeness of Arjan to her, and of how openly he sat, almost inviting her to climb onto him. Arjan glared the other way, into the distance and cursing John once more for putting him in this position.

Sighing loudly again, he decided that enough was enough. He had been wanting to get Sienna alone for months now and this was finally his chance. Moving closer to her and turning to face her, Arjan took Sienna's hand and just managed to say 'Oh, Sienna...' when the recovery vehicle, with its flashing lights casting orange glows on their faces, came into view.

Forty minutes later, the tyres had been replaced and Arjan and Sienna climbed wearily back into the car and headed off into the night. Grateful for the heated seat to warm her bones, Sienna stared out of the window at the lights flashing by and wondered what would have happened if the recovery man had not turned up when he did. Arjan had been so assertive, strong and in control throughout the whole incident, something she deeply admired in a man, and she could still feel the warmth of his hand in hers. And as for what he had said to her... Was he trying to tell her something? Too cold and tired to think straight, she leaned back in her seat and gazed out into the darkness.

It was almost midnight by the time they arrived at the farm, and Arjan pulled up outside John and Bethany's front door. 'What a night…' he said, leaning back in his seat and closing his eyes as he exhaled. Sienna moved to pick up her handbag when she felt Arjan's hand on her arm.

'Sienna, wait…'

Looking up, Sienna found herself staring into Arjan's eyes as he looked intently at her. 'I…'

Arjan got no further in his sentence before he leaned over to Sienna and hesitated, just a fraction away from her face. She could feel his breath on her lips and he gazed at her, his eyes for once giving away conflicting emotions as he decided whether to kiss her or pull away.

'I… Goodnight…'

With that, Arjan closed his eyes and leaned in to her before, ever so softly, he gave her the gentlest of kisses on her lips. Just one kiss, incredibly tender, incredibly intense, and then he pulled away, looking ahead into the night once more. As he watched Sienna get out of the car and rescue her case from the boot of the car, Arjan half-smiled to himself. Progress, at last!

Waking late the next day, a slightly dazed Sienna walked into the kitchen and found John sat at the table answering emails. Standing up and giving her a very perfunctory kiss hello, John called through to Bethany to come and welcome their guest.

'Today is not going to go quite to plan I'm afraid,' John said as Bethany came in with some coffee and a smile. 'Arjan has dropped me in it again, something that he has a habit of doing. He left for the Middle East first thing. He didn't give a reason, just said that he had to get away. But it

114

does mean that I will have to show you the horses myself and you will have to use your imagination a lot.'

'He's not that bad but he can't run as fast as Arjan,' added Bethany. 'Probably as Arjan is so used to running away from so many annoyed husbands! Still, he has done well for himself and after all that business with Rin, it could have gone either way really. More coffee, Sienna? I'll just go and get the croissants, they must be warm now.'

As Bethany returned to the kitchen, John started talking to Sienna about his plans for the farm and how he hoped to start selling horses to the United States.

'That is where you come in, really,' he said. 'You have so many contacts there and you can help me promote my farm. I thought an advertising campaign with ArabHorse to start with – can you speak to Scott for me?'

Sienna nodded, automatically making some notes on her tablet. But while she was aware of John's words and what he needed her to do, she was reeling from the fact that Arjan had left. As she glanced out of the window, watching the conifer trees swaying in the breeze, Sienna wondered whether last night had been a dream. Had Arjan really kissed her? And the things he had said... But now, he had left and once more, he had taken her much-fought dreams with him. And Bethany's words reinforced all that Sienna knew about Arjan to be true.

'So, shall we go and look at the horses? We can go for lunch later and then we can start organising the campaign this afternoon.'

Nodding, Sienna pulled herself together and followed John out into the chilly but bright February day.

Later that evening, when John and Sienna had gone over the promotional plan for JB Arabians once more and John was finally satisfied that everything was perfect, Sienna received a text from Rin.

"Any chance you can come to Belgium soon? I need to talk to you about a few things. Rin."

Smiling to herself, Sienna made her excuses and went outside to call Rin.

'I'm actually in Belgium now – at John and Bethany's. How close are you to theirs?'

'I'm about an hour's drive away, in the other direction I'm afraid. I'm sure that we can sort something out to get you home afterwards.'

'That would be great. I came by Eurostar.'

'Perfect! There's a train direct from here to Brussels Midi/Zuid or I can take you. I'll be at John's tomorrow at 11am to pick you up. Happy you can come!'

Hanging up, Sienna made her way back inside to enjoy an evening with John and Bethany. Contrary to her first impressions of John, as the visit had gone on, she found herself liking him more and more. Bethany was also very easy going, and Sienna liked her straight talking style – she truly said it as it was and that was very refreshing to hear.

The following morning, Rin picked Sienna up at 11am as promised, and they made their way to Rin's home. When she had left Arjan, Rin had decided to relocate to a different part of Belgium, leaving Balen in the north behind and settling instead near Damme, found just outside of Bruges and closer to the Flemish coastline. Rin preferred this part of Belgium, and had settled here with Zoë, her groom who had been with her since her early days with Arjan.

Having stopped for a light lunch and a couple of glasses of wine and a chat in Bruges, they finally arrived at Rin's farm around 3pm.

'Now, let's have a coffee and then you can come and see

the farm! You must also see videos and photographs of my new colt, Ibn Shahja. He is so sweet, and I've just imported him from Australia, and he is now in the Middle East, ready to make his debut. His new owners are very excited about him, and we want to announce Ibn Shahja's arrival in a blaze of publicity. Oh Sienna, I have such hopes for him! He really is wonderful – a sweet, sweet character, and such a show off when he gets in the ring. Do you have milk in your coffee?'

Steaming cups of coffee in hand, Sienna and Rin stepped out into the yard and began to walk around the stables. Having seen the horses there, they returned to the house and Rin showed all the videos and photographs that she had of Ibn Shahja. Sienna could immediately see that he was a very special colt indeed – and also why Rin was so taken with him.

'He is already Australian National Champion at just two years of age,' said Rin 'That is why I can take him to Dubai. To be honest, I wasn't sure showing him there, but it is on his way home, so... And, of course, it is a great way to jump-start his career in this part of the world – just as it would be good for you, too, promoting him.'

Sienna smiled, agreeing with Rin. This was a great opportunity for her and she was thankful that.

Turning her attention back to videos of Ibn Shahja, Sienna agreed that there was something very touching about this young sweet colt. Watching, it was clear to see that Rin had already built up a wonderful bond with this colt, whose coat was a pink-grey at present but was already light enough that he would be white within a year at the most.

With a big, soulful eye, Sienna smiled as watched another video, this time showing Shahja following Rin out of his stable and was then turned loose in a small sand

117

arena. Together, Rin and Shahja played and he followed her across the arena, obeying commands given just by the wave of a finger. Rin had a wonderful rapport with horses, better than she did with most people, and she worked with them in a very natural way. She spurned gadgets and pressure, bringing them on at their own pace. While some other trainers liked to put pressure on the horses, often intimidating them and hurting them in the process, something that seemed to happen across the whole equine industry, Rin was very careful about how she trained and handled her horses. She only put the pressure on, and reluctantly at that, when she herself was pressurised by clients, although on more than one occasion, she had told the client to take their horse and leave her yard. Now, due her successes, she was thankfully able to work with whom she chose, rejecting desperate clients and those that would push her into methods she did not agree with. She had seen the way many handlers treated their horses – beating them through rugs, standing them in water and shocking them with electric cattle prods – and she did not intend to go down that path.

The break with Arjan, however, had proved costly and where once between them they had the pick of the European show horses, she now struggled to keep going as a sole trainer. Losing horses such as Sparkle of Justice, as well as Dance of Glory, after the split had not helped either, and Rin was aware that people were talking about her success in the past tense, saying that she was a has-been and her moment had passed. Such thoughts kept her awake in the night, as well as thinking about Juan and whether he would finally leave his wife for her or if she should just give up. The result of too much stress and too much coffee was taking its toll, but she was determined that Ibn Shahja would turn her fortunes around. Ignoring a small, niggling doubt in the back of her mind that showing the colt in Dubai was perhaps too soon for him, Rin needed Sienna to get the publicity machine working for them.

For now, however, she was happy to relax in the moment and talk with Sienna about how best to promote Shahja, and in the process, help recover the good name that Rin Risley once had.

Two days later, Sienna headed home on the Eurostar, happy with the plans made for Ibn Shahja as well as for Rin. She also had a lot of work to do with John and she was feeling positive about what lay ahead.

However, as the Flemish countryside faded into French, Sienna's vision was suddenly full of images of Arjan's dark, brooding eyes and she thought back, yet again, to that butterfly kiss he had placed on her lips just a few nights before. She really did wonder whether she had dreamt it, it seemed to be so unreal and, of course, she had not heard a word from or of Arjan since. Picturing his eyes once more as they stared into her when they spent time waiting for the rescue truck to arrive, she felt her stomach flip.

'Oh hell,' she thought to herself as the train she was confined in went underground, plunging her into darkness once more.

9

Just a few weeks later and the Dutch boy wonder, Sven Weber, was in the Blue Bar in Dubai, eyeing up the local talent. God, these guys were hot! Yes, he had a gorgeous man at home to warm his bed every night, but life on the road with his boss and his boss's horses was hard. Sven laughed to himself as he took a slug of his beer. His work could never be described as 'hard'. Also working in Arabian horse marketing, he had done well for himself over the years and life was good. As long as the clients kept coming in, he was happy. And as he spotted some British grooms come into the bar, he felt very happy indeed. He had enjoyed a threesome with some of them in Ajman and he was sure they would be up for something this time around as well. Armed with some vodka, he went over to begin his chat up lines, keen with anticipation of sating his appetite later that evening. Once again, Sven thanked his lucky stars that the shows in the Middle East started late in the day, often well after lunch, giving trainers, WAMS, managers and hangers on alike the chance to lay by the pool in the sun, working on their tan lines.

The next morning, Sven and some of his friends sat by the pool at the neighbouring Ibis Hotel with some of their latest conquests, hangovers not easing in the sun but determined to get as much colour as they could before they returned to northern Europe. Sven was 5'11", had curly blonde hair with brown running through the roots. He knew that everyone thought he had highlights, but his grandfather had had the same colouring and he just shrugged off the comments and jokes. His eyes, a playful green, had man and woman alike transfixed but in spite of many offers from a number of women, he was strictly interested in men only. With his freckles coming out in the sun, his full lips drawing furiously on the cigarette that seemed to be permanently glued to his hand, he kept looking impatiently at his phone.

Sven knew that Sienna was arriving today and he wanted to see her. He enjoyed her company and he felt almost a brotherly affection towards her. Besides, Sienna had a way in with many of the people in the industry and he wanted to see what she thought his chances would be with Tony, a newly-single Brit with raven black hair and an easy manner.

Sven and Sienna's initial meeting had been a difficult one when, in the dark bars of the Moorsele showground, he abruptly went up to her and, having barely introduced himself, accused her in front of a group of friends of stealing his clients and taking his business. Faced with this young, fiery Dutch guy, with his blonde curls falling around his face and hands moving agitatedly as he spoke, Sienna quickly realised that he could make or break her and her then fledgling business.

Taking him to one side, and buying him a drink at the bar, Sienna showed Sven a respect that few in the industry had to date. Deferring to his opinion, asking his advice, Sienna slowly assured Sven that she had no intention of taking over his flourishing design business – founded out of a love of IT work and not of horses, although he increasingly came to appreciate the Arabian breed. Leaving Sienna to return to his clients half an hour later, Sven felt slightly less hostile and, over the coming months, Sienna would regularly call him for a chat, to ask his opinion, and she frequently recommended him to clients. As time went on, Sven's wariness of Sienna thawed and from there, the brotherly tenderness that he now felt grew.

From that first meeting, Sven quickly recognised a good, pure side in Sienna's personality that few seemed to have these days; it had turned into a very unscrupulous world, where so many seemed quick to stab each other in the back.

Knowing that, because of her perceived naivety, Sienna would be vulnerable to those wishing to take advantage, Sven quietly went around behind the scenes, protecting her from the rogues. Plus, Sven quickly learnt that he enjoyed working with Sienna and, as an added bonus, his clients liked her, and she was handy to have around when a difficult owner was in town. Smiling to himself as he awaited her arrival into Dubai, he acknowledged that, when Sienna was with him, he always seemed to strike more deals than when he was alone.

Just as he decided that it was getting too hot in the sun, Sven received a text from Sienna, saying that she had just arrived, and he headed into the bar at the Ibis Hotel to meet her. There, the bar was open all day and he and Sienna could quietly have a few vodkas and catch up on what had been happening since they last saw each other.

It was later that evening in the Blue Bar that Arjan and Leap walked in together, Arjan immediately spying Sienna sat at the bar, laughing with some American clients. In spite of himself, and his continued annoyance that he hadn't been able to kiss her in Belgium as he wanted to, Arjan was pleased to see her and before he even realised what he was doing, he quickly made his way over to where she was sitting.

'Hi, how are you?' he asked, kissing her cheeks and inhaling her perfume as he did so. Instantly he cursed himself – she smelt so good and all he wanted to do was take her away from everyone and kiss her. He had dreamed of that first kiss for so long now and he knew that he wanted that and more… He shook his head slightly to himself; again, he told himself that he had to get a grip.

'Good, thank you,' said Sienna smiling. Since the night they had spent roadside in Belgium, he had haunted her dreams more and more and she was encouraged by the texts he kept sending to her. They were light and friendly but also managed to be intimate as well. Sienna was all too aware of his reputation but after his revelations that night, let alone that lightest of light kisses that he had given her, she wondered whether Arjan had decided to hang up his title of 'show stud' and settle down. And she couldn't help but wonder whether it was she that he had chosen to be the one to settle down with.

'Want to join me for a drink?' she asked, deciding that if she didn't ask him now, she never would.

Smiling, Arjan nodded and sat next to her. Across the bar, Sven watched the exchange and frowned. He had heard the rumours around the showing circuit that the pair were getting ever closer, and that Arjan was apparently captivated by someone for the first time in years. Arjan would be bad news for someone like Sienna, but Sven wasn't going to be the one to tell her that. Not yet, anyway. Sighing as he lit a cigarette, Sven knew that he would have to keep an eye on the situation – Sienna was too sweet to be messed around with and Arjan was such a predator, he would undoubtedly play with her as a cat does a mouse before sinking his claws in. The whole of the showing circuit had noticed the looks and exchanges between them, and bets were being taken as to how long it would take Arjan to bed the friendly, yet elusive, ice maiden. So far, she hadn't blotted her copy book and become involved with anyone in the industry. Unless she was careful, Sienna could be about to make a massive mistake and it could seriously damage her business as well as her heart. Arjan would take no prisoners and when, or if, Sienna fell out of favour, he would think nothing of destroying her. Scowling as he finished his vodka-red bull, Sven decided that he needed to be Sienna's quiet knight in shining armour. He enjoyed working with her and she was always ready to listen to him as he lamented his latest stands. The excuse he needed to interrupt them came in the form of Tony, as he sauntered into the bar and stopped to talk to some fellow Brits.

Sven swiftly made his way over to Sienna and Arjan at the bar, pushing himself in between them.

'So? Introduce me to him?' he asked, interrupting them with his typical Dutch manner.

Laughing, only mildly annoyed that her teté a teté with Arjan had been interrupted, Sienna slid off the stool and led Sven over to Tony, working her magic as she brought the two together, even if it was just for one night, which would surely be the limit of Sven's attentions anyway.

Arjan remained seated at the bar, still as a cat, and watching everything going on around him. His brown eyes were brooding as he watched the people moving around him. Every time he decided he wanted to get close to Sienna, she was pulled out his grasp. Downing the last of his beer, he ordered one of his famous Penicillin cocktails as he decided that tonight was not going to be his lucky night, with her at least. He looked around the bar to assess who else was available for some fun and smiled as he saw some potential. Knocking back his drink, he caught Sienna's eye as he went to talk to some hookers, blowing her a big kiss before turning his attention to, once more, getting laid.

Sienna still remembered the kiss from the previous month and she was torn between wanting to go and talk to him to find out more and keeping a cool distance. Arjan was a player, she knew that through and through, but he seemed to have a hold over her that stopped her from walking away. Looking at Sven and Tony, sat next to her talking, her eyes returned once more to Arjan, who was now chatting up two big-breasted French grooms. Cursing her continued interest in the man, Sienna grabbed her bag and headed to the toilets to compose herself. Tomorrow was another day.

Rin paced around the cool of the air-conditioned stables. Juan was not answering her calls and she was finding it increasingly difficult not to be jealous of Arjan, who had seemingly moved on from their lengthy relationship with apparent ease. Rin's fine bone structure and delicate, feminine appearance attracted many admirers, but Arjan's long shadow seemed to hang over her and stop them getting close. She knew that there was a chemistry between Arjan and Sienna, and she wasn't sure why it annoyed her so much – she was just aware that it did. Maybe, deep down, she wanted Arjan to still be in mourning for her but his smiling face and good fortunes in the show-ring provided only an even sharper contrast for her own downward turn in luck. For while she was full of new energy and determination, she still felt very alone.

Rin went into the stable, accepting cuddles from the grey colt standing by the door – Ibn Shahja. She only had a small show string for Dubai, but she was determined to make her mark with each horse. Patting Ibn Shahja, she left the stables and walked straight into Yves. Relations between them had cooled considerably since their affaire had been discovered and he was now dating a new girl, Ella, although there were rumours that theirs was a very open relationship and that bed-hopping was standard. Sighing imperceptibly, Rin wondered why Flemish men seemed to find it so difficult to remain faithful.

Kissing her cheeks, Yves ran his eye over Rin, noticing how she had filled out around her hips since he had last seen her naked. 'How are you?' he purred, smiling seductively to her and bending his knees so that he could lower himself and look in her eye. He was surprised to see dark circles and a forced smile – not what he expected. Rin had always been so full of joie de vivre, no matter what was happening in her life. Checking over his shoulder, he ensured that they were alone before he stole an arm around her waist.

'Why don't we go to your room for a catch up? It's been a while…,' he whispered. Rin shivered as she felt his breath on her neck, and despite her better judgement, she allowed herself to be led to the lifts. As the doors closed and Yves moved in for a passionless kiss, she saw Arjan stroll past, with a brunette bimbo on each arm, and closing her eyes, Rin lost herself to the moment.

Waking later that afternoon, Rin blinked as the setting sun shone into her eyes. Yves was still sleeping next to her, snoring gently as the sun gave his face a healthy golden glow. Rin felt her heart sink, feeling nothing for this boy lying next to her. She was nearly 15 years his senior and while she had been flattered by his attentions when she was with Arjan, now she did not want anything to do with him. She longed for the strong arms of Juan to hold her one more time. But he had gone back to his wife and his promises to her had proved to be empty. Just as her own promises had been to Arjan, she thought wryly to herself.

Rin pulled back the cotton sheets and, naked, she headed to the bathroom, running the shower hot so that steam filled the room before climbing in. Scrubbing herself with the vanilla-scented shower gel she loved so much, Rin was so deep in thought that she didn't hear the hotel door click shut. Yves, on waking, had gathered his clothes and crept away. He had enjoyed his pity-fuck, but he didn't want a repeat performance. Rin was not surprised to return to an empty room – if anything, she was relieved that she didn't have to make small talk.

Drying herself, she quickly dressed and returned to the stables, checking on her horses again before returning to her room and ordering room service. With her phone on mute, she ordered a cheesy Hollywood classic on the television and lost herself in another world for a few hours. She knew that she had to start getting a grip but for now, horrified that she sank so low as to sleep with Yves once more, she just wanted to hide away from the world for the rest of the day.

Visiting the stables the next morning, all the horses had settled into their new temporary home with the exception of Ibn Shahja. Rin was concerned and called the show vet out to have a look at him. Diagnosing a temperature, Rin left the colt to rest and checked over her other horses. Her plan had been for Ibn Shahja to debut in Dubai. The meeting Rin had made with Sienna last month had led to this point, and all her hopes were pinned on this young horse with the soulful eye, and she hoped that he would settle soon. At the moment, it was doubtful that she would even be able to show him, and her heart sank.

Listlessly, she made her way back to the hotel, taking the long route outside so that she didn't have to bump into Yves, Arjan, or anyone of the trainers. She wished that Zoë was there with her, but with foals due any minute at home, someone had to stay behind and take care of the mares. Instead, she had Sian with her, who came from the Welsh valleys and had an impish smile and green eyes that dazzled their way through customs with extraordinary ease. She was great with the horses and had told her boss to go back to her room and rest.

'You look so tired – I'll keep an eye on Shahja and let you know if there's any change,' Sian told her. Nodding, Rin quietly agreed.

Ordering another room service meal, Rin picked at her plate before dozing on her bed, with some drama film on in the background. She was so out of sorts with herself that her routine had gone out of the window. Rin slept through the afternoon sunshine, waking just as it was beginning to get dark. Still disgusted with herself for sleeping with Yves again, she quickly showered again before making her way back to the stables once more.

As she was walking through the World Trade Centre, the location for the show and with the Novotel and the Ibis hotels at either end of the main plaza, her phone began to vibrate in the back pocket of her jeans.

'It's Shahja,' said a panicked Sian. 'I think he's got a twisted gut.'

Breaking into a run, Rin raced the rest of the way to her stables, jumping over abandoned feed buckets in her haste to reach her section for the European horse stables. The vet was already there, and Shahja was dripping with sweat and pawing at his stomach.

'Oh God, please no…' was all Rin said as she went into the stable to help Sian and the vet, who was trying to inject the terrified colt. As his eyes rolled, Shahja fell to the floor and he stretched out his legs stiffly.

'We have to get him up,' the vet said, pushing the colt's back violently from behind in a bid to make him stand. As Sian and Rin coaxed and pulled, and the vet push, Shahja groaned loudly. Holly, Guy's groom, heard the commotion and ran to help, but it was too late. In just a matter of minutes, it was all over and Shahja's breathing became weaker and weaker.

'There is nothing more I can do. I am sorry,' said the vet, as he prepared to leave the stable.

'But there must be something… There must!' Rin cried out, tears spilling down her face as she held Shahja's head in her arms. She could feel the sweat coming off Shahja as she cradled him, and she knew that it was an impossible situation.

Shaking his head sadly, the vet walked away, leaving a sedated, but dying, colt for the three women to deal with; in the Middle East, it was considered unlucky to put a horse to sleep and besides, this colt was now so weak that he would die before any poison entered his system. As Shahja rolled his eyes one more time, and gave his last groan, all three burst into tears, begging him to be okay. But the dancing grey horse breathed no more.

As word spread, Guy appeared at Shahja's stable and put a black curtain up over the door.

'I'll contact the show organiser, get this taken care of,' he said to Holly, as a stunned crowd gathered outside the silent stable. All were shocked, and as they slowly left and went back to their own stalls, they each checked and double checked their horses, making sure that they had enough water, and ensuring that their feeds were dampened down, all just in case.

Rin, stunned and silenced, was led away from the stables and taken to a quiet corner of the bar, where a large brandy was put into her hands. Looking up, she was shocked to see that it was Arjan that had led her away and was now looking after her.

'He was a good horse,' was all he said as, just for a moment, he dropped his hand on Rin's shoulder before walking off to join the subdued group at the bar.

A short while later, Sian joined Rin, replacing her empty glass with a full one.

'I took my eye off my horses Sian,' said Rin with a choked voice. 'I let my own personal misery stop me from seeing what was happening to my horses. I forgot to trust my own instincts. I never should have let them bring him to show in Dubai so soon after leaving from Australia. It was too much for him. He was so young, so beautiful…'

As the tears began to fall again, Rin took a steadying gulp of brandy. 'The only way from here has to be up. This can never happen again. Any of it. It can never happen again.'

Rin didn't show her remaining horses in the Dubai Championships that year, and the celebrations were muted for the duration of the show with Angelina OL's Gold the only high point. As Rin flew back to Europe, her heart even heavier than it had been going out, and she returned to her beautiful farm, Rin gave herself an ultimatum. She would be back on her feet, truly back on her feet, by the end of this European show season, or she would walk away from the Arabian world and find a new path in life. Turning her grief over the loss of Shahja into a hopefully positive energy and inspired by anger at herself for failing the young colt, she opened her diary and began to make detailed plans for the rest of the year.

Arriving back to Belgium, broken, a day later, Rin passed a board advertising equestrian properties for sale. The seed was sown and, as soon as she got back to the farm, Rin went to the internet and began to search for equestrian properties within a 75-mile radius of her current farm. After two hours of searching, she found what she was looking for - a property near Düsseldorf in Germany. Set in the Lower Rhine, in Niederrhein, Rin called the estate agent and arranged a viewing the very next day. With its brilliant paddocks, horse walker, and outdoor and indoor arenas, as well as a luxury apartment for her and one for her grooms, it was perfect. Set in 11 hectares, with pristine pastures and a river running through the property, as well as a small forest, it was perfect. Rin fell in love and, for the first time since that terrible day when Arjan uncovered her deceit, she felt hopeful. By the end of the week, the sale was agreed, and Rin moved her farm from what had only ever felt like a temporary location after her split with Arjan, to the Lower Rhine. Finally, Rin was back in her own place. Later that day, walking down her own barn, hearing the soft sound of the horses eating their hay, Rin hoped that surely now, she would be able to turn things around. Zoë, who had made the move with her boss and was watching her as she looked over the stable doors, certainly hoped so.

And so it was that the end of March saw the Middle Eastern show season reach its finale. There was a small break as the Arabian horse circuit moved to Europe, ready for the season to begin there in late April. Many trainers took the opportunity of a break to travel to shows in America, enjoying the Arabian Breeders' World Cup in Las Vegas. Only in Vegas could there be a horse show in a hotel, and visitors flocked from the world over to enjoy this amazing spectacle, as well as the glamour of the bright city itself.

As the days got lighter and longer, trainers kept a private tally of how many victories they had over their rivals – Guy even went as far to have a whiteboard with the shows listed on it. There, he marked who won which championship at which show, keeping a list of how he fared. With gold, silver and bronze championships available at every show, competition was fierce and personal pride was always at stake. To be beaten by a rival to one title was bad enough, but to continually be taking the bronze behind their golds was just insulting. It made the trainers even hungrier to beat their rivals – second just was not good enough. As a result, behind the stables dodgy deals were done, hands shaking over promises of show wins for gold, a dalliance with a groom, or even bribing a pliable trainer to not bring their horse to a particular show, something reluctantly agreed to as long as the win-bonus was generously shared.

Sienna's focus during this time was the UK and the breeding farms there, yet a little under 200 miles away, across the North Sea, Arjan was sitting outside in the sun, drinking beer with Leap, and wondering how to nail this girl; in every way possible.

'Enough of talking about her Arjan! Either fuck her or move on. I am sick of this! It's "Sienna, Sienna, Sienna" all the time! I want you to sell my colt, not go on about this bloody girl!'

Arjan gave a wry smile and took a slug of his beer.

'Ah Leap, my friend. I will sell him. I have a buyer already lined up. 25% to me.'

'25%? Dream on!'

'I've got 100,000 euro for him….'

Leap laughed. 'I only wanted €40,000. Okay. You take your 25%.' He paused, looking at Arjan speculatively.

'What?'

'I am just wondering how it can be that you, who can get anything he wants and sell things to people who don't even want to buy anything, cannot get this girl. It must be driving you crazy!'

Leap laughed loudly, clapping Arjan on the back. 'Unlucky, my friend! Unlucky.'

Arjan just glared at Leap before lighting a cigarette and staring off into the distance, looking to the west and to where the woman that continually eluded him while haunting his dreams at night was also staring out of a window, looking to the east.

10

Seven weeks on from the horrific loss of Ibn Shahja, Rin was settled into her new farm and was enjoying riding Benji, a seven-year-old gelding who belonged to a friend. Benji had enjoyed success in the show-ring as a yearling before a paddock accident left him with a cut leg and a terrific scar. After a few months of box rest, it was decided that Benji would be better off gelded, so he could enjoy life out in the paddock with other horses rather than living a solitary life as a stallion. Later, he was backed by Rin, who enjoyed the art of educating a young horse about ridden life even though she was more dedicated to the halter side of showing. Every so often, Zoë would ride Benji at a local show, and they regularly won, but he loved life on the farm so much that he quickly became Rin's favourite mount.

Leaving the stable area, Rin headed off out the back of the yard to the track that led through the forest. All around her was a riot of colour as bluebells covered the forest floor to the left and right of the track. The purples, yellows and whites of spring crocuses added to the colour, while under the trees, clusters of daffodils danced in the breeze. Blackbirds called to each other, selecting their mates and making their nests. Germany was firmly in the grip of spring and as Benji broke into a canter, Rin gave a sigh of happiness at the nature all around her. Lifting her face slightly to the sun, for the first time in many moons, she felt alive again.

She had taken the loss of Ibn Shahja hard, blaming herself over and over for not paying more attention to the horses and allowing her personal life to interfere with her professional. Sian, unable to see her boss continue to berate herself, had spoken at length with the vet on call in Dubai that fateful day and he had, finally, been able to assure Rin that nothing could have prevented Shahja's death.

Finally accepting this had been a turning point for Rin. Those clients that had stalled or left after she and Arjan went their separate ways were finally coming back to her. One client that was no longer welcome, however, was Juan. In those traumatic days after Dubai, Juan had, for once and for all, finally decided that the grass was definitely greener on his wife's side of the fence. He had strung Rin along for so many months and arriving back in Belgium, she finally snapped and decided that she'd had enough. She had rung Juan and told him that his horses were no longer welcome at her training centre. Juan had laughed cruelly, saying that without him, Rin was nothing, but she ignored his jibes, went to South America for three weeks to find some new clients and new bloodlines to bring to Europe. As the new show season arrived in Europe, Rin felt reborn.

As Benji fell back into a trot, Rin steered him around the property, inspecting for broken fences as well as the water level on the lake. She pulled him to a gentle stop and they stood, watching the foals playing in the fields before them. Once more, Rin enjoyed the feeling of the warm sun on her face. The last two years had been tough, but she had finally turned a corner. A strong, if small, group of clients had remained loyal to her and she was ready to shine once more.

As she headed Benji for home, Rin felt her phone vibrate in her back pocket. A text from Guy Tindall, who was always so desperate to clinch a deal.

'Sienna is coming to do a brochure on our farm. When can I have that colt?'

Sighing, Rin decided not to answer and put her phone away. There was not a day went by when she didn't feel guilty about involving Sienna in her plans to get back at Arjan. She knew that she would have to make it up to her at some point. At the moment, any mention of her name made Rin feel terrible, and she knew that she would have to act soon.

As for the colt, Raafid was one of her best and that was the only reason Guy wanted him. She knew that many of the trainers were desperate to buy Raafid off her clients, a beautiful colt she had seen while she was out in Brazil. An exotic beauty, this deep black-bay colt mesmerised Rin from the moment she saw him and, in the flesh, he was even more charismatic. A Brazilian National Champion as both a foal and a yearling, Raafid commanded your attention. It was little wonder that people were offering increasingly indecent amounts of money in a bid to secure the colt. Rin knew the way that Guy worked – in his mind, if he had Raafid, he would win championships not only with the colt but also his other horses, and thus get his own owners, the DuPont's, off his back. In the few months between Moorsele and now, the couple had already worked out that Guy was not always the most truthful – but that was not her problem. The fact that Guy wanted Raafid, however, was.

Rin had immediately recognised Raafid's potential and rang her Middle Eastern owners to purchase him before anyone else spotted him. They agreed and had imported him from Brazil at great cost. Now two years old, Raafid oozed charisma and class. Since his arrival into Europe, the colt had steadily taken championship after championship.

Rin had started him off slowly at smaller local shows and then, as his confidence increased and the bond he had with Rin grew stronger, she began to enter him at the bigger shows. Having won the Tulip Cup at the start of May, Rin decided to give Raafid a break until the Frankfurt Show in early June, where Rin fully expected him to take the Junior Male Championship.

As Rin lead Benji to the wash-down area, she thought about what to do for the best. She knew that she would have to tell the client that someone was offering silly money for their colt; she just hoped that the client wanted what was best for Raafid too. Either way, when the time came, it was not going to be an easy conversation with Guy.

In May, a small part of the circuit moved to Austria, and the charming town of Wels. The International A Show there was a precursor to the bigger shows in Europe and it traditionally had been the venue where people debuted their horses to see whether they had the potential to go all the way. Horses that would go on to take the World Championship titles in December would show here first and wow the crowds and judges alike.

Few people went from the UK to this show as it was so far to travel horses. Guy decided to stay in the country for a rare weekend. His plans involved visiting clients, inspecting their newborn foal crop for future superstars, and Wels was the furthest thing on his mind as he loaded an overnight bag into his car and sped off down the A12.

Meanwhile, not so many miles away from Guy, Sienna was standing in line at Stansted Airport, waiting to board her flight to Linz. She was looking forward to the weekend ahead. She loved this show and the charm of Wels just added to the magic of the weekend. Far more relaxed than most of the other shows, this event in Wels allowed the natural beauty of the Arabian horse to shine through and Sienna enjoyed the chance to relax for once while still doing her job.

Two hours later, Sienna landed at Linz Airport and she was met by a driver in the obligatory black Mercedes; truly, she thought to herself, it seemed to be the car of choice for show organisers the world over.

'Good flight ma'am?' he asked as he loaded her cases into the back of the car.

'Yes, thank you.'

Arriving at the hotel in Wels, which was in fact an old converted monastery, Sienna found her check in already done by the organiser of the show and there was just a key to collect. Pressing the button for the lift, she listened to the creaking mechanics of this ancient hotel. She knew from previous experience that the lift was barely big enough to take two people and their cases, and as she waited for it to make its short but unhurried journey from the second floor to ground level, she looked up at the stairs, wrapping themselves around the lift shaft in a steely embrace.

As the lift finally arrived and Sienna waited for the doors to slowly open, Sven came bounding out of the bar like an energetic puppy.

'Sienna, you're here! See you in the bar in a few minutes?'

Without waiting for an answer, he went outside to make a call and Sienna waited for the lift to slowly raise her up to a higher level.

Returning downstairs a few moments later, by the stairs this time, she went into the bar. Dark wood panelling welcomed her, and Sienna ordered a large beer as she sat in a small booth, waiting for Sven to join her. She could see him through the window, walking up and down the street outside, drawing furiously on his cigarette.

As Sienna stared out of the window, she felt the wooden bench she was sat on shift slightly as someone sat down next to her. Turning her head to the left, she found herself staring into Arjan's eyes as he half-smiled at her.

'Hello Sienna. It is nice to see you,' said Arjan, slightly awkwardly as he laid his room key on the table. It seemed all his confidence vanished whenever he was around Sienna, and he became unsure of himself, and that puzzled him.

'Arjan,' she replied, taking a steadying sip of her beer.

Sighing, Arjan briefly closed his eyes before moving slightly closer to Sienna.

'I need to talk to you...' he began, before being interrupted by Sven bounding into the bar and sitting down with them.

Nodding curtly to Arjan, Sven turned to Sienna.

'There's a big dinner tonight in the Chinese restaurant, there's a load of us going. Will you come too?'

'Sure,' Sienna replied, blushing as she felt Arjan's eyes on her, and wondering what it was he had been wanting to say.

'What time?'

Sven glanced at Arjan before answering.

'I'll text you.'

Feeling tension rising between Sven and Arjan, who outwardly remained friendly but less and less so when Sven was around, Sienna finished her beer and made her excuses before heading to her room. Pressing her head against the window, she looked out over the garden and wished that Sven, as much as she liked him, had not interrupted them at that moment. It seemed that whenever Arjan wanted or tried to talk to her, Sven was there, coming between them and dragging Sienna away on some pretext.

Sighing, she started as she heard her mobile phone beep.

'I'll meet you downstairs at 7.50pm. Don't tell anyone else. It is a private event. X'

Having replied, Sienna wondered what to do with herself for the next hour. Checking out the bathroom, she decided that a soak in the bath was a rare luxury that she really needed. Decision made, she ran the hot tap and poured in a generous amount of rose oil, before slipping out of her clothes and into the silky water. 'Peace at last', she thought to herself as she laid back and closed her eyes, forgetting about everything and everyone for a short while.

At 7.45pm, Sienna made her way down the stairs and went outside the hotel for some fresh air. Further up the street, she could see Arjan sitting at a bar, staring at his phone while downing a beer.

'Ready?' Sven bounced up beside her. Turning her back on Arjan, Sienna headed off down the road with Sven for an evening of fun.

'Shizer!' Sven swore under his breath as he looked up from the menu. Arjan had come into the restaurant and was now staring at Sienna, who was sat next to him and talking to one of his clients, oblivious of Arjan's presence. Before Sven could say or do anything, Crispin called over for Arjan to join them.

'Arjan! Come and sit here – everyone budge up,' he brayed in his loud and ragged voice. As people got up and moved, Sienna – to her horror – found Arjan sat next to her with Sven, like a petulant guard dog, on her other side. Glaring furiously across her, Sven lit a cigarette and blew the smoke into Arjan's face.

'What are you doing here?' Sven almost snarled at Arjan.

'I was hungry,' Arjan replied as he pressed his leg firmly against Sienna's.

'You were not invited.'

'Cheers…'

Smiling broadly, Arjan raised his glass of wine, freshly

poured by Crispin who was sat on his other side, and looked at Sven, before leaning in front of Sienna, who in turn was leaning back, one finger in her ear, on her phone and trying to understand a thick Middle Eastern accent. Quickly, and under his breath so that only Sven could hear, Arjan murmured in Dutch: 'You know, life would be much easier if you would just fuck her instead of hanging around like an annoying little dog.'

Not giving Sven a chance to reply, Arjan turned back to Crispin and steadily ignored Sienna and Sven for the rest of the night, although he kept up the pressure of his leg on hers and as desserts were being enjoyed around the table, he stole his hand underneath the tablecloth and gently placed his hand just above her knee. Turning to her, he smiled into her eyes, raising the fingers of his other hand to his lips, warning her to be quiet. As Sienna smiled back hesitantly, having jumped when he first touched her, Arjan felt triumphant. It had taken him 18 months, but he finally had Sienna where he wanted her. Still amazed that it had taken so long – 18 minutes was a usually long time for any women to fall under his spell – and he felt a surge of adrenaline. Finally, she would be his. And who knew where the road would lead them – a thought that kept crossing his mind and alarming him. Surely, he was the one that just needed to fuck her and get Sienna out of his system for good, and then he could stop obsessing about her. But even as he thought that, Arjan knew that he was very likely to be deluding himself.

Sienna sat stock still, barely taking in the conversation around her. She could feel the warmth of Arjan's hand through the fabric of her trousers and the look in his eyes when he had just smiled at her... She was lost. She knew that she was powerless to resist anymore – and what good would it do anyway? She was also trying to understand the undercurrents between the two men either side of her, not sure why Sven had gone from being happy and friendly to glaring at everyone and refusing to eat anything.

As everyone stood up to leave, Arjan helped Sienna on with her coat, an action that was noted by many. Sven glared at Arjan, having chosen to drink and chain-smoke his way through dinner rather than bother to actually eat. Grabbing Sienna, he headed out of the restaurant, deciding that it would have to be now that he would speak to her about Arjan and his terrible ways. God knows that someone needed to put her in the picture. The love he felt towards Sienna was purely brotherly, but he didn't want to see her used by the biggest rake in the industry. She was a sweet girl and she deserved better than that. Lighting yet another cigarette, he readied himself for what was not going to be a pleasant conversation.

Unfortunately for Sven, Crispin chose that moment to bend his ear about why his horses weren't winning and that he had better take a title this weekend or he would be moving his horses away from his trainer, who was a friend of Sven's.

Sienna walked behind them, seemingly in a world of her own. Arjan, it seemed, had vanished into the night and Sienna decided that she needed some time on her own to think things through.

'Come to the bar and have a drink with us Sienna love,' said Crispin.

'I think I'm just going to head straight to bed actually. Thank you for a great evening though,' she smiled.

Hugging Sven, who whispered to her that they urgently needed to talk tomorrow, Sienna pressed the buzzer to call for the lift, feeling just woozy enough from the wine not to be able to face the spiral staircase. Miraculously, it was already on the ground floor and she waited for the doors to open before going in. Turning around, she pressed the button for the second floor. Just as the doors were beginning to close, a boot wedged them open and Arjan stepped into the lift with her.

'Sienna…,' he murmured as the doors closed at a steady pace behind him and the lift slowly jolted into action.

'Finally…' he whispered as he took a step towards her and put his arms around her, bringing his lips gently down on hers. For one glorious minute, they kissed while the lift slowly took them higher and higher. As it juddered to a halt on the second floor, Arjan reluctantly released his grip on this gorgeous woman, smiling down at her and taking her hand to lead her out of the lift.

'Finally,' he murmured one more time, almost to himself, before kissing her again, this time a light butterfly kiss.

'Sweet dreams…'

Knowing not to push her too far and thrilled to have already kissed her so soon after finally stealing her heart, Arjan quietly made his way down the stairs to the first floor and his room. He might have walked quietly but there was triumph in his stride, with his chest puffed out before him as he went down the winding staircase. Finally, he had Sienna just where he wanted her and Arjan couldn't resist getting out his phone to send a quick text to Leap, who had decided not to come to the show this time.

'I've kissed her – game on!'

Arjan paused before sending the message, however, something inside stopping him, and he decided to delete it. Touching his lips with a wry smile, Arjan chose to keep the news to himself for just a little longer, not least so he could see the look on Leap's face when he finally told him he had Sienna under his spell. Game on, indeed…

Meanwhile, on the floor above, Sienna closed the door

to her room and leaned back against it in stunned silence. Her heart was pounding and her knees felt weak. She revelled in the moment, securing it in her memory, reliving it over and over again.

Eventually, Sienna made her way further into her room and collapsed on the bed, staring at the moon through the still-open curtains.

'Arjan...' she said to herself as she rolled over, recalling the feel of his arms around her, the taste of his lips on hers and how marvellous it made her feel. Smiling to herself, she fell into a deep sleep. Cupid's arrow had finally hit her, and it had hit her hard.

Sienna felt that she was walking on air as she made her way to the showground the next day. She was fully aware that she was falling for Arjan – and had been for the last year or so, if she was being honest with herself – and she felt nervous about seeing him again. As she arrived ringside, she joined her clients and politely went through the motions but all the while, she was looking for Arjan. Now that it was the morning after, she was doubting whether she had done the right thing by kissing him, and she knew she would feel better once she had seen him again, and was impatient to do so.

She didn't have long to wait. He had the first horse in the first class, which she had sponsored, and Sienna sat and politely watched as he trotted a showy grey filly around the arena. As she marked off the horses as they came in, she could see Arjan watching her from across the arena. As the last horse completed her trot, Arjan led the class around for the walk stage.

'Good morning...' he smiled at her as he passed the table the first time around. The second time, having checked that her clients were otherwise engaged, he blew

Sienna a kiss, and then focused on the task in hand – winning the class and then the following day's championship for his client.

'Sienna, if you would like to come and present the prizes please,' said Léonie, the Show Organiser, leading Sienna into the arena. Over her left arm, she carried a basket containing trophies and sashes for the horses in the Top Five.

Arjan had won the class. As Sienna went to hand over the prizes, Arjan felt that it was he himself who had won her, not the horse the sash. As he kissed her on the cheek, he inhaled the bright floral scent that she always wore, which smelled of roses and freesias, and he knew that that scent would always remind him of Sienna.

'Congratulations,' Sienna said as she posed next to Arjan so that the photographers could have their moment.

'You are the better prize,' said Arjan quietly. 'I would like to keep it to ourselves for now… I just want to enjoy this moment first before it becomes public.'

Arjan had an ulterior motive for saying this. He knew that Sienna's friends, Sven especially, would warn Sienna off him even more if they knew that they had kissed. He wanted Sienna to fall for him even more before she was warned off, knowing that by then, she would be so far under his spell that she wouldn't care what her friends said or thought.

Squeezing Sienna around the waist, she wondered just what had been started with last night's kiss and, hoping that she wasn't blushing, she moved on down the line to the second-placed filly. As she turned to pose for the camera once more, she saw Arjan watching her out of the corner of her eye and felt happy to go along with whatever he wanted.

Back in his hotel room, Arjan was getting ready to go to dinner with his clients, who were very happy after they had won every class that day.

'Something is making you smile, Arjan!' they had laughed as they clapped him on the back in the stables. 'We want to see more of this!'

Arjan was just wondering whether he could wrangle an invitation for Sienna to join them at dinner when there was a knock at the door.

'Leap!' Arjan exclaimed in surprise as he opened the door. 'What on earth are you doing here? I didn't think you were coming to Wels this year.'

'I wanted to surprise you! I have a present – my new girlfriend has a sister, she is very bendy... I brought them with me. Besides, I want to see one of the stallions showing. I might breed to him – or buy him. So you need to get your commission hat on Arjan.'

When he didn't reply, or even register any interest in the sisters, Leap stood and looked thoughtfully at him.

'Is she here then? Sienna?'

Nodding, Arjan walked back into the room, leaving the door open for Leap to follow. Or leave. All thoughts of taking Sienna out with his clients, before walking her to her room, kissing her again and slowly removing her clothes, layer by layer, now lay in tatters and he knew that he had to keep a front up or Leap would suspect. He knew him too well. He felt differently when he was with Sienna, and the kiss last night had been the best first kiss he had ever had. Deep down, he knew that this would be more than just a fling, and having kissed Sienna, he was finally prepared to admit it to himself. But he wanted to take his time to get used to the idea before everyone else found out. And now Leap was here. And Arjan knew that he was weak.

'Sisters, hey?'

Arjan forced himself to sound jovial but all he could see was Sienna's face as she closed her eyes to accept his kiss.

'Yes – and you know what fun they will be! And they are downstairs waiting for us now, all keen and ready, so get a move on.'

Walking back from the showground much later, having stayed behind to talk about putting a book together on one of the bigger farms, Sienna glanced into the Chinese restaurant as she went past. Fancying cosying up in the hotel bar with beer and schnitzel, and perhaps a nightcap with Arjan later, she was horrified to look in and see him sat there with Leap and two buxom blondes, one of which had her hand on his crotch while he laughed.

Running back to the hotel, Sienna tried to make sense of what she had just seen, coming up with excuses and believing none. She was all ready to head straight up to her room when Crispin and Katherine appeared and pulled her to the bar, too full of their own self-importance and self-promotion to take in Sienna's distress. Sven, however, sat at the bar doing shots with some of the grooms, did notice and knew that Arjan had to be at the root of it. He had been aware of Arjan's play on Sienna last night and he was still smarting at the Belgian's words to him. With his eyes glinting dangerously, he downed another shot and motioned to the bar man to pour the same again.

Having gone through the motions and sat and talked horses and breeding programmes with Crispin and Katherine while they ate vast steaks and drank three bottles of red wine, Sienna was finally beginning to make her excuses and head upstairs when Leap, Arjan and the two blondes fell laughing into the bar.

Seeing Sienna staring at Arjan in horror, frozen to the spot, Sven stood up, ready to jump to her defence if needed

147

as well as hitting the pompous Belgian across the bar, something he would happily do at a moment's notice, with or without encouragement. Leap, too, noticed the reactions of Sienna and Sven, and leaned towards Arjan, laughing saying too loudly:

'So – nothing happened with you and Sienna then? You sly old dog…'

Glancing at Sienna, aware of his best friend ready to make a scene and for some reason, wishing that it wasn't all so public, Arjan made a choice, a choice that he could not explain either at the time or later when he stared at his reflection in the mirror, alone with just his guilt-ridden conscience for company.

'That frigid bitch? Don't be stupid.'

And with that, knowing full well that the whole bar had heard him, he grabbed the nearest blonde and shoved his tongue down her throat.

Stifling a sob, Sienna fled from the bar, aware of shouts ringing out behind her. Not waiting for the lift, she ran up the stairs and unlocking her door, threw herself down on the bed, sobbing as she did so. How could she have been so stupid? And how could she have even thought for a second that Arjan might change. Men like him never do. Ignoring Sven pounding on her door, Sienna sobbed into her pillow, fists clenched as she realised just how foolish she had been to let her guard down. This was the second time that Arjan had upset her so strongly and she was determined that it would never happen again. But like so many, Sienna knew that she could not resist the bad guy and even as she cried, she knew that she was lost.

The next day at the show, Arjan felt wretched. He had been an utter bastard to Sienna, and he knew it. Maybe Rin was right when she said that he was incapable of love and destroyed everything that he touched. He could see Sienna and in spite of smiling at her and saying 'hello' every time he passed, she steadfastly ignored him. He could hear Leap, telling everyone what a legend Arjan was, and how he had put 'the Irish girl' in her place. Clenching his fists and grimacing rather than smiling as he was called forward with the grey filly as Junior Female Champion, his feelings the polar opposite of what he had felt the previous day, Arjan glared at Leap laughing in the audience.

Leaving the arena, he pulled out his phone and sent a quick message.

'Sienna, I am sorry. Please let me explain, just give me a minute of your time. See you later at the open house. A xxx'

Pressing send as he made his way back to the stables, he glanced past the security fencing to see Sienna getting into a car. But instead of turning right to head off to the farm, where the open barn was held every year after the show, the black Mercedes instead swept to the left and to the airport, taking Sienna and his pathetic apologies out of his life. And once more, Arjan only had himself to blame.

11

Back in Belgium once more, Leap invited Arjan over to his farm for the afternoon so that he could show him the new foals born at Leopold Arabians. Born into a very rich family, with old money going back as many generations as he could be bothered to count, Leap had never had to want for anything. Arabian horses had been his obsession, however, and he constantly dreamed of breeding the next World Champion. But while he had many disposable thousands, he didn't have enough disposable millions to bribe his way to the glory spot. Every year, Leap made his breeding plans and, a year later, he excitedly asked Arjan over to review the outcome. As Leap walked down the luxurious foaling barn, he couldn't help but feel that he had excelled himself this year. Or rather, his mares had.

Arjan arrived, his BMW leaving a trail of dust as he careered down the driveway. Leap greeted him at the door, an espresso in hand as he clapped his friend on the back.

'I think I have done it! I have bred a World Champion! Come and see this filly, she was born at 2am and wow – I have never seen anything like her!'

Arjan grinned. 'You always say that!'

'This time, I mean it. Come - see! We are about to put her out of the first time.'

The men made their way around to a walled garden. In the middle was a raised platform, with weatherproof rattan chairs covered in Middle Eastern drapes, a low table and a big pot of coffee. Below this platform was a small arena, thus providing the perfect place to sit and watch the horses. All around, flowers let off their gentle perfume, bees buzzed busily between the petals, and Leap bounded up the steps.

'Come on Arjan! Jeez, I am there for you in everything and you can't even get excited about what I have to show you? Come on!'

Arjan stepped up on to the platform, smiling affectionately at his friend. 'Calm down, Leap. Let's see if she really is as special as you say. We have been here many times before, remember?'

Brushing Arjan's words aside, Leap nodded to a waiting groom, who then called around the stables. Moments later, a bay mare appeared, with a brilliant chestnut filly foal at foot. The filly had one small white star on her forehead, and no other markings. Although she was just 12 hours old, the filly trotted confidently ahead of her mum, ears alert, neck naturally raised and carried beautifully, and she already showed great, natural, free movement. She still had to unfold fully from being inside her dam, but she painted a startlingly beautiful picture.

'Well?'

Arjan lit a cigarette, never taking his eyes off the foal. Leap had done it. He had finally bred something with that extra *je ne sais quoi*, that special something that you could never fully and completely describe, but you knew it when you saw it. And there it was, dancing in front of Arjan's eyes. He inhaled deeply on his cigarette, trying to gather his thoughts. After sitting in silence and just staring at the filly for a minute, Arjan finally spoke.

'Well, Leap. I think you've done it. After all those years of trying, you have finally bloody done it!'

Clapping his friend on the back, Arjan leapt down off the platform, graceful as a cat, keen to get closer to this dancing beauty in front of him.

'She is going to need a good name,' he called back.

'I was thinking of Golden Aura LA,' Leap said as he

joined Arjan in the grassy arena.

Arjan laughed. 'Golden Aura? No! Something special. How about…,' Arjan paused.

'Sienna LA?' Leap couldn't help but make a sly dig at his friend. 'Seriously, when are you going to just screw her and move on?'

Arjan scowled at Leap, who quickly realised that he needed to back off from the subject.

'Iridescent LA. How about that?'

'Maybe… Let's go and have a beer and think about it. And please. No more about Sienna. It is all your fault that it went wrong in Wels anyway. I had her eating out of my hand before you showed up!'

'Only eating from your hand isn't quite what you had in mind,' Leap laughed back in his face. 'Face it. Sienna is impervious to your charms, and you'll never have her.'

Scowling again, Arjan list another cigarette.

'Cut the shit, Leap. Let's go and see this little beauty – Iridescent or whatever she will be called – close up.'

Putting his arm around Leap's shoulders, the men headed to the yard, names proving impossible to find for such a beautiful filly. As far as Leap was concerned, he had done it. He had bred a World Champion. Now it was over to Arjan to campaign her, show her, and win with her. After a few hours of talking and drinking champagne to celebrate the new arrival, Leap came up with the perfect name.

'Aria LA,' he grinned, as he raised his glass towards the stables. 'My first World Champion.'

12

The showing circuit moved on into a long, hot summer. Even Guy was getting tired of wheeling and dealing – all anyone wanted to do was go to the beach and relax with friends there. So when the Menton Show came around at the end of June, everyone flocked to the south of France to enjoy just that – friends, sun, sea, and, for a few hours at least, Arabian horses.

To give it its full title, the Mediterranean & Arab Countries Arabian Horse Championships was held next to the beach. Just a stone's throw from the Italian border, the show was held in the Porte de France. While situated next to the shingle and sand beaches, the show itself was held on sand-covered concrete. With the late June weather invariably meaning blisteringly hot weather, the show was loved and hated by trainers in equal measure. While the late starting of the show, and the idyllic location, meant that there was plenty of time for topping up their tans and having long, cool cocktails as they watched the show, it also meant extra work for the grooms as they strived to keep the horses comfortable. Vast electric fans were brought for the stables and the star horses were watched around the clock to ensure that they had enough water, ate their feed, and didn't start to run a temperature. Add in the hard going underground, and up to a third of the horses going home lame, all in all the trainers preferred to go and watch rather than risk putting their potential World Champion out for the rest of the season. But the kudos of winning in Menton was huge, and those that won there would often go on to wow the rest of the world come autumn. It was well known that if you won in Menton, then you were likely to end up winning a medal of some colour or another in Paris later that year.

Rin had brought just one horse with her, Raafid. This elegant black-bay colt had already proved this season that had the potential to reach the big time. His owners from the Middle Eastern were new and enthusiastic. However, they didn't understand that it took time between a horse winning a title at a small show and taking the glory at one of the main shows. They were pushing Rin to, in turn, push Raafid to reach the top as quickly as possible. Rin resisted, knowing that if this young colt did too much too soon, it would ruin him for life. Rin, however, was canny enough to know that if she didn't have a big win soon, then she would be all but over. The titles Raafid had already won were all good and well but these clients wanted to win big among tough competition – something that was not so easy to do but it was crucial to the owners that they had this kudos.

As she settled Raafid into his stable, with Zoë stationed outside with her nose in a book and ignoring all the advances of the Italian grooms, Guy came around the corner, his cool demeanour for once blustery.

'I have to have that colt!' he all but shouted.

'And hello to you too,' said Rin as she secured the stable door behind her. 'He is not for sale – I told you.'

'Not yet, but he will be by Sunday when you fail – again – to get him into the Top Five. Just save yourself the hassle and do the deal now.'

Sensing Zoë tense behind her, Rin felt annoyed. 'And how do you know that? His owners are happy.'

Guy laughed cruelly. 'Think what you like Rin – I know different! And he will be mine by the end of the show.'

Turning, Guy raced away, keen to get in on the next deal and ignoring the trail of destruction he left behind.

'Ignore him, he is always full of hot air,' Zoë said as she

tried to quietly comfort Rin.

'But he's right... Raafid deserves to be at the top of his game and I am holding him back...'

Fighting tears, Rin turned to around look at the beautiful colt in his stable.

'His eyes – he has such big eyes... Just look at him – he deserves so much' she said, as the tears began to fall and Raafid nudged her jeans pocket, ever hopeful of being given a minty treat.

Zoë sighed, not liking what she was going to have to say to Rin next.

'Then you know what you have to do... Just this once, put your personal feelings aside and push Raafid a little and get the win. There is plenty of time between now and the next show, and you can work on him plenty more at home and get him shining. You are going to have to Rin – or you'll lose him... Besides, who is to say that you are holding him back? You know in your heart what is right.'

Hugging her boss, who she had worked for since she was 16 years old, Zoë busied herself with water and feed buckets so that she wouldn't have to look at Rin making one of the more difficult decisions of her life. When on when, she wondered, would Rin get the break that she deserved? Ever since she and Arjan had split up, it seemed that her life was on a constant downward spiral and Zoë knew that Rin deserved better than that.

Saturday afternoon was hot, bright and sunny. People made their way from the Hotel Napoléon, overlooking the Garavan Bay, across the road and down to the restaurants that lined the seafront. Guy was wining and dining his clients, plying them with vintage Perrier Jouet pink champagne while he enjoyed a refreshing sparkling water. He was showing that afternoon and he needed to be alert, not least as he was convinced that Raafid would be his by this time tomorrow.

'I can get you 20 breedings to Dancing Lyric, no problem,' he said as he scooped up his fresh oysters and picked lobster out of the shell. 'He might not be at public stud, but I have a way in.'

His clients, Pierre and Marcia DuPont, nodded, Pierre looking particularly keen. Dancing Lyric was one of the superstar stallions of the day and his stock were winning the world over. Born in 2008, this iridescent chestnut with a flaxen mane and tail had won every title going as a youngster and was one of the few horses to win in three continents – the United States of America, Europe, and the Middle East. Dancing Lyric had passed on his winning ways to his progeny and having sold over 500 breedings in just three years, his book was now closed. Guy had enjoyed a fling with the woman who owned him and was convinced that he would be able to get all the breedings he wanted. "A service for a service," he thought to himself as he topped up Pierre and Marcia's glasses.

Pierre looked impressed and gulped down most of the exquisite champagne in a mouthful. Marcia was less impressed, recognising Guy as a womaniser. She and Pierre had been childhood sweethearts and he was only too happy to support her with her love for the Arabian horses. Having ridden for most of her life, Marcia was new to the halter showing world. That did not, however, make her a fool, she thought to herself.

'I can get Raafid too, it is all but done,' said Guy confidently – and arrogantly, Marcia thought. She liked Rin and wanted to support the female trainers; there were precious few of them in the industry, and she certainly didn't like this arrogant Englishman's attitude towards herself; he was dismissive of her, instead trying to wow

Pierre with his flashy attitude. Smiling vaguely, she looked out to sea and came up with her own plan. Guy might think that he was all that, but Marcia had other ideas.

Rin stood sweltering in the collecting ring, the heat bouncing off the ground around them and reflecting the sun on to the horses' legs. Raafid stood quietly next to her, looking every inch the contender. His strong legs and beautiful face ensured that he stood out and, measuring almost a hand higher than the other colts, all eyes were upon him. Rin had taken him for a walk earlier that day and had tried to intimidate the colt – but she just couldn't bring herself to do so. She would rather lose him than lose her integrity, and while she understood Zoë's concerns, she just couldn't do it.

Raafid was so tall that he towered over Rin, and anyone coming to stand by his shoulder to talk to Rin would be hidden from view. Rin watched a petite raven-haired woman come up to her and stand in front of her, hidden from view, and talk intently to her. Not a flicker of emotion crossed Rin's face, no one could tell of her relief, and as the raven-haired lady walked away, so a cloud finally lifted from her face. Finally able to breathe again after months of self-doubt, she threw her arms around Raafid's neck, startling the colt only slightly.

'Let's go and show them what we're really made of,' she whispered. 'Come on boy.'

Forty-five minutes later, Rin and Raafid stood top of the class, his owners thrilled to have finally won.

'I must talk with you immediately, I have some news,' Rin said to them as they left the arena. Nodding, they agreed to meet her in their suite at the Napoléon in half an hour.

Walking along the sea front that evening, Rin and Zoë made their way to one of the many bars and selected martini cocktails from the menu.

'To Raafid,' toasted Rin.

'And to you,' smiled back Zoë as they chinked glasses.

As Rin sat back peacefully, Zoë noticed that her friend looked more like her old self. A corner in the long road that Rin had been on had finally been turned.

Guy sat with Pierre and Marcia during the championships, ready to strike as soon as he could. While he was not shocked that Raafid had won, he was upset that he had done so with Rin at the end of the rope. He knew that the momentum wouldn't continue through to today – Rin would blow it in the championship as the pressure became too much, and he could then make his way over to the clients and steal the horse from under her nose.

'And the Junior Male Championship is…'

The dramatic pause followed as a rider, dressed in authentic Arabic costume, rode around the arena on a white stallion to the colourful group of flags in the corner. Selecting one, the rider turned in triumph and rode back to the centre of the ring. Guy was surprised to see her holding a French flag – there were no French horses entered, as far as he knew.

'RAAFID!' cried the commentator as Rin ran into the arena, throwing her arms around the colt and almost stumbling to her place at the top of the line. Zoë followed, wiping tears of joy off her face as she hugged both her friend and the colt.

Marcia stood up and looked at her husband. 'Shall we?'

Pierre nodded, standing and following his wife as they made their way through the VIP arena and out into the blazing sunlight to stand next to Raafid. Hugging Rin,

Marcia patted her new colt on his neck while Pierre took the prize. It was her who had visited Rin in the collecting ring the previous day, and had secretly purchased Raafid, having firmly decided that Guy was not the man for them. Marcia's only condition on buying Raafid was that Rin not only continued to show the colt, but also all their other horses too. Rin, overjoyed, had accepted and Marcia's offer was enough money that it had pleased her clients. While Pierre was the one that did all the talking, Marcia wore the trousers and so it was with great satisfaction that she turned around to see a puce-coloured Guy sat in the VIP tent, watching them, hand clenched so tightly around his glass of water that it cracked.

Guy was waiting for the DuPont's as they left the arena.

'What the fuck?' he angrily asked Pierre, grabbing his elbow as he did so.

Pierre glanced down at Guy's hand on his arm.

'Rin is a better person than you will ever be, it is as simple as that,' he said as he shook off Guy's hold.

'We have a transporter on its way to your farm to collect our horses as we speak. I trust that there will be no hold ups when it arrives.'

Without looking back, Pierre put his arm around his beautiful wife's waist and led her to the stables to admire their new colt. While he would have done things differently, he always respected his wife's wishes – and she was always right, at the end of the day. Patting the black-bay beauty Raafid, Pierre knew that his wife had truly worked her magic this time and as he looked into the smiling faces of Rin and Zoë, such a contrast with Guy's belligerence, he was glad that his horses were moving to Germany to join Rin's yard.

As Rin opened up a bottle of champagne to share with Zoë and the DuPont's, she cast her mind back to how Guy had taken Sparkle of Justice from her, and then how she had lost Ibn Shahja, all those months ago. The pain that she had felt then, along with her desire for revenge towards Guy, had lessened considerably. She was happy to have Marcia and Pierre as her clients, and the last of the emotion from that dark day finally faded away. Now, she just felt joy and as she raised her glass to the couple, she leaned against Raafid's door, laughing as he tried to sip the champagne from her glass. Things had finally come full circle for Rin – and she was a better person for it.

13

While there were shows every week, the summer was also a quiet time for many. Rin had welcomed the DuPont's with open arms and through their kindly praise and excellent word of mouth, their friends had also now sent their horses to her training centre. Rin and Zoë were constantly on the road, and with both in such a good mood, the effects were clear to see as they began to clean up at every show they went to. One championship quickly turned into two, and then three. New staff were taken on to help with the influx of horses coming from across Europe and the Middle East, all keen to cash in on Rin's success and ensure that they, too, were in the winner's circle.

With this newfound success came a newfound resolve. Having enjoyed a great training session with a weanling foal that morning, Rin went into the house and picked up her iPhone. Scrolling through the list, she found the number she wanted and dialled.

'Sienna? It's Rin… Please, can we talk?'

And so it came that Sienna made her way to Germany to see Rin and her farm. When Rin had called her, she had poured her heart out and bared her soul to Sienna, explaining why she had acted the way she had, and apologising profusely for the outcome. She explained what had happened with Arjan and, especially, with Juan, and how she had gone into free fall for a while. Sienna, relieved to have finally understood some of the pain Rin had suffered, tentatively agreed to visit the farm with a view to putting together a beautiful brochure on the horses.

As Sienna drove up the E40 away from Calais and

towards Niederrhein, she could see echoes of Arjan everywhere, remembering the drive that they shared on a dark night those months ago. If she thought back hard enough, she could almost feel the touch of his lips on hers, and it made her heart break anew every time she did so. Taking a deep breath and knowing that she had a job to do and that she should do it well, Sienna focused on the drive and hastened to Niederrhein. Arriving at a practical but impressive property, Sienna got out of the car and went to find a revived Rin.

The DuPont's were also there, and Sienna quickly took to this friendly French couple. It was they who wanted the brochure made, to showcase not only their horses but also the faith they had in Rin. That night, they dined together in Rin's vast dining room, red wine flowing and laughter filling the room as they recounted tales of their time in the industry.

The next day, the hard work began. A photographer arrived, pre-booked by Rin, and horse after horse was brought out to be captured in the early morning sun and then the magical, late afternoon pre-dusk glow. When the sun was high in the sky, Sienna spoke at length with Marcia and Rin about the running order of the brochure, which horse would appear where, and what text would be needed. Realising that a story would enhance the brochure, Sienna put a call through to one her writer friends in England, Sophia Morgan, who had worked with Rin before. With the story arranged, it was time for more photographs before, once more, opening another bottle of wine.

Three weeks later, the brochure was complete. Gold embossed with an intricate, artistic logo, the DuPont's horses looked amazing. It was the perfect marketing tool to take to the upcoming title shows.

Just a few weeks later, Arjan arrived at the UK International Arabian Horse Show – or UKIAHS for short – held near Braintree at the Towerlands Equestrian Centre. The name of the venue, Towerlands, was how everyone referred to the show. Arjan got out of his car and cautiously looked around. He knew that he was on Sienna's home turf and he knew that more than a few people were shocked at the way he had behaved. Even Leap, on learning the truth of the kiss after dragging it out of him, had berated Arjan.

'I know that we joke but you really led her on. You've played with her as a cat does a mouse for too long now. I never would have lined you up with that girl had I known you kissed Sienna. You really are a shit at times Arjan.'

Knowing that Leap and his belligerence in lining him up with the girl was part of the reason why things had gone so spectacularly wrong in the first place during that ill-fated weekend in Austria did not warm Arjan to his friend, and he slowly started to keep his distance. The trouble now, though, was that he was in the UK, at a show by himself, and he knew that Sienna had several allies.

Walking away from the stables and over to the main building, Arjan headed to the bar. Just as Sienna had stopped dead in her tracks in Wels, so he too did here. For there was Sienna, sat holding hands with Peter Gilliard, the smooth commentator who was also some 18 years her senior. Like Arjan, Peter also had colourful reputation and he frowned as he saw them sitting there, holding hands. Peter glanced around and saw Arjan but did not allow even a flicker of recognition to cross his face. In fact, nothing gave away what either man might be thinking.

Arjan nervously approached the table, fatalistically drawn to them. He could not keep his eyes off their hands, of Peter rubbing his thumb over Sienna's hand, and holding it so tightly, so naturally.

'Hello…'

Sienna looked up, a guarded look on her face.

'What's going on here?'

The words were out before Arjan could stop them. He wanted to be the one sat there, holding Sienna's hand. Not Peter. He should be the one taking Sienna to his hotel and making love to her all night. He shuddered as he thought of Peter's old body climbing on top of her youthful one and he hoped that such a thing hadn't already happened.

'We're just talking,' said Sienna, lowering her gaze to back to Peter's reassuring grin.

'Talking…?' said Arjan, as if he had never heard of the concept. He walked slowly around them, all the while staring at their hands, a million thoughts rushing through his mind and wanting to do nothing more than take Sienna's hand and run away with her.

'Are you okay Arjan?' Peter asked, slightly pleased at the turn of events if a little unnerved by Arjan's intensity.

'Yes. Why wouldn't I be? Why wouldn't I..?'

Arjan stopped talking and looked directly at Sienna.

'I missed seeing you at shows recently.'

Sienna shrugged, her heart still aching with desire for him but knowing that he should never be trusted.

'Okay. Then, I will see you later.'

Arjan turned on his heels and marched back to the stables.

'You okay?' Peter asked Sienna.

Sienna smiled, although there were tears in her eyes.

'Yes, the first time was always going to be the worst. Thank you for getting me through it. Now, where were we? I'm sorry again about your mare, I hope she pulls through.'

Squeezing his hand, Sienna took hers back and picked up her phone.

'How ironic that Arjan would see that exact moment

when we were holding hands!' she laughed as she paused mid-text. 'I think it threw him a little.'

Peter grinned, thinking that it wasn't ironic at all; he had carefully planned to find Sienna once he knew that Arjan had arrived, and to give this arrogant Belgian a taste of his own medicine for once. 'I think it threw him a lot. Anytime you need me to be a suitor for you, I'm happy to oblige ma'am!'

Although he would never say it out loud, Sienna reminded Peter of Esme in many ways, especially through her natural innocence, although he knew that some would call it naivety. He had a strong urge to protect her from all that was evil in life and, if he was honest, he wanted to bed her too. But for his own protection, he would never allow that fantasy to become a reality, keeping it strictly for moments spent by himself in the shower instead.

Towerlands was an amazing venue and the indoors was decorated with a large cut-out logo, much copied around the world, depicting an Arabian horse with its tail, in Union Jack colours, over its back. In between were sponsor banners, and flags hung from the ceiling. With the bar leading straight off the show-ring, there was always something to entertain – be it the coming together of two people in a passionate kiss or old scores settled with a slap. The heat of the August bank holiday weekend only added to the hot, den-like atmosphere of this show and it was increasingly popular among handlers, owners, and spectators alike.

One of the best things about the UK International Arabian Horse Show was the British supporters. Always vocal, they loved to cheer for their favourite horses and if a British contender made the championships, the cheers would be deafening.

This year, over 200 horses were entered, a record, and with ridden and in-hand classes, including geldings, the show promised to be a packed two days of equine entertainment and fun. People arrived in their droves, taking their spot in the stands and opening up their thermos flasks and lunch boxes, enjoying a sandwich while they waited for the first stirs of music to signal the start of the show. The excited chatter among the crowd only intensified as the horses started to come into the arena – always to the music *Sandstorm* by Darude – and by the afternoon, the atmosphere inside was always electric. Come Sunday's championships, there was standing room only and the roof was repeatedly raised as favourite horse after favourite horse came in and put on a powerful trot as they stormed around the arena, showing their true Arabian beauty and spirit.

Rin, Guy, and Arjan all had key horses entered and each hoped to win. Rin had brought Raafid and he looked amazing. She had high hopes that he would win the Junior Male Championship that weekend, and her confidence in him as a future sire grew with each outing.

One thing that UKIAHS did better than any other show was the Saturday night entertainment. Previous years had seen *UKIAHS has the X Factor* take the room by storm and lined up this year was Miss UKIAHS, a parody on Miss World. A number of male trainers and grooms had been approached and, plied with free vodka and beer, they had agreed to do two rounds – one in evening wear, the other swimwear, which included bikinis.

As ever, the ballroom was packed to bursting as people crowded in to see some of much-fancied eye candy saunter around in next to nothing. Three breeders had been chosen to give points for each contestant and there was much hilarity as trainers pretended to be distraught with their scores, flouncing off in layers of chiffon and satin.

Peter, already half-cut after an afternoon in the bar, decided to commentate for the event, and his throwaway comments had the audience in stitches. Yves was among those competing, and he took Peter's comments in the good nature that they were intended with, although he was upset to lose to a gay groom from eastern Europe who had once been in a band and was used to wearing heels.

As the catwalk was cleared away, the disco began and the UKIAHS party theme song, *Reach for the Stars*, came on over the loudspeakers. The revelry began in earnest and Arjan, Yves, and Peter all made their way on to the dance floor. It was going to be a long night…

The polar opposite to this came the following morning, as 9am Sunday was always something of a relief at this show. Here, the classes started with the gentle beauty of the ridden Arabian. With two classes held before the pace stepped up for the halter, the ridden allowed competitors and spectators alike to recover from the night before and enjoy a wonderful reminder of the versatility of the breed. With classical music playing elegantly in the background, the stands slowly filled up and as the last of the ridden horses made their way out of the arena, there was a polite and respectful ripple of applause. The ridden champions were always announced later in the afternoon, allowing spectators to see the very best of the best and thus appreciate the all-round nature of this wonderful breed of equine. Before the fast pace and excitement of the mare and stallion halter classes, everybody welcomed this serene start to the day.

Guy woke on Sunday in a good mood and, to his

surprise, without a hangover. Arriving early to the stables, he checked his horses. Cursing as he ran his hand down the leg of Angelina OL, he checked again. He could definitely feel heat coming off her foot. Calling for Holly to ring the vet, he found an abscess. "That's her year over," Guy thought grimly. With her retirement from the show went his best chance of a championship, and his good mood darkened.

Finally, it was time for the championships to begin and, in spite of all the arena doors being open, the heat was almost stifling. Rin waited to go into the ring for her trot-around with the big-moving Raafid. His confidence grew with each show and everywhere he went, he captured the hearts of the public. The judges agreed, and he was duly called forward as unanimous Gold Junior Male Champion.

It was the Stallion Championship that everyone was always so keen to see, and Sunday's line up was impressive. Spectators were truly excited to have six such top-class horses to admire, and they came from across Europe and the Middle East. In true British style, however, there was one that they cheered for more than the others. If there was ever a British entry, then the audience almost raised the roof as they cheered and shouted loudly for 'their' horse.

Today, the horse in question was Master Design GA, an incredibly beautiful and exotic chestnut stallion imported from the United States and owned by Rhodri Jones. He had won his class with the highest points of the show, and his youngstock had also enjoyed success in the junior classes. As Master Design came into the ring and powered around the arena, the British audience cheered their hearts out and the noise was deafening.

Peter kept the tension up to the last minute as he revelled in commentating at his home show, calling in first the Bronze and then the Silver placed horses. 'And ladies and gentlemen! Your Gold Champion Stallion is… Master Design GA!'

As Rhodri ran into the top spot with his trusted chestnut steed, the British crowd went mad. And as the national anthem for the United Kingdom, *God Save the Queen*, belted out around the arena, there was not a dry eye in the house. Decorated in his gold garland, Master Design just stood there and took the applause, gently nudging his human and searching for the treats that he knew were in his pocket; he also knew that he thoroughly deserved them.

Sienna arrived home at 9pm, weary but exhilarated after a great weekend at the show. Her clients had done well, and she had enjoyed going out with some of her close friends for dinner on the Friday night. From then on, the show was a blur although she had missed Saturday night's party after she and Rin celebrated a win in the afternoon a bit too much, giggling and taking their time over dinner before they realised that it was too late to return to the showground. Somewhere along the way, Rin was developing into a good friend and a great client. From that early support Rin gave her when Sienna first set up Essentially Arabian, Sienna had always liked her, but she had been confused by the coldness that the woman gave to her. While she knew that there was a connection to Arjan, Sienna chose to judge Rin on the person that she knew rather than on the idle gossip she heard in show-ring bars around the world. After Menton, when Rin had finally explained it all, the last barrier between them dropped and they became very close friends.

Kicking off her heels, Sienna relaxed. After all the emotion and excitement of the weekend, it felt so good to be back in her flat, with some peace and quiet around her.

Pouring herself a large glass of Pinot Noir, she checked her phone for messages. Amid all the e-blasts from farms celebrating their successes and arrivals, there was one from Arjan. She had managed to avoid him ever since Wels, although he had tried hard to talk to her. Finally, realising that she was not going to answer his calls, Arjan had stopped ringing. Towerlands was the first time she had seen him since Austria, and she was pleasantly surprised with how painless it had been. Still, she was intrigued to see an e-mail from him and taking a large slug of red, she put the glass down and sat on the sofa to open his message.

Dear Sienna

Please know that I never meant to hurt you. All the excuses in the world won't change things. But you going off with Peter is a big mistake – he is worse than me. And much too old for you. You made yourself look ridiculous at the show. And if you would stop acting like a child and just talk to me, I am sure we can work things out.

You need me to support you to get on in this industry. I am sure I can make things easier for you. Or not.

Grow up will you, and call me.

Arjan .

Shaking with anger, Sienna re-read the e-mail. How dare Arjan say those things to her – and how dare he insinuate that something was going on with her and Peter. And what if there was! Arjan had made his feelings towards her perfectly clear and now he had sent this message... After his anger this weekend towards her every time Peter had spoken to her, which Peter made sure was frequently, Sienna was furious. What right had he, Arjan, to tell her how to live her life, especially after seducing her and then insulting her and walking away in Wels. Her heart, already slightly hardened against Arjan, hardened just that little bit more as she felt her euphoria from the show vanish in an instant, and she damned the man for still having that much power over her.

14

If Arjan was jumpy at the UK International Show, he was even more so as Aachen came around. He knew that he had treated Sienna very badly, but he couldn't help it. He couldn't bear the thought of her with Peter and, as he considered this realisation, he wondered, not for the first time, if he was actually in love with the girl. He hadn't loved anyone since, or before, Rin and after catching her with Yves, he vowed never to love again.

Shaking himself out of his self-indulgent stupor, he loaded up his Mercedes Benz M-Class and headed over the border to Germany. From Balen, it was a relatively short drive, and he was there in no time. Throwing his car keys at the valet, Arjan carried his lightweight suitcase into the hotel, choosing to stay at the Holiday Inn, the main hotel for many of the show people. The first person he saw when he walked into the building was Sienna. She was standing with her back to the door, checking in, and Arjan felt his heart stop a little. 'Hello Sienna,' he said as he cautiously approached the reception desk.

She turned, her blue eyes crystal cold as she almost

looked through him, before gathering her bags and walking to the lift. As the doors shut behind her, she leaned against the wall of the moving lift. How she would get through the weekend, she didn't know, but she knew that she had to. For the sake of her business, she simply had to.

Later that night, Sienna was in the hotel bar with Crispin, Katherine, Guy and Peter, enjoying some very British company and very British humour. Standing to go to the bathroom, she realised that she was tipsier than she had thought, and she giggled to herself slightly. Spying Arjan at the bar, and in a forgiving mood due to the amount of wine she had consumed, she went up behind him. Deliberately, provocatively, Sienna leaned into Arjan's back and put her arms around his waist. Inhaling the unique scent of her perfume, knowing it was her, Arjan instinctively leaned back into her, both of their hearts skipping a beat although they were almost too drunk to notice.

'We need to talk,' she said, before walking away, only just registering his nod as she headed off to the bathrooms. Checking her make-up, she expected Arjan to be there waiting when she came out, only he was nowhere to be seen. Shrugging, alcohol masking her disappointment that he had, again, snubbed her, Sienna made her way back to the British corner where Peter had already got another round in.

'Cheers,' she said, smiling broadly as she pushed all thoughts of Arjan to the back of her mind.

It would be the final day of the show before Arjan finally plucked up the courage to talk to Sienna. He had so much to apologise for – Wels, the e-mail, the women, ignoring her, treating her so badly – and yet he still hoped that Sienna would fall into his arms, reassure him and tell him that she loved him. It was a long shot, but Arjan surprising himself as he hoped that she would.

Getting his phone out of his pocket, Arjan sent Sienna a quick text message.

Meet me in the bar in 10 minutes. Axx

Taking a quiet spot by the window, Arjan ordered two vodkas and sat there, nervously waiting. After five minutes, he drank his vodka nervously, downing it in one. After another five minutes, as Sienna had not yet arrived, he downed her drink too, holding the shot glass in his hand and staring intently into it.

'I don't think you will find the answers in there.'

Sienna's gentle Irish lilt cut through Arjan's thoughts like an arrow and he dropped the glass on the table as he looked up at her. She was wearing a pale blue top with grey sleeves, a colour that only served to make her skin more translucent and give her cornflower blue eyes more clarity.

'Sienna… Please, sit…'

She perched on the edge of a chair uncomfortably, wondering what Arjan had to say, but ready to turn tail and leave if he began to insult her again.

'I don't know where to start…' he floundered.

'Try the beginning. Wels?' she said, somewhat sharply

Arjan looked up at her, staring deeply into her eyes. She felt her stomach flip and cursed her body for betraying her. Arjan was still easily the best-looking man on the circuit and the mere mention of Wels brought forward memories of broken dreams and promises, and of a kiss that she had replayed in her head over and over again.

'I was a prat. An idiot. You didn't deserve that. Leap led me astray…'

'Arjan, you're a grown man! You could have just said "no". Honestly, any excuses you come up with right now just make you look stupid.'

Riled, Arjan snapped back, 'I know!' Taking a deep breath, he added, more softly, "And then when I saw you with Peter…'

'Nothing is going on!'

'But it made me so jealous…'

Sienna paused, absorbing the fact that Arjan had finally admitted some sort of feeling towards and about her.

'Why are you jealous? There is nothing going on between Peter and I. Or you and I,' she added as an afterthought.

'But there should be….'

Arjan reached across the table and took Sienna's hand.

'There should be,' he repeated, as he gently began to rub his thumb over her fingers, staring into her eyes all the while.

Sienna paused. She wanted to allow herself to be caught up in the moment, but the memory of those women, calling her frigid, and then him calling her childish in his e-mail, all held her back and she went to pull her hand away.

'Please…' he whispered, holding on tightly to her as she tried to free her hand. 'Please give me one more chance to prove to you how much you really do mean to me…'

Again, Sienna hesitated. Then, slowly, half wanting to say no, she nodded.

As Arjan went to smile and lean to kiss her, she held up her other hand in warning.

I have spread my dreams under your feet; Tread softly because you tread on my dreams.'

'What's that? I don't want to tread on your dreams,' said

Arjan, confused.

'William Butler Yeats,' smiled Sienna. 'Tread softly, Arjan. Tread softly.' And with that, she allowed him to gently, tentatively, kiss her.

Rin walked past the bar in Aachen at that precise moment. She saw Arjan finally lock lips with Sienna, registering the look of triumph on his face as he kissed her, something Sienna wouldn't have seen as her eyes were closed. Rin wondered whether to warn the girl, but she didn't want to jeopardise their newfound friendship. She just hoped that Arjan wouldn't hurt her in the same way he had Rin. Yes, she had cheated on him in the end, but he had never once been faithful to her.

Be careful with her – don't destroy her. R.

She sent the message to Arjan, deciding to do no more for now but that a warning of some kind was needed.

15

The seasons changed once more and after the colour of autumn in Aachen, with the trees a blend of vibrant yellows, reds and oranges, the skies seemed to become a uniform grey as winter was slowly approaching across Europe. Slowly, the trees were losing their leaves and the fields were mud-brown as farmers worked to sow the seeds for next year's harvest. Still, the days stayed bright and mild, and this helped keep the horses' coats in show condition with just the aid of a couple of rugs and a slicker, rather than having to pile on the piles of duvets and blankets as grooms had in the past.

In his gym at the top of the house, Guy was pounding out the miles on his running machine, glaring at a film of Raafid taking the Gold Junior Male Championship in Aachen just a few weeks before. It still ate him up that he had never been able to get the colt, in spite of being so close to having him. It also irritated him that the DuPont's didn't speak to him anymore. To his mind, he had not done anything wrong and, never stopping to consider why they didn't speak to him or why he had not got the colt, Guy dialled the number of a farm in Brazil, keen to import a new colt to show in Paris and wow the crowds with – there was no answer. It had been a long time since he had stood in the championship spot, and he needed to get back up there. Angelina OL had never fully recovered from her abscess at Towerlands, which turned out to be far more serious than anyone had realised, and while she was now relegated to being a broodmare with Guy determined to find the right stallion for her and breed the next World Champion.

Turning the running machine down to a walk, Guy called one of the more prominent horse breeders in South America and began to wheedle information out of him. He certainly used his family trait of city slicker charm to great effect, and within five minutes, he knew of a two-year-old bay filly, Bint Sanatra, that had caught the eyes of many at the Brazilian Nationals. Hanging up, Guy pounded the never-ending track impatiently as he waited for a video of Sanatra to be sent to his phone. Liking what he saw, he rang the breeder back and gleaned more information from him.

One further telephone call, followed by sweating it out on the running machine while he waited for Bint Sanatra's owner to speak to his wife, and then Guy got the call he needed; the deal was done and for $300,000, Bint Sanatra was on her way to England.

Stepping off the running machine, Guy wiped the sweat off his face, and then put in a telephone call to Sienna. While the ink wasn't yet dry on the contract, it was never too early to start putting the wheels of hype in motion, and by the end of the day, Guy had successfully sold Bint Sanatra on for $500,000. He would finally have something good to show in Paris, and with the thought of making $200,000 profit that day turning him on, he took Ally to bed and imagined himself lying on a bed of dollar bills as he climaxed on top of her.

Across Europe, preparations were being made for the climatic end of the year – the Paris World Championships. There was no other prize that the trainers – and owners – wanted to win so much, and the days and weeks leading up to the show saw meticulous planning.

After being jilted the previous year with his beloved Passionate Presence, Luca decided not to take her to Paris and instead, took his even more precious wife, Alessandra, to the Maldives for a surprise holiday away from the children. Leaving his phone behind, Luca took care of Alessandra's every want and desire, and thus put himself back on her good books to be away for weeks at a time over the year ahead.

Having had a long conversation with the DuPonts, Rin decided to show Raafid in Paris before giving him a break from the ring. He had already enjoyed a successful year, with gold titles at every show he went to across Europe. 'We are not interested in showing in the Middle East,' said Marcia over dinner one night. 'What matters to us is that Raafid has a long and happy life – and next year, we would like to stand him at stud at your farm. We think it is time that he proves himself as a sire and gives the shows a rest.

'However, we are French and Pierre dreams of showing a horse in Paris! So, let us go and have fun. Anything else will be a bonus.'

With the pressure off, Rin couldn't help but compare her Paris experience this time to years gone past, when she was either riddled with anxiety and guilt over the horses, or joy that they had done so well. Knowing that the DuPonts would be happy regardless of where Raafid came ensured that it was a very relaxed Rin and Zoë who drove their show string down to Paris.

Finally, the time had finally arrived for the World Championships to begin once more. Sienna still hadn't slept with Arjan, partly because she had only seen him once since Aachen, but also because she wanted to be sure of him first. While her heart was running away with her, her head warned her to be cautious. With his track record, and how Arjan had already promised her the world once before, and then promptly kissed the next woman passing, Sienna felt that she was right to take her time.

Instead of going to the European Championships in Verona, she had gone to Santa Ynez in California with Rin on what had been a very successful business trip for the pair of them. Rin had hopes to open a partner training centre somewhere else in the world, as well as in Australia – a feeder for bringing top horses into Europe and vice versa – and many promising opportunities had come out of this visit as a result. As Rin and Sienna drove along the coastal roads, the horse show in Verona was the furthest thing from Sienna's mind – as was Arjan.

Sienna hadn't mentioned Arjan to Rin. Not only did she want to be sure of him before she told anyone, Sally aside, who was naturally very wary on her friend's behalf, she wasn't sure how Rin would take the news. Deciding to wait until there really was something to tell, Sienna had kept her feelings for Arjan, and the many text and WhatsApp messages he sent, under wraps. However, she and Arjan had planned to spend as much time together during the Paris World Championships as possible, including extending their stay for two extra days after the show had finished.

Arriving on Thursday afternoon, Sienna checked into her hotel room at the Mercuré and had barely even taken her coat off and thrown it on the king size bed before there was a knock at the door.

'A delivery for Miss Stevens,' said the Bell Boy, handing Sienna a large gilt-edged box wrapped up in thick black ribbon. Thanking him, Sienna closed the door and laid the box on the bed. Untying the ribbon, she took the lid off to reveal layer after layer of cerise pink tissue paper, with a note from Arjan on top.

For later tonight… xxxx

Unfolding the tissue paper, Sienna removed a beautiful deep purple and black lace baby doll nightie, one that was designed to be tasteful rather than slutty. Holding it up to herself in front of the mirror, Sienna smiled as a thrill of anticipation ran through her. Laying the baby doll out carefully on the bed, she unpacked, showered and made her way downstairs for the evening.

As luck would have it, however, Arjan was held up in the traffic and by the time he had finished at the stables and wearily made his way up the small hill from the showground to the hotel, it was gone midnight. Dragging his suitcase behind him, his suit carefully stored in a separate lightweight bag, Arjan pushed through the revolving doors into the hotel foyer, making his way to reception over on the right. In spite of his late arrival at the stables, his clients were there and were increasingly demanding. Seemingly oblivious to the fact that Arjan and his grooms were setting up the stable area, they called for wine and music, and sat there while the booth was built around them. Any hope that Arjan may have had that his hints to leave might be listened to, his clients instead stayed for hours, talking about the following year and their hopes for the coming season. Arjan knew he couldn't just hurry them out and leave – this was business after all – but all he could think about was Sienna lying on a bed, wearing nothing but the baby doll nightgown he had sent her.

Finally, Arjan received his room key and immediately tried to call Sienna but her phone was off. Sighing, feeling tired but horny, his dick in need of release after all those thoughts he had entertained of Sienna for the past few hours, he looked around the bar. There was always so much talent at these shows, and Sienna need never know…

Friday was always a busy day as the World Championship qualifying classes got underway. Each training centre had their own hospitality area and before the first class began, clients lingered enjoying coffee and croissants, many oblivious to the rising tension among the handlers and trainers, who either smiled and were hospitable or were nowhere to be seen. Slowly, as the countdown to the 10am start approached, the clients finally drifted to the VIP area leaving just the trainers and a couple of grooms to make their way to the collecting ring, where they would take their horse from another groom. With the thick leather lead rope in their hands and everyone standing back from them, the trainer could breathe. Now it was just them and the horse – it was time to show.

As all this was going on around him, Guy waited quietly in the corner of the collecting ring, ready to show Bint Sanatra, who was as flashy as her video had promised. She easily made it through to the Top Ten and both he and his clients were satisfied. Sanatra was Guy's only horse in Paris this year and it was with a grim look on his face that he spent the rest of the day leaning over the wooden railing of the collecting ring, inhaling the scent of sawdust, leather, show sheen and horses. As he watched his rivals take their horses into the big lights of the main arena, he vowed that, next year, life would be better.

Rin had Raafid to show once more during Saturday's male classes, and she also had two fillies and two mares, one in each class, to show in today's classes. Meticulous planning meant that, while it was just she and Zoë at the show, all four horses were prepared and ready. Once one class was over, Zoë was already there in the collecting ring with the next horse ready to hand over to Rin before taking the previous class's star back to the stables.

To her delight, Rin won with one filly, was third with another, and took second place in each of the mare classes. With all four females through to Sunday's finals, Rin was in a good mood when she headed up the hill back to the hotel.

Waiting at the pedestrian crossing as the French traffic raced past was Sienna, and Rin eagerly caught up with her.

'Hey! How are you?'

Sienna turned, smiling at Rin. She was a very different person these days to the angry, tortured lady that she had first met all those years ago. Rin had truly turned her life around, with losing Ibn Shahja a true low point in her life, and now that things were better, she was always ready to share her happiness.

'I want to talk to you about a new brochure – I know, I know, it's only five minutes since we had the last one done! But I have an idea for something different and I think you will like it… I also have some clients I'd like you to meet. Can you join us for dinner tonight?'

Crossing the road as the lights changed, Sienna hesitated in her answer. She was desperate to see Arjan, but she had turned down seeing clients last night for him and ended up alone in her room with a bottle of red wine and room service. Knowing that there was no guarantee Arjan would be able to make tonight, and very aware that she was there to work, Sienna agreed.

'Great! We will meet in the bar at 7pm and then go on from there. There's a cute little restaurant down the hill that I like going to or we might even head into the centre of Paris. Be good to have you with us.'

With a hug and a wave, Rin headed off to the lift and walked quickly along the corridor of the seventh floor, eager to get back to her room and make plans for the season ahead. For this new, re-energised Rin, it was never too early to start planning and as she watched Rin head to her room with "purpose" written all over her face, Sienna couldn't help but smile to herself.

Sienna saw Sven sat at the bar and, as he waved her over, she went to join him.

'Drink?'

'Hot chocolate – I'm frozen!'

Laughing at her choice, Sven ordered another vodka red bull for himself and a chocolat chaud, with a measure of brandy added to it, for Sienna.

'I'm not ordering you a girly drink like that – it has to have alcohol in it! So, what gossip..?' began Sven as the bar slowly began to fill up with friends and clients. Intrigued by what he was telling her, Sienna sat engrossed for a couple of hours, drinking cup after cup of brandy-laced hot chocolate before realising the time and that she was meant to be meeting Rin in half an hour. Giving Sven a hasty kiss goodbye, Sienna raced upstairs to get ready herself ready.

As Sienna stepped into the lift and the doors closed on her, Arjan arrived back from the stables. Looking around the bar, and not seeing her anywhere, he looked up the open lobby to the floors above them. Seeing Sienna rushing along the corridor and imagining that she was going to get herself ready for him, Arjan smiled to himself before going to join Leap and John at the bar for a quick beer.

At 7pm, the bar was packed as people came back from the centre of Paris, returned from free-flowing hospitality at the showground, or came down from their rooms after sleeping, screwing, wheeling, or dealing.

Sienna met Rin at the bar and enjoyed a glass of champagne before they headed into Paris half an hour later. Arjan was nowhere to be seen and to be honest, Sienna forgot all about him as she was so fascinated by the stories that Rin's client, Omar, was telling them about his Arabian mares and foals.

'It is an old Bedouin tradition that we never let a foal drop to the ground when it is born,' Omar said. 'Instead, we receive the foal in our arms and handle it carefully, washing the foal and stretching its delicate limbs. Although this custom has now died out in many parts of Arabia, there are some of us that still do this, preserving the heritage of our Bedouin grandfathers.

'Another wonderful thing from Bedouin tradition concerns our Arabian mares. We never tie her up, and when we are out in the desert, the mare and her foal will wander in and out of the different tents, carefully stepping over sleeping children as she enters and exits each tent. They are loved and rewarded, and we treat them with the greatest care imaginable. The mares are so important in our history, and we truly treasure them.'

Paying more attention to Omar than to who was in the bar, Sienna didn't see Leap, who duly reported back, via text, to Arjan that Sienna had gone out that night with Rin and some Arab clients. Just stepping out of the shower, Arjan was surprised that Sienna had not made plans to see him that night, but it did free him up to have some time drinking with the boys before she came back. 'Time for a Penicillin,' he thought to himself as he wrapped the towel snugly around his tapered waist and, looking into the mirror above the sink, pushed his dark wet hair back off his face.

Three hours later, Sienna, Rin, and friends arrived back in the hotel bar which, by now, was heaving with people. Sienna saw Arjan as she made her way to a table, and smiled as she caught his eye.

Now slightly drunk, and also trapped by some Middle Eastern clients who wanted to go out into Paris for a late dinner and some fun, Arjan could only look over at Sienna and smile at her. Just as she needed to go out earlier and do her work, he now needed to be here and do his.

'Who is good for brochures and design these days Arjan?' Ahmed asked him.

Without hesitating, Arjan motioned to Sienna, who was at that moment engaged in deep conversation with a judge.

'Sienna Stevens. She's bright, innovative. And she has a very big heart,' he added at the end, surprising himself.

Ahmed laughed. 'She sounds good – we can meet her tomorrow. Come, our restaurant is waiting.'

Helpless again, Arjan was forced apart from Sienna for another night.

Tomorrow, darling xxxxx

He quickly texted to Sienna before following Ahmed and his friends into the waiting cars.

Waking early on the Saturday morning, Sienna checked her phone for messages. A photo message came through from Peter, along with the words *'Sorry darling xxx'*. The image clearly showed Arjan in the men's toilets, trousers down and head back, eyes closed, with a woman on her knees in front of him.

Tears stung Sienna's eyes as she stared and stared at the image before her. After a few moments of sitting in shocked silence, she picked up the phone and rang Peter in his room.

'Peter... When?'

'I'm sorry darling. Late Thursday night, when he got back from the stables."

'You sure...?'

Peter sighed, hating to hurt Sienna and wanting to

185

throttle Arjan. It seemed that the whole world knew that Arjan was no good for Sienna apart from the girl herself.

'I saw him chatting her up and then going into the loos. She followed him within minutes – I went in and there they were. They didn't even stop, just carried on until he came. I am sorry….'

Sienna mumbled something incoherent and hung up, not trusting herself to speak anymore.

Her mobile, still in her hand, vibrated as another new message came through.

Dinner tonight? And dessert at yours? Axxxxx

Screaming with rage, Sienna threw her phone across the bed, leapt out and picked up the baby doll nightie, hanging off the chair next to her, ripping the straps and tearing the flimsy material into pieces. As a new wave of Arjan-induced humiliation rolled over her, Sienna gathered up the pieces ready to throw publicly back in his face later. He had gone too far this time. No more second chances. It was over.

After the classes had finished on Saturday, Guy was in the stables, having been invited by a potential client to look at a horse he had purchased a few months ago and who had been shown by a friend in Paris as a favour. Glancing over the stable door, Guy realised that it was Sparkle of Justice, or Claude, the chestnut colt that Rin had lost after failing to win with him at the European Championships – Rin's ruin, he had referred to him as at the time. Claude hadn't stayed with Guy for very long before Juan changed trainers once more, sending him to Luca. Together, they took the Reserve Junior Male Championship in Paris last year before Juan, now completely bored with the Arabian industry and wanting to cut ties with it, had sold him on for a huge price.

His new owner, Davey Baynes, had looked around for a new trainer as he didn't understand the Latin temperament of Luca. Davey was keen for Claude to go one better now that he was a stallion and while Guy realised it was a tall order, he was pleased to have been asked. Heaven knows he barely had any clients left at the moment! Having nodded at the horse, he sat down with Davey to talk about how best to show him in tomorrow's championship as well as how to campaign him for the following year.

'Well, he would need to be stabled with me,' Guy was saying. 'My fees are £200 a week basic keep, a £100 showing fee per class, a £250 win bonus and a £500 championship bonus; to show in the championship costs £250. All transport, hay, feed, farrier, dentist, and back treatment is extra on top of that, as well as £200 a month for a dedicated groom to look after him.'

Davey visibly paled. His wife had been the one to fall in love with the Arabian horse and he was happy to spoil her. He had no idea, however, that it would cost this much.

'Mr Baynes, I can see you are an intelligent man. You get what you pay for in any business, you know that I am sure. And I am the best of the best. Sparkle of Justice made World Elite Top Ten this morning with one of your friends showing him, and I am sure that we will do well together tomorrow. Holly! Get Mr Baynes some wine – I am guessing that you are a red man.'

Nodding, Davey allowed himself to be bowled along by Guy and before he knew it, he was signing the year-long contract Holly was holding out.

'This takes us through to Paris next year, Mr Baynes. And we still have tomorrow to enjoy yet. Your good health…'

Raising his glass, Guy's eyes misted over, and he already began to calculate just how many horses he could sell to

Davey in that time, and just how he could line his own pockets in the meantime. Smiling to himself, he downed a large mouthful of the Bordeaux and glanced over to Holly, before winking discreetly to her and motioning to her to bring over another bottle.

Rin was delighted to have won one of the two colt classes with Raafid that morning, and Pierre and Marcia DuPont were thrilled with how well their horses were going. Walking past the stables and seeing Guy stretching his claws into another unsuspecting client, they felt sorry for the pale faced man sitting there, hands clasped around a glass of red wine as if his life depended on it while his wife sat, rapt and eager, listening to every word that Guy said. The pair of them would learn soon enough about Guy's ways but they would not be the ones to tell them the bad news.

As they followed Rin to the stables to see Raafid, they became aware of shouting.

'Sienna! It was not like that!'

'No? Tell me, Arjan, what was it like then? She just happened to be in the gent's loos and tripped, her mouth landing on your cock while your trousers just happened to be around your ankles?'

There was the sound of ripping and as Rin, Marcia and Pierre rounded the corner, they saw an enraged, fiery Sienna shaking the contents of a carrier bag over Arjan. Pieces of lightweight purple and black lacy material fell down over him, and Rin was shocked to actually see tears in Arjan's eyes as he gazed imploringly at Sienna.

'Sienna, please…'

'No! You have done nothing but play with me over the years and finally, as we finally get close, you would rather cheat on me than have a cold bed for just one night. One night! You are a total, utter bastard, Arjan. You can get lost!'

As Sienna turned to walk away, head held high, Rin found herself beginning to slowly clap.

'Well done Sienna! And I agree – he is a total bastard. Come, join us.'

Putting an arm around Sienna's shoulders, Marcia and Rin led Sienna away while Pierre could only look at Arjan, covered in lace and chiffon and surrounded by his big-name clients, including some from the Middle East, many of whom were looking at Arjan with a mixture of horror and distaste, the women visibly moving away as if they might catch something just by being in such close proximity to him.

'I think you made a mistake, monsieur.'

Leap, standing as usual in the corner with a beer in his hand, could not believe what he had seen. Laughing, he clapped Arjan on the back.

'And you still didn't have her? What happened – stud?'

For once, Arjan turned round and howled in rage at Leap.

'Just fuck off will you! It's all your fucking fault anyway!'

Seeing the wives of his Middle Eastern clients visibly flinch at his choice of words, Arjan marched out of the stables and headed back to the hotel. If he ever found out who sent that photograph, he would kill them. But as the cold air finally swept over him, marginally cooling his rage as he stomped up the hill, he knew that he had no one to blame but himself. Sienna was lost to him – and it was all his fault as he couldn't keep his trousers zipped up. Crossing the road, he muttered 'first class prick...' to himself and, on reaching his hotel, he ignored everyone and headed straight for his room and a bottle of whiskey.

The following morning, Arjan's clients had to find someone else to show their horses in the final day of the prestigious World Championships as their trainer had mysteriously vanished. Having checked out in the early hours of the morning, after the last stragglers had finally left the bar and gone to bed, Arjan had headed straight to the airport. As he glared out of the taxi window, the twinkling lights of Paris muted by his sunglasses, Arjan was keen to put as much distance between himself and the scene of his crime as possible. But before he boarded his plane for South America, he organised a delivery.

And so it was that upon arriving back to her cosy London home on Monday afternoon, following the remainder of the Paris show where she had been swept up in euphoric celebrations as Raafid took the Junior Male World Championship title, Sienna found a dozen red roses with a note attached, waiting for her at the foot of her door.

"I am a stupid man. Forgive me. Axxxx"

Trying to be determined not to let her heart melt, trying not to picture his hypnotic brown eyes smiling before her, Sienna unlocked the door to her flat, stepped in, and firmly closed it on the inevitability of the situation and dropped the roses on the table next to her. If only you could turn emotions off like a tap. Loathing herself, she knew that Arjan was still in her heart, in spite of everything that had happened between them, everything he had done wrong, and there wasn't a damned thing she could do about it. Throwing the flowers into the bin, Sienna switched off the hall light and went straight to her bedroom, throwing herself on her bed and staring, unseeingly, out of the window at the world going on around her.

"Damn you Arjan Vermeulen," she thought to herself. "And damn me for loving you."

16

Sue Dickinson waited at Abu Dhabi International Airport for her visitors to arrive. Every February, the United Arab Emirates hosted an International Arabian Horse Show, held at the beautiful Abu Dhabi Equestrian Club, and she was one of the organisers. Born in the United Kingdom, Sue had spent her childhood as a dedicated member of the Pony Club before training as a jockey. At 19 years of age, she had come across her first Arabian horse and her path had altered. She had left her home in Surrey and her family behind and headed out to work in the Middle East. That was 30 years ago and not a day went by when she regretted her decision. She had seen the world, thanks to the Arabian horse, and she had worked with some of the most famous names in the industry. At 5'4" with honey-brown eyes and honey-brown hair, she had attracted a lot of interest from a number of men but had kept her distance. In a world where it was difficult to keep one's private life private, she had succeeded, and no one knew that she was married to a local, and that they were as deeply in love today as they were when they had first met 15 years ago.

One of Sue's roles was to meet and greet people when they arrived in Abu Dhabi for the show – the judges, the DCs, and all kinds of media people. Today, she had two judges and Sienna on her list, and was waiting for the plane to land so she could get them to the Intercontinental Hotel, the preferred hotel of many. Sienna, however, was staying with her and she was looking forward to hearing all the news while they shared a bottle of wine later.

'So, you and Arjan are finally over,' Sue asked as she

placed the bottle on the table between them.

'Yes. It has to be. He's no good for me. I just wish…'

'I know.' Sue tactfully paused before changing the subject.

'And Rin – she's going ahead with her new training centre in Australia?'

Swallowing down a mouthful of wine, Sienna nodded, eyes smiling.

'Yes, she is! She's so excited about it. It is such a great idea, to have a place out there to bring on the young horses before shipping them over to Europe to show. God, I am so glad that I never told her about me and Arjan – she just saw the aftermath in Paris when I threw the lace over him. She had warned him off me, you know. It's so funny how you can get people so wrong at times.'

'Or just that when you meet people they are in a different place to where they should be? Rin was never a bad person, but she allowed events to get the better of her. She should have left Arjan years ago, but I guess that we are all guilty of staying for the wrong reasons.'

'True. How is Ahmed?' asked Sienna with a smile.

'Wonderful,' sighed Sue. 'He's away this weekend on an endurance ride. He was so looking forward to seeing you again but needs must. He is coaching the local Abu Dhabi youth team now, you know. It's given him a new lease of life – not that he needed one!'

As the women laughed, a desert moon came rising up over the Arabian Gulf, blushing as their conversation moved on to more risqué topics before, finally, they made their way into the house and to bed.

Waking early, Sienna went outside Sue's house and sat on the balcony, enjoying the early morning sunshine. She loved Abu Dhabi and the Middle East – the scents and the

193

sounds were all so evocative. She loved hearing the call to prayer and with the sweet-smelling flowers in the garden around her, the Middle East seemed full of exotic promise to her.

The Middle East was renowned for being the cradle of the Arabian horse, being where this fantastic breed was first found. The true origins of the Arabian horse remain a mystery, even today, and there were clear differences between an Arabian and other breeds – not least as it has one less rib and two fewer vertebrae than other equines. Known for its flight of foot as well as its beauty, the Arabian horse was the founder of the more well-known Thoroughbred horse, which was born of the Godolphin Arabian, the Darley Arabian and the Turk Arabian. The fact that the origins of the Arabian horse remain unclear has meant that, over the centuries, a multitude of myths have formed and a deep and continued fascination about the breed persists.

Sienna loved these myths and fables that surrounded the Arabian breed, not least the legend of the four winds, a story that is engrained into the hearts of all those that love this majestic animal. This legend comes from a traditional Bedouin, or Arab tribe, story, whereby Allah created the Arabian horse from the four winds: spirit from the north, strength from the south, speed from the east, and intelligence from the west. While doing so, he said:

"I create thee, oh Arabian. To thy forelock, I bind victory in battle. On thy back, I set a rich spoil and a treasure in thy loins. I establish thee as one of the glories of the earth... I give thee flight without wings."

Sienna recalled that different versions of this legend have Allah saying to the south wind:

"I want to make a creature out of you. Condense."

From the material condensed from the wind, he made a bay/burnt chestnut animal. This particular legend continues with Allah saying:

"I call you horse. I make you Arabian and I give you the chestnut colour of the ant. I have hung happiness from the forelock which hangs between your eyes and you shall be the Lord of the other animals. Men shall follow you wherever you go; you shall be as good for flight as for pursuit; you shall fly without wings; riches shall be on your back and fortune shall come through your meditation."

With the origins of the Arabian horse firmly fixed in the Middle East, and the Arabian Peninsula in particular, Sienna always loved returning to this part of the world. The moment she stepped off the plane and breathed in the humid, scented air, her mind was filled with the mythology that went hand-in-hand with this part of the world, with visions of deserts and mountains, Prophets and Kings, Bedouins and their ever-faithful steeds.

Through her travels in the world of the Arabian horse, Sienna had learned that many of these stories and names continue down to the modern Arabian world. Al Khamsa, for instance, means 'the five', originating from a myth about the Prophet Mohammed and how he chose his foundation mares, testing their loyalty as well as their courage. The most popular version of this myth states that after a long journey through the desert, the Prophet Mohammed let his herd free so that they could race together to an oasis so that they could drink. But before the herd reached the water, the Prophet called for the horses to return to him and just five mares responded, faithfully

195

returning to their master in spite of their desperate thirst. And so these five mares became his favourites, known as Al Khamsa, and they became the founders of the five main strains of the Arabian horse: Keheilan, Seglawi, Abeyan, Hamdani and Hadban – or Keheilan, Seglawi, Abeyan, Managhieh and Shuweymah if you look at a different version of this tale. Through her travels, Sienna had learned that there were many breeders around the world that claimed that the modern Bedouin Arabian descended from these same five mares, and that direct descendants could be found in their barns.

Whatever the truth of these stories Sienna, like many, could not fail to be caught up in the romance of it all. Coming to the Middle East and watching Arabian horses here either in shows or private presentations, always felt like coming home and, for Sienna, there was nowhere else in the world more special to see these horses.

With the sun now rising in the sky, and the bustle of morning life now filtering through from the noise of the city outside, Sienna headed back into the house to find Sue and organise breakfast.

Meanwhile, on the other side of the city, Arjan was organising the horses, who had finally arrived at the Equestrian Club and were settling in before the show. Checking the horses under their slickers, he called to Suzanne, his loyal groom, about which horses needed extra rugs on that night to try to keep hair growth to a minimum. His mind was not on the horses, however. He knew that Sienna was there, and he was filled with a mix of anticipation and dread upon seeing her in equal measures. Leap had teased him non-stop for being caught with his trousers down and for losing his stud reputation, but no one realised just how deeply Arjan felt for Sienna. He had

196

surprised even himself over winter, thinking about her constantly and wondering whether it was too late… He had never heard from her after he sent the flowers, and he had no idea whether or not she had received them. He had also started to write countless messages to her, e-mails, letters, and texts, only to tear them all to shreds or delete them and gaze into the bottom of his whiskey glass in despair as photographs of a laughing Sienna filled his Facebook page as she celebrated Christmas and New Year with friends and family.

There had been many a night when Arjan had just sat there, looking out of the window on to a dark, winter's night, with the rain making rivulets down the glass before him, reflecting his own tears. He had replayed memories of moments with Sienna over and over in his mind, remembering the feel of his arms around her in the bar in Moorsele, the shy smile she gave him in Aachen, her surprising passionate fury in Paris. And, of course, the feel of her soft, soft lips below his as she finally gave in and kissed him, the moment when he first though he had died and gone to heaven before, once more, he pressed the self-destruct button. *Dear Darlin* by Olly Murs seemed to sum up his mood and now, finally, he and Sienna were in the same part of the world once more.

Sienna had missed the first shows of the season as she had chosen to go the US and had been busy with clients there, but finally, she was here in Abu Dhabi, staying with friends who would no doubt be keeping a close eye on her. Arjan longed to get her alone but he knew that would not be possible – there was no way that her friends would risk Sienna being hurt once more. Determined to see her, however, he slowly began to make his plan.

Sienna arrived early at the showground hours before the

show itself was due to start. She loved the Abu Dhabi Equestrian Club and that wonderful feeling of seeing Arabian horses in the desert, where they came from and where they belonged, always warmed her. Even if, she thought to herself with a wry smile, all you could hear was traffic and all you could see was grass.

Taking herself to the old arena, long since abandoned for a newer, bigger version, she climbed to the top of the grandstand, looking out over the original showground below her. She had so many memories of wonderful horses, seen here under the floodlights, filled her mind. She remembered the mighty chestnut stallion Spartacus TO doing battle to take the title, and the graceful femininity of the grey mares that contrasted so sharply with the power of the boys.

There had been many a night spent here, when the desert sun had long sunk in the skies, casting a chill over the showground, but still Sienna and her friends remained seated, eager to see who would win the classes, which horse would emerge victorious that evening.

Basking with the feel of the sun on her face, so welcome and reviving after being at home in the English winter as well an unseasonably cold New Year in Scottsdale, Arizona, Sienna leaned back in her seat and closed her eyes. Feeling herself unwind, she relaxed for what felt like the first time in months; it was certainly the first time since Paris, that much was sure.

Sienna must have drifted off to sleep as she was startled by the sound of a step, and then a shadow falling across her face. As she opened her eyes, she found Arjan standing over her, close to her, and before she even really registered his presence in full, he leaned in and kissed her.

Unable to stop herself, Sienna allowed the kiss to happen, winding her fingers through his hair and pulling him closer to her. Arjan's hands gently reached around Sienna's back, moving his body into the space between her legs as he kneeled before her, absorbing the kiss. Finally, finally it would happen, he thought to himself. Finally, Sienna and Arjan would become an item. Finally. The utter despair Arjan had felt since Paris melted away as his fingers inched up underneath her top, feeling the softness of her skin, such a sharp contrast to the increasing hardness of his body.

Groaning, he finally pulled away from her and looked deeply into her eyes.

'Oh Sienna! I have missed you so much.'

Sienna nodded, allowing herself a small smile, before leaning in to kiss him once more. She knew that Arjan had already used up more chances than he deserved but she could not get him out of her head, and until she did, she was unable to move on.

Later that day, Sienna arrived back at Sue's house, the smile on her lips and the flush on her skin being caused by more than just the sun. She and Arjan had enjoyed a long, lingering lunch together before heading to one of the many nearby beaches where they walked for what felt like miles with the sand warm beneath their bare feet and their fingers entwined. They shared a mixture of contented silence and talking, slowly revealing more about themselves to each other, and laying themselves bare. Returning her to Sue's, Arjan had leaned over and kissed her once more.

'I will see you tonight. I have to see some clients now but come to the stables around 9pm. I have a lovely surprise planned for you.'

Sienna smiled to herself as she went into the house, heading straight for the shower. In spite of everything, she still felt something for Arjan and spending all that time alone with him today only served to make these feelings stronger, and they also seemed more real. As she washed the sand and the dust of the Middle East out of her hair, Sienna thought that tonight might well be the night – the night she finally gave in and succumbed to the charms of Arjan Vermeulen.

Arriving at the stables as the sun began to set, Sienna realised that she was an hour early having set her watch to the wrong time when she landed. Nevertheless, she was keen to see him, and she made her way around to the yard where Arjan had his horses stabled, passing a very nervous looking groom on the way. Arriving at Arjan's row of stables, she headed to the middle stable which, at every show, was used to house bridles, whips, clothes, horse shampoo, horse make up, and so on as well as a table and chairs for entertaining friends and clients, brochures on Arjan's farm and a fridge full of wine and beer; even though it was the Middle East, a blind eye was frequently turned as long as things didn't get out of control.

The stable door was very firmly shut, and pausing for a second, Sienna knocked on it nervously, butterflies suddenly entering her stomach. As she knocked, she heard some groaning coming from inside and she idly wondered whether one of the grooms was getting lucky. But, to her horror, as she went to turn away and leave, it was Arjan's husky tones that called out 'Come in you dirty whore – but only if you're going to…'

Throwing open the door, Sienna was greeted with the sight of Arjan lying back in a chair, completely naked, with a hooker on her knees in front of him, clearly giving him a blow job. A second hooker was standing behind him, massaging Arjan with her breasts which were slick with oil, repeatedly sliding them over his shoulders and against his face, where he kept trying to grab her nipples with his mouth and tongue. Over in the far corner of the room on a table was the romantic surprise Arjan had planned for later – a dozen red roses, some champagne all set in an ice bucket, and a picnic basket complete with blanket.

Opening his eyes, Arjan registered with horror that it wasn't the promised third hooker but instead Sienna who was staring at him. Cursing himself once more for his weakness and agreeing to this promised pick me up courtesy of Leap, all he could to do was say her name as she, too, stared at him in horror.

Trying, and failing, to move the woman from in front of him and stand, Arjan could only stare in shock into Sienna's eyes, calling her name out loud, as the prostitute's expert sucking and cajoling finally paid off and he came into her mouth. His eyes never left Sienna's once the whole time and as he automatically gripped the back of the hooker's head, keeping it fastened around him, he could only mouth her name one more time.

Sobbing, Sienna ran off into the night, back to her car, and drove wildly away from the showground. Realising that he had now lost her for good, Arjan slapped the hooker at his knees across her face, bellowing to both of them to get out before throwing on his jeans. Spying the flowers and champagne in the corner, he swept his arm through it all and they smashed on to the floor. He then upended the table, the remainder of his planned romance falling into ruins, before throwing on the rest of his clothes and going out into the sultry Middle Eastern night. His only aim was, once more, to get balefully drunk and to try and forget about the beauty of Sienna's blue eyes – and of how they had looked at him with such horror and disgust as she realised, for once and for all and, with a damning sense of finality, that he was a man always ruled by his dick and one who would never change.

Slamming shut the door of his car, Arjan headed into central Abu Dhabi and a random rooftop bar. Ignoring everyone, he proceeded to drink his way down a bottle of whiskey and smoke through a packet of cigarettes. The only thing that jolted him from his haze was when a waitress walked past, her rose perfume wafting on the gentle Middle Eastern breeze and reaching him. As the aroma of roses reached him, a scent that reminded him of Sienna ever since they had first kissed properly in Wels, Arjan finally shed a solitary tear for the woman he truly loved. He knew that after tonight, she was lost to him forever – and he knew, without doubt, that it was all his own fault.

Sienna, meanwhile, was sobbing and drinking wine with Sue, pouring out the whole sordid story to her. Never again would she allow herself to be humiliated by Arjan Vermeulen. It was truly over this time. He was dead to her.

17

Just one month later, the circuit moved to Dubai for the International Arabian Horse Championships. Based at the World Trade Centre, the show was run by the ruling family of Dubai and was a very prestigious event. No expense was spared in making the arena look wonderful, the horses' stabling area bright and airy, the judges' gifts the most expensive, or in making all visitors feel welcome and well looked after. This was the one show that all the Middle Eastern studs wanted to win, and for Alejandro Orlando Suarez, this was no exception. Born in Spain, Alejandro had been captivated by horses from a young age and he loved riding them as often as he could. He trained in classical dressage, something that made his stance as he walked seem even more alluring. He went on to take courses at the local university on equine management. Slowly, he worked his way up through the ranks before leaving Spain and getting a job firstly in an artificial insemination centre in Germany, and then moving on to stud and breeding management at a higher level. A job offer from the Middle East followed and Alejandro excelled. His career continued to rise and now he now worked for one of the bigger Arabian horse farms in Bahrain, and they regularly expected to leave the arena with championship titles. Anything less wouldn't do, and it was Alejandro's job to ensure that not only did the horses stand the best chance possible in achieving the prize, but also that any ruffled feathers among grooms, handlers and his owners were soothed before, during and after the classes.

Demands on Alejandro were high, and he was a man always on a mission. From his ex-wife, constantly calling about their two children, to his over-familiar boss who thought it acceptable to call him at 3am 'just to talk about breeding plans', Alejandro found it increasingly difficult to have any kind of life, such were the daily pressures that he faced, and his Latin tastes of wine, women and song had become decidedly tempered in recent months.

Standing at 5'11", Alejandro had wonderful Mediterranean skin that tanned easily and became darker as the summer went on. Now in his early 40s, his once dark hair was turning salt and pepper in colour, and with his dark eyes – the exact colour of a quality dark chocolate bar – he regularly had swarms of women falling at his feet. When he smiled his face, weathered from riding and working outside in all weathers, lit up, and lines and wrinkles that would have looked aged on anyone else created character and charm instead. Not a naturally vain man, Alejandro knew that he was in the peak of his fitness, running daily and playing football once a week, all in a bid to stop the clock approaching 50 years and taking him unawares. He knew that women swooned around him on a very regular basis, but with his deep-rooted Catholic upbringing, he kept his distance from them. The greatest sadness in his life had been when he and his wife, childhood sweethearts who married as teenagers, had split up. She had, without question or hesitation, followed him from Spain to Germany, and then on to the desert heat of the Middle East, supporting him in all he did. However, with the children growing up, and Alejandro's increased focus on the stables he worked for, they had drifted apart and had fallen out of love with each other. While they still cared deeply for the other, both decided that it was best if Alejandro moved out and in spite of seeing the children daily, the hole that being surrounded by a family had left in his life was huge. However, working in the Middle East had meant that his estranged wife and children would have been sent back to Spain if they were no longer together, and Alejandro had quickly moved back to the marital home, albeit it to a separate wing of the house. Filling his time with horses, his children and frustrated dreams, Alejandro continued to live each day as quietly and carefully as possible. His life was on hold, but he accepted this fact. It wasn't as if it was forever and besides, his family had to come first.

Now, standing in his room at the Novotel Hotel, one of the two hotels situated within the World Trade Centre, Alejandro stared at the message that had just come through on his phone.

'I land at 5.30pm. Be at the hotel by 7. Can't wait to see you! XX'

Sighing in exasperation, Alejandro flipped the phone case shut and marched out of his room. In a bid to inject some passion and energy into his life, he had endured a one-night stand with a French girl at the Abu Dhabi show the month before. Thinking that this girl, Delphine, could offer emotional comfort rather than just sex, had been Alejandro's mistake, and it had been a disaster, in more ways than one. Not only did she want a repeat performance at shows across the Middle East and Europe, but she had been telling people about what had happened. Alejandro, meanwhile, didn't even want to talk to Delphine, let alone look at her. The moment her hotel door had slammed shut on the two of them, Alejandro knew that this was not what he wanted. In need of a release, he had gone through the motions and hadn't been able to get away from the room quickly enough afterwards. Undeterred, Delphine was bombarding him with a stream of increasing explicit messages and even photographs, and she was clearly

205

expecting a repeat performance tonight.

Slamming the door to his hotel room shut, Alejandro ran down the stairs to the hotel lobby and headed towards the neighbouring Ibis Hotel, a slightly different journey to the showground but one that meant he didn't have to go the conventional route where he was more likely to be seen.

Declaring himself off passion and relationships, even if they were just for one night, he decided he would stay at the stables until 10pm, before taking the longer route outside the Centre back to the Novotel so that he could avoid Delphine and her over-attention.

As he walked through the Ibis hotel, the air-conditioned coolness keeping people at a chilled 18°C instead of the baking 36°C outside, he glanced into the bar area and saw a couple of women having lunch. Even in spite of his new declaration, his Latin temperament allowed him to assess every woman that he saw as if she were a work of art, quickly casting an expert eye over them to look for beauty where others perhaps did not see it.

One of the women was older, in her 40s, with peroxide-blonde long hair hanging down her back. She was instantly recognisable as Corinne, the long-suffering wife of a French trainer, and he knew her well; not someone he would step out of his way to talk to, but Alejandro would happily pass the time of day with her if he saw her in a bar.

But it was the woman opposite Corinne was the one that made Alejandro hesitate in his tracks, just for a second. There was a woman he had never spoken to but had seen around on the circuit for the past few years. Sienna Stevens. Now in her early 30s, her hair was dark brown, unusual for British girls these days as all of them seemed to be intent on being a fake white-blonde, a look only achieved by ultimately destroying their hair and meaning that they had to have it cut off. Sienna's hair hung in waves, rather than the regimented straight lines that every woman in the world seemed to favour; Corinne's hair looked as if it had been ironed and in contrast to the softness of Sienna, she looked fierce and uptight, the harsh lines taking away from her natural beauty.

Sienna's eyes sparkled blue, enhanced by a clever use of eye shadow and eye liner, and as she licked her lips after sipping her wine, Alejandro noticed how pink and kissable they looked. In every single way, she was different to the girls that regularly frequented the showing circuit and Alejandro felt a stirring in his groin as he watched her. In less than a minute, he had made all these observations, and he found that his feet were walking towards the bar rather than out of the door to the stables.

As he approached the table, he became aware of the heady, over-sexual scent of Corinne's perfume, a stark contrast to the subtler, floral fragrance coming off Sienna. To Alejandro, she smelt like a glorious English day and he was transported back to a summer holiday spent in the UK and being in the gardens of Windsor Castle with his parents as the sun shone down and he and his sister ran among the rose beds.

'Salut Alejandro!'

Corinne was looking up at Alejandro expectantly. He didn't even realise that he had stopped walking and he had to shake himself slightly to return to reality.

'Bonjour, ça va?'

Alejandro automatically leaned down to give Corinne a perfunctory kiss on each cheek.

'And… Hello…'

Without waiting for Corinne to answer, Alejandro had turned to Sienna and held out his hand, which she duly shook. Sienna looked up at the face in front of her, noting the way his cheeks dimpled as he smiled, the laughter lines around his eyes, which were a hypnotic deep brown, and the flecks of grey creeping into his hair, and smiled. In spite of being sworn off all men after the crushing final humiliation by Arjan on her in Abu Dhabi, she could feel his allure and was instantly captivated. At that same moment, Alejandro was lost, and he just stood there, holding Sienna's hand, staring deeply into her eyes, his smile growing by the second.

'Alejandro Suarez. I work for Alambrado in Bahrain.'

'Sienna Stevens. I own Essentially Arabian.'

Corinne laughed, breaking the spell between them.

'Are you going to let go of each other's hands? Join us. Drink, Alejandro?'

Pulling himself back to reality, and suddenly grimly aware that the news of this meeting would be all over the showground by the end of the day, Alejandro smiled at Sienna once more before carefully loosening his grip on her hand and turning to Corinne.

'I have my driver waiting, I am needed in town. Maybe another time.'

With a slightly stiff and formal bow, Alejandro headed towards the door, not daring to look back as he heard Corinne's laughter ringing out around the hotel foyer.

18

It was almost 10 months later that Sienna walked through the mall in the Kingdom of Saudi Arabia with a client, Francesca Huttingson-Brown, the Head of Arabian Racing in the UK. They were visiting Al Khalediah Arabian Horse Festival and having opted to catch up on some sleep after getting to the hotel in the early hours of the morning, they were wandering through the mall and looking for something suitable for lunch.

As they stopped in the food court, Francesca scowled at the Subway store in front of them. 'Everything is spicy. Why is it all spicy?' she said in her loud, braying voice. As Sienna wanted the floor to open up and swallow them, she saw him. Alejandro. Their eyes met, and he swiftly changed direction and walked towards her.

Thrilled to see him, terrified he was going to kiss her, a big no in Saudi Arabia, Sienna took an involuntary step back and held out her hand as if to ward off evil.

'Don't kiss me!'

The words hung in the air and Sienna realised the ridiculousness of them as soon as they left her lips. Of course he wouldn't kiss her; he knew the protocol of the Middle East far better than she did. Looking fresh and cool in pale linen trousers and a duck-egg blue shirt that set off his Mediterranean colouring perfectly, Alejandro was slowly eating ice cream from a tub, thoughtfully and slowly sucking each mouthful off the small plastic spoon.

'How are you? So good to see you here – a nice surprise,' he smiled. It was as if Francesca didn't exist, and the hundred other people around them in the food court were not there either. Sienna felt something move beneath her, and as she realised that she was staring intently at Alejandro, she felt herself blush.

'Actually, I do need to talk to you,' she blurted out quickly. 'One of the magazines has a proposal for your farm with your stallion…'

'Call me when you get back to the hotel. Here's my card.' Alejandro handed Sienna a gold-embossed stiff piece of card, with 'Alejandro Suarez – Manager' written on it in a fancy font. Bowing slightly, Alejandro walked away from the two women, heading straight back to the hotel to freshen up before Sienna rang.

Two hours later, Sienna and Alejandro were still sat in the coffee lounge at Al Faisaliah Hotel, the grand and official hotel of the show guests. They had quickly conducted their business within five minutes of sitting down, long before the coffee they had ordered had even arrived and had spent the rest of the time getting to know each other, talking about absolutely anything and everything.

Alejandro looked at his watch. 'I have another meeting to go to… The woman you were with earlier, is she a friend?'

'No, a client.'

'Would you like to have dinner with me tonight?'

Sienna paused, feeling herself blush in spite of her trying to act relaxed and cool.

'Yes, okay.'

Alejandro raised his hand and the hotel concierge came over immediately.

'Sir?'

'Where is the best place to go for dinner here?'

'The Globe is the best place, sir. You see the golden orb on top of Al Faisaliah Tower? That is the restaurant, and it offers a beautiful view of the city of Riyadh.'

Alejandro raised an eyebrow at Sienna, who nodded.

'Please book a table for two for 8.30pm. Is that okay?'

Sienna nodded once more and, leaving Alejandro to make the arrangements, headed back to her room to shower and get ready.

Feeling like a teenager going on a first date, Sienna checked with Francesca as to how she looked – not that it mattered as she was hidden underneath her black abaya. 'Have a fun evening – I've ordered room service and a film,' Francesca smiled as Sienna headed down to meet Alejandro.

Having passed through strict security to access Al Faisaliah Tower, they waited for the lift to come. Going up the 240 metres in the lift to the restaurant, with the Bell Boy accompanying them, Sienna felt like a movie star. From one lift, they stepped into a smaller, much more personal one that took them the last few metres up into the Globe itself. The doors opened to reveal a dimly-lit room, with discreet lighting providing privacy for diners. 'This way sir...'

They followed the waiter to the table, with Sienna gasping as she saw Riyadh all lit up beneath them, beautiful in its sparkling splendour. Waiting for Sienna to be seated, Alejandro looked around him, satisfied that there was no one there that they knew, knowing that they could have a private dinner in peace without being worried about people gossiping about them.

The menus arrived, on gilt-edged, stiff card, and Sienna stared at the muddle of words before her. She could feel the nerves rising up in her stomach and she concentrated on breathing deeply rather than studying the menu. Distraction came in the form of a telephone call, to Alejandro from his children. This gave Sienna time to take in the magic of her surroundings and calm herself. "Honestly", she chided herself, "you're like a kid on a first date!"

Speaking swiftly in Spanish, Alejandro said his goodbyes and turned his phone off.

'Now, you have my full attention,' he smiled. Sienna's stomach somersaulted again. 'Have you decided what you would like to eat?'

Flushing, Sienna shook her head and studied the menu, which was very western in its tastes. 'I'm going for something light,' said Alejandro as he selected soup and chicken. Sienna quickly chose chicken pâté and king fish, one of her favourites in the Middle East, just as the waiter appeared.

Having ordered their food, the menus between them removed, Alejandro leaned forward to Sienna and smiled.

'You smell wonderful,' he murmured. Sienna smiled to herself, pleased that she was having an effect on this incredible man. 'Tell me more about yourself, your hopes, your dreams.'

Sienna started talking, about how she had always loved horses, how they had always been a part of her life, and of how she was enjoying her new career. Alejandro waved his hand in the air as if brushing a fly aside.

'No... Tell me about your real dreams – the ones that you long for privately and no one ever asks you about.'

Sienna paused, slightly taken aback at his directness. Opening her mouth to begin speaking, she paused again as the waiter delivered their starters.

Alone once more, Sienna began, hesitantly. 'Well... I guess a lot of my dreams are the same as many other women's – to find someone to share the rest of my life with. To find someone who I love and who loves me. To grow old and happy and contented with them, regardless of how we change physically, the wrinkles we get, the way our bodies fail us. An unending, enduring love…'

Embarrassed by her frankness, Sienna busied herself with the pate and toast.

'Silly, isn't it?' she said, as she took a bite of her food.

Alejandro was surprised by how open Sienna was; most women didn't show such a vulnerable side, especially so early on in a… In a what? He was startled to find that, in spite of his self-enforced celibacy, he was already developing feelings for Sienna and that he wanted to take things further than just one dinner this evening. Conflicting emotions ran through him as he smiled at Sienna.

'Not at all. How's the pâté?'

Swiftly changing the subject back to safer territory, he tried some of Sienna's offered pâté on toast, appreciating the flavours of cumin and coriander than ran through it.

The rest of the meal passed by in a blur, as they talked about places they had travelled to, horses they had seen, people they had met, and countries they wanted to go to but had not yet visited. Everything was discussed apart from relationships, love and romance.

Before they realised it, the waiter was back at their side, asking whether they would like to see the dessert menu.

'Sure,' said Alejandro, passing it to Sienna to study. 'What would you have?'

'Tarte tatin,' she replied.

Alejandro nodded to the waiter, asking for one tarte tatin with two spoons. Smiling casually at Sienna, she felt her stomach squirm in anticipation. From the moment they sat down, she had been aware that this was more than just a business dinner; it had had been more than just business since they sat down for coffee that afternoon, but this intimate sharing of a dessert seemed to be the confirmation that Sienna needed.

Lingering over coffee, a plate of petite fours remained untouched. Glancing at them, Alejandro thought how much his children would have enjoyed them but with four more days left in Saudi, they would have gone off by the time he arrived back home.

As Alejandro paid the bill, Sienna went to the bathroom to give herself some space to breathe. It had been a very heady evening, and without alcohol to mask and blur the feelings, too; they had glanced at the list of non-alcoholic wines offered in this strictly dry country, the high cost of them putting off any curiosity to try them. Looking in the mirror in the mirror-covered black-walled toilet, she saw that her cheeks were flushed and that her eyes had gone the brilliant blue they always went when she was very happy. Reapplying her lip gloss, Sienna adjusted her headscarf and smoothed down her abaya before making her way outside to where Alejandro was waiting.

Having gone down the first, short lift with the Bell Boy, he then reached into the second lift to press the button that would take them all the way back down to the ground floor, and it was quickly apparent that he would not be joining them on the journey back to reality. Alejandro started asking questions about how high they were and how long the lift took to travel; 25 seconds, was the answer. Sienna switched off to his typical man questions and tried to stand nonchalantly in the corner of the lift, leaning back into the corner, hands resting lightly on the rails either side of her that went around the inside of the lift.

As the doors closed, it was immediately obvious why Alejandro had been asking such questions. Turning around to look at Sienna, the black scarf of her abaya fighting an ever-losing battled against the softness of her brunette hair, he smiled.

'You don't need to wear that in here,' he said and took a

214

step towards her. Without hesitating, he put one arm around her back and pulled her to him and kissed her. The combination of love's first kiss and the elevator plunging down to earth made Sienna's knees go weak and she was glad of the metal supports around the lift walls to cling on to. While after such an intense evening, such a kiss was not unexpected, but it still caught Sienna by surprise. Stepping away from her just in time, the doors opened, and they walked out past security back to the hotel.

Feeling like she was in a dream, the couple walked past people they knew enjoying a late dinner in the hotel restaurant. Alejandro frowned; they would be gossiping tomorrow. Walking Sienna to her lift and then to her room, Alejandro paused at the door. 'I think I'd better come in to say goodnight,' he said as he closed the door behind them.

Suddenly as nervous as a cat faced with a giant dog, Sienna fidgeted in her room, closing curtains and turning down the lights and generally staying away from Alejandro. Her ex had teased her that she was frigid and, after everything that had happened – or not – with Arjan, she was worried that she would be a let-down, especially with such an experienced man as Alejandro.

'Come here,' said Alejandro as, grabbing her as she went past to fix more lights, he pulled her to him and pinned her against the wardrobe, hands either side of her shoulders so that she could not escape. Looking deeply into her eyes, he smiled at her. 'Just relax,' he said, as he leaned in to kiss her.

The kiss increased in its intensity and Sienna smiled through the kiss, putting her hands up and around his back as she did so. So muscular and broad, she was aware she was in the hands of an expert, one full of passion, inspired by her. She allowed her guard to finally drop and gave herself over fully to the feeling of Alejandro's lips pressed against hers, the lingering of his hands over her body, amazed at not only the feeling inside her but also at the effect she was having on this sensual man.

Gently undoing her abaya, the black nylon material fell to the floor leaving Sienna in more standard combination of grey trousers and a fitted cerulean blue top, which flattered her figure and brought out the hypnotic colour of her eyes. Alejandro's kisses moved from her mouth to her neck and gently, he turned Sienna around in is arms and took a step forwards, so that she fell back onto the king-sized bed as her knees buckled beneath her.

'Oh Sienna…' he murmured into her hair as his hot kisses slowly trailed down her neck and to her breasts before returning once more to her mouth. Sensing that he had to be gentle with her, Alejandro leaned over and turned out the light, with the room almost instantly illuminated by the night time lights of Riyadh outside, shining in through the half-closed curtains. Seeing his mouth smile, Sienna pulled his pale green shirt out of his jeans and placed her hands on his smooth skin. Groaning slightly, he kissed her deeply before reaching down to remove her top.

Waiting for Sienna to get used to the moment, knowing how much she had resisted all the men on the circuit so far, Alejandro felt a moment of tender triumph as he tasted her soft skin beneath his lips before deftly reaching around to her back and unhooking her bra in an instant. 'Definitely an expert,' Sienna thought wryly before surrendering herself to his gentle touch. Adder-like, his tongue toyed with her nipples, arousing her far greater than any man had in years, and she arched her back to him.

'Oh Alejandro,' she moaned as he moved her arms above her head, holding them there with one hand while he played with her nipples with his mouth and fingers. Groaning, she struggled to free herself and pulled him closer, wrapping her legs around him and pulling his shirt off over his head.

Eyes now fully accustomed to the light, Sienna took in the dark tan, the hair curling on his chest and the broad shoulders, before he rolled over and pulled her on top of him. Fear of being just another conquest caused her to utter 'this is as far as it goes' to which Alejandro closed his eyes as he groaned inwardly before whispering 'I understand.'

For two or more hours, the pair twisted and turned on the bed, kissing each other nearly all over, Sienna teasing Alejandro through the tightness of his jeans, amazed at the size of him and wishing she wasn't so cautious, before finally, feeling relaxed and happy, she rolled over and lay face down on the bed. Alejandro moved next to her and traced his fingers across her lower back, his lips across her shoulders and she could feel the smile on his face as each kiss landed on her. Moving his hands to intertwine with hers, the feather-light kisses continued, before they just lay there in the semi-dark, listening to the other breathing, both contented with the world and smiling to themselves.

As Alejandro finally left Sienna's room, the morning call to prayer sounded and Sienna fell back into her tussled bed to try and sleep. All she could feel was Alejandro's lips all over her body and she ached for him. After everything that had happened with Arjan, she was so wary of the men in this industry. But Alejandro had moved her more than she had ever been moved in her life.

As the first fingertips of the sun finally came gently over the horizon, heralding the beginning of a new day, Sienna finally closed her eyes and fell into a happy, deep and dreamless sleep.

Waking later that day, Sienna recalled the events of last night with a huge smile on her face. Turning her phone on, she received a text from Alejandro, asking her to collect his show numbers from the hotel, where they had been left by a groom and he had deliberately forgotten to bring them so that he had an excuse to arrange to meet Sienna the minute she arrived at the show.

Leaping out of bed, Sienna jumped into the shower, aware that her skin still burned with the feel of Alejandro's kisses on her body and as the water coursed down over her, she couldn't help but smile as she noticed her lips stinging with stubble burns. Getting ready, throwing on whatever came to hand before covering herself with her abaya, Sienna made her way down to the hotel's impressive foyer to collect his numbers and made her way out to the bus that would take them to the show, through the impressive drive between Riyadh and Tebrak.

For the hour's journey, Sienna just stared out of the window, eyes oblivious to the incredible, dramatic landscape that passed her by. Arriving at the show, past the numerous, strict security checks, Sienna texted Alejandro to let her know she was there before making her way to the VIP seats where she would sit with Francesca for the rest of the show.

Seeing Alejandro already there, waiting for her, she smiled as she approached him across the carpeted VIP area. Carefully, he took the show material from her and gently stroked the underside of her wrist as he did so.

'Thank you for last night,' he murmured quietly. 'You were amazing.'

All Sienna could do was smile as Alejandro's groom immediately came running up to them, gabbling away quickly in Spanish about a problem in the stables. Smiling to her as he walked off, Sienna felt her stomach lurch with excitement and anticipation of what was to come.

The rest of the show passed by in a haze of longing;

Alejandro passing Sienna whenever he could just to look at her, smile at her, talk to her, either a passing word or a longer conversation, and to touch her hand or her arm in a guarded moment. As she finally flew home back to the cold of England several days later, both were hooked, with Alejandro trying to work out a way to make this all possible, and to allow love to come back into his life once more.

Arjan, now a shadow of his former self, was the only one who noticed the intense looks between the couple. After all, he had been on the receiving end of them himself so many times, but not like this. He knew that Sienna had fallen hook, line and sinker for Alejandro – it was obvious from the look on her face – and that it seemed that her feelings were reciprocated. He heard from an Italian magazine owner that the pair had been seen walking back from the Globe Restaurant late last night before disappearing into a lift together and getting out together on the same floor.

Jealous to the core, Arjan was determined to come between them and stop anything happening with the fledgling lovers. He was full of bitterness – it should have been him spending the night with Sienna, not Alejandro. He conveniently forgot what a bastard he had been to her, and seeing Alejandro stop to talk to her once again, he marched off angrily to the stables, cigarette gripped tightly in his hand, glowering at everyone he passed.

Since that fateful night in Abu Dhabi, Arjan's life had been on a downward spiral, much worse than when he and Rin had split up, and he was drinking more than ever. It was only now that he realised he had truly loved Sienna, and it was his own weakness and obsession with getting laid that had ruined any chance of them ever getting together. Denied, by his own stupidity, of his only chance of true happiness, Arjan took to hitting the bottle in a bid to forget all about his loss. It was the only option - being numb was preferable to being awake to his feelings. Friends fell by the wayside and clients were beginning to look elsewhere. Arjan was on a freefall spiral downwards, and he was unable to see it or to stop himself. Only Leap stayed with him, refusing to move his horses elsewhere, believing in his friend in spite of what everyone was saying about him – that he was finished, and a has-been. In just a few short days, Arjan had automatically lost his status both as Lord of Misrule and King of the Ring.

Returning to Europe for a short break before the season continued in the Middle East, Arjan headed straight for home, slamming the vast wooden door behind him with a resounding bang, and went straight to the liquor cabinet. Even Leap was unable to get through to Arjan and night after night, the proud Belgian would just sit there, bottle of whiskey to the side of him, cigarette clenched between his fingers, and he would go through photograph after photograph of Sienna on the internet. On the rare occasion he would find one of them together, in the show-ring when Sienna had been presenting the prizes, he would stare at the image for never-ending minutes.

Taking another slug from the bottle, he would stand up and walk to the window of his farmhouse, and just stand there, staring up into a starless sky. Wondering just why he had allowed it to all go wrong. And how to stop Sienna and Alejandro from getting together. Scheming against them seemed to be the only thing that gave him pleasure these days, even though it ate him up inside, taking his every waking minute and his every subconscious sleeping thought.

19

Life had gone full circle and it was time for the Abu Dhabi Show once more and in spite of what had happened there the previous year, Sienna was looking forward to going to the show. This part of the Middle East had always captivated her, and she felt very at home there. Not only that, but in the two weeks between Saudi Arabia and Abu Dhabi, Alejandro had kept in touch daily, calling her whenever he could, and resorting to text and WhatsApp messages the rest of the time. Their feelings for each other grew stronger daily and Sienna was counting down the days until she could see him again. Arjan was a distant memory to her and looking back, she wondered just how, and why, she fell under the Belgian's spell for so long. He was half the man that Alejandro was. And while she didn't actively avoid Arjan, she didn't go out of her way to be in the same part of the showground as him.

Staring out of the window as the plane raced through the late afternoon sky, Sienna was mesmerised by the changing landscape below her. The clouds, with the pale light bouncing off them, looked like the skeleton of a dinosaur's back. Watching the clouds flying past below her, Sienna noticed the snow on the mountain tops, so smooth and perfect that it seemed to have been placed there by an artist. Tiny villages were hidden in between, some catching the last rays of the day's sun, others destined to never quite be in the sun's golden glow.

Slowly, the sky became a blue rainbow – showing colours from deep aqua to a luminescent icy blue. It was perfect through every shade, and Sienna noticed the edges – the yellow of the sun and the white of the horizon –

perfecting its heavenly glaze. Sipping her wine, Sienna thought how it almost seemed as if the sun was warming the engines from behind them as they raced towards dusk – just as her heart was being warmed by Alejandro and she was flying through the skies to be with him. She was headed towards the land of midnight dreams and promises and, with Sienna close to an unsighted heaven, it seemed like the perfect place to make wishes and hope for dreams to come true.

Eagerly, Sienna looked ahead for the first tell-tale stars of the East, anticipating the beauty that they would bring, stark and silent in the deep indigo blue sky. As she stared, the first hint of pink appeared on the horizon, the dusk making its first appearance. Soon, all around them would be dark and Sienna's desire to arrive in Abu Dhabi grew as all the colours faded around her. Nights long-reaching fingers enveloped the plane as the last hues of pink and purple faded away; no matter how many times Sienna watched this moment, the same scene was never painted twice. Sighing happily, she leaned back in her seat and closed her eyes. Outside, the stars were appearing, ready to welcome her back to the Middle East, the place where her heart seemed to truly belong.

A short while later, Sienna walked out of Abu Dhabi Airport, smiling up at the stars in the sky and inhaling the almost tropical scent of the Middle East – the hot, humid night, the bougainvillea, the musky smells of spices and the exotic. She was met by Sue, who could not believe the change in her friend from one year to the next.

'You look amazing! What's your secret?' she asked, only worrying slightly when Sienna whispered in reply: 'I might be falling for someone…'

After the way Arjan had treated Sienna, Sue didn't want her to make the same mistakes again. This time, however, she had a feeling that things were very different. She had never seen Sienna look as she did now – she was glowing and vibrant and full of confidence – and Sue could only hope that this was a good sign.

Arriving at the showground the next day, Sienna made her way straight to the arena. She had overslept, and she was running late. The first class was already in, with Guy running around a liver chestnut filly. Spying Alejandro standing in the collecting ring, Sienna dumped her bags at her VIP seat and made her way around to him.

With a big smile on his face, Alejandro embraced Sienna as closely as he dared.

'It's so good to see you – and you smell so good,' he murmured. 'Can we have dinner tonight?'

Nodding, Sienna felt full of happiness. The chemistry between them, something that she had thought so much about during the past two weeks, hadn't all been a dream. As she stood next to Alejandro, discussing the horses, Sienna found it hard not to put her arm around him and lean in for an embrace. "Maybe later," she hoped to herself, very aware that they could not let anyone know about their relationship just yet.

As she made her way back to her seat, something that took a long time due to the number of people that she had to stop and speak to, she saw that Sue was sitting there, with a big grin on her face.

'Well, I think it's safe to say that you've picked a good one this time. I approve!'

Sienna just nodded, smiling shyly, and turned her attention to the horses coming into the arena. Sue was one person that she never had to worry about knowing and she allowed herself a quick excited grin to her friend before controlling herself once more.

Guy, Rin, Luca, and Arjan all had horses here, and part of the magic of the Middle Eastern shows was that there were also the local handlers, bringing in horses and running them amok among the more seasoned professional handlers. Chaos regularly ensued and it was not uncommon to have three or four loose horses a day, lead ropes flapping around their legs as the horse careered around the arena, other handlers trying to avoid their horses being injured by a stray kick while at the same time, trying to catch the loose horse and bring some normality back to the show so that it didn't run into the cold, late hours after the sun had set and impinge on their socialising time. At one memorable show, a handler was doing a wonderful, dramatic run around the ring with his horse when he tripped on some grass, did a somersault, and then landed back on his feet and carried on running as if nothing had ever happened, the horse not even breaking her stride beside him! The moment had been caught on camera and circulated widely around social media, with the handler in question now something of a legend among the local showing community.

Bint Sanatra was the first big winner among the European trainers that day, now a three-year-old filly and full of beauty and vibrance. With her exotic head and huge, black eyes, she captivated judges and spectators alike. The local DJs, who arranged the music for the classes, had taken to playing My Way every time she was called in as champion, which all added to the relaxed feel of this show. While Guy may not have many fans among those in the industry with him, people couldn't help but watch when he brought out this dancing filly. She was so beautiful and had a natural presence that made other trainers envious and breeders wish that this was the filly they had bred.

It was much later in the day that the show finally

finished, and the trainers arrived back at the hotel. Not bothering to go to their rooms, Guy made his way into the hotel bar. Sven was already there. Nodding to each other, Guy went to the far end, away from Sven, to order a neat whiskey. Sven sat there, chain-smoking and looking constantly at his phone as well as over his shoulder to see who was approaching. Arjan came into the bar with Leap, and he just glared at Sven, who he also held responsible for his failed romancing of Sienna. Ignoring Guy, the two Belgian men sat away from the others, drinking shots and eyeing up any woman who walked past.

Arjan sat still as a cat watching a bird once more, keen to see if Sienna came in as he wanted to quiz her about Alejandro. He still couldn't get the woman out of his head and even Leap was horribly aware that Arjan was a shadow of himself these days. No matter what Leap did, and how many women he lined up, Arjan just didn't care. Arjan would ultimately, however, leave the bar unhappy once more. Sienna was staying at Sue's and had no intention of going anywhere near the rest of the crowd. On Sue's invitation, Alejandro was dining at hers tonight, giving the blossoming couple more time together to find out more about each other. After a magnificent and traditional Middle Eastern meal, Sue retired to bed to watch a film, leaving Sienna and Alejandro alone on the balcony, sipping brandy and listening to the sounds around them and breathing in the aromatic scent of the bougainvillea.

They were both talking, shyly, to each other, getting to know more about what made the other tick.

Alejandro laughed. 'It's crazy! I feel so shy around you right now, and yet we were in bed together just a couple of weeks ago.'

'I know. It was a special night…,' Sienna smiled back.

Leaning over, Alejandro gently kissed her on the lips.

'It is difficult, Sienna. So difficult. You move me in a way that I have not felt since I was a teenager. And yet, I have to hesitate. And I don't want to. But I have to. I must...

'You see, Pasha and I were childhood sweethearts. We loved each other from when we first started high school and as soon as we left, we were quickly engaged. It was a totally natural thing to do. All my life – through school, through university, any of my studies – I never looked another woman. I only had eyes for Pasha.

'Finally, we had two children. Two girls. I would have loved to have had a boy, but it was not meant to be. But they were my three girls, and I loved them intensely. I would have given them my world. We moved to the Middle East and they had everything that they could possibly have ever wanted. More, probably. But the one they couldn't have enough of was me. I wanted to get on in my career, and the only way to do that was to throw myself into my job and work for the promotions that inevitably came my way.

'The girls were home-schooled by a local school teacher. You can probably imagine what happened. I came home early one day to surprise them - only to get the surprise myself. The girls, Maria and Ana, were working quietly in the reading room, their classroom as such. I asked where their teacher was, where Pasha was, and they said that they had gone upstairs together to talk about something important.'

Alejandro paused, taking a small sip of his brandy and looking to the skies before he continued.

'I went upstairs and there they were – in our bed. The woman I had loved all my life had betrayed me. As you can imagine, the rows that followed were fearful. Sometimes, Pasha threatened to leave and take the girls with her. They were only eight and ten years old at the time, and I couldn't bear to live my life without them, so I begged Pasha to stay. We tried living in different houses, but it raised too many questions. So I had to move back in with Pasha and the girls again. I made some excuse about Pasha having a visiting hysterical girlfriend as to why I had moved out for a week, and that was that.

'Since then, Pasha and I have lived separate lives. It suited me fine. I had my work. But then, I see you in that Italian restaurant in Dubai – and I perhaps fell in love for the second time in my life. But what can I do? Tell Pasha that I have met someone and risk that she will take my children back to Spain? Or stay as it is, saying nothing and only being able to dream of you and longing every night before I go to sleep to have you in my arms again?

'So, I guess what I am saying… If you can bear it, please give me time. Please give me time to arrange things with Pasha, calmly. In a way that will mean that she won't have another screaming match and not threaten to leave with my girls. But that instead, if the time is right, she may – just may – be happy for me and stay in Bahrain with my children. It has been almost three years now, but I just need a little more time. And I know that I have no right to ask that of you.'

Finishing his speech, Sienna took Alejandro's hand and squeezed it, looking him deeply in his eyes as she did so.

'Of course I will give us time Alejandro. After all that has happened between Arjan and me, I need time, too… Time is a wonderful thing. So yes, I will give you all the time that you – that we – need. And a little bit more. I probably fell in love with you the moment that I saw you in that mall in Saudi Arabia. And I am not going anywhere.'

Smiling, Alejandro moved closer to Sienna, taking her face in his hands, and staring into her eyes. There was no need for words as he just drank in this amazing woman in front of him, and then gently kissed her on the lips.

'Time,' he said, as he kissed her again, more passionately this time, his arms pulling her body close to his, lifting the hem of her shirt and feeling her soft skin under her top, feeling himself harden with instant pleasure.

Sighing, happily, he eventually let Sienna out of his embrace and sat back. 'If I don't leave now, I am going to make love to you here on Sue's balcony, and I don't think that she would be too happy if we did that! I will see you at the show tomorrow?'

Kissing him a yes in reply, Sienna led Alejandro through Sue's house and said goodbye at the door, reluctantly opening it to let in the warm night air as he made his way out. Alejandro's driver was waiting to take him back to the hotel and, with one last look at Sienna, he left.

The next day, Sienna was woken by a call from a client in the United States. They had sent her a first-class plane ticket, and they needed her at their farm immediately. Messaging Alejandro, Sienna wrote:

"Time will always wait for those that deserve it. I have to go to the US but will be back for the Bahrain Show. See you there? Love S xx"

Fully expecting to be back in the Middle East within two weeks, Sienna relaxed into her first-class seat – a luxury that she was not used to, as most clients just paid enough to get there and nothing more. As she sipped her champagne, Sienna remembered how Alejandro had looked at her the night before and she knew that she would give him all the time that he needed to sort his situation. Sienna admired how he placed his children above everything else, even his own happiness, and even if it meant that she would have to wait, she knew that it would be worth it.

Alas, the trip to the US took far longer than originally planned and she missed the Bahrain Show. A client then called from South Africa, begging her to fly to Cape Town as quickly as possible, as they wanted her to help orchestrate a 10-day photoshoot and video campaign. Feeling shattered after such a crazy few weeks, Sienna decided to stay on in Cape Town and enjoy a few days off before heading back to the Middle East for the Dubai Show. All the time, Alejandro kept in constant touch, and they messaged each other as often as they could. She could not wait to see him again.

20

Four weeks later, a car pulled up outside the hotel in the early hours of the morning. 'Finally,' Sienna thought to herself as she paid the driver. 'Drink. Bed. Sleep.'

Entering the foyer, the Novotel in the Dubai World Trade Centre was eerily quiet. The marble floor reflected the lights from the ceiling, but instead of the noises from the bar that she expected to hear, there was just the sound of the reception staff murmuring to each other. Sienna knew it was already gone 2am, but she still expected to see some of the stragglers from the show circuit around – Arjan, Peter, Yves, and Sven for sure. But there was nobody visible and everywhere she looked, the place seemed unusually empty.

She checked in quickly and, dragging her bags behind her, headed straight for the infamous Blue Bar. The scene of many a crime over recent years, it was here that the great and the good of the showing world created havoc. While the shows in Saudi, Abu Dhabi, Qatar, Bahrain and Kuwait all preceded Dubai, this was seen as the first major show of the season, as well as the Middle East version of Paris. It was here that many of the European trainers, grooms, competitors, media and assorted hangers on came together for the first time in that showing year. As winter changed to spring, the Dubai Show provided everyone the opportunity to shake off the dark and cold nights and instead think about summer, sex and the desire to win. As Sienna approached the door to the bar, she hoped that she might be able to get a drink before it closed; after that long journey, heaven knows she needed it. Pushing the door open, Sienna was hit once more by a wall of quiet. The lights were already dimmed with just the bar illuminated with one lone barman standing there, wiping the final couple of glasses.

'We're closed. You a guest?'

Sienna nodded, showing her door key and stub that she still held in her hand.

'One drink.'

'Vodka cranberry.'

Leaving her cases by the door and settling herself on one of the bar stools next to the dim bar, Sienna was gratified to see the barman half-fill the glass with vodka before adding the cranberry juice.

'I have to go now. Thirty-six dirhams please. Thank you'

Flicking the switch and leaving Sienna framed by the dimmed lights around the top of the bar, depicting different faces of musicians such as Jimi Hendrix, Jim Morrison and others on the bar below her, the barman left the room.

Illuminated by blue, Sienna sighed. A hellishly long flight around the world had left her exhausted. She had been looking forward to seeing some friends but would have to wait until tomorrow now. She looked down at her hands, tanned light-gold from three weeks spent in the South African sun, where she had been before returning to London for just one meeting, held at Heathrow Terminal 5, before boarding the plane to bring her to Dubai. Sienna knew that she looked good and that none of her friends had seen her look like this before: golden and rested from days spent in the sun rather than a frozen winter. She was also a dress size smaller from feasting on summer salads rather than warming stews. It had been a successful trip, helping an already established stud farm plan how to get into the global market, as well as travelling between Johannesburg and Cape Town visiting clients, but Sienna was looking forward to getting back into the Middle

Eastern and European show circuit.

Taking a slug of vodka, Sienna started as she heard a movement in the corner of the room. Peering into the darkness, she couldn't see anything. Suddenly nervous, she wished that the barman hadn't been quite so generous with his measures – she wanted to finish her drink as quickly as possible, leave this dimly-lit room and go to bed.

The sound of a table being pushed back made Sienna leap off the stool, but before she had even taken a step away from the bar, Alejandro walked into the spotlight.

Everything about Sienna stopped: her heart, her breathing, her thoughts. She just stood and stared at the man before her, sweet Alejandro who had taken her in his arms less than two months before and ravished her. Sweet Alejandro who had haunted her dreams every night since then, since Saudi Arabia. Sweet Alejandro, and her, alone in the bar.

'Hello Sienna.'

'Hello Alejandro.'

Sienna allowed herself to be taken in his arms as he dropped a kiss on both cheeks.

'It's good to see you. You look… Amazing.'

Smiling, Sienna settled back on the stool.

'Thank you. Three weeks of living out of a suitcase can have that effect!'

Alejandro stepped closer to Sienna. She could smell his aftershave and the faint, lingering scent of the stables. She could see the 5 o'clock shadow darkening his chin. She could see his eyes, dark like deep pools of melted chocolate, fixed upon her.

'I missed you in Bahrain last month.'

'You did?'

Faint with longing, Sienna steadied herself with a sip of her drink. Alejandro was so close now that she could feel the pressure of his body against her knees.

'Yes. I kept looking for you, before remembering that you weren't there. I missed you. Four weeks is too long to wait to see you.'

Looking into Sienna's eyes, as clear blue as the daytime sky, Alejandro felt any resolve he had fade. He had tried not to fall for Sienna, tried not to fall in love. But she occupied his thoughts every waking second. And his dreams, too. Walking out of her room in Saudi and just being civil and normal with her the next day as there were so many people around was the hardest thing he had ever had to do. He wanted to throw her down and kiss her all over, make love to her until dawn broke, and then fall asleep in her arms. He wanted to lay his head on her soft, gentle breasts, to hold her hand in public and tell the world, that he, Alejandro, had won the heart of this girl. It was he that she thought of when she went to sleep at night. He that made love to her as the dawn broke. The show in Abu Dhabi had also been difficult but as they had been unable to even snatch five minutes alone together, apart from the evening at Sue's, it had, in a way, been slightly easier. Looking into her eyes, Alejandro lifted his hand to gently trace her cheek.

'So soft. So beautiful...,' he muttered, almost to himself. Stroking her hair, Alejandro gently cupped Sienna's face between his hands and gently kissed her lips; a repeat of their first kiss. But this time, new feelings were unleashed inside them both.

'Mmmm...,' Alejandro murmured. 'I really have missed you Sienna.'

And with that, Alejandro kissed her with passion, burning Sienna's lips with his bruising kisses. His hands were stroking her face, her hair and slowly moving down to her breasts.

'Oh Alejandro…'

Sienna threw her head back as, involuntarily, her legs opened and then wrapped themselves around Alejandro as he stepped in closer to her. She enjoyed the sensation of his lips moving down her throat, down her collar bone, and then beginning to kiss all over her breasts. Pulling her halter top down, unhooking her bra, Alejandro looked into Sienna's eyes, seeking approval to continue, before kissing her nipples. His tongue flickered over them, making Sienna groan and her back arch with pleasure. Moving to her left breast, Alejandro's fingers replaced his tongue on her right breast, driving Sienna to complete distraction as her nipples stood to attention.

'Oh Alejandro…'

Feeling Alejandro hard against her groin, Sienna made to move her hands down to his flies, but Alejandro grasped her hands, holding them where they were. Not threatening, just masterful, he played with her breasts, teasing her with his tongue, kissing, licking, sucking, biting and pulling.

His eyes sought out Sienna's again. 'Can I go on?' they seemed to ask. 'Yes,' hers replied, knowing that they were both under a spell and that the silence must not be broken.

Freeing her hands, Alejandro reached down to undo Sienna's trousers and, with her help, eased them off and also her knickers. Sat on the stool, naked under the spotlight, Sienna wondered whether she was in a dream, especially when Alejandro dropped to his knees, parted her legs and began to kiss her. Sienna steadied her breathing, feeling like Julia Roberts in *Pretty Woman*. As Alejandro's kisses trailed over her thighs, Sienna pulled him up, so she could kiss him, revelling in the taste of her in his mouth.

'I want you…,' she whispered, loosening his belt.

Eyes locked, Alejandro released himself from his pants and hesitating for just a second, his eyes continually searching hers, he thrust into her, pausing as he hid his length in her.

'You sure?' he whispered into her hair.

'Yes,' she murmured, kissing his mouth, his neck, any part of him that she could reach.

Alejandro groaned as he came far too soon.

'I'm sorry...'

'Don't be,' Sienna smiled, enjoying the feeling of him inside her, feeling herself spasm gently around him.

Kissing her slowly, luxuriously, Alejandro smiled at Sienna, holding her gaze.

'I have wanted to do that for months,' he confessed. 'Ever since we first met here last year. Oh God...'

He kissed her again, more gently, more intimately, smiling, pulsing and radiating happiness. 'Let's go to bed,' he said, helping her on with her clothes. Sienna just smiled and took his hand.

As the door swung shut, the barman returned to the almost-full glass, put it in the sink, and switched off the light. No need for him to order a blue movie that night, he thought, as he left the room.

Walking to the stables the following morning, Alejandro had a spring in his step and a smile on his face. Stopping to talk to the girls who rode the farm's ridden horses, he could barely take in anything they were saying. All he could think about was Sienna and the fact that finally, they had a chance to be together. It was such a fickle world they lived in. The trainers seemed to be in a different bed every night and there was a string of groupies that worked their way around them. Sienna had always stood apart and been different – it was that sense of individuality that had attracted him to her, as well as her beauty and intelligence.

As he rounded the corner, Alejandro saw Arjan ahead.

He knew that there had been chemistry between Arjan and Sienna, and that it had gone on for years, but he wasn't sure how far things really had gone. Certainly, rumours had been rife, and the circuit had been full of gossip about Arjan and Sienna; it had been impossible to both escape and ignore it, even though he didn't know Sienna at that time. Alejandro's face clouded slightly as he heard the other man, his possible love rival, talking about her.

'She still won't talk to me! I mean, come on…'

His grooms were laughing with him, egging him on with his impressions. Alejandro stalked past, deliberately ignoring this arrogant Belgian as he discussed the woman he'd fallen for as if she were a piece of dirt.

'If only she'd put out earlier, then it might have been better for her…,' Alejandro heard Arjan say as he rounded the corner. It took all Alejandro's strength not to go back and punch him in his arrogant jaw.

Determinedly walking on, and arriving at his own stables, he saw that Marco was already there, checking the day's show horses and discussing timings with the grooms.

'Ciao Alejandro. Did you have a good evening?'

Alejandro just smiled at Marco, his eyes flashing as he recalled the feel of Sienna moving underneath him. He had left her sleeping off last night's sexual excesses in bed and was already looking forward to a returning to the bed for a pre-show sexual workout; God, he loved these late starts to the championships!

'Great. You?'

'Quiet…,' Marco studied Alejandro's face. There was something different there, a look that he had not seen since Saudi. 'Do you know if Sienna is here yet?' he asked idly. As Alejandro tried to hide the smile that crossed his face, Marco's suspicions were confirmed. 'And, how is she?' he added, laughing as he clapped his friend on the back.

'I don't know what you mean,' said Alejandro, hiding another smile and blushing slightly as he went into the filly's stable, checking her legs for any knocks or bumps.

By the time they left Dubai, Alejandro and Sienna were unofficially a couple. With the hotel so busy, it was easy to be able to come and go unseen between each other's rooms, and rather than socialise in the bar until 1am, they would each go in for drinks and leave within 20 minutes of each other before meeting up. With the classes starting at 3pm, this left plenty of time for making love and talking to each other about their hopes and dreams, for now and the future. The moment he had seen Sienna in the mall in Saudi Arabia, their fate had been sealed. All they had to do was keep it a secret for now, just until Alejandro had told his ex-wife and arranged with his boss that his family would not be sent back to Spain. While keeping secrets were something notoriously difficult to do in the Arabian industry, Alejandro was hoping beyond hope that this would not get out, not yet. He knew that the conversation with his boss would not be an easy one, nor with his ex-wife, but he hoped against hope that he would be able to talk them both round. Already, Alejandro could not imagine a life without Sienna, and it scared him just how quickly and deeply he had fallen for her.

21

Unfortunately, Alejandro didn't have to wait long before he and Sienna were discovered. Feeling overjoyed with her newfound love, Sienna decided to, for once, stay on and enjoy the Sharjah Show. An International B Show, Sharjah is found between Dubai and Ajman and is one of the seven emirates that make up the United Arab Emirates, the others being Abu Dhabi, Umm Al Quwain, Fujairah and Ras Al Khaimah. With Sharjah being a dry state, many that attended the show chose to stay in nearby Ajman, with the sumptuous Kempinski Hotel Ajman being the hotel of choice.

Persuading Sue to come and stay with her, rather than venture the 180km or so back to Abu Dhabi each night after the show, Sienna checked into the hotel. The Kempinski really was a stunning hotel and with access to a private beach, and thus the clear waters of the Arabian Gulf, surrounded by white sands, it was an ideal location for a break, albeit it one centred around a horse show.

'Wow, what a room!' Sue said as they opened the doors to the first of two neighbouring rooms. Stepping out on to the balcony, Sue breathed in the fresh sea air and felt glad that she had agreed to stay over. A little bit of luxury every now and again did the world of good.

Smiling at her friend, Sienna opened the door to her room and caught her breath. For there, scattered over the bed, were hundreds of rose petals. Next to the bed was an ice bucket, with a bottle of Laurent-Perrier Rosé ready to be opened. As Sienna allowed the door to close behind her, the telephone next to the bed rang.

'I'll be there in three minutes,' Alejandro said. Sienna

could hear the smile in his voice as she replaced the receiver. Putting her bags down, she waited for the knock at the bedroom door, with a smile of her own on her face.

A few hours later, Sienna reached across the dishevelled bed and rang Sue next door.

'Ah, there you are!' laughed Sue. 'I wonder what you possibly could have been up to!'

Sue was one of the only people that knew about Sienna and Alejandro, and she was more than happy to keep her friend's secret. Heaven knows, after all that Arjan put her through last time Sienna was in the country, she deserved some happiness.

'We're getting hungry and wondered about heading down to the Bukhara for dinner? Half an hour?'

Sue readily agreed, and very soon, the three of them were sat in Bukhara, a beautifully decorated Indian restaurant where the menus come on carved pieces of wood and the scent of the tandoori-inspired cooking mixes with the smells of the Middle East to create a potent mix. A favourite with the showing community, Alejandro knew that they were taking a risk eating together so publicly, but felt that, with Sue there as well, they should be safe enough to be seen as just 'talking shop'.

With the low lighting and candles on the table, the three sat down in a corner and surveyed the menu, with Alejandro also casting an eye over the wine list. Most of the champagne earlier had been licked off rather than drunk, he recalled, smiling wryly to himself, and he fancied a good bottle of red.

Hearing the sound of laughter coming through the door, Alejandro was dismayed to look up and see Arjan, Leap, and John come into the restaurant. Taking the table on the other side of Bukhara to them, Arjan sat in the seat

239

opposite and it was only when he looked up and saw Alejandro, Sienna and Sue that he reacted. A dark cloud fleetingly passed over his face, before a slow smile began to play around his mouth.

Wondering what mischief he could be thinking up, Alejandro's alarm grew as he saw Arjan order a round of Penicillins. Dragging his attention back to his own table, Alejandro hazily selected some food and wine off the menu before glancing back towards Arjan. Lighting a cigarette, never taking his eyes off Sienna, Arjan blew the smoke towards the ceiling and downed his drink in one.

A few rounds later, and Arjan was feeling vengeful. He had no horses to show in Sharjah but, angry with the world, he wanted to be there and to cause as much trouble as possible. He had noticed the way that Sienna and Alejandro had looked at each other in Saudi Arabia, seen their closeness in Abu Dhabi and even more in Dubai, and now here they were, dining together in Ajman. Yes, Sue was with them too, but a maiden aunt was hardly going to add any excitement to the evening. It had to be a cover for Sienna and Alejandro. Arjan was a poisonous, toxic mix of self-loathing and revenge, a heady cocktail and one that John and Leap were seemingly unaware of, as Arjan had grown so used to putting an impregnable mask on his emotions.

Seeing that Sienna's group had finished their meal and Alejandro was occupied with paying the bill, Arjan abruptly stood up and went over to where Sienna was sitting. Leap, glancing around, and unaware to that point that Sienna was there, tried to get up and follow Arjan, but John pulled him back down.

'Let him deal with it. It's the only way he'll get over it and move on. God knows we are sick of hearing nothing but "Sienna" come out of his mouth for the past few years… Come, more drinks!' John said, calling the waiter over as an afterthought. He had a feeling Arjan would be needing at least one after this.

Sienna and Sue both had their backs to the room and so when Sienna felt a pair of hands on her shoulders, she immediately thought that they belonged to Alejandro. Smiling, she began to lean back but almost immediately, caught a whiff of cigarette smoke as someone moved down to whisper in her ear. Flinching, she tried to pull away, but the pair of hands held her roughly down in her chair.

Finally, Arjan had the chance to go in for the kill, something he had wanted to do ever since he realised he had lost Sienna all those months ago.

'Sit there and listen, you frigid bitch,' Arjan muttered. 'I know what's going on with you and Alejandro. I know he's fucking you. And I know that could cost him his job – and his family. So what's it to be, Sienna? One night with me so that I can get what I want, and what you owe me, you little cock tease, or I blow your relationship with him wide open.'

Sue gasped in horror, not only at Arjan's words, but at the menace with which he said them. The force he was pushing Sienna into her seat with was intense and she could see Sienna's skin pale under his hold. With a cry, Sue turned anxiously in her seat towards where Alejandro was paying.

Immediately, Alejandro crossed the short distance to where they were sitting, just as Leap also ran over to Arjan.

'Arjan, come on. Leave them,' said Leap, putting a cautionary hand on Arjan's arm.

'Fuck off Leap! This is nothing to do with you. Sienna and I are just talking, aren't we Sienna?'

Not waiting for an answer, Alejandro grabbed Arjan by the arm and pushed him away from Sienna.

'You've just confirmed my thoughts – you are fucking her, aren't you?'

Alejandro glanced over to Sienna, who shook her head ever so slightly.

'I think you need to take your friend outside and sober him up,' Alejandro said to Leap. 'Ladies…'

Deliberately putting his hand on the small of Sue's back, he led the two ladies from Bukhara and out back up to their rooms. Shaking violently, Sienna had red marks on her shoulders where Arjan had put his hands.

'It's nothing. Don't fuss,' she said as Alejandro showed concern. 'I need to sleep.'

Shutting both Sue and Alejandro out of her room, Sienna shut the door on them and fell, shaking, on to her dishevelled bed. When would Arjan get out of her life, once and for all? Rubbing the marks on her shoulder left by Arjan's hands in a bid to get rid of them, Sienna wished that Arjan were as easy to remove. Lying down on her bed, Sienna just stared at the ceiling, wishing that she had never become involved with Arjan, and wondering why he wouldn't let her go after all this time. Reaching for her phone, she messaged Alejandro.

'See you tomorrow - I love you xxx'

Sighing, Sienna fell into a troubled and restless sleep.

The Sharjah Equestrian Club had a vast, indoor arena and the VIP area was always a grand affair found amid concrete, versatile surroundings. Huge, plush gold chairs and sofas were lined up in rows, with a small dark wooden table between each set of seating. Chilled water bottles on doilies, bowls of sweets and nuts, plates of dates, plates and forks, and show catalogues and pens were on the tables, all ready for people to help themselves to as they arrived to watch the show. The biggest sponsors, and the most senior of the Middle Eastern royal families, took the seats in the very front rows, allowing them easy access to the arena to either collect or present prizes. Behind them, still in the VIP area, sat those heavily involved in the industry, and Alejandro had arranged for Sienna and Sue to have some passes. As they sat down on a sofa as soft as a cloud, uniformed waiters carried trays of food and fruit cocktails around, offering people traditional Middle Eastern fayre to enjoy as they watched the horses head into the arena.

Today was Saturday, championship day. As with all the shows, the championships were always a high-profile affair but like Paris, Sharjah had an end of season feel to it being the last show in the Middle East before everyone headed west to Europe. The result of this was a more relaxed atmosphere but anticipation for the gold, silver and bronze honours was still very much there.

Sienna and Sue looked through the catalogue, noting the horses that had impressed during the two days of showing, and watched the action unfold below them.

Alejandro had kept a discreet distance from both Sienna and Sue since the first night, when they had arrived in Ajman. Furious that Arjan had uncovered his secret affaire with Sienna, Alejandro hoped that no one else had realised. Talking anxiously on the phone to his boss, he realised that he had got away with it for now, but he knew that both he and Sienna would need to be a lot more careful in the future. It also underlined how important it was that he was able to speak to his ex-wife as soon as possible and to get something sorted. He knew that he needed to make things official between him and Sienna, and soon.

Rin had arrived in Sharjah early on Saturday morning, ready to see the best of the show and also speak to Sienna about a new project for her farm. Sitting next to Sienna on a chair, with the table in between them, she laughed as she saw a group of girls hanging around Peter.

'They love your English commentator,' she chuckled.

As the brass band prepared itself to make its way into the ring, Rin caught sight of Arjan, lurking by the entrance. Always able to read Arjan's mood, having spent so many years with him, Rin was shocked to see a black expression on his face, which gave away just how angry he was and, as he fell over his own feet, she realised that he was also extremely drunk – a volatile combination. Just as she was about to say something to Sienna, the band started up and made their way, not quite marching in time, into the arena.

Arjan, full of bitterness towards Sienna and Alejandro, had stayed up drinking the night before and he arrived at the showground in a dangerous, drunken mood. Scowling and growling at everyone he passed, people stayed out of his way. Having transferred some whiskey to a water bottle, Arjan was openly swigging the liquor as if it were apple juice.

As the officials made their way to the arena to stand before the band and officially introduce the show, Arjan seized his chance. Jumping into the arena, where the brass band were preparing to play the UAE National Anthem, Arjan began to grab the instruments and throw them around, crashing drums and trumpets to the ground.

'You are all losers!' he shouted to the shocked VIP area as officials came running in from all sides of the arena to try and catch him.

'Fuck you all!' he shouted, as he knocked over a band member and raced around the ring. Everyone stood, ready for the National Anthem, shocked into silence by what they were seeing before him. Those that knew, loved, and loathed Arjan could only stand there watching in horror as he created carnage before his eyes. Leap, who had been sitting up in the stands with a Middle Eastern client, tried to run down and into the arena, but his way was blocked by security, who had appeared as if from nowhere. Looking over to the VIP area, Leap could see the various Royal Princes of the Middle East and their families being hurried out of an emergency exit and groaned, putting his head in his hands as he realised that his friend had finally imploded.

Peter, deciding that things were getting out of hand, made his way towards where Arjan was currently standing.

'Arjan, mate…'

Peter never made it any further in his sentence as Arjan turned and yelled at him. 'You fucked her too! I know you did!' he cried, as he punched Peter in the face, sending him flying backwards, down and on to the sandy arena floor.

Running sideways, sticking his fingers up at the VIP audience, Arjan finally fell over his own feet and ended up face down in the sandy surface of the arena. The officials jumped on him and dragged him back to the collecting ring. Arjan's richest Middle Eastern client was already waiting for him as Arjan was pulled, kicking and bucking, out of the ring.

'How dare you insult us and our women so much! I am booking you a one-way ticket to America. I suggest that you use it and never come back here. You are a disgrace.'

With that, the client walked off, and security dragged Arjan, who was still bucking and kicking, to a waiting car and threw him into the back seat.

Thirty minutes later, the car pulled up at Dubai Airport. The security man, who had travelled with them, opened the door and threw Arjan out on to the pavement, chucking his rucksack after him, which Leap had had the foresight to throw into the car before the doors slammed shut.

Lying sprawled on the pavement, Arjan watched the door of the black Mercedes slam shut. As it sped off, leaving him choking in exhaust fumes and nausea, a very drunk Arjan hazily wondered whether his career was over. Realising that people were stopping and staring, some even taking photographs of him on their phones, he struggled to his feet and made his way into the terminal.

America. After all the trouble he had endured in Europe over the previous years, it seemed like this could well be a golden ticket out of here. Throwing his rucksack over his back, which contained just his mobile phone, his wallet, and his passport, with everything else in the hotel room back in Ajman, Arjan made his way to check in. Mentioning his client's name at the Emirates check in desk, Arjan noticed a look of alarm pass over the check in attendant's face, before he was issued with an economy ticket to Boston. Barely registering anything, he staggered off to security.

Boarding the plane an hour later, Arjan gazed unseeingly out of the window at the Middle Eastern land vanishing beneath him underneath cloud cover, the enormity of what he had done slowly beginning to hit him – along with the world's biggest hangover. Europe and the Middle East would be closed forever to him now. His reputation was in tatters and he was all but through in the Arabian world. As he realised that he might never find work again, and he had thrown away the life he had worked so hard for, he groaned aloud and shoved his fists into his eyes, alarming the passengers all around him. In a bitter twist of irony, the woman sat next to him got some rose hand cream out of her bag and began to rub it into her skin, releasing the aroma that reminded him so painfully of Sienna. As his groan turned into a primal scream, the plane continued on its journey, ignoring Arjan's pain and anguish, and taking him to an America he never wanted to see; not like this.

Back at the showground, the organisers had tried to

carry on with the championships as best they could. Everyone was in a state of shock. Sienna, distraught, had been taken back to Sue's house along with Peter, who was nursing a black eye. Alejandro had quietly whispered to Sienna that he had better stay where he was, and he would call her later. Briefly touching her hand, he marched back to the collecting ring to check on his horses, which were standing there patiently waiting for their now much delayed championship.

Rin, who had been at the show to wow new clients as well as talk to Sienna, felt a moment's sadness that Arjan had fallen from grace so much. Where it had all gone wrong for him, she could not say, but she knew that the events of her frolicking with Yves had not helped and had probably been the start of the incredibly self-destructive journey that Arjan had been on. Shrugging off any feelings of guilt that she may have felt, she got in the car and made her way to Sue's house, wanting to check in on Sienna and also craving some European normality away from prying eyes.

Guy, watching from the sidelines, was briefly shocked before smiling at such a dramatic fall from grace. He didn't allow himself long to gloat, however, as he turned his attention back to Bint Sanatra. If she took Gold here, it would be a clean sweep of all the Middle Eastern shows, something that had never been accomplished before, and he was thrilled when the pair was called forward as Gold Champion. Leaving the arena, past band members still shocked at Arjan's outbreak, Guy headed straight for the airport and home, not bothering to give Arjan a second thought. However, he saw Arjan at the airport, limply making his way through the gate to board his plane. Guy stood and watched, a twisted smile on his face. Finally, his greatest rival was out of the way – for good.

As for Leap, he made his way back to the hotel, and

ordered a bottle of whiskey for his friend. Goodness knows when they would meet again. Raising a glass to the skies, Leap knew that he had his own business and reputation to think about, but he felt sad anguish that Arjan had fallen so dramatically from favour.

'Safe travels, my friend,' he said, as he poured another glass and looked to up to the increasingly inky-black skies.

22

Returning to Europe, which for once was enjoying a warm spring, Rin readied herself for the season ahead. She was excited about the horses that she had to show this season and also the new centre that she was opening up in Australia. It was a gamble, but it was one that she felt she could pull off – with the support of friends and clients, of course.

The first thing on her list was to have a new brochure done for the farm and she fired off a text message to a friend, arranging a photo shoot for the coming weekend, weather allowing. She then sent another message to Sienna, asking if she could visit the farm anytime soon. Rin left the house and headed outside, feeling the sun warming her face – her training centre, Arabian Elite, was finally just where it should be, on the up.

As she made her way outside, thinking back to when Arjan had found her and Yves together, all those years ago, her mobile phone vibrated in her pocket. It was Sienna, saying that she could visit anytime in the next two weeks. Smiling, Rin replied to book a flight to Germany as soon as possible and that she would pick her up from the airport.

As she walked through the barn, Rin reflected how funny it was that Sienna had gone from someone she didn't really know, and wasn't very sure of, to someone that she liked. The time Rin spent with Arjan seemed so long ago now, and she was glad that Sienna, while hurt and humiliated, had not been destroyed by him. Arjan truly seemed to turn all he touched to rust, and she couldn't help but wonder how he would get on in America. Looking back, Rin knew that she would forever be embarrassed by her dalliance with Yves but in hindsight, she realised it was a necessary step she'd had to go through to get her to finally shift Arjan out of her life.

Pausing by Raafid's stable, Rin patted him. He stood there quietly, eating hay from a net, and dropping most of it over the door as he turned his head to survey his barn with every mouthful. Scooping up the hay, Rin threw it over the door to him and patted him some more. He had a big season ahead, with lots of visiting mares. Since his big win in Menton last summer, as well as his win in Paris, lots of breeders had booked their mares to him and she had already had to collect and freeze a lot of semen for export.

'You're in for a fun time, my boy!' she smiled as, giving him one final pat, she moved on down the barn.

In the stable next to him was a two-week old filly foal, sired by Raafid. Rin liked to keep her horses as naturally as possible and so she stabled stallions near their progeny for the first few weeks. This filly was beautiful. Also black, she had a single white star and four white socks. She was bred and owned by the DuPont's, and Marcia, in particular, was delighted with her.

'We have to come up with a good name,' she kept saying to Rin who, being suspicious, had not chosen a name before the foal was born as it went against Bedouin beliefs. The DuPont's had, however, registered "DP" as their suffix, with those letters going after the name of all the horses that they would breed. Marcia kept phoning Rin with suggestions, and the trainer was delighted at how much interest these owners were taking with their horses.

For now, the filly was known as 'bint', the Arabic word for daughter, with 'ibn' meaning son. Looking at the filly, Rin was certain that a star had been born, a fact that only added to her excitement. Raafid had proved her early faith in him and once again, Rin counted her blessings that it was the DuPonts who had ended up purchasing this incredible horse, thus securing him a home for life. Watching the filly play, Rin headed back to the house with a huge smile on her face. Finally, life had gone full circle again and she was truly back where she belonged.

Leap sat in the walled garden at his farm, watching Aria LA parade before him. He was devastated by the loss of his friend to America and, in spite of constant messages, neither he nor anyone else had heard a word from Arjan since he had been unceremoniously thrown out of Sharjah.

Leap blamed Sienna. He knew that he shouldn't, but it was easier to put the blame at her door rather than look into himself. Deep down, Leap knew that he had a part to play in Arjan's downfall; that if he had not led his friend astray so much, he would probably still be here in Belgium, getting ready for the season ahead. For over 20 years, Leap and Arjan had been partners in crime and Leap felt lost without him. John was not the same – he had his wife and children, and his idea of a good time was a dinner party with other couples, talking about local schools. Leap missed Arjan's high jinks, his wicked sense of humour, his way with the ladies, and the fact that he was as close as a man was to his brother. Leap knew that life had changed for him as well as Arjan, but he knew that he had to try and pick up the threads of his life and build it back again.

Lighting a cigarette, Leap took another look at his filly. Now three years old, she was still unshown. Arjan had kept saying that she wasn't ready. Watching Aria LA, Leap noted how elegant she was, so effortlessly graceful, and that she carried herself so well. Studying her for a moment longer, before raising his eyes to the sky, Leap made a decision. Reaching into his jacket, he pulled out his phone and began searching through the numbers.

Two days later, Rin opened up a stable door and tied a fresh hay net up in the corner. Any moment, she knew that Leap would be arriving with his filly. His call had come as a complete shock. She had heard rumours that Leap had bred an amazing filly a few years ago, but as Arjan had not shown her, all thoughts of her had long been forgotten.

Rin acknowledged that it had taken a lot for Leap to call her. She realised that a lot of water had passed under the bridge since she and Arjan had split up, and even since she had first tried to seduce Leap all those years ago. However, Leap was very much Arjan's biggest supporter. She knew that Leap must have swallowed a lot of pride before he picked up his phone. In many ways, she was flattered that, in spite of everything, Leap had chosen her over the other trainers. Rin was prepared to let bygones be bygones and forget all the years and months that Leap had spent telling anyone who listened how she was a rubbish trainer.

Hearing the sound of a small lorry pull into the yard, Rin went outside to meet them.

'Rin.'

'Leap.'

The two looked at each other for a moment, before Leap grinned and held out his arms.

'It's been a long time,' he said as he hugged her. 'Now. Are you ready to see this year's World Champion Filly?'

As Rin nodded, Leap undid the lorry and led Aria LA out. Rin just stood and stared.

'Leap, over the years, you have been wrong about so many things,' she began, her face breaking into a big smile. 'But for once, I think that you just might be right.'

Long after Leap had left, and Aria LA was safely ensconced in her stable, wrapped up in a slicker, rug and bandages to both protect and hide her beauty, Rin picked up her phone and rang Sienna.

'I have a very special project for you,' she enthused. 'Only I best not tell the owner yet that I will be dealing with you… It's Leap and Aria. he's done it – Leap has done it, and he's bred the next big thing.'

Over the phone, standing in her kitchen in London making a cup of tea, Sienna felt her stomach flip as she knew that she would have to work with Arjan's best friend once more. The only comfort was that Alejandro was in constant touch, and she felt that neither Leap nor Arjan could hurt her anymore. The time that she had spent with Alejandro in the Middle East had cemented their feelings for each other and in the aftermath of Arjan's eviction, Alejandro had become almost territorial over Sienna.

Hanging up on Rin, Sienna was thoughtful. She messaged Alejandro to tell him the latest twist.

Don't worry, my love. Your professionalism will shine through, and soon Leap will love you like we all do xxx

Grinning, and reassured, Sienna replied, more interested in the 'love' part of the message than anything about Leap. That was for another day.

Abandoning the tea, Sienna poured herself a glass of red wine and she sat back on the sofa to face-time Alejandro. The sound of laughter was soon ringing out around her flat, Sienna's eyes sparkling with happiness at that this amazing man was making her way into her life and, even more so, into her heart.

23

Alejandro and Sienna had arrived in the south of France two days early for the show, which was admired by many and run on the seafront of the Pearl of France, Menton. Having enjoyed a night in Monaco, Alejandro had driven the coast road to Menton, with Sienna feeling like Grace Kelly as they sped in their hired open-top sports car alongside the Mediterranean Sea.

Since they had arrived, a few people had seen them together and the rumour mill was in overtime about whether this was the next hot couple on the circuit. With neither Sienna nor Alejandro confirming or denying their relationship, everyone was trying to get proof of their status, eager to be the first one to break it to their friends that Sienna, the elusive British rose, had been ensnared at last. Both Sienna and Alejandro knew that they had to be careful, that there was so much at stake with his family. He had not yet had a chance to speak to his boss in Bahrain to see what could be done, although Pasha had agreed, in theory, to each of them moving on, she didn't yet know that he already had. Alejandro deeply loved Sienna and he knew that she was his future. For now, they just had to try and keep things discreet until he could get home and talk to his boss.

Checking into the Hotel Napoléon, Alejandro surprised Sienna by booking them into a suite. The Cocteau Suite, named after the French writer Jean Cocteau, author of *Beauty and the Beast*, was light and airy, with two sofas by the window as well as a balcony. Walking out onto the balcony, Sienna took in the beautiful blue sea, settled in the bay beneath her, as well as the sights and the smells of the

Mediterranean. She had her own room as well, booked as a precaution, but this beautiful space was to be their home for the coming days.

The couple had deliberately arrived in Menton before the show started, giving them the chance to spend some time together before the masses arrived. Knowing that discretion would be necessary from Saturday morning onwards, Sienna was revelling in the thought that she would get to spend some secret time with Alejandro away from prying eyes.

The next two days passed by very happily. Exploring the area, and venturing into Italy, Alejandro and Sienna enjoyed long, sunny days, picnics under the shade of trees found in fields off the beaten track, mountain views, and making love in the sun as well as in their room.

Thursday night saw them enjoying a final evening in Menton town before the flights began to arrive bringing in the many international visitors. Taking a moonlit walk on the beach at 11pm, Sienna and Alejandro walked hand-in-hand, barefoot through the gentle waves at the edge of the shore. Pausing, Sienna turned her face to the moon overlooking the sea, and Alejandro stole his arms around her, pulling her to him and kissing her neck. To any passer-by, they were just a romantic couple in love; and as they stood there under the stars, the sound of the waves crashing against the shore the only interruption against their thoughts, Sienna and Alejandro truly were just that. After standing there, arms around each other, for half an hour or more, Alejandro gently took Sienna's hand and led her back to the hotel.

Sienna woke early with a smile on her face. Last night with Alejandro had been magical and she ached in all the right places. Stretching sleepily, she looked across at the sleeping figure of Alejandro next to her, noting the way his eyelashes gently grazed his cheek and his slow, steady breathing.

As the light Mediterranean sun crept in from around the curtains, Sienna stretched. Wide awake, she decided to leave Alejandro to sleep and she crept out of bed and went to the bathroom. Turning on the big waterfall shower, she cleaned her teeth while the water warmed up to the right temperature. Glancing at herself in the mirror, Sienna hardly recognised herself. Her eyes were bright and shining, she had colour in her cheeks, and she seemed to glow with happiness. Smiling to herself, she stepped into the shower, closing the glazed glass door behind her.

Humming gently, Sienna began to wash her long brunette locks, shampoo coursing down her body as it was swept away by the torrent of water. With her arms up and her fingers entangled in her hair, Sienna felt a pair of hands creep around her waist, moving up to her breasts and holding them while a pair of cool lips kissed her shoulder.

'Good morning...,' Alejandro murmured as he covered her shoulders in a steady stream of subtle kisses. 'I think you've missed a bit...'

Reaching down with his hands, he found Sienna's sodden bush and moved his fingers in between her lips. Groaning, Sienna turned around to meet him and Alejandro pushed her up against the wall of the shower, parting her legs with his knees as he did so. Bending to kiss her breasts, Alejandro grabbed the bottle of shower gel and poured some into his hands. Rubbing her slowly and sensuously all over, Alejandro kept his eyes on her as he gently massaged her arms, her stomach, her hips and her back.

Leaning in to kiss her, Alejandro crouched down slightly so that he could get a better angle and, slowly and gently, entered her. Sienna gasped, raising one leg to wrap around him and feeling him thrust deeper into her. A leisurely morning fuck swiftly turned into a passionate moment, with the intensity overtaking both of them.

As the torrent of water cascaded down and over them, Alejandro felt his orgasm grow and with a few final thrusts into her, he came.

Resting his head on her shoulder, Sienna kissed his now-soaking hair, relishing the feel of him against her, inside her. Smiling, she whispered into his ear, 'And good morning to you too...'

An hour later, the couple sat on the balcony, enjoying the feel of the sun on their faces as they finished their breakfast. Sienna was scowling at her laptop, trying to understand some vague instructions from a client who seemed to want a short film made about their horses that afternoon – when the horses were in Brazil and not in show condition.

Alejandro laughed as he watched her, 'You do look cute when you're cross Sienna!'

Smiling, Sienna relaxed slightly, looking across at Alejandro reading his newspaper; unlike most men she knew, he lingered more on the business pages than the sports pages.

'I'm not cross. I just get fed up with clients and their unreasonable demands.'

'Relax – they are just that. Demands. Now finish your coffee and let's go for a walk.'

After another blissful day over the border together in Italy, Sienna and Alejandro strolled hand-in-hand along the seafront at Menton. Once again, the moon was sparkling on the water and the midnight-blue sky was filled with twinkling stars. From the bars littered around the edge of the sand, laughter carried up through the night towards them.

Having enjoyed a wonderful Italian feast in the dimmed light of the Coté Sud Restaurant, Alejandro and Sienna left and slowly walked arm in arm along the top of the promenade. Knowing that most people in the Arabian community would be in the bars below, they felt safe as they strolled leisurely along, knowing that few people, if any, would see them.

Stopping some distance away from the last bar on the sea front on the Porte de France, Alejandro turned to face Sienna, gently running his finger down her cheek. Under the moonlit skies, she almost looked ethereal, her blue eyes looking like deep pools of water in the night. For the hundredth time, Alejandro counted his blessings that he had met Sienna. He had never felt this way before and he knew that they belonged together.

As Alejandro tenderly leaned in to kiss her, he was aware of giggling behind them and a flash. Yves and Pierre had secretly been following them and as the couple turned to face the noise, there was another flash as Yves' iPhone went off in their faces, temporarily blinding them.

With a cry of rage, Alejandro stepped forward towards the laughing men, who just turned on their heels and ran down the steps, back to the bar, shouting 'Alejandro and Sienna! It's true!' Sienna stood, staring, feeling the happiness that had surrounded her the past months evaporate away. Alejandro was an intensely private man and his position, managing a farm in the Middle East, meant that any relationship had to either be kept very low key or very, very official. While she knew that Alejandro was finally going to speak to people when he got home and had already asked if he could have a meeting, they had just been pre-empted. With Yves and Pierre now in possession of photographs of them together, Sienna knew that it was only a matter of time before they would be on Facebook with themselves duly tagged and everyone in the Arabian world watching, all eager for the latest scandal and gossip.

'Sienna…,' Alejandro began as he turned to face her, but was immediately interrupted by his mobile phone ringing. Taking it out of his suit pocket, a cloud passed over his face as he registered the number of his boss. Swearing under his breath, he looked at Sienna as he answered the phone.

'Si?'

After just a few short minutes, during which time Alejandro stayed incredibly quiet and Sienna was lulled into a trance by the sound of waves crashing gently on the shore, Alejandro hung up.

'They sent him the photographs. He already knows. I have to go.'

Turning, Alejandro took a step and then stopped before turning quickly back to Sienna. He took her in his arms and kissed her brutally and passionately, before jogging away from her back along the Quai Bonaparte to the hotel. As Sienna watched him go, a sense of deep foreboding overcame her. Alone on the promenade, the sound of merry laughter carrying on the breeze, Sienna leaned heavily against the railing. As if in a stupor, she walked along the promenade and down to the seafront, away from the bars, where she sank on to her knees in the still-warm mixture of shells, stone and sand. Oblivious of the pain as they cut her knees, she just stared into the distance, out to sea, seeing visions of Alejandro in her mind's eye.

Back in his hotel, Alejandro paced in his room, arguing with his boss. He was not prepared to give up Sienna, but the implication was clear: continue this relationship and incur the wrath of his more senior bosses or give her up and settle for the easy life. There was a third option, too; marry her. But this was something neither could consider right now, and besides, Alejandro's divorce was still hanging over them and he knew that his ex was not just going to give up that easily. Everything had been so amicable between them since they split up but as soon as she learned that he was in love with someone else, jealousy raised its head and she refused to let him even speak to the children on the phone when he was travelling. Frustrated, Alejandro knew that an impossible choice faced him.

'But it is a serious relationship… You can't… But I… Yes. I understand.'

Alejandro hung up the phone and stared out of the window. He saw Sienna walk along the pavement, head hanging, shoes in her hand, and looking forlorn. Before she could look up, he angrily pulled the curtains closed and turned his back on the window, balling his fists into his eyes, choked at the decision that lay ahead.

Sienna closed the door to her room. Alejandro had been very careful to book two rooms, but they had spent all their time in his, enjoying the king size bed and the fabulous room service on offer. Her room, by contrast, was barren and void of life. The bed covers were still firmly tucked in, apart from the one corner opened by the turn-down service, the welcome note and chocolate were still on the pillow, and the television was still running its welcome screen. Sienna's suitcase lay half-closed in the corner, clothes spilling out and over the sides from where she had randomly grabbed items for their days out. The room looked soulless after the man-made warmth of the suite she had shared with Alejandro, and it reflected the emptiness that she now felt in her heart.

Not bothering to turn on any lights, Sienna slid down the back of the door, rested her head on her arms and, hugging her knees to her, silently began to cry. The irony crossed her mind that this was not the first time she had been in this exact position inside a hotel room, but the pain she felt this time was one of her heart potentially breaking. She knew better than to contact Alejandro now. He needed to think, to consider, and she needed to give him space. All she wanted to do was run down the corridor and pound on his door, tell him how much she loved him and plead with him, but she knew better than to push things. Once again, the Arabian horse world had interfered in her life, just for its own pleasure, and once again, she feared that she had come out the worse for it.

The show went by in a blur. Sienna had been tagged by at least fifty different people on Facebook as the photographs Yves had taken went viral across the global Arabian community. With both of them being so well known in the industry, everyone was intrigued by what was going on and everyone had their piece to say. While a few people called her a home wrecker, not knowing the truth about Alejandro's situation, the majority of the comments, which Sienna looked at in despair, seemed to suggest that the world was delighting in her fledgling relationship, the one which, ironically, these photos had seemed to destroy. Alejandro was full of officiousness, doing his job and hiding behind his Ray Ban shades. With a forced, grim smile on his face every time he went into the ring to collect the prizes, Alejandro was fixed and cold and no one dared to cross his path. Anyone that attempted to speak to him was studiously ignored and people were cut dead if they tried to block his path between the ring, the stables, the show and the hotel.

'Sienna!'

Alejandro was leaving the ring as he heard her name called. Scowling, he tried to identify who was talking to her. He needed to talk to her himself, but there had never been a quiet moment to take her to one side. He had nearly made his decision, but he wanted to give Sienna a chance to have her say. As he angrily stamped the sand off his shoes, he wondered once again why life had to be so difficult. And why people had to interfere in what was not their business.

'Sienna,' the voice was saying with a loud American twang. 'You must come and have dinner with us tonight darling. I have some clients over and you simply must meet them. No, I won't take no for an answer. We'll pick you up in an hour. Ciao.'

Catching her eye, Alejandro scowled at Sienna before realising it was not her fault. He smiled, too late, as Sienna had snatched her bag and fled back to the hotel. He paused, wondering whether to go after her. Shaking his head imperceptibly, Alejandro instead turned and headed down away from the show and that action and towards the beach. Here, he found a deserted bar with just locals for company. True to form in the Arabian world, but an act that was alien to him, oblivion was now Alejandro's only goal.

Sienna struggled through dinner with the American clients. Trying to be entertaining and engaging, but falling short of either, she decided that the best thing for her was to return back to the hotel and try again tomorrow to impress these important clients.

Feigning a migraine, Sienna assured them that she would be okay on her own and that the fresh air would do her good, and quietly began to make her way back to her hotel. Passing a bar on the seafront, she saw Yves and Leap outside, the former smoking a cigarette and talking animatedly into his phone. Spying her, Yves quickly ended his call, a broad grin on his face.

'Hello Sienna.'

Sienna didn't look at him, continuing to walk down the path, and ignoring him as best she could.

'Oh, come on!'

Sienna hesitated for just a second at Yves' words, which was all Leap needed to go in for the kill. While he felt sorry for Sienna, he hated what had happened to his friend and his anger spilled over towards her.

'How's Alejandro? Oh, not together anymore? Good – after all you did to Arjan!'

Laughing, the pair clapped each other on the back and headed back into the bar, calling to their friends to tell them about the latest pain inflicted on Sienna. Her own anger rising, Sienna flicked a quick V sign at their retreating backs before carrying on down the street. She was shocked that Leap had been so vicious, he was generally so laid back, but she knew that he blamed her for Arjan's deportation. Stung, she rushed back to her hotel and closed her ears to the laughter ringing out behind her.

Unknown to her, on the promenade above, Alejandro was hanging onto a lamp post for support, watching the exchange. He watched as Sienna carried on walking back to the hotel alone, her hand rising up to her face as if to wipe away tears. In his many years in this industry, he had faced heart against head dilemmas on countless occasions, but none as devastating as this: take what could possibly be true happiness with the girl he loved but at the risk of losing his job and the very real possibility that his family could be sent back to Spain, or lose Sienna but keep his job and continue providing financial security for his family. His Latino background made him proud and he hated the thought of not being able to provide for his children. But Sienna... He had never felt this way about anyone before.

Meet me tomorrow after the last championship.
We have to talk. xxx

Still watching her, Alejandro pressed 'send' on his phone and registered her picking up her phone before heading to the nearest bar. He couldn't face seeing the look on her face as she opened the message and read his words – all he wanted to do was forget about the hell he was in and return to a time before the world had found out about their love.

Impatient for the show to finish, Sienna tapped her fingers on the table. 'And the winner of the Best Female Head is…' Peter droned on, milking his position as commentator and all the glory – and groupies – that it brought him.

Deciding that she had had enough, Sienna leapt up from her seat and headed away from the show to a more deserted part of the seafront, out along the Porte de France and the Quai Napoleon and along the Promenade du Soleil. Seconds later, Alejandro joined her. Sienna's heart leapt.

'You should be watching the championships. You have horses in there.'

'I have an early plane to catch. My boat to take me to Nice leaves in 20 minutes. I guess they organised a boat to make sure I made it.'

'But you weren't meant to leave until tomorrow!'

'Things change,' Alejandro shrugged. 'Come. Let's walk.'

The pair headed away from the showground, walking as close together as they dared until they were out of sight. Looking over his shoulder to make sure they weren't being followed, Alejandro glanced at Sienna and then took her hand, pulling her to him. Reaching out with his arms, he pulled her into his embrace and tenderly kissed her forehead.

'Oh Sienna…'

Leading her down onto the beach, Sienna felt her stomach begin to turn and twist. Surely this wasn't it? She saw a boat sat there, the Middle Eastern flag flying in the bow, and she knew that the boat was meant for Alejandro. Glancing up at a plane flying overhead, Sienna noticed that the heat was just starting to leave the day and that the sun was slowly sinking.

'I love you Sienna,' Alejandro began.

Sienna smiled, opening her mouth to speak, but Alejandro put a finger on her lips.

'I love you Sienna. But I cannot be with you. I am sorry. You have no idea how sorry I am… But my children have to come first, there is no option. My happiness has to take second place to that. If I stay with you, then they will send my children back to Spain and I will hardly see them, and I need to be involved with their lives. I am so, so sorry. Please, please believe me when I say that I truly love you, and that this is the hardest decision I have ever had to make in my entire life…'

Gently, Alejandro kissed Sienna on the lips, savouring the moment and the feel of her soft lips below his, before looking sadly at her, drinking in the way her hair curled around her face, down to her breasts, memorising the exact shade of the blue of her eyes, burning it to his memory forever. Leaning in, he kissed her forehead and then walked away, heading to the jetty that would lead him to the waiting boat. Not daring to look back in case his resolve faltered, Alejandro stepped into the boat and, immediately, the engine fired up and the boat pulled away though the water, heading for Nice. Still he dared not look back, and his mouth was set into a grim line as he did his best to control his feelings in front of his boss's private secretary, who had travelled out with the boat to ensure that

Alejandro boarded it.

Sienna stood and watched him walk away from her, his broad back so taut in his sky-blue shirt, and felt her heart break as she realised that she would never put her arms around him again, or feel his body pressed to hers. Her lips, still slightly damp from his kiss, would never again be bruised by the passion building up between them. It was over. The realisation that he was gone hit her in the stomach, as she knew that he would, and could, never change his mind, that his young family would always come first.

Standing alone on the beach, the sun beginning to slowly dip low in the sky to embrace the sea, Sienna stared until the boat had long vanished from view. As the sun set around her, tears streamed silently down Sienna's face, and she continued to stand, staring out to sea. Her heart had not only been broken, it had been smashed into smithereens, and it hardened against those that had forced their hand, revealing their relationship before they were ready, and able, to tell the world. Before they had been able to clear the way to ensure that no one was hurt, and to ensure that they could happily and officially be together. Before they had a chance to tell the right people in their own time, and in the right way. Now, she was on her own, her heart broken. The tears would not stop falling, and slowly, Sienna sank once more on to the shingle shore, the warm waves of the Mediterranean lapping around her knees.

As the stars came out hours later, Sienna was still motionless on the beach, watching that distant point where Alejandro had disappeared from her, all alone and totally empty inside. Meanwhile, the sounds of cheers and laughter from the nearby bars echoed all around her, reinforcing just how truly alone she was.

24

After spending almost two months crying herself to sleep at night, Sienna came out of hibernation for the Polish National Championships and sale. She knew there was just the faintest chance that Alejandro would be there, but she also knew that it was more likely he would not and as she threw some clothes into her case, she tried to distance all thoughts of him from her mind.

Meanwhile, in another part of Europe, Sven grunted as he climbed off his boyfriend. A long night foaling a difficult mare had resulted in a huge row between them, each of them claiming that they knew what was best and neither listening to the other. These rows were slowly becoming more and more frequent, and Sven felt increasingly detached from his other half. Sex was still the only way that either knew to make things better and as Gerald lay there, panting as he got his breath back, Sven watched him as he pulled his jeans on, feeling a moment's revulsion towards him.

'I might have to go to Poland this weekend,' he said, not bothering to kiss him before he left the room. Lighting a cigarette between shaking fingers, he pulled his phone out of his back pocket and sent Sienna a message.

'Will you be in Poland?'
'Yes x'
'Great. See you there.'

Stopping to pat his dog, who was the only person who Sven genuinely seemed to give affection to these days, he made his way to his office and, fixing himself a double espresso, he booked a flight to Warsaw.

Poland was seen by many as the home of the Arabian horse. The horses bred there, especially at the famed State-run studs of Janów, Michałów and Białka, were world-renowned for their terrific movement and the white mares especially were famed for their ethereal beauty. Every August, the week-long event, Arabian Horse Days, drew visitors from the world over to the hallowed grounds of Janów Podlaski, found over 200km north-east of Warsaw and not far from the Russian border. This group of visitors formed a more genuine and dedicated group of Arabian horse lovers than at many of the shows and the Polish traditions were greatly enjoyed by everyone. The highlight of the week was the Pride of Poland, where a carefully selected group of mares went up for auction, often attracting bids between €500,000 and €1,000,000. Some Sheikhs had been known to pay well over a million euros, just to ensure that the coveted Polish beauty that year made her way to their barn rather than that of a rival's. While these larger studs in the Middle East vied to secure such mares, visitors from across the rest of Europe were just happy to take home an incredible broodmare, with fantastic bloodlines, to enhance their own breeding programme.

Much of the allure of the Arabian Horse Days was the charm of the location. The nearby village of Zaborek was where many people stayed, a quaint miniature village where Polish was the only language spoken and the laughter went on long into the night.

Sienna arrived at Warsaw Airport, her heart still broken from Alejandro's decision. Two months had not yet passed and as she went around every corner, she longed and dreaded seeing his face in equal measure.

Sven arrived in Warsaw minutes after Sienna. Spying her

across the luggage carousel, he noticed that Sienna had lost a lot of weight and that she looked pale and gaunt. Determined to cheer her up – and also share his woes about his declining relationship – Sven vowed that they would have a fun and decadent weekend. Calling over to her, Sven smiled at her before going around and giving her a huge hug.

'So good to see you! Got your bags? Good. I've got a car – let's go.'

Taking her arm, Sven led them out of the airport and, having found the hire car, headed for Zaborek. With the windows wound down full and Sven's iPod churning out Euro pop as they sped through the streets of Warsaw, Sienna felt her spirits lift for the first time in weeks.

Arriving at the showground that afternoon, Sven went straight to the free bar at the back of the VIP area and began to load himself up with vodka. He had left Sienna sitting with his American friends. The longer he spent in her company, the more he wanted to either kill Alejandro or Yves for breaking her heart. She was a shell of her normal self and seemed to just be functioning, barely going through the motions. There was no doubt that her business would suffer if she didn't pick herself up. And that would also impact on him, as they had lately been working together closely. He cared a lot about Sienna as a friend, but it was also very much in his interests to help her get back to her old self.

As he downed his vodka and looked around the girls chatting with their friends before the classes began, Sven marvelled at how many of his male friends had fallen under Sienna's spell. Wary of her at first, she had then fallen straight into the bracket of 'friend' for him and he looked at her purely in a brotherly way. It intrigued him how so many of his friends looked at her as something more. She had helped him so much during his difficult times with Gerald, and he wanted to make her smile. So many of his friends struggled to make a woman smile and feel special, and the only way that they could was to flirt with them and later, take them to bed. Maybe if one of his friends shagged Sienna, she would have a smile back on her face once more? Certainly, it was an idea…

Sienna sat still with her hand clenched tightly around the glass of vodka cranberry Sven had organised for her. Since she and Alejandro had split up, she hadn't drunk this combination and it brought memories flooding back. It painfully reminded her of that night in Dubai, the night that they had finally given in to their feelings.

'Well honey, my Arabians are the best in the world! You gotta come see them.'

Turning politely, Sienna smiled vaguely at Kris Green who was sat next to her. His was a line she had heard a hundred times before, and she always found that it was the buyers, not the breeders, who could never see the faults in their own horses. She would turn up at their farm, a huge marketing plan in mind based on all she had been told and then have to adjust the high-end ideas to mediocre horses.

Sven put his arm around her shoulder, making her jump.

'Sienna, I would like to introduce you to some new clients of mine, Sergei and Mikhail. They run the famed Karlov Stud in Russia. They are here with their trainer, Jesus Angelo, to buy some horses.'

As Sienna stood for the introductions, she shivered as she caught sight of the look in Sergei's eyes. The way he was looking at her filled her with a sense of menace; he wasn't just undressing her with his eyes, he had her across the table and was fucking her.

'Nice to meet you,' she said meekly, holding out her

hand and pulling herself together.

'The pleasure is all mine,' Sergei snarled as he took her hand in an unforgiving vice-like grip. His eyes were an icy steel-blue, his hair a white blond, and he was so well toned that his face had an almost skeletal appearance. Finally releasing her hand, Sergei penetrated Sienna with his stare and even after he had stepped back from her, he refused to look away.

Mikhail, by comparison, was softer in the face and body, with brown shady eyes that seemed closed off as Sienna looked at him. 'Muddy waters,' she thought to herself.

Unbeknown to most of those at the show, Sergei was the more sinister of the two men. Part of the underground Russian Mafia ring, he was merciless and did not stop until he had got what he wanted. His colouring added to his sense of menace; when he smiled, his eyes stayed cool and hateful, glaring at the subject until they agreed to anything. Mikhail was softer, brown-haired, brown-eyed, and more innocuous; you could quite easily miss him in a crowd and people regularly did. With such a talent, used to alerting Sergei that people were turning against him and needed to be dealt with, Mikhail was a strong part of the Russian team and was Sergei's right-hand man. He would go in with the softly, softly approach before Sergei stepped in for the kill.

Jesus stood in the background. He was an up and coming Portuguese trainer who had fallen in love with the Arabian horses on his frequent trips to Spain and was determined to get in on the action. At 5'8", dark and tanned, with huge dark brown eyes and a wicked glint in his eye, Jesus was 100% gay, but he would happily service the needs of a woman if it helped his career. He really would stop at nothing to achieve what he wanted – the lights, the glory and the garlands – and he didn't care who he trampled on and hurt in the process. He was known for trotting around the ring, the horse loose on the end of the rope, while he pranced alongside like Bambi's sister. Once seen, he was never forgotten.

For the past few months, he had been working for the Karlov Stud in Russia. The Siberian weather did not agree with his Latin love of all things hot but needs must. If he did this job well, he could lay claim to being the trainer who took the Russian horses back to the top of the show-ring. Besides, the supply of Slovakian grooms that made their way through the farm was too enticing to miss.

Sergei and Mikhail ran the stud between them; aggressive alpha males, they had little time for gay men, but they recognised Jesus' determination to get to the top, as well as his love for the vast sums of money that they put his way, and they knew that they could use him well to their own advantage. Truly a fearsome combination, Jesus learned quickly how to stay on the right side of his Mafia bosses, never pushing his luck and quickly carrying out whatever was asked of him regardless of his own personal feelings. He wondered whether he could add 'detachment' to his CV. It might help him when looking for his next job.

The three men stood there, two of them eyeing up the girls as they walked past in their short dresses, long bronzed legs shivering in the cool of the evening. Standing beside them and feeling uneasy, Sienna made to leave.

'No. I want to learn more about you.'

Sergei didn't ask, he commanded. Taking Sienna's arm by the elbow, he led her to an empty table at the back of the VIP area. Feeling uncomfortable, she frantically made "come and rescue me" eyes to Sven, but he was too busy helping Mikhail chat up two buxom blondes from Switzerland to notice her.

'There's nothing much to tell, really,' she stuttered. 'I come from England, I love horses, especially Arabians, and that's it.'

Sergei looked at her, assessing her.

'And is there a Mr?' he asked, casually glancing down at her left hand.

'No… There was – but not anymore.'

'So you are all alone….'

Sergei allowed the words to hang in the air, watching to see how much they hurt Sienna, waiting to see whether she allowed her emotions to come through to the surface or whether she would contain them.

'I guess…' she said sadly.

'Such a waste…" He paused again, allowing the words to linger once more.

"Come, let us drink vodka and watch horses! I want you with me all evening. Beauty and intelligence combined is a rare combination and I think we could work very well together, no?'

Sergei leaned into Sienna and it took all her strength not to shudder in horror at him. If he metaphorically had her across the table earlier, he now had her on her knees… Ignoring the shiver running through her, along with a deep sense of foreboding, Sienna meekly stood and followed Sergei to the bar where they joined Mikhail, Jesus, and an ever-excitable Sven.

'Sienna – look, this is the colt I have told you about! Etros! If all goes well, he will be coming to the Netherlands with us. What do you think? Come closer to the ring so that you can see him properly.'

Happy to lose herself in horse talk, Sienna concentrated on Sven and Etros, ignoring the menacing feeling of Sergei's eyes boring into the back of her head.

Etros went Polish National Champion Colt on the Sunday morning, much to the delight of Sven, who was bouncing up and down in his chair, puffing away furiously on his cigarette. This classy and huge-moving grey certainly wowed the international audience, as well as the judges, and as soon as the photographs had been taken and the colt had left the arena, Sven scuttled off to the stables to move the hoped for deal a little further along.

Sienna remained seated at the table, watching the mares competing for the golden title of Senior Female Champion. While Poland was admired the world over for all of its horses, it was the ethereal grey mares that everyone so easily fell in love with. Each foal born in Poland was given the same initial as the dam, and these families were known the world over through this letter. A beautiful ethereal grey mare called Emandoria, out of a mare called Emanda, is part of this 'E' line, known for its floating greys that had done so well the world over. Add the flamboyant, dark bays, mainly from the 'P' mare line and it was little wonder that people flocked here, year after year.

As the title winners were called forward, Sienna's thoughts turned to Alejandro. That first year when they had met, but barely knew each other, had included a lot of random encounters around the world. Janów Podlaski, with its beautiful tree-lined driveway and history found around every corner, had been one such place. With the show-ring contained by stands and VIP tents, Sienna had made her way to the back of the viewing area to get herself a drink between classes. Standing languidly at the bar was Alejandro, intently watching the horses from the previous class leave the arena. He was bidding on horses in the auction for his boss, and there was a relation in this class.

'Sienna!' seeing her standing next to him, Alejandro was all smiles. Swiftly calling the barman over to mix her a mojito, Alejandro and Sienna stood there for the rest of the day, talking about horses, life, and family, all the while sipping the extra-strong vodka cocktails. It was with great reluctance that Alejandro dragged himself away back to his hotel in Warsaw that night, while a rather tipsy Sienna went back to Zaborek.

Sitting watching the mare champions leave the arena, Sienna recalled that afternoon and felt as if another knife had been plunged into her heart. Would she ever get over Alejandro? Sighing deeply as the Best in Show horses came in, she seriously doubted it.

Sven, returning to the show, saw Sienna sat alone, deep in thought, and he went over to her.

'Come,' he said softly. 'Come and meet Etros, then we'll have lunch.'

Gently taking her arm, Sven led Sienna out the back of the VIP area and to the stables. Even though the show was over, in anticipation of that afternoon's auction, the stables were a hive of activity and it was easy to lose yourself to the world of Arabian horses as you wandered around the stables, checking out each horse.

Sunday in Poland was where all the action happened, as not only was the morning given over to the championships, the State Studs put some of their best mares, as well as some more average ones, up for auction. To own a Polish mare, bred at Michałów, Janów or Białka, was a dream for many people, and it was often through the silent sale that these dreams came true, not forgetting the frenetic main auction where bidding was high and vast sums of money were spent in the blink of an eye.

Sven had several clients all keen to bid on the horses, and after the Polish National Championships finished and he having taken Sienna to the lunch tent to dine with Kris Green, he spent much of his time on the phone, pacing up and down outside the stables and smoking cigarette after cigarette as he confirmed with his clients which horses they were bidding on, and how high he could go with those bids. He had hoped that Kris would get it together with Sienna, but there was clearly no chemistry between them.

Besides, Etros was Sven's key concern. By the famed Polish stallion Ekstern and out of one of the beautiful E-line mares at Michałów, Emanda, this two-year-old grey colt was all show and class, full of pizzazz and excitement. Available through the private auction, there was a lot of interest in him and Sven already had dark circles under his eyes having been kept awake the night before by nightmares that he had been outbid and that Etros went to another farm rather than that belonging to his rich clients. Sven knew that the chances of being outbid were slim, as he had an open cheque book, but in this world, nothing was guaranteed.

As the auction began, Sven's chain smoking increased, and Sienna found it slightly amusing to watch him. Kris, having promised Sven to keep an eye on her, stayed by her side. He, too, was bidding on a horse and decided that it would be fun to let Sienna place the bids. Having secured the mare he wanted, in spite of paying €10,000 more for her than planned, he arranged for more Polish vodka to be brought to their table and, keeping Sergei and Mikhail at arms' length as they gave him, too, a feeling of unease, Kris slowly and happily got drunk.

Sven, however, was a bag of nerves until Etros came in. Bidding was instant and it was fierce, and Sven thanked the heavens that he had the open cheque. Having secured the stallion for €750,000, it was the final moment before the hammer went down and another bid came in, pushing the price up to €800,000. Sven whipped his head around, trying to see where the bid had come from, but there was no clue.

Nodding, he added another €50,000 to the pot and the mysterious bidder came in again. Realising it was a telephone bid, and not knowing who he was bidding against, Sven dug deep and raised the bid on Etros to €1,000,000. Gasps and applause came from all angles, and Sven crossed his fingers that it was enough to secure this promising young colt. Sienna, too, crossed her fingers, anxious for her friend. But she need not have worried.

'Going once... Going twice... Sold!' the announcer almost rushed through, as if he, too, knew that Sven and his group of clients was going to be the better home for Etros. Everyone cheered, not least as it was rare for bidding to go over the one million mark. Sven was very popular, and there was little doubt that Etros would make his mark on Europe and, if the rumours were to be believed, the US as well. Sven jumped into the arena and, taking the lead rope from the Polish handler, he did a lap of honour with Etros. The photographers went mad, and Sienna and Kris were among many that gave this new partnership a standing ovation.

As a grinning, over-excitable Sven finally returned to the table, amid a hearty hale of backslaps and drinks being thrust in his hand, he hugged Sienna and arranged for yet another bottle of local vodka to be brought over to them.

It was a very bleary-eyed Sienna and Sven that boarded the coach to take them from the hotel to Janów the following morning. From there, having enjoyed a serene parade, they went to Białka before eventually arriving at Michałów the next day. Sven was happy to see Sienna relax finally and take more of an interest in her surroundings rather than just going through the motions as she had been since that day in Menton when her heart had been shattered. Kris had already flown home, as had Sergei and

Mikhail, and it was good just to have some time together, enjoying some of the best Arabian horses that this part of the world had to offer. As they sat either giggling in the back of the coach, enjoying shots in the bar together, or entranced by the horses shown before them, Sven felt like he was sat with his little sister, and she certainly drew out the best in him.

A text from Gerald, however, did burst Sven's bubble slightly. It seemed that his long-term boyfriend was finally showing signs of having had enough of being expected to be Sven's horse groom and secretary while Sven himself was off gallivanting around the world. The message was short.

We need to talk. I've had enough.'

Sven was not sure that Gerald would be there when he returned home. Pushing such thoughts to the back of his mind, he concentrated on keeping Sienna happy and occupied. He was busy checking out the gorgeous horses to be seen at each stud, making plans on which horse he could arrange to purchase for his clients next. Sven also had one eye on the gorgeous groom handling the horses; after all, he was only male …

25

By the time Aachen came around again, Sienna had finally eased her broken heart. She closed it off to those that had caused her so much pain, and as she packed, she included a bottle of single malt for Sven as a thank you for looking after her so well in Poland. After a week in the sunshine of that tranquil country, she finally felt more like her old self and she was back on track for the forthcoming busy Title Show season. She also included in her packing a vibrant red top, purchased deliberately to show that she was back on top, and that nothing would beat her.

Only Sven had seen how truly devastated she was by the events that happened in Menton, and after the initial shock the night after things had started to go so wrong between herself and Alejandro, Sienna never outwardly showed Yves and the others how hurt she was – she was determined to be professional to the end. And while he was thousands of miles away, she was determined Arjan's name would never be mentioned again in her presence. He was truly dead to her, and to have others throw Arjan's misfortunes at her feet in Menton had been the final straw.

Arriving at the Aachen show on the first morning, Sienna immediately headed around to the show office to get the VIP passes for her guests. As she rounded the corner, she saw Yves sitting on a fence, smoking a cigarette. Chatting into a mobile phone in fluent French, he quickly ended the call when he saw Sienna. If he felt bad for what he had done, he never showed it, but he knew that he had to be nice to her as he needed her to promote him to her clients around the world. It was truly a case of he needed her more than she needed him, and they both knew it.

'Hey gorgeous! How are you?'

Sienna barely slowed her walk. 'Fine… In a hurry,' she muttered over her shoulder. Her hands gripped into a fist and she struggled to not turn around and go and slap Yves around the face. Ignoring him calling after her, she paused out of view, just inside the collecting ring. "Get a grip. You have to work with these people," she said to herself. Taking a deep breath, she rounded the corner into the show office and walked slap bang into Alejandro.

Silently, she stood before him, unable to even utter a "hello". It felt as though all her breath had left her body.

'Sienna…,' he said, unable to keep his sense of longing out of his voice.

Staring at each other for what felt like hours, the couple just stood there, locked in an intense myriad of feelings – love, desire, sadness, longing, pain, heartache, passion… As they stood, a dressage rider shoved past them, abruptly ending the moment.

'I hope you are well. See you at the show.' Alejandro bowed slightly, eyes closed in anguish, before walking off down the corridor, fists gripped tightly in unexpressed rage. Deflated, Sienna leaned against the wall for support. She knew that she'd see him in Aachen; she just hadn't expected for it to be so soon after she arrived, or for it to wind her so much. As she stood there, she realised that she loved Alejandro as much as ever, and that the three months apart and with no contact had not changed a single thing.

Alejandro headed straight for the stables and locked himself in an empty stall. Burrowing his fists into his eyes, he tried to stop the stem of tears that were threatening to escape. He still loved Sienna so much, but he had to put his children first. It was an impossible choice – be a father and lose the woman he loved or be with the woman he loved and lose his children. Either way, it felt like he could not win - his personal happiness would be compromised one way, and his family the other.

Banging his fist against the wall, Alejandro's pain was intensified by the fact that his ex-wife, Pasha, had taken a lover and was happily flaunting him in front of Alejandro's nose. As Pasha remained in the family compound in Bahrain, it was easier for her to move on as so many people visited the area every day. For Alejandro, however, he had to keep his nose squeaky clean so that his family weren't sent away. It was an impossible situation and not for the first time did he curse Yves and his friends for sharing his fledgling romance with the world before they were ready.

Deep down, Alejandro also wondered whether he was slightly to blame; he had tried to talk to Pasha when he returned from Dubai and Sharjah, but she had thrown such a tantrum and threatened to kick him out, with no access at all to the children, that he decided to wait a while longer before talking to her. Having called her briefly from Menton, he had got Pasha to agree that they needed to talk. However, it all ended up being immaterial as Yves' photographs had alerted his boss before he had a chance to explain that this was a real, serious thing, not just a passing fancy. With the reputation of the stud farm at risk, Alejandro's boss had been extremely clear that he was to have no further contact with Sienna apart from on an open and professional basis.

Breathing deeply, Alejandro struggled to pull himself together before he finally left the stable and headed off to meet his boss for coffee and a pre-show meeting with the trainers. As he walked past his grooms, they were shocked to see Alejandro's expression. They knew that their boss was a proud man and that, since Menton, he had been different – more distance, more distracted, and more easily upset. But they didn't know why. Seeing him leave the stable with his lips tightly drawn together, grazed fists balled by his side as he walked, they raised their eyebrows to each other, wondering just what was going on and why their boss, so in control of everything and, at times, emotionless as he just got on and got the job done, seemed to be losing it.

As Alejandro left the showground, he kept his head down, looking only at the ground before him and nothing else. He couldn't risk catching sight of Sienna again; the pain was just too much to bear.

Meanwhile, elsewhere in the stable block, Guy Tindall was shouting angrily at all around him. He had finally met his match and his new boss was playing him at his own game. Having sold a string of young Arabian horses to him at vastly overinflated prices and having pacified him continually that they would come good in time and deliver the championships he had promised, the owner had just made a surprise visit to the showground.

'If I don't win a medal this weekend with at least two horses, I am taking them all away and putting them with Rin. She gets results. You have failed. This is your first and last warning,' Lucas Curtin had said before calling his wife, Adrianna, over to him and returning to the Holiday Inn for a brandy. Lucas and Adrianna were extremely rich, and it was that which had drawn Guy to them in the first place. With her long, blonde hair, Adrianna constantly trailed furs over her shoulder and looked disinterested in everything around her. On meeting her, Guy was convinced that he could charm her into spending ever-increasing amounts of money on the horses that he wanted to have in his stables. He had not, however, counted for Lucas in the equation. Tall, dark, brutally handsome, Lucas was raised in Switzerland by a string of international nannies and had gone to Harvard to study Technology and Operations Management. A shrewd businessman, it was he that had decided on having the Arabian horses. Adrianna, little more than a trophy wife, was happy to go along with Lucas' plans as long as she was kept in the lifestyle to which she had become very accustomed.

Watching Lucas and Adrianna walking away from him, Guy felt more tense than usual. With the DuPont's gone, and firmly settled with Rin, he needed a big money client to continue his ambitions. Tension made his nerves shorter than ever, and he felt impatient with everything and everyone around him. Even Davey Baynes had not lived up to early promise, deciding against entering the world of Arabian horses after that first terrifying show where he had envisioned his life's savings going straight into Guy's pockets. Having been badly frightened, Davey took Sparkle of Justice home where he was promptly gelded and backed. He became his wife's happy hacker horse, and Sparkle of Justice loved his new life. Petted daily, and told how wonderful he was, he led the life of riley and enjoyed long rides out over stubble fields and snow, always being careful to look after his rider. Guy, meanwhile, still cursed when he thought about how much money he had spent on wining and dining the Baynes', and thinking about them now did nothing to improve his humour.

'Will you just get the banners up, the curtains up, and get a move on with it! Jesus, do I have to do everything myself!'

As Guy roughly pushed Holly, his comely groom, to one side and marched out of the stable block, he saw Ally bearing down on him. Seven months pregnant with twins, she had started following him to shows in Europe when she could travel in the horse lorry with him. Thank heavens it would be the Middle East soon, he thought to himself, and Ally would be busy with their children and unable to follow him around the world so easily; it would also be their only children if he had his way. He didn't need complications in his life, nor reminders that he was getting older, and he had secretly booked an appointment to have a vasectomy when he returned home. With Lucas breathing down his back, and Ally curtailing any extra circular activities, Guy felt like a trapped lion and he needed some release. Seeing Holly sit down outside the stalls, lighting a cigarette with a trembling hand, he decided to deflect Ally and brusquely sent her back to the hotel to charm Lucas and ply him with brandy before turning to appease his grumpiness with his groom. Given that he couldn't do anything right with his girlfriend, what difference would it make anyway? Besides, Holly was wonderfully grateful for any and all attention Guy bestowed upon her and he needed all the hero worship he could get right now.

Rin watched the proceedings with amusement – it seemed that every time she saw Guy at shows, he was either trying to win over a client or being shouted at by one.

Checking her stalls, she was happy to see that she had a good string of horses at the show. Making her debut at a major show was Aria LA. This chestnut filly had matured with confidence since her arrival at Rin's yard, and she had gone to a smaller show at the end of August. In spite of Rin's concerns that she was a three-year old filly who had not yet been shown and may not be able to cope, Aria took the ring like a natural, full of pizzazz and self-importance. She left as Junior Female Champion, and Rin and Leap were now ready to present her to a wider audience.

One thing that had amazed Rin was how easily Leap had come around to Sienna. After her initial call, way back in April, Rin had been worried that Leap would refuse to use Sienna's considerable experience and expertise in marketing through a sense of misplaced loyalty to Arjan. However, having sat and spoken with Leap, and gone through Sienna's initial plans, Rin was amazed that he embraced not only the marketing ideas, but also Sienna herself.

'I think, over the years, I have been too hard to you,' said Leap when the three of them met for a meeting in July. 'I think – no, I know – that Arjan truly did have feelings for you. But he always was weak when it came to women. You must both know this. I was cruel to you in Menton and for that, I am sorry. I am sorry for all you went through with Arjan, and all you are going through now with Alejandro.'

Shaking Sienna's hand, Leap sat back and listened to Sienna's plans for making Aria LA the most well-known filly on the planet before she even stepped into the show-ring.

The plans had worked. By the time of the small show, people were already keen to find out more about Aria LA, and they screamed and cheered when she came into the ring. Now, one month on, her name was on everyone's lips and all the promotion and speculation before Aachen was about Aria. Rin knew that she had to deliver - but she also knew that this was the filly to do so with.

Time and time again, she marvelled that Arjan had chosen to never show Aria LA. She would have won at any show easily and who knows, he might have still been in Europe. Leap wouldn't talk about it whenever Rin tried to discuss it with him, and she had a feeling that Arjan was, by the end, just plain lazy. He had missed his chance of a golden moment, and she was determined not to do the same.

Aachen was the favourite show of many breeders, spectators, and exhibitors from across the world. While the VIP area encroached on the show-ring, making the space allowed for the horse to trot ever restricted, the seats in the main stands were always full to bursting with cheering crowds, all keen to see these wonderful Arabian horses show.

The calling card of Aachen was the music; at the start of each class, Verdi's *Triumphal March* rang out, signalling that the horses were ready to begin their trot into the ring. The power of the music, combined with beautiful Arabian after beautiful Arabian trotting into the arena, was an emotional combination. By the time of the mare classes, typically full of huge-moving Polish princesses, emotion levels ran high and even the most tired breeders and the most stale of trainers, were reinvigorated to begin breeding again or in trying to show their horses that little bit better.

Aachen drew to a close, and Guy managed to scrape a bronze championship placing in the most uninspiring of the final classes. Lucas had gone into the arena to collect his much-paid for award and as the national anthem of Germany played for the Gold Champion Colt, he whispered out of the corner of his mouth to Guy. 'You've survived for another show. If I don't see improved results by Verona, you're through.' With that, Lucas marched back to the VIP area, grabbed his wife, and went to meet his driver before heading back to his private jet and their weekend home in Marbella.

Badly shaken, Guy stormed out of the arena and taking a bottle of whiskey from his hospitality area, locked himself into his horse lorry and drank himself to oblivion. Even the calls of Ally and Holly could not persuade him to unlock the door and as a result, it was a very hungover man that loaded the horses the following morning. Resolving that he would never be in this position again, where others would tell him what to do and call the shots, Guy grimly drove the lorry back to England himself, with Ally following in the car. As the ferry lurched across the turbulent North Sea, Guy threw up the remains of the whiskey, and an even more steely determination entered his already loveless heart.

The weekend after Aachen, Rin decided that she needed some fun in her life. She enjoyed being back in Germany and nearer to her family and was thankful every day that Zoë had made the move with her, but she knew that there was something missing. She had finally moved on with the horses, and now it was time to move on with her life, too.

Realising that she had a rare weekend off, Rin decided to pay a visit to the historic city of Bruges and enjoy 24 hours away from the horses. She had always wanted to visit Bruges and had always been too busy. Also, deep down she felt that it was a romantic place to go and neither Arjan nor Yves had wanted to visit. Juan had arranged for them to have a weekend there, but his wife had called saying that one of the children was ill. While Juan suggested that Rin went on her own, she hadn't. She did not want to be reminded of all that she could have had at that time, if only Juan had the gumption and balls to leave his wife.

Now, however, it was a glorious October day and still on a high after Aria LA's Gold Junior Female Championship the week before, Rin wanted to go and explore this beautiful part of Belgium. Booking a hotel for the night, Rin made to leave, slightly sad that, as much as she begged, Zoë would not leave the stables, saying that she had things she wanted to get on with and do quietly, and told Rin to go and enjoy herself and not rush back. Privately, Zoë felt that it would do Rin good to get out by herself, away from anyone at all involved with the horse world. As much as she loved her boss, Zoë knew that Rin wasn't always good at relaxing and a day out would do her good.

Driving down the E34, having navigated her way around Antwerp, Rin felt happier than she had in months. For the first time since before Arjan had left, she was planning an open day. With the support of Zoë, she had truly turned her business around in these past months and she felt free and happy as she drove along, singing along to the radio.

Arriving in Bruges and deciding to go on a river cruise so she could take some photographs, Rin found herself standing next a tall good-looking man from Brussels. Stepping on to the boat, he held her hand and half-smiled at her. By the time the cruise had finished, Rin's camera lay untouched in her hands, but she knew all about this dashing stranger. Making their way to the Market Square, they walked past the Belfry and Cloth Hall and settled into one of the many restaurants outside for something to eat.

Rin learned that this gentleman's name was Paul and that he worked for an international company. Having decided, like Rin, that it was a beautiful day to be enjoyed, he too had taken himself to Bruges for the afternoon in an effort to free his mind from the challenges of his job. Like her, Paul had thrown himself into work over the past few years and he felt that it was days like today that reminded him that he was alive and to go and enjoy life.

As the sun began to set on the medieval city, Paul reluctantly said that he had to leave as he had an early flight to Zurich. He and Rin exchanged telephone numbers and a slow kiss. Finally, she had buried the last of her ghosts and could start again and allow new love into her life. The distance from Niederrhein to Brussels wasn't so far, and she was sure that they could meet up again and make things work. All these thoughts went through her mind as she smiled up at this handsome stranger, whose chance meeting had put her life on to a different path once more.

26

The next stop on the Arabian circuit was another title show, this time the European Championships, held in the north Italian town of Verona. With its wonderful history – including Juliet's tower and the impressive complete amphitheatre, that was still in use today – there was much to enjoy about this weekend other than just the horse show.

The trainers, however, hated the show here. As part of the larger Fiera Cavelli, or horse fair, the Arabian horses were just one fraction of the show here and as such, their part was small. With Italian officials to be negotiated, as well as Italian bureaucracy, the challenges of getting a horse from A to B were not as straight forward as it seemed, and so it was only a dedicated group of trainers, and those owners eagerly after a coveted Triple Crown title, that made the difficult journey over the Italian border.

Sienna had decided at the last minute to stay away from Verona. Unlike many others, Sienna loved the show, as she always spent an evening in Old Verona with clients, watching a play or an opera, as well as spending too much money at the various shopping halls that there were on the showground. However, Sally had suggested that a break would do Sienna good and so had booked a girls' weekend for them in Dublin going back to Sienna's roots and drinking more Guinness than would be good for them. Not bothering to tell anyone that she was not going, Sienna cancelled her Verona hotel and instead, made her way to Stansted with Sally and boarded a short-distance flight over the water to the Emerald Isle.

On arrival, Alejandro was devastated to be told that Sienna had neither checked into the hotel, nor had she a room booked. He was hoping to be able to spend some time with her, just for a coffee, so that he could try and explain things to her now that things had settled down a bit. He still missed Sienna desperately – from her smile and her laugh to the way she listened to people sharing their horse stories for the thousandth time, and the fact that she cared so much. Checking into his suite, booked for him by his boss, the vast king-sized bed seemed to mock Alejandro and leaving his case by the door, he went to stare blankly out of the window without even bothering to turn the lights on.

Appropriately enough, the rain was cascading down the glass, blurring his vision once more. He had to get a grip; there was too much at stake with this show to start falling apart now. Alejandro's boss had a super young mare entered, and she had already taken Gold in Aachen. Hopes were high that she could go all the way and take the Triple Crown title, but Alejandro felt empty inside.

In the room next door, Rin and Paul lay naked in bed together, curled up in each other's arms.

'I have never met anyone like you,' Rin marvelled. 'I never knew that I could feel this way.'

Paul laughed, burying his lips in her neck.

'That is because I have special powers – I actually cast a spell over you in Bruges that day. That is why you cannot eat or sleep without me!'

Laughing, Rin rolled on to her stomach and grinned at him, her green eyes almost azure in colour, she was so happy.

'After Arjan…,' she began.

'Not him again! Arjan! I hate the guy,' groaned Paul, who was only half-joking.

Prodding him in the ribs, Rin smiled at him.

'I'm serious – listen! After Arjan, I never thought I would ever find love again. He had worn away my confidence so much as he cheated on me, week in, week out. Then I had that stupid fling with Yves…'

'Who I also hate…'

'Yes, Yves who you also hate, and then I thought I was in love with Juan – I know, I know, you hate him too! But I was only looking for a father figure with him, I realise that now. I didn't really love any of them. You have opened my eyes to so much Paul, it feels so real with you, so comfortable. I think I am falling in love with you – truly.'

Rin fell silent as she gazed up at Paul, wondering if she had been too honest, too soon.

Tightening his arms around her, Paul buried his lips briefly on her hair before nudging her to lift up her face. Kissing her slowly on her lips, Paul stared into her eyes, pausing for a second and just drinking in the moment.

'I'm so glad you said that – I am falling for you, too,' he said, kissing his way down her body. Rin smiled to herself, aware that she had finally found true happiness.

At the showground, there was a hive of activity as grooms and handlers prepared for the show while the finishing touches were put into place in the arena. This was a show with a true sense of theatre, and it was agreed by all that ANICA, the Italian Arabian Horse Society, ensured that the show-ring was the most dramatic on the circuit.

Horses entered the ring through two huge Egyptian-style columns, with a sphinx the opposite end, all lending to the Egyptian feel. No one quite knew why the Italians had decided to recreate Egypt for their Arabian horse show – although a great many horses descended from this region – but certainly no one minded, and it lent a sense of fun to what was often a tedious show.

Held in November, there was always a truly cold gasp in the air as grooms left the relative snugness of the stables and walked over to the ring. Extra blankets were needed to keep the horses warm and their coats in condition – as well as to lay over the grooms unlucky enough to be sleeping in the stables at this show. By 2am, any semblance of snugness had surely gone, and waking at that time often meant an uncomfortable rest of night, trying to warm your bones again and get comfortable before daylight came once more.

Over at the showground, Guy was incredibly tense. With Ally now very pregnant, she had thankfully decided to stay at home, and he knew that within two or three weeks, he would become a father for the first, and only, time. His secret operation had gone well and having booked himself to one of to the top doctor's in London and spent a few days recovering in a swanky hotel, Ally was none the wiser. It wasn't the thought of fatherhood, however, that was making Guy feel so tense. The Curtin's had made it very clear to him that he was on his last chance. With three horses at the show, Lucas was expecting at least two championship placings, if not more, and the pressure really was on.

One of the more expensive horses Guy had purchased for them was Dancing Legacy KG, a beautiful grey mare with a huge trot, expressive eyes, and a perfectly dished face. Bred in the United States by Kris Green, Dancing Legacy had yet to meet expectations in Europe and it was with her that Guy was desperate to prove himself. That chance, however, would have to wait until the Paris World Championships as only horses bred in Europe could be shown here at the Europeans. Guy had two horses at the show for the Curtin's, a yearling filly called BM Affectina, who was a very flashy grey, and a vibrant and striking chestnut colt with a flaxen mane and tail called Jambalaya.

Wrapped up in furs and leather, the Curtin's entered Guy's stable area.

'They travel well?' asked Lucas as he looked over the door at BM Affectina.

Guy nodded, nervously licking his lips as he became fully aware the enormity that the coming two days would have on his career.

'Holly! Get the Curtin's some wine!' he called as he showed Lucas and Marcia to the seating area before bringing both horses out for inspection. It really was a case of now or never for him.

Rin watched the scene with Guy and the Curtin's play out before her with interest. As she stood there watching, she felt a pair of arms slip around her waist and squeeze her tight. Turning her head, she felt a kiss drop on the side of her face and she smiled up at Paul. At 5'11, Paul was very handsome and everywhere he went, he turned heads. While tall and with brown, smouldering eyes as well as brown hair, it was true that he bore a slight resemblance to Arjan. However, Paul invariably had a smile on his face and a happy-go-lucky carefree attitude. He also treated people with respect and, having been so shoddily treated by both Arjan and Juan, not to mention Yves, Rin was enjoying being treated like a cherished girlfriend rather than just someone to keep a bed warm at night.

Paul had insisted that he wanted to know about as much as Rin's world as possible and so he had taken time off work to accompany her to Verona.

'This is the guy who stole Sparkle of Justice off you?' he asked, nodding in Guy's direction. In spite of the cold of the November evening, Guy was sweating with fear and expectation and the tension that he was feeling was clearly expressed across his face.

Rin nodded.

'Somehow, I don't think he's a threat to you anymore!' laughed Paul as he took Rin by the hand and led her back to the hotel. Calling to Zoë to check the horses, and to keep an extra eye on Aria LA, who was being plagued by fans, Rin could only be swept along in the moment and finally, after all those years of cheating and being cheated on, she felt safe. She was very settled and in love with Paul, and Rin was happy to share her happiness wherever she went, and she waved at Zoë as she headed off.

Zoë smiled as she watched her boss be led away by her handsome boyfriend, happy that, at last, she had found happiness. Having been with Rin for so long, she had seen the men come and go, and she was so happy to see her finally so happy with someone. Besides, Paul was very good looking, and she had already cheekily asked Rin if he had a younger brother!

Later that evening, wandering through the streets of Verona, Paul pulled Rin down an alley.

'There is something here I want you to see,' he said. 'Here it is – Juliet's balcony, made famous in the play *Romeo and Juliet* by Shakespeare.'

As the couple stood there, hand-in-hand, watching the lit-up balcony above them, Paul recited from the book he had read earlier while Rin was training her horses.

'The house dates back to the 13th century and belonged to the Dal Cappello, or "Cappelletti", family. This balcony is where Romeo promised Juliet eternal love in that famous, tragic play.

'If unmarried people touch Juliet's statue, it is meant to bring them luck and help them find the love of their life. I think we should hold hands, touch the statue and kiss…'

Smiling up at Paul, Rin leaned in towards the statue and kissed her boyfriend while touching this talisman of love. Unfortunately for Alejandro, he happened to be passing at the same time and this outward display of affection did nothing to ease his own heartache. Heading to a nearby restaurant, he sat at the bar and ordered a carafe of red wine; he knew that he had to get a grip, but at the moment, everywhere he looked seemed to remind him of Sienna, and the labour of lost love.

With Guy tense, Rin loved up, and Alejandro dejected, it was an interesting group that made their way to the collecting ring the next day to wait for the yearling fillies to make their way in for the first class. Holly was quietly standing there with BM Affectina, soothing the filly and brushing any dust off her coat that settled as the other horses went past.

'Ready?' she asked Guy as he came to take the lead rope from her. Grimacing as he saw Lucas appear by the entrance to the arena, Guy nodded, motioning for Gary, a young groom he had just taken on to help Holly, to start shaking a bag behind Affectina so that she entered the ring with a huge trot rather than taking a couple of strides to warm up.

Aware of Lucas watching his every move, Guy ran as fast as he could around the arena with Affectina, before standing her up in front of the judges. From a team of six, the five that were assessing this class made their way around the filly, judging her from every angle before asking the Ringmaster to tell Guy to walk the filly before them. Smoothing her mane down, and pushing her forelock from her eyes, Guy paused for a moment to calm the filly before walking Affectina away from, and then back towards, the judges, thus helping them evaluate her legs and conformation. After a final brief stand, Guy trotted the filly away from centre of the ring and back towards the entrance, waiting for the next horse to trot in before he exited back to the collecting ring.

Holly was there to greet him. 'She looked amazing!' she said, hugging Guy before taking Affectina from him. 'She moved brilliantly, and her stand was superb.' Patting the filly enthusiastically, Holly led her away and awaited the scores.

'And now, we have the points for horse number 12, BM Affectina, owned by Lucas and Adrianna Curtin and shown by Guy Tindall. BM Affectina was bred in Holland and her score is – 91.25!'

Patting the filly again, Holly grinned up at Guy. 'You're in the lead – and I doubt whether the last horse will bother you. Well done!'

'Still a long way to go…,' replied Guy, talking half to himself as he took BM Affectina back from Holly, ready to make his way into the ring as for the winner's presentation.

As Guy shook hands with the sponsor for the class, represented by Alejandro, Lucas and Adrianna came to stand beside their filly.

'A good start, that I will grant you," said Lucas, shaking Guy's hand. 'But the show has only just started. I want more – more wins for all this money you have taken from us on, so far, false promises. Come.'

Signalling to Adrianna to follow him, Lucas made his way down the line, shaking hands with the other owners who had horses in the Top Five before returning to their VIP booth.

Aria LA was next to show, with Rin allowing the filly to take in the enormity of the ring and its staging on the first walk around, before asking her to trot in her individual show. Aria LA seemed to dance before everyone's eyes, and she received a glut of 20s from the judges to score 93.75 points, a huge score. Guy scowled as Rin left the winner's circle, but there was no denying the filly's quality.

After a tense lunch with the Curtin's, Guy took Jambalaya into his class and was delighted when this young colt, in only his second show, took second place. Even Lucas seemed pleased for once, in spite of not winning.

'You see? This is what I am talking about. Results. It seems you just needed a little persuasion. I want more – the championships are tomorrow.'

Sweating, Guy could only nod as the Curtin's left the showground to go out for dinner with some rich friends. Relieved that they had left, and also relieved to have been placed well in both classes, he caught Holly's hand as she rushed past him with the show halters.

'Hey… Why don't you come back to the hotel with me for a – more comfortable evening? Gary can look after things here for the night.'

Flushing pink with excitement, Holly readily agreed and, having given Gary gabbled instructions, walked back to the hotel with Guy, ready for a whole evening with this vain, handsome, argumentative man, her boss who had her truly wrapped around his little finger.

Putting an arm around her shoulder and pulling her into him as they arrived at the hotel, Guy grinned wickedly and whispered to Holly: 'Let's have a jacuzzi and some champagne. Oh – and I could do with a massage…'

Leaving her to open the door to his hire car herself, Holly could feel her heart fall a little as she realised that, even in an evening of lust, she would still be nothing more to him than just a fuck and someone that worked for him. After that night spent together on his parent's sofa all those years ago, Guy had shown just enough interest in Holly to keep her hanging on, but he had also started seeing other women within a matter of months. 'You're my special girl,' he always told her whenever she protested, and to ensure her loyalty even more, Guy had hired her and made her Head Girl at his yard. As Holly finally began to see through the cloud of lies and realised that she would never be anymore more to him than something convenient, she stood and briefly looked up into the night sky. Deciding to push all such thoughts to the back of her mind, and aware that she now had a lot to think about once she was back in England and safely on home soil, Holly chose to just focus on the here and now and enjoy the evening ahead, with all that it had to offer. As she shut the car door, she realised that as well as being the first whole night they will have spent together in years – and it could also well be their last.

The following morning, Holly found that she could hardly walk as she arrived at the stables and she automatically checked over Jambalaya and BM Affectina before their championship classes. The night spent with Guy had, much to her surprise, been wonderful. Relaxed after his win, he had made an effort and ordered room service – steak and champagne – and had even given Holly a back massage before smacking her bottom firmly and pulling her up onto all fours. Entering her, admiring his reflection in the mirror, Guy's focus was not on Holly but on winning Gold with his horses. As he came into Holly with a cry, he inwardly crowed as he saw himself taking the top honours. Falling straight into a deep and dreamless sleep, Guy barely acknowledged Holly's presence the next morning as, once again, nerves that he wasn't used to feeling kicked in.

Guy's nerves weren't for nothing. Aria LA had commanded her filly class the day before and he knew that she would be impossible to beat. All he could do was hope for the Silver medal behind her – and hope that was enough for Lucas. Aria LA wowed everyone once more to be named unanimous Gold Junior Female Champion. Guy waited nervously for the Silver to be called and was happily surprised when Peter announced that this was another unanimous decision, with the title going to BM Affectina. Lucas punched the air with delight and even gave Guy a hug when he went into the ring to collect his huge trophy. Jambalaya followed this success with a Silver Junior Male Champion title, and so it was a happy group that made their way back to Tindall Training Centre's stalls for a champagne celebration. Once again, however, the hard work of clearing up was left to Holly and Gary, although Guy did find time to pin Holly in the corner of Jambalaya's stable and kiss her.

'Paris next,' was all he said to her as he left with the Curtin's to go out for dinner without a backward glance. Holly, meanwhile, was left to load the horses up into the transporter that would take them back to England before clearing out the stables ready for the next occupants.

While Aria LA and BM Affectina may have been the junior stars, the senior honours went to an incredibly over-emotional Luca. Bringing out Passionate Presence once more, this regal beauty had only grown more beautiful with age. Now a mare, and having already had a foal, she had already taken her return to the show-ring with enthusiasm. Passionate Presence first showed in Aachen and had taken the Gold title there. Now, here in Verona, surrounded by chanting and cheering supporters, she had won her class and taken the Gold Senior Female Championship. Unable to stop crying, Luca had leapt up on to Passionate Presence's back and, bareback, ridden her around the arena, his fingers knotted into her mane and one arm aloft.

Grabbing a bottle of champagne from a celebrating reveller, Luca, emptied the bottle of bubbles over his head and Passionate Presence. Laughing wildly, crying, cheering, Luca came to a halt in the centre of the ring. Dropping the bottle, he wrapped both arms around the beautiful mare's neck and covered her in kisses. All watching, including those beaten to Silver and Bronze places, cheered and there wasn't an unsmiling face in the crowd. Even Guy managed to clap Luca on the back in acknowledgement of his win as, finally, exasperated officials managed to herd Luca, Passionate Presence, and several football teams of hangers on out of the arena and get the show back on track. Reflecting later, many agreed that it was moments such as this that made all the heartache worth it. They were truly special and reinforced that amazing bond between horse and handler like no other.

Alejandro, meanwhile, endured a disastrous Verona. Nothing seemed to run smoothly for him anymore and it turned out that headcollars had been left behind in Bahrain, the handler missed his flight and Alejandro spent a very tense couple of hours trying to find someone to replace him – at the right price, with the right talent, and the right attitude. Then the first horse due to be shown went lame, a second got stable cough and hacked their way around the arena, and a third tucked up on the journey and ended up on a drip to revive her. Their Gold Champion Mare from Aachen looked like a different horse, and the trainer could do nothing with her to make her show and sparkle. A small gasp was heard as she left the ring unplaced in her class; truly, anything could happen at these shows – and frequently did.

Still painfully aware that he was searching for Sienna everywhere he looked, Alejandro managed to struggle on to the end of the show and, with less than glorious results, boarded a plane back to Bahrain. There a surly Pasha greeted him, fed up with looking after the children while she ranted that Alejandro was off having all the fun. "If only she knew," Alejandro thought to himself sadly. 'If only she knew…"

27

'Where are we going? Can I take the blindfold off yet?' Rin giggled as Paul let her from the car out on to what sounded like a busy road. 'Almost – just one moment...'

Turing Rin around, Paul whipped the blindfold off her face, and she blinked as her eyes accustomed to the light once more. She was at Frankfurt Airport – and Paul had two small cases next to him.

'I know Paris is in 10 days, and I know there are a thousand things for you to do, but I wanted to get you away for a very brief break so that you can go to Paris energised and ready to go. We're off to Dubai.'

Squealing, Rin put her hands up around Paul's neck and kissed him. While she would never choose to go away at this time, he was right. She was only taking Aria LA to Paris - all her other clients had agreed that the show was too political this year, and they would rather the horses had a good rest before the Middle Eastern shows started up as several had been invited to attend.

As she boarded a plane to Dubai with hand in hand with Paul, the handsome stranger from Bruges who had since become her boyfriend, Rin marvelled at the luck that had meant they had both been in the same place at the same time that sunny October day. Paul had booked them into a spa hotel in Dubai for three days, and two nights, of peace and tranquillity together, and as the plane took off, Rin realised that she was more than ready for this mini- break.

Their hotel was located in the trendy Bur Dubai and Paul arranged a surprise for Rin on the second night there.

'Ready?' he asked, smiling at Rin. She nodded and he took her hand, led her to the lift, and inserted a card key into the elevator before selecting the button for the hotel's top floor.

At Rin's questioning raised eyebrow, Paul responded with: 'I know the right people'. Smiling to himself, he remained silent as the lift made its way to the very top floor.

The doors opened and, still holding Rin's hand, Paul led her out through the doors and on to the roof. Here was a table set for two, lit by candles, and with some champagne chilling on ice in a bucket next to it. Beyond was an infinity pool, lit by underwater lighting, the blue and purple hues contrasting beautifully with the inky blue-black of the night sky. Even though it was early December, the temperature was a balmy 18°C, and dipping her hand into the water, Rin found that the pool was heated. To the right of where they were standing was a bamboo screen that housed a hot tub and hid it completely from view.

Smiling, amazed at the scene before her, Rin turned to Paul, putting her arms around his neck and kissing his lips.

'This is amazing! I love you!'

Without thinking, the words escaped her lips before she could stop them, and Rin immediately froze in horror.

Paul gently kissed her back.

'It's okay – I love you too.'

Smiling, he turned and nodded to the waiter who had magically appeared behind them.

'Just open the champagne please and leave us. We will dine in an hour and a half.'

With the champagne poured, Paul led Rin to the bamboo screen and the bubbling hot tub. Stripping off, he climbed in and took Rin's glass from her while she admired his bronzed, toned chest, his winter tan heightened by a week spent doing business in Istanbul a month earlier.

'Care to join me?'

Rin smiled, and undid the straps of her dress, which fell to the ground in ripples around her feet. With her small breasts having no need for a bra, she slipped her snow-white knickers off and climbed into the hot tub beside Paul, feeling goosebumps shiver all over her as her body adjusted to the feel of the bubbles against her skin, and the intense warmth of the water against the relative cool of the night-time air.

Paul passed Rin her glass and she took a sip of champagne before he leaned over and kissed her once more. Deeply, hungrily, Paul's mouth searched Rin's passionately before he took both of their glasses and put them to one side. Pulling Rin to him, Paul eased her onto his lap and kissed her deeply once more.

'I meant it, you know. I love you.'

Smiling, Rin leaned in closer to him. Straddling him properly, she gasped as she felt his cock rising up against her.

'Don't worry, we won't be disturbed.'

Glancing around, Rin realise that Paul was right and all she could see was the night skyline of Dubai, and carefully, she lowered herself onto Paul's cock, feeling him slide deep into her. Gasping again, Rin began to rock her hips back and forth against Paul as he groaned and pulled her in closer to him. As the bubbles continued to froth around them, the intensity of Rin's motion increased, and Paul also began to move, pushing against her as the tension began to build up inside him. Kissing her long and hard, taking her breath away, Rin began to tighten around him, calling out his name as she threw her head back and he leaned in to inhale the smell of her skin and kiss the hollow of her neck. A second later, he came, too, pulling Rin deeply into his lap, pushing into her as far as he could while she spasmed around him.

'I love you,' they both whispered at the same time, giggling as they realised they spoke at once. Holding each other close, Rin closed her eyes and acknowledged that she had finally come full circle. Her heart had finally been melted, and Paul was the one for her.

After a lazy swim in the underwater-lit pool, Rin and Paul climbed out and put on the dressing gowns that were thoughtfully hanging by the bamboo screen. They had just settled themselves down at the table when the waiter discreetly appeared with a plate of appetisers for them and a bottle of Cloudy Bay.

Toasting each other, the couple's giggles and chatter rang out over the Dubai rooftops, but there was no one to hear them. They were utterly lost together, lost in their own special world.

Barely a week later, Rin stood in the spotlights of Paris once more – this time with Aria LA. She had won not only the World Championship, but also the European Triple Crown, which was incredibly difficult to win. In order to do so, a horse had to take Gold titles at Aachen, the Europeans and Paris, all in one season, and very few horses achieved this accolade. Listening to the Belgian National Anthem being played for Leap, who as breeder and owner had tears in his eyes and the biggest smile on his face, Rin once more felt a stab of pain for Arjan mixed with her euphoria.

'It should be him here – with Aria,' she managed to say to Leap, her words catching in her throat as, to her surprise, tears threatened to overwhelm her.

Leap looked at Rin for a second, before embracing her in his arms. 'She is the right horse for you – and you are the right person for her. Arjan would never had made it.'

Smiling, Rin nodded and leaned into Paul, who was

proudly standing next to her with a packet of mints in his hands for Aria.

Leap turned to Rin once more: 'How do you fancy sending Aria to America? I think we could have some fun with her there in the mare classes.'

As the spotlights faded, Rin was seen throwing her arms around Leap in excitement, while Paul quietly stood there, sharing mints with this most beautiful filly.

The next class saw Etros make his show-ring debut for his new owners, trotting confidently around the arena and stealing the hearts of crowd and judges alike as he did so. As they chanted his name, he was named Gold Champion Colt, much to the relief of Sven, who grabbed a bottle of champagne and, having shaken it, sprayed it over everyone in the ring with him. A passing photographer captured the moment, of laughter and smiles for once instead of grimaces and outrage, the lights from the ceiling bouncing off the champagne, while Etros stood there calmly in the centre of it all. Sienna was sent the photograph the next day, and immediately began to contact the magazines to see which would enter the bidding war to run it on their next cover. Her phone did not stop beeping as the offers came rushing in, and she rang Sven regularly to update him. Finally, in that moment, her pain at losing Alejandro was starting to ease slightly, and she allowed herself to get caught up in the excitement and dramas surrounding Etros.

In a Paris full of memorable moments, the highlight, however, was Passionate Presence. To universal delight, this ethereal white mare took the Gold Senior Female Championship and with it, she also took the European Triple Crown. If Luca had been all flamboyance in Verona, in Paris he broke down and cried like a baby as he tried to lead Passionate Presence in to take her title. In the end, the other handlers had to help support him and take him to their place in the spotlight. With the beautiful World Championship saddle donated by His Majesty the King of Morocco in front of her, Passionate Presence enjoyed all of the applause, carrots, and mints that came her way as the photographers vied to get the best shot of her. Once again, the carousing went on long into the night and Luca slept clutching the World Championship trophy. For once, Alessandra didn't mind not being in his arms; she knew just how much this win meant to her husband, and she was overjoyed for him. Waking the next day, Luca made slow and tender love to his wife, the frantic urgency of recent weeks having finally left his system. He was on top of the world, and nothing was ever going to change that.

Guy found Paris stressful for more reason than one – the main being Ally. The twins had been born the minute he got back from Verona, and he was not enjoying fatherhood. Ally insisted on sending Guy pictures of the two girls, Sophia and Olivia, to his phone every few minutes, or calling him to say that one of them had just done "something cute". Feeling that his orderly life was turning into a constant misery of nappies, screaming, and projectile vomiting, he handed his phone to Holly, saying that he didn't want to see or hear anything else about the twins until the show was over. He then stormed off, leaving it to Holly to deal with Ally every time that she rang.

Unbeknown to Guy, however, Ally was taking great pleasure in badgering him with the photos of her girls. "Yes, my girls," she thought to herself as she put them into the double buggy and prepared to go for a walk around the Essex countryside. All those months ago, when Guy had bailed on the New Year Ball to go to the Middle East, Ally had checked his phone while he was in the shower. Seeing the message to Mike Dann, she was surprised to see a naked photo sent in reply from someone who very definitely was not a man. She recognised the girl, Miranda, immediately, as she had seen her strutting around the showgrounds for years, full of airs and graces and really thinking that she was something special. Going back through the messages between Guy and Miranda, Ally had found evidence of years of his cheating on her. As she heard the shower go silent, Ally put the phone back and decided that, as per her original plan, she would go to that night's ball – alone. Only she would go one step further and get her revenge on Guy for all the sleeping around that he had done.

As soon as Guy had left, his long list of orders fell out of Ally's head as she rang up the local beauty salon for an urgent appointment. Emerging three hours later, having been spruced, waxed, buffed, and manicured to within an inch of her life, Ally sailed into the local hair salon for more pampering. By the time they had finished, Ally barely recognised the woman looking back at herself – eyes sparkling and captivating, hair tamed and curled into soft waves, and lips painted a deep crimson red.

Arriving at the Hunt Ball that night, Ally walked into the hall and the room went quiet. Man after man wanted to know who she was, not recognising Guy's downtrodden girlfriend for a moment. Ally decided to remain anonymous as it added to the allure, and she felt herself swept away on to the dance floor time and time again by a never-ending stream of good-looking men.

All the anger and frustration that Ally felt came out in a carefully, if swiftly, laid plan. Selecting the young buck that looked most like Guy, she motioned for them to find a private space. Barely believing his luck, this young man with blonde hair and blue eyes bounded up the stairs after her, following her into an empty room.

Turning to face him, Ally felt her face gently taken into this nameless man's hands. As he kissed her on the lips, first tentatively and then with a rising passion, any doubts that Ally may have had fell away as, for what felt like the first time in her life, a man truly made love to her, worshipping every inch of her body.

Three weeks later, Ally took the pregnancy test. She smiled. It was positive.

Guy was none the wiser.

Now, nine months on, with the girls born and resembling Guy in looks if not character, Ally finally felt the love that had been missing all her life. Sophia and Olivia filled the hole that her loveless relationship with Guy had created, and she still got to be with her beloved horses. That was enough; for now, that was enough.

28

With the show season over and having returned replenished and refreshed from her time in Dubai with Paul, Rin finally had a chance to put into action the plan that had been going through her mind ever since she had been riding with the gauchos in Argentina and where she had first came across the Barrett family from Australia. They showed her photographs of a country with unimaginable and endless possibilities as well as so many beautiful and undiscovered horses. Her subsequent flying visit, to see the ill-fated Ibn Shahja, had ensured that Rin had fallen in love with the country. So much so that, ever since she had returned to Germany, Rin had been unable to get Australia out of her mind and she had decided to visit the continent properly during the European quiet season, straight after Paris and before the Middle Eastern shows kicked off. This also had the advantage of being at the height of the Australian show season and as soon as she could, Rin booked her ticket. Paul decided to stay behind and work on his business, and the couple shed a few tears as Rin boarded the plane to the other side of the world for just over three weeks.

On this visit, Rin travelled around as much of Australia as she could, starting in Queensland, down to New South Wales, then on down to Victoria and finally, flying out from Western Australia after spending a few days there. She visited all the farms that would have her, discovering that the amazing Australian hospitality that she had heard so much about was very much true. Rin was able to relax into their summer sunshine, glad to be away from a particularly cold winter in Germany where the local Snow and Ice

Festival did not, for once, need to import any snow.

But it was there in Victoria that Rin discovered a young colt that was full of potential. She knew that he would be a great addition to her show string in Europe and would be just what she needed for the season ahead. The colt's name was Valentine and he was an eye-catching black-bay with just a white star and no other markings at all. Rin was certain that Valentine would add extra qualities to the horses in Europe that were maybe lacking. Rather than being ultra-exotic as so many of the horses in Europe were becoming, this Australian colt had substance and character as well as beauty and type. Rin was hooked, and she immediately began to look to form a syndicate to import this charismatic colt to Europe.

More to the point, however, Rin knew that Australia was, as yet, an untapped market, partly caused by its huge distance from the rest of the world. She was determined that she would be the one to source the best horses from there and bring them to Europe and the Middle East. Making her way to Perth International Terminal in Western Australia, ready to board the plane back to Brussels via a stopover in Dubai, Rin got out her phone and prepared to send a message to Sienna – she needed her help to get Valentine to Europe, and to start making her bigger dreams a reality.

Guy woke on New Year's Day with a raging hangover to the sound of heavy pounding on the front door. Rolling over in bed, he just about registered that the clock showed 8.30am. Ally wasn't in bed; in fact, it looked as if she had not been there all night, and other than the banging on the door, the house was in silence.

Cursing quietly, Guy hauled himself out of bed and made his way down the stairs. Through the tinted glass, he could just make out the figure of a man with what looked like a briefcase. "What the…," he thought to himself.

Answering the door, wincing as the bright light of a new year hit his eyes, Guy looked at the man in front of him.

'Mr Guy Tindall?'

Guy nodded vaguely in return.

'Mr Jason Hunt here, from HMRC. We would like to talk to you about your tax bill.'

Already pale from his hangover and lack of sleep, Guy went ashen as the words said by the man in front of him fully registered in his brain.

"Tax? I…'

'We have sent you several letters, Mr Tindall. Made several calls – both on the phone and in person. You have chosen to ignore them all and not get back to us. So we are now issuing you with a summons. You have seven working days to pay back all that you owe, or we will see you in court.'

Hangover rapidly receding and his brain beginning to function with startling clarity, Guy felt his bowels loosen as he realised that his worst nightmare had caught up with him. Taking the letter from the HMRC man at the door, he managed to ask how much he owed.

'£750,000. Happy New Year, sir.'

With that, Mr Jason Hunt turned on his smart heel and retreated to the warmth of his car. He never liked issuing final notices but that amount, given on a day like today, would have major implications. As he drove away, Mr Hunt looked in the mirror and saw that Guy had not moved. Turning the corner, the receding figure of Guy vanished out of his sight – and mind. Job done, his attention was now focused on a New Year's Day party.

Left alone in the cloud of dust, Guy finally looked down at the envelope in his hand and slowly ripped it open. There it was, in black and white. Well. Black, red and white. He owed the government £750,000. Staggering backwards, Guy closed the door and called for Ally.

Her name reverberated around the house. It was only then that he realised that he couldn't hear Sophia or Olivia either. Rushing upstairs, taking the steps two at a time, he went into the nursery and found it empty. Going back to his bedroom, he found that Ally's side of the bed had, indeed, not been slept in. Fumbling for his phone, he called her.

'Where the fuck are you?'

'Happy New Year to you too Guy.'

'Never mind that! Where the fuck are you? We need to talk. Now!'

'We do. Yes. But probably not about what you are expecting.' Ally paused for a moment and Guy could hear the twins in the background.

'Ally!'

Sighing, Ally said: 'I've left you Guy. I've finally had enough of being treated like a doormat. So I've taken the girls and we've gone.'

This time it was Guy who was silent as he digested this. He needed Ally right now - not for the reason she may think, but because over the years, he had done a lot of deals under her name. Ally didn't realise it, but she was a very rich woman indeed - and he needed her to liquidate those assets before the courts caught up with him.

'Darling, I know I've not always been the best partner, but I love you and the girls. Please, come back,' he wheedled.

Ally laughed. 'I don't think so! And don't pretend that you care about Sophia and Olivia either. It's a little late to pretend that you love them.'

Ignoring the dig, Guy continued.

'Ally, I need you to come home. Now. I've, err… I've had a visit from…'

'The taxman,' Ally finished for him. 'Yes, I know all about it. They threatened to come and see you in the new year about the money that you owe. I just didn't think that it would be today. How poetic.'

'You knew!' Guy spluttered, incapable of coherent thought, that quiet little Ally had been that secretive. 'You bitch! You knew, and you didn't say anything!'

"No, why should I? After all you have done to me. That affair with Miranda and sleeping with all those other women. And Holly. Everyone! You have never once been faithful. Oh – I should let you know that Holly left as well last night. So you need to go and do the horses, I imagine they're hungry right now. Gary has the time booked off, so you can't expect him to do them.'

'What do you mean, she's left! There's no way Holly would do that to me!'

'That is where you are wrong, Guy. She got a better offer from Rin and like me, she was fed up of being used. She found me packing when she came to hand in her notice. So she has gone, too. Goodbye Guy. I'll see you in court. We can talk about maintenance then.'

Cutting Guy's expletives off, Ally felt a mixture of sadness and relief. Turning to smile at her precious daughters, she took in their beautiful, innocent faces.

'It's just us now, darlings. Just us. We don't need daddy Guy in our lives anymore.'

Turning her phone to mute, Ally slipped it into her handbag, her hand brushing against an envelope of papers as she did so. Smiling, Ally recounted how, after Guy had screamed abuse at her once again last night before going out drinking and leaving her to see in yet another New Year on her own, something had finally snapped.

Ally had broken into Guy's safe – he was so vain that he used a combination of his birthday and the date of his first big win as the code – and she had gone through all the paperwork and money that she found tucked away inside. Slipping £1,000 of cash into her purse, enough to get her and the twins away from Guy, Ally picked up some of the papers and began to read. It seemed that Guy had been doing a lot of buying and selling in her name - and the signature he used was most certainly hers. "Probably all those times that he yelled at me to just sign the form and go and pack his case," she thought to herself.

Reading on, Ally discovered that – through Guy – she had a lot of shares in the FTSE stock market; a flat in Mayfair; and a savings account with close to £300,000 in it. There were a few other items as well such as a Porsche car and a start of the art Land Rover. Ally put all the documents, keys, and cash into an envelope.

She had already been planning to leave Guy for a while – ever since the night she found the naked photograph of Miranda on his phone – but discovering the contents of the safe had been the final straw. She never had any money to buy new clothes for herself or the girls, and yet Guy had all these riches squirreled away. Gathering up her precious children, Ally got into her run-down car – the kind that made it through its MOT each year on a wing and a prayer – and drove as far from Colchester as possible, before finding a remote hotel for the night. For Ally, lying in bed and watching the television a few hours later, never had the sound of Big Ben calling in the New Year sounded sweeter; for her, they were ringing for her freedom.

Back in Colchester, realising that Ally was not going to answer his calls, Guy ran into his office and went to his safe. He desperately needed to find out just how much money he had in assets, and what he would need to liquidate. Seven days was not long, and he didn't have a second to spare. Unlocking the safe, Guy decided that he didn't need Ally to get him out of this hole, he would just forge her signature as he had so many times before.

Rifling through the contents, Guy's ashen face resembled a death mask as he realised that not only was some money missing, but that a lot of documentation was too. Howling with rage and disbelief, the debtor's chair appearing in his mind as he frantically searched again, Guy found a note.

After all you have done, and all you have not, this should be a good start for me and the girls. I will see you in court for the rest. Ally.

Disbelief, anger, and fear hit Guy all at the same time and, as he collapsed on the floor in shock, he felt the weight of the world caving in around him.

Ally decided that she wouldn't tell Guy that the twins were not his, not yet anyway. She wanted to make him sweat a little longer for all that he had done to her over the years. When Holly had come in to hand in her notice, she had tearfully told Ally everything – about her, about Miranda, about all the women at the shows around the world. Distraught and apologetic about her role in it, Holly had been amazed when Ally just laughed and hugged her.

'Please, don't worry. I knew about Miranda and I guessed about you. But I am leaving him now, and it really doesn't matter anymore.'

'You're leaving him? But what about Sophia and Olivia?'

Ally smiled at the girl standing before her but decided not to tell her the truth. It was best that only she knew.

'I think we will all be better off without him. But what are you going to do?'

'I have been talking to Rin at some of the shows. She is

doing so well, and she needs someone else to help Zoë. After Verona, where Guy promised me the world and then left me with nothing once more, I knew that I needed to get away. In Paris, Rin made me an offer and I must take it. I am sorry to leave you…'

'Don't be. Go! Let Guy realise what it is like to clear up some of his own mess for once!'

Hugging her, Ally let Holly go. 'Good luck,' they both said to each other at the same time. Laughing, the two women finally felt the first sense of camaraderie between them, something that Guy had always stifled. Whether they could have been friends or not was immaterial now – Ally was going, and she was done with the horse world.

Her final task had been to warn Gary that she was leaving. Knocking on the door to the flat that Gary lived in above the stables, he had eventually answered with just a pair of faded Levi's pulled up over his hips; over his shoulder, Ally could see the blond hair of his partner, Hugo, through the bedroom door. Smiling, Ally apologised for the interruption and quickly explained what was happening.

"I understand, he's a real bastard," said Gary. "Just take care of yourself. We're off to friends later and unlikely to be here when His Nibs finds out what's going on. Good luck."

With a smile, Ally turned away and headed back the house to gather up the last of her belongings. For the first time in a long time, she finally felt free.

Having moved into a small cottage, rented on the other side of Colchester, Ally tracked down the Land Rover and was settling into a new life for herself, Sophia and Olivia. As she hung the washing out on the line, Ally revelled in the normality of it all. It was a beautiful day in early January, the skies were blue, and the sun was warm on her face.

Wrapping up the girls in their winter clothes, hats and mittens, Ally pushed the double buggy out of the drive and went for a walk by the river. As she stopped to feed the ducks, Sophia gurgling excitedly, Olivia sleeping, Ally was surprised to hear a vaguely familiar voice saying hello to her.

Looking up, Ally took a step back as she realised that she was face to face with the young buck that she had met, and bedded, at the ball; the father of her children.

'Fancy seeing you here! How are you? And who do we have here?'

Leaning down, it was the buck's turn to take a step back as he looked into the buggy and saw his own eyes staring back at him.

'What the...! I think we need to talk.'

Nodding, Ally expected the worst and was surprised when he slipped his hand into hers.

'I cannot tell you how much I missed you when I woke after the ball and you weren't there. I am sure that you have your reasons – and now there are two of them! Let's go and have some coffee and fill in the blanks. I'm Will, by the way.'

Smiling shyly, Ally returned the pressure of Will's hand and they walked off back down the bank towards town, sharing the pushing of the buggy together.

Unaware of how duplicitous his ex had been, and how she was now finding true happiness for the first time in many years, Guy went to find a solicitor a few days later as he had been unable to raise anywhere near the kind of money needed to keep the taxman at bay. Walking into the firm, he was impressed to be met by a very smart, very savvy woman with a brilliant mind and a killer pair of heels.

Eyeing her up slowly, Guy beamed his brilliant smile,

and prepared to wow her. By the end of the meeting, Guy was groaning as his new solicitor was on her knees in front of him, giving him the best blow job that he had enjoyed in a while. With her scarlet red lips leaving their mark on his cock, Guy felt that he had finally met his match in a woman. Regardless of the outcome of the court case, he was determined to keep seeing her.

A few weeks later, over in Belgium, Leap choked on his coffee as he read the morning papers.

LEADING BRITISH HORSE TRAINER JAILED FOR TAX EVASION IS ASSAULTED IN COURT

Guy Tindall, one of the UK's top Arabian horse trainers, was jailed yesterday on tax evasion. Mr Tindall owed Her Majesty's Government the total of £750,000. Unable to make any payment at all, Mr Tindall was sent down to HMP Colchester for 10 years.

In bizarre courtroom scenes as he left the court, Mr Tindall's ex-girlfriend, Ally Holmes, shouted out that the children were not his. We understand she has twin girls and had led Mr Tindall to believe they were his. As a result of finding out about the pregnancy, Mr Tindall had undergone a secret vasectomy.

Also in court was Mr Tindall's mistress, Miranda Hallerton, who laughed when she heard that the twin girls were not Mr Tindall's – although she was seething when she learned of the secret vasectomy. A screaming match ensued as Ms Holmes told Ms Hallerton that Mr Tindall would not remain faithful to her. Laughing, Ms Hallerton was then horrified see QC Ms Wakeley kissing the defendant as he left the court.

In a curious twist, Ms Holmes then left the

court with Will Taylor, her new beau and the
father of the twins. The couple have seemingly
only recently got together, in spite of the
twins being over six months old.

Arranging a prison visit, Ms Hallerton then
attacked Mr Tindall with her stiletto, just
missing his eye. Stitches were required, and
all visits to Mr Tindall have been suspended
until further notice.

Laughing hysterically, Leap wished, not for the first time, that Arjan was there with him. Taking a photograph of the news report, he sent it to Arjan's telephone and Facebook account. However, as before, there was no way of knowing if Arjan received it. No one had heard of or from him in months. Still chuckling to himself at the tangled web Guy had managed to get into, Leap tore out the page to keep for prosperity. Once he knew where Arjan was, he would frame it and send it to him.

'To you, my old friend,' he said as he raised his coffee cup to the skies. 'Wherever you may be…'

29

Jesus Angelo arrived in London with two jobs to do. Firstly, he had to put a suitcase stashed full of money into a safe in a top London bank. Secondly, he had to take Sienna Stevens back to Russia with him.

Ever since Poland, Sergei and Mikhail had not stopped talking about Sienna, and they were relying on Jesus to bring her to them. She had haunted their lustful dreams since they had met her – all blue-eyed innocence and virtue. They wanted her out here, but they knew she wouldn't come if they asked her directly, especially as so many people such as Sven and Kris Green had warned her off them. The other problem they had was that Alejandro seemed to have her enraptured, although they had not been seen together in months. Maybe now was the time to strike, while she was feeling alone and, hopefully, vulnerable.

Jesus had been tasked with luring Sienna to Russia – not easy to do in a wintery January, when it was freezing in London and positively Arctic in Russia. Jesus was also vaguely aware that such a move could be fatal to her, but he had to use Mikhail's bland charm and his own sense of allure to convince her to come. Otherwise, it would be his head on the block, and he wasn't ready to lose it just yet.

Getting out his phone, he called Sienna.

'Darling! It's me, Jesus Angelo. We met in Poland – I work for the Karlov Stud, remember?'

Surprised to hear from him, Sienna murmured that she did remember him and how could she help him.

'I'm in London, ghastly cold grey place, and I wondered whether you'd like to meet me for dinner? I'm at a bit of a loose end really, and you would be helping me out no end if you could join me for dinner.'

Agreeing, with nothing better to do that night than curl up with a hot chocolate and watch Bridget Jones for the thousandth time, Sienna agreed, and went into the shower to start getting ready.

They met at Hawksmoor on Air Street, Jesus positively salivating at the handsome young men around him. Full of chatter, he drank his way through three bottles of red wine and barely let Sienna get a word in the whole night. Having bored her to tears, Jesus made his pitch to get her on the plane to Russia tomorrow. By this time, coffees and brandy were being drunk, and Sienna was amazed at his capacity to drink so much without passing out.

While initially reticent, getting Sienna to Russia proved to be easier than Jesus had dreamed of. Her defences were still down, and she was at a low ebb without Alejandro around and a new year stretching out ahead. Jesus was good at picking up the weakness in a person, as well as their talents, and he had flattered her mercilessly until she finally gave in and agreed to go with him. Jesus had cautioned her about telling anyone where they were going, saying that the Directors wished to keep it a secret so that they could make a big splash in an American magazine, and with her heart still bruised, Sienna decided to go and have an adventure, rather than playing it safe as she had done all her life. With barely a thought of the full implications, Sienna agreed and before she knew it, she was on a British Airways flight from London to Moscow. In their business cabin, Jesus chattered non-stop to her the whole time, twisting her up in different conversations, ensuring that her thoughts and logic were blurred even more than normal.

After flying from London, Sienna and Jesus arrived in Moscow and they then caught the train down to Vladikavkaz, where Mikhail had greeted Sienna warmly.

Any doubts Sienna had about her being so deep in Russia on her own still lingered, but Jesus had promised that he would look after her and protect her, and she just had to trust him. Still, as she arrived at the farm and stepped out into the icy cold, she felt a shiver go through her, one that wasn't only caused by the temperature. Looking around her, Sienna couldn't help but wish she had told someone where she was going.

'Over there is the famous stallion statue… And there is the stallion barn; I love it there! And there are the famous mountains, used as the backdrop to so many photographs…'

Finishing the brief tour, Jesus led her into a room where Mikhail and Sergei were waiting with some traditional Russian vodka. Jesus went over to the tray of drinks, back to the others, and busied himself for a few seconds away from the rest of them.

'Welcome to Russia!' they toasted as, glancing at Jesus, who imperceptibly nodded as he handed Sienna a glass of vodka. 'Down in one – it's the custom,' Jesus said playfully as he put his drink to his lips.

Pausing, Sienna watched the three men around her drink their shots and look at her expectantly. "Here goes…," she thought as she brought the cool, fiery liquid to her throat and swallowed, her eyes smarting with the strength of it. A minute or so later, she swayed slightly.

'Long journey,' she muttered, as Jesus took her arm.

'Of course it is ducks. Now, come on. Let me show you to your room so that you can get some rest. This way.'

Waving blithely at Mikhail and Sergei, Jesus led Sienna out of the room and down a long corridor. Turning right at the end, Jesus suddenly exclaimed that he had gone the wrong way and doubled back on himself, heading in the opposite direction. Feeling tired and slightly dizzy, Sienna followed him as they twisted and turned their way through the building. She was sure that some of the rooms looked familiar – surely, they were going around in circles? Talking non-stop, Jesus continued on his journey, finally leading Sienna through the house to where the Directors sometimes stayed, before taking her to her room.

Unbeknown to Sienna, Mikhail had warned Jesus to take a deliberately confusing route, so that Sienna would be disorientated and unable to find her way out easily, and Jesus was happy to chat inanely to Sienna and distract her even further. He had been promised a bonus of £10,000 if everything went as planned, on top of what they were already paying him.

'Ah, here we are,' said Jesus, overly friendly and full of smiles as he ushered Sienna in through a door. In a daze after the flights and Jesus' constant chatter since they left the hotel in London that morning, as well as the winding route to her room, Sienna was barely aware of where she was, and she allowed Jesus to close the door behind them.

'I just need to check your bag – security; you know what they are like,' said Jesus.

Sienna handed him her handbag, looking around her at her new surroundings as she did so. She was so tired that she didn't notice Jesus slip her mobile out of her bag and into his pocket. Nor did she notice him take her passport before he handed her bag back, smiling winningly at her. 'Perfect – I knew it would be. You look done in ducks, you should get some rest.'

Jesus shut the door quietly behind him, locking it silently and only pausing for a second to wonder about what horrors he had just committed this young woman to. Shrugging off his fleeting doubts, he made his way down the corridor, carefully and quietly locking the end door as ordered. With a locked fire escape the other side, Sienna was already a prisoner; she just didn't know it yet.

Sienna stood in the middle of her room after Jesus had left. As she had expected from his stories, it was stark and bare, and symbolic of the country she was in. Just one thin, threadbare rug lay on the naked wooden floor and a harsh, woollen blanket lent the only colour to the room. The bed, a single, was metal and old fashioned, and there was just a thin, ripped piece of once-white netting against the window, the only protection against the sun that would rise later the following morning.

As sleep slowly came to embrace her, an exhausted Sienna peeled back the blanket and, fully clothed, crept between the white sheets, mended holes clearly visible. As she was finally drifting off to sleep, a sound outside her room startled her. Without arrogance, she knew that she had caught the attention of many, and she was on high alert as to any dangers, knowing only too well what could happen to her. She had seen the way Sergei and Mikhail had looked at her when they met her in Poland, and she had struggled to put that unease to the back of her mind as she boarded the plane to Moscow. With Jesus chattering non-stop to her throughout the journey, she hadn't had time to be concerned but now, alone in her dark room, her senses were on edge, and the noise outside her window had only heightened them. She wondered whether she dare turn on the light and find her mobile phone; again, she cursed herself for not telling at least one person where she had gone. Before she could even think about moving, however, sleep enveloped her, even though her mind was still wondering what to do. The arms of Morpheus embraced her deeply as Sienna fell into a drug-induced sleep, unaware that Jesus had tampered with her shot of vodka earlier.

Waking later, Sienna felt very disorientated and was not sure how long she had been asleep. She was woken by the sound of someone at the door and struggling to come to her senses, she was relieved to see that it was only Jesus who put his head around the door.

'How do you feel ducks? Oh, you don't look well…'

Sienna tried to sit up in bed, but it felt as if her arms and legs did not belong to her.

'I think you need to rest. You go back to sleep and I'll pop along in an hour or so and see how you are.'

Unable to answer coherently, Sienna just looked as the door closed. On the other side, Jesus silently locked the door once more, before getting out his mobile phone.

'All going to plan. The Benzodiazepine is working a treat. Give it another few hours and she's all yours I reckon,' he texted through to Mikhail.

Again, Sienna was not sure how much time had passed and once again, she was woken by the sound of someone at her door. This time, however, she felt more lucid and, pulling herself up in the bed, she looked over to the door. Through the chink of light coming in underneath, Sienna could see someone standing outside. Holding her breath, now registering the light of the moon coming in through the window and falling on the door, Sienna could only watch in horror as the handle turned and the flimsy lock gave way against the gentle force used behind it.

Scrambling out of the bed, ready to run, she saw that, to her relief, it was Mikhail who stood there, framed in the light from the hallway. Definitely the lesser of the two evils and also the one that, she hoped, she could charm more.

'Sienna,' he purred. 'How do you find Russia? I hope you are not too cold.'

Sienna smiled warily, unsure of herself and feeling a

sense of menace at his arrival. 'It is fine, thank you. I am looking forward to getting out tomorrow and exploring.'

Mikhail just gazed out of the window, quite clearly giving the impression of someone not interested in what she was saying and also adding to her anxiety about his being there in her room.

Turning around, he started blankly at her. 'Sure. Come – sit down.' He motioned to the bed, the only place to sit, and Sienna nervously sat down. She wished again that she had already checked her mobile to see if she had a signal, but she was so tired that she hadn't.

'You seem tense. Why?'

'Oh. Just a long journey, you know.'

'I think you seem sad, as well.'

This comment caught Sienna by surprise. As Mikhail sat down on the bed next to her, she looked at him cautiously.

'Alejandro. We all know that he's not been around for months, that you haven't seen him… You seem to be saving yourself for him – you shouldn't.'

The words hung in the air and the huge ache that Sienna had held hidden in her heart came to the fore under such seeming kindness. A single tear escaped and made its way down her cheek.

'Such a waste…' Mikhail whispered, leaning into Sienna and gently brushing the tear away. 'Such a huge waste.'

With that, Mikhail kissed her. Sienna began to recoil but with his hand firmly on her back, she was unable to move.

'You deserve some happiness. Alejandro has gone – it's time to move on,' he purred, kissing her neck. Sienna felt a shiver go through her and, in spite of all the doubts she had in her mind, her body felt numb and unresponsive as Mikhail gently lay her down on the bed and slowly began to remove her clothes.

30

Sienna was woken by the weight of a man on top of her. Mikhail, she automatically assumed, knowing that he had gone to sleep beside her. But this man felt different – not just heavier and stockier, but a lot more aggressive.

As her eyes flew open, Sienna felt her legs being forced apart and in the same moment, as she registered Sergei's cold steel-blue eyes glaring triumphantly down at her, he brutally thrust into her, causing her to cry out with pain.

Muttering to her in Russian, Sergei yanked Sienna's hair back, pulling her head to the side as she struggled against him, trying to push him off her. As her hands finally managed to reach his shoulders, she was met by three strong, sharp slaps – one on each cheek and then a third, back-handed against her left cheek again. All the while, Sergei was thrusting into her, ripping her inside and bruising her body as he crushed down on her.

Feeling blood begin to trickle down between her legs and tasting it in her mouth, Sienna finally found her voice and let out a scream. Her horror, surely already at its limits, mounted as the bedding next to her moved and the sheets were pulled back to reveal Mikhail smiling and laughing at her. He rolled over and reached up to hold Sienna's arms back so that Sergei could focus on his own satisfaction.

'Welcome to Russia darling. This is one communist hardness you won't forget.'

As Sergei gave his final, hard thrusts, crying triumphantly as he came, Mikhail leaned into Sienna and kissed her neck, an act so reminiscent of the hours before that she thought she was going to throw up. Tears began to spill from her eyes, sliding down her face. As Sergei ground to a shuddering halt on top of her, Mikhail continued to hold her arms until all the fight had left her body.

'Dirty British whore,' Sergei muttered as he roughly pulled out of her. Rage ignited in Sienna, but as she struggled to free herself from Mikhail's once-tender embrace, Sergei just looked at her.

'Bored now,' he said, as he smashed his fist into her face.

How many hours had passed, Sienna didn't know. When she woke, the grey light outside gave no clue; it could be late morning or late afternoon. A glance at the door showed that a new lock had been fitted – with her firmly bolted on the inside and no possible way out.

Slowly, the horrors of the previous night came back to her. And with it, the nerve endings in her body began to react to the pain. Rushing to the sink, Sienna threw up, wincing in pain as the aches in her face came into sharp focus. In the cracked, dirty mirror, Sienna stared at her reflection, wondering who the woman was looking at her with tears streaking over a mix of blood and bruises which lay across her face. She collapsed on the floor with a sob, battling isolation mixed with a rising fear that they might come back. And what if they didn't? Who knew exactly where she was? Reaching for her bag, she searched for her mobile phone but could not find it anywhere. Tipping the contents of her bag onto the floor, she hastily pushed the fallen items aside as she looked in vain for what could be her only salvation. In despair, she sat back realising that her phone wasn't there and that any of them – Mikhail, Sergei or even Jesus – could have taken it. She was utterly alone.

Jesus opened the door tentatively. He wasn't sure what he would find inside. Sergei and Mikhail had been laughing and joking non-stop since the night Sienna arrived. He had seen them both coming out her room early one morning, high-fiving each other. Having then left her alone for 36 hours, they had told Jesus to take her some water and make sure she was still alive.

Flicking on the light switch, cleverly positioned outside the room, Jesus scanned the room in the dim light from the solitary bulb hanging from the ceiling and finally located Sienna. She was sat on the floor in the corner of the room, hugging her legs to herself and her head was bowed down to her chest.

'I've brought you some water,' he said, putting the dirty glass on the table.

Not looking up, Sienna mumbled something at Jesus.

'What?' he said, impatient to leave the scene of his crime.

Glaring up at him with hate in her eyes, Sienna asked again, 'Why did you bring me here?'

'Money, darling. You were the easiest ten grand I've ever made.' Jesus couldn't quite look Sienna in the eye as he said this, but the feeling of sleeping on a mattress of cash was something he was going to savour.

'Sweet dreams,' was all he said as he turned off the light and bolted the door, plunging Sienna once more into the horrors of darkness.

Hours passed again before someone came – Mikhail, full of smiles, although he, too, was unable to quite meet her eye. He carried a tray which housed some stale bread, dried up cheese, and a glass of water. Jesus stood by the door, looking bored and picking dirt out from under his nails.

'Good morning. I hope you are enjoying Russia,' Mikhail said as he put the tray down. 'You still have yet to see the best of our country. And tonight, Sergei's brothers are here, all looking for a little sport. You have 16 hours to prepare yourself and wait for the fun that is to come.'

With a chuckle, Mikhail swept out of the room past Jesus, his long leather coat swinging as he marched down the corridor, leaving Jesus alone with Sienna to prepare the room for that evening's fun.

For the first time in his life, Jesus felt uneasy – not a feeling that came naturally to him. He had met some of Sergei's brothers before and, having been paid handsomely, had been their willing sport for a few hours. To say that the older brothers were rough was an understatement, and there was a good chance that the coming hours could be Sienna's last on this earth.

As he closed the door and locked it behind him, Jesus pulled Sienna's phone out of his back pocket. While he knew that he couldn't save her himself, and wasn't totally sure that he wanted to, he should at least let someone know where the girl was. Turning the phone on, he searched for Alejandro's number and sent him a brief message. Having made sure the message was sent, Jesus dismantled the phone and threw the battery into the bin and stamping on the SIM card before tossing it out of the window and into the snow, where it vanished instantly without trace. It was now a race against time as to who reached Sienna first – Alejandro, or Sergei's violent brothers.

Sat in the darkness, Sienna felt despair so deep that she never knew it was humanly possible to feel. As the last fingers of dusk vanished into the inky-blue black of night outside, Sienna felt the sense of panic begin to return. The snow was piling up below the window, and she knew that she would freeze to death even if she did manage to escape. Pulling on as many clothes as she had, Sienna started in terror as she heard another noise at the door. Surely, they couldn't be here already!

Holding her breath, Sienna looked quickly around the dim light of the room and seeing a painting on the wall, she grabbed it and tried to smash it against the window. Amazingly, the pane of glass broke, and she slammed the painting frame around the edge of the window pane so that she could dislodge the jagged glass that remained.

Glancing over her shoulder, Sienna saw the shadow of one lone figure outside the door and she wondered whether it was Jesus come to get her. As she braced herself to make the jump out of the window into the snow below, she hesitated as there was a gentle knock on the door.

'Sienna?'

Hardly daring to breath, Sienna couldn't believe the voice that had just said her name.

'Alejandro?'

Never in her life had she been so pleased to hear the heavily-accented tones of Alejandro Orlando Suarez.

'Stand back!'

Sienna heard the sound of a crash, followed by a curse, and then another louder crash and Alejandro burst into the room. As he straightened himself up, Alejandro looked to where Sienna was still standing by the broken window.

'I'm so glad I found you,' he said, taking her hand and pulling her forward towards to him.

'Christ!' he exclaimed as the bright light from the corridor showed up the bruises on her face, her swollen, cut lip and the scared look in her eyes. 'No time to talk – we have to get out of here. But oh, my darling…' Dropping a tender kiss on her forehead, Alejandro grabbed her hand and together, they ran out of the room. Heading to a fire escape at the end of the hall, which was already open somehow, Alejandro pushed the door shut and pulled Sienna in close behind him. 'I have a car outside – come on.'

Tripping in her haste, Sienna slid across the snow in her bid to keep up with Alejandro. Too scared to look anywhere other than ahead and holding tightly onto Alejandro's hand, Sienna stifled a scream as she heard the sound of shouts coming from inside the house. Throwing herself in the passenger seat, she had barely even closed the door when Alejandro was already on the power, slamming through the gears and trying to get as much distance between themselves and the Russians as possible.

Watching them silently from the top barn of the stables was Jesus, tightening the girth on one of the fastest horses at the stud. As he threw his saddle bags full of money over the horse, he swiftly mounted and fled north to the border; he knew that if he was caught, he would be killed. The Russians had lost their sport and it wouldn't take them long to figure out that he, Jesus, was responsible.

With headlights dipped, Alejandro went off the road into a freshly-ploughed field, carefully following the tracks rather than creating new ones. At the end of the field was a copse of trees, and Alejandro quickly slammed on the brakes. 'Hurry – we have no time to lose,' he said, opening the car door. Sienna followed, unsure of what was happening, but very aware of the fast-approaching noise of several cars hot on their heels.

'Sienna!' Alejandro said urgently, grabbing her hand and running through the trees. With snow everywhere, Alejandro was aware that they were constantly leaving tracks – their only hope of escape was to go through the copse of trees and head to the forest. 'I have everything prepared – there is no time to explain. Just trust me – and please, darling, hurry!'

As they ran across the open ground, the sound of the cars got ever closer, headlights creating beams behind them as they desperately tried to close the gap between themselves and the thick, heavily overgrown forest. Shouts and the slamming of car doors carried across the dark of the night towards them, just as they reached the first of the trees. 'Hurry!' Alejandro urged again, half-pulling, half-dragging Sienna behind him. 'We're nearly there.'

Turning right at a huge Siberian pine tree, Alejandro stopped abruptly and started to pull a mass of branches to one side, uncovering a small motorbike. 'Get on,' he barked at Sienna, who promptly obeyed him. The cries and shouts getting ever closer, shadows and shapes started to appear in the moonlight, menacing down on the stationary couple.

Alejandro started the motorbike and, after just pausing a moment to make sure Sienna was holding on tightly, began to expertly weave his way through the trees, heading through the forest and away from the following men.

Leaving no footprints behind in the dank forest earth, Alejandro and Sienna fled unseen through the forest and out across the fields. Behind them, in the distance, lights were racing along the road, giving chase to a prey they could no longer see.

Alejandro finally pulled up outside a deserted property and turned the engine off. Hiding the motorbike behind a nearby bush, he grabbed Sienna's hand and took her down the side of the house and in through the door. Turning to barricade the door, he let go of Sienna and she sank to the ground where she stood, shaking frantically.

Moving to her, he gently took her in his arms and pulled her to him. 'You're safe now,' he whispered as he stroked her hair. 'You're safe.'

Sinking to the floor, Alejandro just held Sienna as she shook violently and sobbed silently, too shocked to let any noise pass her lips. As he held her, Alejandro relived the past few hours, and his urgent dash to reach her. He had been in Italy, sitting outside on a balcony chatting to clients, when his phone beeped with an incoming message.

Cursing, as his phone had been busy all morning, he snatched the phone off the table ready to turn the sound off, but his eyes were caught by the incoming message. As he had done so, he immediately went pale, not only as it had come from Sienna, but as she was obviously in trouble.

Sienna is being held by Sergei and Mikhail in Russia. They have already attacked her. Tonight, they could kill her. If you want to see her alive again, you really should hurry.

Standing up so abruptly that his chair fell on to the floor with the force of the movement, Alejandro ran back to the house, slamming the door firmly behind him as he fled through the house and jumped into a car, instantly dialling numbers trying to get to Russia in time to save Sienna.

Driving a breakneck speed to the airport, Alejandro had called in every single favour that he could in order to reach her in time – private jets, speeding through border controls at a breakneck pace, palms liberally greased in order to ensure that Alejandro was not too late. Not only that, he had contacted friends in Russia to ensure a safe path from the Stud where Sienna was being held prisoner to somewhere where no one could ever find them. As he held Sienna in his arms, Alejandro couldn't help but think that it was ironic that, just days ago, his divorce came through, but he hadn't wanted to contact Sienna just yet in case she was getting on with her life. And all the time, that life had been in danger.

Alejandro's fear of being too late to save Sienna was what had kept him going on what felt like a never-ending journey from Italy to Russia, and it was only now that she was in his arms that he could begin to breathe again. The relief at his finding her alive – and then his horror as he took in her badly beaten up body and the force of realisation hitting him that he came so incredibly close to losing her forever – would be a moment that would stay with him forever and haunt his nightmares for years to come. Now that he had her in his arms again, he silently vowed never to let her go.

After what seemed like hours of just holding her, but in fact was just minutes, Sienna had calmed enough to allow Alejandro to lean back and look at her. 'Unless we want to freeze to death, we'd better get a fire lit. Don't worry, we're far enough in the wrong direction that they won't find us here. Go and sit down on the sofa – there's some blankets there for you.'

Sienna did as she was told, pulling the furs over her as she curled up in the corner of the sofa. Alejandro quickly and skilfully lit the fire and was back at her side in an instant, this time with a bottle of vodka and a box. 'Here, have a sip of this. It will help – with the nerves and the pain.'

Like a patient doctor, Alejandro waited quietly while Sienna drank some vodka, the harsh taste reminding her of Jesus' betrayal.

'Now, I need to examine your injuries,' he said. 'All of them I'm afraid. I need to see just how bad things are. I promise, I won't hurt you and I will stop anytime you want me to. Is that okay?'

Too scared of crying again, feeling scared of what was to come and the anticipation of pain, Sienna could just nod mutely at Alejandro's words.

Talking through everything he was doing, Alejandro began his examinations with Sienna's face. Gently, he smoothed her hair down before bathing the cut around her eye, a cut that Sienna didn't even know she had. 'He was wearing a ring, I guess,' Alejandro said quietly and almost to himself. 'Bastard.'

Slowly, under Alejandro's familiar, tender touch and comforting words, Sienna began to relax for the first time in days. His fingers were slowly soothing her aching skin, as he bathed her face and neck, applying ointment as he went. Gently, he undid her shirt part-way, wincing as he saw dark bruises across her breasts. Slowly, carefully, he bathed her wounds, all the while talking to her, saying what he would be doing before he even touched her.

As Alejandro finished, he gently kissed Sienna's forehead once more. All was quiet for a moment, each alone in their thoughts as the fire crackled in the hearth.

'Can I go on?' he asked, his voice no louder than a murmur. Hesitating, Sienna nodded, gratefully accepting another slug of vodka. Gently, Alejandro removed the rest of Sienna's clothes, stripping her down to her underwear before looking in her eyes for assent, before carefully taking them off as well. The last time he had done this, they had been in the raptures of passion; now, the emotion was as far removed from there as it could be, and he steeled himself to look at her. His breathing stopped as he took in all the cuts, bruises and abrasions all over her body and he had to make himself focus on the task in hand. Clinically, he assessed the damage and bathed the wounds that were in easy reach. Handing her some liniment soaked in alcohol, he looked at her with concern.

'I think it is best if I leave you alone for a moment to clean yourself with this. It will hurt a lot, but it will sterilise any infection and help the healing process. I am so sorry…'

Dropping yet another kiss onto her forehead, Alejandro left the room to give this woman he felt such a tremendous and intense bond to a moment of privacy so that she could face the final stage of her immediate ordeal with dignity.

Returning a few minutes later, he said nothing and just took Sienna in his arms, lying them down on the sofa under the furs, watching the flames flicker in the hearth. There was no need for words, they just lay there surrounded by silence, each alone in their thoughts as their bodies moulded together in harmony.

31

The sound of screaming woke Sienna. It took her a minute to realise that the screaming was her own and as she felt the movement of a man next to her, the hysteria intensified and she punched him, trying to push him away as hard as she could.

'Sienna! Sienna! It's me – Alejandro!'

It took Sienna a few moments to realise the truth and her screams gave way to sobs as, once more, Alejandro gently held her in his all-encompassing embrace.

'It is okay, it's okay,' he soothed into her hair as he just held her tightly to him, wondering when this ordeal would begin to repair itself for her. He knew that it was a long way from being over, and that the nightmare Sienna had just endured would continue for days if not weeks; he hoped for her sake that it would not be months.

As Sienna calmed herself, she saw that the sun was beginning to shine through the window and she began to relax in the daylight. At the same moment, Alejandro saw the daylight and tensed, knowing that it was time for them to move on before the Russian mafia tracked them down.

'We need to go soon,' he said. 'Sergei will be looking for us again – and he won't be happy to have had his prize taken away from him so soon.'

Already dressed, Sienna covered the ashes over in the fire and gathered the blankets to take to a car that Alejandro's friends had left there for them, while Alejandro loaded the few supplies that they had into the trunk. Fully prepared for the flight ahead, he also had a jerry can containing more fuel, which he put into the boot of the car.

'We have to get to the border,' he said, looking around them as they shut the doors. 'Once we are there, we are safe. And then I'll explain everything. Ready?'

Sienna nodded, taking his extended hand and smiling as he kissed it. 'Let's get some distance between us and these complete and utter bastards.'

Looking back, Sienna would always look on the next 36 hours as some of the scariest of her life. Alejandro's plan was to head to Georgia, then across into Turkey and then fly to sanctuary from there. As they neared the Georgian border, they found that the Russians were waiting for them, having used the underworld to track them down. Sienna would later learn that as soon as Alejandro received Jesus' text message, he had instantly called in every single favour owed to him from friends across the world. And having brought horses from just about everywhere, there were a considerable number of friends to call on. Hence everything had been set up by local friends who, unless you knew, had no outward connection to Alejandro. These favours included the bike hidden in the woods, the house all prepared for their silent arrival, and, as Sienna was to discover, the gun.

Meeting them near the Georgian border was Hasan, an old friend of Alejandro's from his university days. Hasan would be the person to ensure that they got over the border safely and as soon as they realised that the Russians were following them and that they were determined to get their prey, Hasan had done everything he could to protect them. As soon as he got Alejandro and Sienna to, and over, the border, he laid a false trail, heading north back into Russian and dropping clues along the way at service stations. By the time the Russians realised that they had been duped, it was too late to find Alejandro and Sienna, who had long since vanished. Hasan's contact had been waiting for them and with not a second to spare, they had hurried through Georgia. As the Russians retraced their steps, they encountered conveniently set-up police road blocks, which not only halted but also captured some of the Russians.

While Hasan vanished once more into the background, and to safety, Alejandro and Sienna made their way into Turkey, where they made a beeline for Istanbul. Knowing that airports would be covered, Alejandro arranged safe passage for them on a fishing boat and then a bigger vessel and from there, it was a flight to Spain before taking another boat to Mallorca. Here, they decided to lay low for a few weeks and Alejandro checked them into an innocuous, yet palatial, hotel suite overlooking the Balearic Sea. In her heavily traumatised state, Sienna barely noticed that he booked the room under Mr and Mrs Orlando, with Alejandro using his middle name as a disguise.

The pair slept soundly for 24 hours before waking, twisted tightly together in each other's arms. Finally feeling safe in their hotel room, Alejandro left Sienna dozing while he went to the room next door and rang for room service. Waking Sienna half an hour later, he suggested that she have a bath while he made some telephone calls.

'I have called for the hotel doctor to come and see you, just to get you checked over,' he murmured gently to her. As Sienna began to protest, Alejandro held up his hand.

'For my peace of mind, Sienna. You have been through a lot. You either see a doctor here or I take you to a hospital.'

As he said this, there was a knock at the door. Looking at Sienna, she nodded and, getting out of bed, wrapped a dressing gown tightly around herself.

'I hear you've had a bit of an ordeal young lady,' said the

doctor as he came into the room and sat down on the bed beside her. His business-like formality immediately set Sienna at ease. 'I just need to examine you, it won't take a moment, and I hear that Alejandro has already looked after the worst of your injuries.'

As Sienna nodded, and the doctor began talking about never being too careful with these things, Alejandro discreetly closed the bathroom door, leaving her to face this final step alone.

Almost an hour later, Sienna gingerly lowered herself into the steaming bath, bubbles falling over the edge, such had been Alejandro's indulgence when running the bath for her. Sliding back, Sienna closed her eyes and felt a sense of peace surround her for the first time in days. A tap at the door interrupted her thoughts.

'Can I come in?' Alejandro stuck his head around the door. In his hands, he carried two glasses and a bottle of champagne. Sienna smiled at him and nodded.

'I have just spoken to one of my contacts,' Alejandro began. Sienna smiled to herself, loving the way that he was always so official, even at times like this, and that he never gave any information away on just who these contacts were.

'As we know, the police had already arrested some of them. Now, they have Mikhail and Sergei as well. Hoping for a reprieve, Mikhail cracked immediately and told them the whole story, how they planned this since Poland... They wanted to break you mentally and sell you to the sex trade – educated white women go down well in Russian apparently, if you pardon the pun. They planned for Mikhail to romance you, to make you fall for him, and then Sergei would take over. But Sergei was jealous after things went too far between you and Mikhail, so that's why he broke into your room that night and raped you so brutally.

They are in jail on the cold front now… I doubt whether anyone will ever see them again, that is if they are even still alive. Certainly, Sergei won't let Mikhail live after spilling the truth so easily.

'Jesus, meanwhile, has vanished. He went off into the night on one of their best horses. I am sure he will turn up again; his kind always do.'

Sienna was silent as she took all this in. There seemed to be nothing to say, no need for words about these men who had tried to ruin her. She shivered slightly, in spite of the warm water lapping around her skin, as she fleetingly thought of how close she had come to dying.

'Thank you, Alejandro. For everything.'

Alejandro shrugged off her thanks.

'There's something else,' he said as he put the drinks down. Taking a step towards her, he hesitated, and then saw the look in her eyes, concerned at his hesitation.

'This…' Gently, searchingly, he took Sienna's face between his hands and after just a moment, Alejandro leaned in and kissed her on the lips, a kiss so light that it was as if a butterfly had touched her.

'Is this okay?' he asked, his dark eyes full of love for her, not wanting to hurt her.

'Yes,' she whispered, kissing him back and allowing herself to be caught up in the moment, forgetting the past few days, thinking only of the here and now. His lips gently pushed against her bruised lips, fingers slowly trailing circles down her back and arms until he, too, finally lost himself in the moment…

Epilogue

Six months later, Sienna Stevens became Sienna Suarez as she married Alejandro. Rin loaned the couple her beautiful farm in Germany to hold the ceremony, and from the main entrance gates to the wedding location, crimson red silk ribbons were tied around the miniature grey-green olive trees that lined the way.

The wedding itself took place by the lake, with a group of ethereal white mares in the distance, watching with interest at what was happening. A selection of carefully invited guests sat waiting for the bride to appear while Alejandro stood nervously at the front, hardly believing his luck that Sienna was about to become his wife.

After a delay, just long enough for Alejandro to get nervous, the music changed from general background music to *Kiss Me* by Ed Sheeran, Sienna's favourite song and one that reminded the couple of happy times spent together; and the promise of many more to come.

Alejandro's ex-wife, Pasha, had grudgingly agreed that their children could be at the wedding, and it was they that led in the bridal procession, one daughter scattering crimson rose petals from a basket and looking adorable in crimson silk while the other solemnly carried the rings on an ivy green velvet cushion.

Rin and Sally Watson, Sienna's best friend, followed, with big, beaming smiles on their faces. Finally, Alejandro looked down to the end of the aisle and caught the first glimpse of his wife to be. Zoë was leading in Raafid with Sienna riding him side-saddle. She looked amazing in ivory lace, satin, and silk, with flowers in her hair, and a shy, love-filled smile on her face. Raafid, who took his role very seriously and carried his charge very carefully, drew to a halt next to Alejandro, who gently took Sienna by her waist and pulled her down to stand by his side. 'You look amazing... So beautiful,' he whispered as the vicar cleared his throat, ready to start what would be a magical ceremony.

As the sun came out on this small, intimate scene, Sienna and Alejandro made their vows in front of their family and close friends, before embracing for one of the longest, most passionate first kisses as husband and wife in history. Sienna was every inch the blushing bride while Alejandro exuded happiness and pride. Finally, Sienna was his. No more games. No more pretence. No more excuses. This was it. They were finally together and this time, nothing would tear them apart.

Acknowledgements

As I said at the beginning, *Sandstorm* has been a long time in the writing, and to have it here in print is the realisation of a huge dream for me. I still love the characters in *Sandstorm*, and I would love to say that we are all strong enough to walk away from the Arjan's of the world, as Sienna should have done early on. But so many of us still love a bad boy and keep going back for more until we can reach our own 'enough is enough'. May we all grow to be strong like that.

Thanks absolutely must be said. First and foremost to Shannon Lawlor, a brilliant Canadian artist and a dear friend, who so kindly let me use her image *The Yearling* as the cover. She is one of the strongest women I know, and her talent incredible. The superb designer Hanneke Lambert, who designed the cover that captures so much of my vision. Renowned UK horse photographer Marilyn Sweet for letting me use her shot of Master Design GA on the back cover, draped with his British National Championship Supreme Garlands. And of course, his owner Rod Jones for allowing this gorgeous stallion to grace the pages of this book, both inside and out.

To my amazing friends who patiently read and re-read *Sandstorm* in its many guises over the years: Paula, Clare, Charlie, Diane, and Carol. Your advice and sense-checking has been invaluable, as have the emotional outbursts – Diane, I am looking at you when I saw that! And of course, my parents, who have been banned from reading the book, but their love and support has, as ever, been amazing.

Finally, the biggest thanks goes to the incredible horses I have met, as well as the many friends I have made, around the world through travelling with the Arabian horse. Time spent in a paddock, idling on a veranda, watching a horse captivate in the show-ring or at a presentation – these are the moments that fuel my dreams and my creativity. The horses are the true heroes, the friends an added blessing.

Samantha xx

About the author

Born in beautiful Norfolk, England, in the 70s, Samantha grew up surrounded by the countryside and Arabian horses. It was inevitable that her life would end up being married to the Arabian – first as a committee member for the local Arab group, and then as the co-founder for the award-winning publication The Arabian Magazine. Samantha has since travelled the world, writing acclaimed articles for both her own and other Arabian horse publications.

Samantha has previously published *progress*, a collection of her own poetry and photography, which sold out its first run in less than six hours.

Sandstorm is Samantha's first full-length novel and the first in the Arabian Storm Series. She is now underway on her second novel, *Firestorm*.

Away from writing, Samantha loves to cook and appeared in the 2019 series of MasterChef. Her passion for cooking has led to her doing cooking demos across Norfolk and a pop up with friends to raise money for local charity. During lockdown, she began a series of interviews through her website The Delicate Diner, aimed at celebrating the local food and drink scene. Samantha also enjoys photography and loves to combine her words with images taken around the world.

Samantha still lives in Norfolk. You can follow her through social media at The Delicate Diner and The Arabian Magazine. Her website is samanthamattocks.com where you can find full details of *Firestorm* and other works as they become available.

Photo credit Richard T Byrant.

www.samanthamattocks.com

Made in the USA
Columbia, SC
04 September 2020